Bedeviled Sea

FORTUNE FAVORS THE BOLD

UNDER THE QUEST FOR ADVENTURE AND RICHES LIES
THE QUEST FOR HIDDEN TRUTHS.

Jerry Earl Brown

Books by Jerry Earl Brown

Bedeviled Sea
Snowmen
The Crevasse
Earthfall
Darkhold
Under the City of Angels

www.jerryearlbrown.com

For Jodie

In Gratitude

MY THANKS GO to many who have provided advice and feedback through the years, like fellow writers John Champlin Gardner, Clive Cussler, John Dunning, Jeff Long, Theodore Sturgeon, Edward Bryant, Connie Willis, Cynthia Felice, George R. R. Martin, Dan Simmons, John Stith, Steve and Melanie Tem, and others whose names are beyond recall.

Also, to literary agent Phyllis Westberg and her assistant Karen Gormandy; to editors Sydny Weinberg and Karen Haas at Bantam, Susan Allison at Berkley/Putnam and Paul D. McCarthy at Simon and Schuster.

As for *Bedeviled Sea*, I owe much thanks to those who read the book in manuscript or advance-copy form, and provided feedback: Novelist and professional editor Ann Howard Creel, Master Scuba Diver and member of the Professional Association of Diving Instructors L. D. Taylor; Jeanne Erickson, Cheryl Grenko, Lisa Fisher, Pamela Hermann, Jan Roberts, and Nancy Bartman.

Most of all, my thanks and my love go to my wife, Jodie, who has for so long supported my work with unflagging faith and fervor.

About the Author

Jerry Earl Brown was born in East Texas. He enlisted in the U. S. Marine Corps when eighteen.

Before seeing his first novel published, he sold stories and articles to various men's and outdoor magazines. His novels run the gamut from science fiction to present-day mystery/thrillers, with a cutting-edge science or metaphysical element in most.

A certified scuba diver and member of the Professional Association of Diving Instructors, he has traveled extensively and loves the sea. But his home for many years has been in the Rocky Mountains.

Bedeviled Sea

CHAPTER 1

Pirates

THE SUNKEN U-BOAT Kyle Dawton had found refused to give up any secrets. It lay in three pieces on its port side at a varied depth of 242 to 276 feet. Embedded in sand and heavily encrusted within and without, it had somehow managed to lie hidden here a mere six miles off the Florida Keys for over seven decades without discovery. Dawton figured this improbability had to be explained by the fact it looked more like part of the deepwater reef than a busted-up World War Two warship.

But he had felt its being here before he found it.

He and the other three divers with him had been looking for another sunken ship in these waters for days when Dawton felt a pronounced alteration of mood from that of a routine sunken-wreck hunt to an irresistible pull in the direction of the reef. When he realized what lay before him, he was momentarily transfixed with wonder and disquiet.

Once he realized what it was, he'd summoned the other divers. Together, they were able to make out the conning tower, torpedo compartment, engine room, and the general configuration behind its thick coral veil. With the help of their remotely-operated-vehicle called *Ogler*, they'd set to work poking around and through it, trying to determine if it would be worth the labor, the risk and cost, to lift the pieces one by one and keep them relatively together.

Their decision was about to be sidelined in a way Dawton could have done without. When he later looked back on what unfolded, he wouldn't be able to say the same for partner and co-owner of the Argos Salvage Company, Wayne Chizzick.

They'd found some bones, a couple of skulls, other items that when cleaned in the lab of the salvage ship overhead turned out to be the German submariners personal paraphernalia. As Dawton scanned the boat once more, he saw under the sediment and coral a mystery within which microscopic polyps had produced a macroscopic shroud. The wreck worked its tentacles into him, moving like the arms of a spectral octopus through his thoughts. Why had he felt it to be here before he saw it? What had happened to sink it? What had become of the wives and children and girlfriends of the dead Germans? What had the men who died here been missioned to do, having come so close to the American coast?

These musings vanished with a sudden prick of apprehension, an inkling that something was wrong up on their salvage ship even before he heard Chiz call the ROV operator on *Salvador* anchored above and heard Rob Palmer's answer.

"Move *Ogler* in closer to the U-boat's engine room," Chiz told him.

"Wayne, this is topside." The usually steady and strong voice of Palmer was curiously choked with tension. "We . . . we've lost control of the robot." That tension in Palmer's voice suggested something worse than what his words conveyed.

Puzzled, Dawton turned his handlight outward through a gap in the wreck's bulkhead, toward the ROV. Enclosed in *Ogler's* titanium frame, the SUV-sized mechanical workhorse sat twenty yards away on the seafloor, silent and still as the surrounding limestone. Even its lights had gone out.

In the U-boat's engine room, Chizzick spoke into his diving helmet's headset, "Topside, this is Wayne. What's wrong?"

Palmer did not answer.

And as Dawton kept his light trained on *Ogler*, the tether line running down from the ship to the ROV abruptly dropped in a heap of coiled cable at the robot's side.

"Rob?" Chizzick said into his headset, "can you hear me?"

Kyle moved closer to Chizzick, pulled on the sleeve of his drysuit and pointed a gloved finger at the fallen tether. He then tried reaching the other two divers at the wrecksite who were forward in the area of the U-boat's torpedo room.

Brad Shinley and Ed Sanchez answered, reporting that they too had seen the tether fall.

"Let's go," said Chizzick. He didn't have to say "up."

Guided by their underwater GPS units that received satellite input from a transmitter buoy off the ship, their ascent was anxious but methodical, broken up by necessary decompression stops. At a hundred-foot depth they could clearly see the hull of a boat on the surface that should not have been there: about thirty feet in length and nine in the beam—lying back near the stern of the salvage ship and snugged up against her starboard side.

Chizzick again tried to raise Palmer with no success. He was the first to break the surface. Dawton, Sanchez and Shinley came up right after. Bobbing in the mild swells like floating ducks, they looked up at the ship's maindeck rail and saw a man holding an automatic rifle on them, silhouetted against the ship's white superstructure as if cut from a comic-book cliché.

"Come up!" he commanded. "Come up the ladder and don't try anything funny!"

Sounds like a goddamn cliché too, thought Dawton. *Only he ain't very comic. And having been below 200 feet for almost two hours, maybe I'm narced and hallucinating.*

Pulling loose his fins and unsnapping his helmet enough to push it from his face, as did the others, Dawton followed Chizzick up the midships accommodation ladder encumbered by hoses, cylinders, camera, and other gear. He was worried about Chiz, a former Navy SEAL who'd done three combat tours.

Once on the deck, Chiz sat down without permission from the gunman and, with his hands undoing snaps and buckles, watched what he had to confront with the eyes of a Rottweiler being offered red meat. Former Marine Ed Sanchez looked much the same. Dawton, an ex-Navy salvor like Shinley, who enjoyed a little excitement and adventure now and then but thought armed combat a glorified form of lunacy, would much rather have been with a lusty lady somewhere on a beachside picnic.

The gunman looked jittery and their stares weren't making him feel any better. He had a handradio and yapped into it: "The divers are up! Four of them. I need another gun down here!"

Dawton looked up at the bridge. Another "gun" was coming down, resembling his shaven-headed, tattooed and ear-ringed comrade except his skin was the color of charcoal and his head a mop of dreadlocks.

"Get 'em face down on the deck!" this one yelled.

Still in his loose-fitting drysuit, Chizzick was nonetheless up and at the one standing over them before the other gunman made it halfway down the bridge ladderway. Chiz was so fast that Dawton couldn't see just what he did but whatever it was, in a flurry of jabs, ducks, twists, and kicks, he quickly deprived the gunman of his weapon and dropped him to his knees. As the rifle clattered to the deck, Dawton was closest and jumped to retrieve it. With the gunman down and apparently out and the other having reached the deck, Dawton tossed the rifle to Chiz, certain he could make better use of it.

The thug at the foot of the ladderway commenced firing.

Bullets struck the metal deck around them, whirred and zinged over the tops of the maindeck shops and machinery midships as Dawton and the other divers scrambled for cover behind the boom-crane control station.

All except Chizzick. He ran forward like a happy madman and was quickly out of sight.

"What the fuck," said Sanchez, pulling his diving knife from its sheath. As a Marine Corps grunt, he was the only member of the present salvage crew besides Chizzick who'd seen armed conflict.

Dawton didn't figure he had to have seen it to know he never wanted to. Nonetheless, they had to do something fast and as the second and only other partner in Argos Salvage, he said to Sanchez, "Go check their boat out, Ed, see if anyone's there we'll have to deal with. Brad and I will move forward to see what we can do there. Okay?"

"Got it," said Eduardo Sanchez and started scooting backward, deeper into the maze of equipment, shops and deck housings between them and the ship's stern.

Keeping low, Dawton and Shinley began to make their way forward. The gunfire was now concentrated only in the area of the bridge. Stopping short of its ladderway to hide against the bulkhead of the storage shed just below, Kyle stole a look around the corner and saw the black gunman sprawled face down on the deck at the ladderway's bottom step with his dreadlocks blood red and the rest of him bleeding in enough holes to have departed this earth.

Kyle was certain that Shinley didn't want the fallen man's weapon any more than he did. But he decided he'd be better off with it than without it and reached from his hiding place to grab the gun as he heard Chizzick shout from above.

"Get 'em! They're headed for their boat!"

From the bridge, Chizzick fired the assault rifle at the port side of the ship where there were targets Kyle couldn't see. With sweaty palms, he checked the dead badguy's submachine gun. Never having held such a weapon before, having had only minimal weapons training in the Navy but having grown up with guns in rural Oregon, he knew enough to slide the bolt far enough back to make sure a round was in the chamber. Hoping its extended magazine was at least half filled, he let the bolt go home again and said to Brad, "Go find out what's up there." He jerked his head at the bridge. "Find our crew. I'm joining Ed."

Brad Shinley nodded, ashen-faced. Certain he didn't look any better, Dawton swallowed against the acrid taste in his mouth and started running aft.

He could tell from the gunfire on the port side that Chiz had to have dropped from the bridge back to the main deck as the pirates must have done, avoiding a slower escape down the ladderway. Based on the gunfire noise and the direction it was coming from, Kyle judged that the pirates were firing back and numbered no more than two or three, all apparently running from the wildman who was raining bullets on their parade and trying to send them all to picaroon paradise before they reached their boat. Wanting to determine if his guess was accurate, Kyle kept glancing forward to see past obstructions as he ran rearward toward the stern.

A pirate sprang from the edge of the A-frame crane's control station aft. He saw Dawton and fired.

Kyle scampered in behind some crates with the adrenaline stoking his blood. He fired back but all he hit was the glass in the window of the control station.

The pirate jumped straight into the water but it was Chizzick's approaching fire he was trying to escape rather than Dawton's. Another came close behind the leaper and did the same. A third wanted to follow but had been snagged by Sanchez. This one went down with a bleeding slash across his thigh, courtesy of Ed's knife.

Chizzick was suddenly there and vaulted over them to reach the rail.

Kyle joined him.

The two gunmen who'd leapt into the water were now in their boat. One fired at Chizzick and Dawton to force them back from the rail as the other started the engines. Ducking for cover, they quickly pulled away from the ship. A cabin cruiser with a fiberglass hull designed for speed, the boat took off to the north at a good 20 knots and climbing. Chizzick emptied his magazine at them, yelling curses and laughing like a loon at the same time.

"Well," said Kyle, gasping to regain his breath, "you must've scared the crap out of them, Rambo. They're long gone."

"Let's lower the RIB."

"What, and go after them? Let the Coast Guard do that."

"There's no telling when they'd get here," said Chiz, his black hair up and flapping in the breeze like a flag. "Come on! Let's get those sonsabitches!"

⋅⊷⧯⊷ ⊷⧯⊶⋅

After combat in Iraq and Afghanistan, Wayne Chizzick had twice undergone treatment for post-traumatic-stress-disorder but was still volatile and flat-out rabid when his hackles were up. There had been situations in which Kyle could talk some sense into him and situations in which good sense was the first casualty. Kyle knew the present situation was of the latter kind.

Salvador's workboat was an ex-Navy rescue craft; a 20-foot rigid-hull inflatable with two 110 horsepower outboards in the stern. It could do up to 50 knots and needed to in order to overtake the pirates' cruiser which was almost a mile away before they got the RIB into the water by winch.

Of the three pirates still on *Salvador,* the one Sanchez had slashed was tied to the rail with rope; the one at the foot of the ladderway had eight gunshot wounds but was amazingly still alive; and the one who'd held the crew at gunpoint on the bridge and in the captain's quarters was out with a blow to the head by Shinley. The Coast Guard had been called and was sending a cutter. Sanchez had been shot in the hip and leg and was being seen to by *Salvador's* medic. Now freed, *Salvador's* crew stood at the starboard rail with Shinley and watched Chizzick and Dawton take off in pursuit.

Dawton had tried several more times to persuade Chizzick to let the Coast Guard take care of the pirates. Such attempts were met with steaming and stubborn silence. But once the two partners were in the water with the RIB revved to max, Chizzick yelled over the noise of the outboards, "The fucking Coasters would never find them once they got here! Give me the heading!" He handed Kyle the binoculars on the shelf under the steering console.

As the bow of the RIB slapped over the chop, Kyle held to the console's side for stability and located the distant cruiser through the persistent spray. "About—" Kyle glanced at the compass on the console—"between three-one-zero and three-one-five! They're headed for the Keys!"

At the wheel, Chizzick turned the workboat slightly to port. On a north-northwest heading, the RIB's bow pointed straight toward the fleeing cruiser. They were six nautical miles south-southeast of the Matecumbe Keys. Off to the northeast stood the Alligator Reef lighthouse, sticking out of the water like a miniature offshore oil derrick whose platform had slightly sunk.

With a westerly headwind and two-foot swells, the RIB was nonetheless doing between 42 and 46 knots and slowly but surely gaining on the cruiser. Feeling the submachine gun hanging against his chest, Kyle Dawton had more time to consider what they were about to do and not only did he not want to do it—especially since he had yet to know its details—he did not even want to think about it. His cheerless ruminations produced only a doubtful hope that they would lose the pirates but the Coast Guard would get them.

Alligator Reef was soon behind them and they were crossing the Hawk Channel. Dawton kept the binocs up. The cruiser was maybe a thousand yards ahead, its heading changed to roughly 320 degrees.

"Looks like they may be going for Indian Key."

Chizzick said nothing. Grinning into the sea spray that had him soaked, he swiped a hand across his face and like a leopard after a gnu kept his eyes on his prey. The picture was not pleasant to Kyle's eyes and he fought off thinking what the pirates' outcome might be, however deserving, if Chiz caught up with them. But as Kyle watched, the cruiser kept well northeast of Indian Key and did not cut its speed. In another couple of minutes it was past the small island and into Indian Key Channel, plowing straight for the Lignumvitae Bridge.

Though they'd seen maps and charts of these waters and drove by them in car across the Overseas Highway from the Everglades to Key West, the two had not ventured here in anything afloat. Looking over the side, Kyle judged the depth of the bottom to be averaging about ten feet. Beyond the bridge, it might become shallower. The RIB's draft was less than three feet and the cruiser's was likely comparable. No doubt Chizzick figured the RIB could go anywhere the cruiser could.

The roaring workboat rose and fell, slapping the waves like a thing wanting to be airborne but inexorably slamming back to the chop. Through the binoculars, Dawton saw the cruiser pass under the bridge with plenty of vertical clearance. It kept going straight northwest at about 310 degrees but once past the bridge it turned more north. Kyle suspected these guys knew where they were going.

Luring their pursuers into a trap maybe.

He kept watching the bottom and watching the cruiser with the glasses. Glassing the water to port and starboard, he could tell by its differing hues that shallower depths lay to the west.

Still heading north, the cruiser suddenly swerved to the northwest some thirty degrees. In that direction lay a sizeable key, as keys went. Kyle couldn't remember the name of it but with the glasses he could see a pier that led into some palms and well-groomed grounds.

He jerked his attention back to the cruiser and saw it go right on by the pier.

The distance separating the two craft was now less than a hundred yards. The RIB's speed needle was nudging 50 knots. But the channel they were in seemed to be narrowing. Coral shoals and what might have been sandbars were flying past, closing in. The bottom was much easier to see despite the cruiser's wake, which meant it was becoming shallower.

"Better slow down, Wayne," Kyle yelled. "This is getting hairy!"

Chizzick said nothing and he didn't slow down. The cruiser was maybe eighty yards away. It suddenly swerved farther to the northwest, skirting a shoal that for the RIB was dead ahead. Chizzick throttled back to adjust but the RIB was still going too fast when he made the turn. It rolled hard to starboard and though it did not capsize, it listed far enough to throw Chizzick out of the cockpit and Dawton over the rubber gunwale. As he hit the water, he heard the propellers of the RIB's engines scrape rock. Fighting to resurface, he got his head above the froth and saw the workboat come to a zigzagging but inevitable halt with its engines growling and sputtering toward silence.

Spitting saltwater and treading it, Dawton let go a sigh of relief as Chiz, up from the deck and cursing, blazed away with the M15 carbine at the fleeing pirates and their boat.

CHAPTER 2

Fortune Hunters

TWO MONTHS LATER, Dawton and Chizzick sat in a Miami restaurant with Wayne's father and a friend the latter introduced as William Cooper ("Call me Bill, boys.").

A fifth chair at the round table stood between the two older men, curiously empty.

At first, Wayne and Kyle assumed the dinner was Curt Chizzick's idea but soon learned that it had sprung from Cooper. Like ex-Admiral Curt, Bill was semi-retired and in his sixties. Both men in their individual ways had a refined yet rugged look but whereas the admiral was lean and flinty-eyed and reticent, Bill was broader in the beam and more generous of voice. Though he'd served in the Navy till his forties, his last leg of professional activity had been in the diplomatic corps, about which he treated them all to several ribald accounts. The admiral laughed a little but offered nothing of the sort in return. And watching him, Kyle easily recalled that in addition to having served aboard several ships during his career, Curt Chizzick had also done a stint in the Office of Naval Intelligence.

Ribald Bill listened intently and laughed heartily at the two divers' account of the pirate attack; an account told mostly by Dawton with Wayne almost as silent as his dad but occasionally inserting a tetchy revision. Knowing Wayne wasn't at all happy with the story's conclusion, Kyle merely said as a wrap-up, "Then we ran aground and the badguys got away. So while the Coast Guard finally got there and arrested the ones left on *Salvador*, the two who got away, at last report, haven't turned up since."

Wayne had nothing to add or amend to this but a curse of frothy disappointment.

Bill kept looking at the admiral's son with a smile but also a wary squint as if he thought Wayne could detonate without notice. Maybe Curt had told him about Wayne's combat experience and his having undergone treatment for "hyper arousal" and PTSD.

As for the U-boat they'd found, Kyle had wanted to raise its broken carcass for its historical value. Wayne had scoffed. "History per se," he'd said, "ain't worth the breath it takes to talk about. Just the same old crap rehashed over and over again with different characters, venue and costume. Bringing that thing up wouldn't be worth the cost, the work, or the risk." It wasn't the first time in the years Kyle had known him that Wayne had expressed, however sardonic, some depth of thought; but it was the first he'd expressed any aversion to risk. The real reason Wayne didn't want to bring the old World War Two sub up lay in that phrase "worth the cost," meaning they would glean a scant return moneywise in salvaging her. Thus, in owning sixty percent of the partnership to Kyle's forty, Wayne had scuttled the job. Photos, sketches, descriptions and location were turned over to the U.S. Navy and the Florida Keys Maritime Authority, in compliance with Admiral Curt's advice. The admiral, after all, was chairman of the Argos Salvage board, their chief source in military and government contracts, and their primary investor.

The waiter returned to the table and Bill Cooper ordered another round of drinks. And it soon became obvious that the reason for this dinner wasn't to exchange tales of dalliance and derring-do.

Though the admiral hadn't laughed or commented once during the pirate account, his craggy and dour visage had cracked now and then with a thin, one-sided smile which could have been as much grimace as grin. Before him on the table was a manila folder he'd taken from a briefcase at his feet. He pulled from it several sheets of official-looking paper. "These are the title to your new ship and the permits to have aboard weapons with which to defend yourselves. It's all spelled out in the permits what's restricted and what's legitimate in resorting to their use. No cowboy crap." He looked at his son and at Dawton. "Understood?"

"Yeah," said Wayne grudgingly.

Kyle heard in that terse response the fact that Wayne and his father had already had the "cowboy" conversation at least once. He could not imagine the strings the former Navy flag officer had pulled to obtain the weapons permits and could not say he was terrifically glad he'd pulled them. They were salvage divers, for chrissake. But then piracy, long seemingly a scourge of the remote past, had re-raised its grim and gory head around the globe.

Having scanned the papers, Wayne passed them to his partner. Kyle didn't look at the gun permits; he would do that later after (hopefully) getting over the shock of being part of a gun-toting salvage crew. His interest was in the new ship: a mothballed Navy salvor laid down, launched and commissioned in the early eighties and decommissioned in 2003 that Admiral Curt with his clout and connections had bought for a song the previous year and which had been undergoing overhaul for the needs of Argos. Up to this point, Argos Salvage had been leasing other ships like *Salvador* or hiring out to other salvage companies for work. But while chief shareholder and board chairman Curtis Chizzick had bought the old Navy salvor for a mere quarter million, it had cost three times that to refit, refurbish, and equip.

"The bad news," said the admiral, "despite those two fairly lucrative wrecks you guys found back in '07 and '08, Argos is dropping into the red."

This wasn't news at all. "You think we don't look at the books?" said Wayne.

"I think you'd better prepare for a sea change," said Papa Curt.

Dawton looked up from his perusal of the ship's specs. *Say what?*

"With your concurrence, of course, Bill is coming aboard as an investor," said Curt, "and that will help." He looked over at Cooper and treated them all to one of his thin-lipped smiles. "But he comes with strings attached."

Cooper chuckled like the seasoned diplomat he was. He said to the two younger men, "Curtis tells me that you guys have treasure-hunting ambitions."

Wayne said nothing. But Kyle could tell his interest if not his unease had just jumped a notch. When the two first went to Wayne's father with the idea of forming a salvage company, they'd admitted finding an old sunken wreck with a cargo worth millions was their ultimate dream. With monetary backing but little comment about that dream from the admiral, and with some of his friends willing to invest in the company, they'd formed Argos. It often seemed to Kyle that Papa Curt owned the whole kit and caboodle, or acted as if he did. Certainly,

Argos would not have come into existence or could have stayed operative up to this point without him.

Kyle said to Bill, "Yessir, we do."

Cooper stirred his drink. "Well, I'm sure you're both aware how in recent years treasure hunters with their own ships have been encouraged, or shall I say pressured," he smiled sympathetically, "into hiring a marine archeologist or two, as part of their permanent staff, to placate those who accuse said treasure hunters—regardless of the risk and the efforts they take in the way of preservation—of being little more than looters motivated only by profit, who have little respect for the historical sites they 'loot.'" Bill paused to let these observations sink in but got no response from either diver, both of whom felt their suspicions on the rise. Glancing at his shiny Rolex, Bill said, "Do either of you have any objection to having a third partner?"

"Why?" blurted Wayne, his eyes snapping to that vacant chair between the admiral and the diplomat, and then to the restaurant's foyer. People were queued up and waiting to be seated. People were leaving.

"To ease the money crunch and provide that archeology team I was talking about." Bill Cooper's gaze settled on Dawton. "Kyle, I understand, if I may be so blunt, that you're in hock to your eyeballs; not only to the admiral here but also to Wayne. I know from the admiral that Wayne is unwilling to let go his sixty percent ownership. But what about you? Would you be willing to split your forty to pay off most of your debts?"

Kyle Dawton loathed talking about money, debt, ownership, partnerships, or any other sort of ship except the kind that sailed the seas. And he guessed that fact explained why he was so deep in debt. Wayne was in debt too, to the admiral. But this "sea change" was beginning to take on the aspects of an earth shift personal to Kyle Dawton. "I might. But that depends on who this anonymous third partner would be."

"Of course." Cooper looked at the foyer. "There she is. Right on time." He waved.

The young woman who emerged from the entrance crowd and waved back was tall and striking. She wore a tasteful dark pants suit that contrasted and complimented her tanned face and blond hair.

As the men stood, her eyes swept the three she was about to meet in a quick but probing glance. Those eyes were a deep and lustrous dark-blue in the low restaurant light. But it wasn't just her eyes that made Kyle Dawton uneasy; it was everything about her. In looks at least.

"My daughter Victoria," said William Cooper proudly. "The archeologist."

"Call me Vic," said she as the introductions went around. Vic wore small pearl earrings and a minimum of makeup. No wedding ring. She had a warm but reserved smile that intrigued Kyle Dawton.

Both he and Chizzick were all but speechless.

"Victoria," said the beaming pop as the admiral pulled out that fifth chair and Ms. Cooper lowered herself into it, "is also a licensed technical diver with plenty of experience underwater. Honey," he said to her, "we were just talking about you."

We were? thought Dawton incredulously as he sat back down with the rest. *This is the proposed third partner?*

As the talk went around the table, he noticed that Wayne had less to say than before but from the way he kept moving in his chair and gulping scotch, he had to be wrestling with a rule he'd declared when they first formed Argos: the company would have an all-male staff and crew aboard ship. (Front office excepted.) In contemplating Victoria Cooper, that rule was no doubt undergoing reassessment.

While Bill and his daughter did most of the talking at first—the admiral, of course, never said much on any occasion and the two younger men were still dumbfounded—it became clear that she already knew quite a lot about Argos Salvage and its two partners. She praised Wayne and Kyle and their past salvage work but didn't overdo it. Her intelligence, her voice, her manner, had Dawton wondering once more if he was narced and hallucinating. As well as having done little to enhance her looks, she seemed naturally at ease and self-assured with four men, three of whom were yet strangers. The uneasiness Kyle was beginning to feel was like that of a man on the edge of water in which, despite all his experience and skill in that element, he could jump in and drown.

After they'd ordered dinner, Wayne threw Victoria a few questions about her diving and shipwreck experiences which she answered with expert detail but without conceit.

"So," said Kyle, "you've been working mostly for the University of Miami and National Geographic?"

"For the last six years," she answered. "Before that, I was with Woods Hole, before that, in college."

"What college?"

Bill filled in: "The University of Florida and Texas A&M," he said.

Both very good schools for nautical archeology.

Kyle said, "Vic, you strike me as a woman who would not reach this point without knowing what you were getting into. My guess is that you already know we're a couple of ex-Navy yahoos whose post-high school-and-Navy education has been of the hands-on and pretty much self-taught variety. We get into gun-fights with brigands and now have gun permits that will allow us to be armed aboard our new ship." He assumed she knew about Wayne's PTSD and his treatments for it but in any case, this wasn't the time or place to mention that. "Our crew and our divers are all male and we—"

"That can change," said Wayne.

Oh.

"Can you shoot?" Wayne asked. "Ever fire a weapon?"

Kyle suppressed a groan.

"Yes," said Vic.

"She can shoot very well," said her father, who apparently had no problem with Annie Oakley Victoria joining a salvor that had its own arsenal.

She glanced at Bill and then at the admiral, and said with another one of her thoughtful but nonetheless disarming smiles, "I've been well informed."

Kyle said, "Okay. Good. But . . . judging from your background, I take you to be a serious and dedicated scientist. Guys like Wayne and me—we're in the salvage game for adventure and the big-money strike." Though this wasn't completely true in Kyle's case, he wanted to hear what she'd say to it.

"Both appeal to me," was her rejoinder.

"But what if it came to a conflict between—What if you—and you'd have an archeological team working with you—what if the archeo guys want to preserve everything in situ, say, whereas we glorified looters want to bring everything up and sell it to the highest bidder?"

She regarded him with a steady gaze that seemed to know he was overstating the case just to draw her out. "I suggest you have it written in a company contract for all to sign precisely what you require."

"Damn good idea!" said Wayne.

But Kyle wasn't finished.

"So, one more question. Why do you want to join us?"

She said, "Oh, there's an adventurous vein in me too. I'm tired of doing only exploration and research. I've wanted a change for a long time. Dad's told me about the finds you've made. I'd like to be part of something like that, find a sunken wreck with high value."

Well informed? There hadn't been that many "finds." But had she also heard about what Wayne liked to call Kyle's hunches, his "feeling" that a couple of the wrecks they'd found were near where he "hunched" they'd find them?

"I would love to join you," continued Victoria, "on terms I think you've already been told about. But whether you want me as a partner or not, I want to tell you about a sunken fifteenth-century British privateer that may lie north of the Cay Sal Bank. With reputedly a prize cargo. If we—or you without me—found it, I think you'd satisfy both monetary and archeological interests. I've done a lot of research—"

"That location's pretty vague," interrupted Wayne. "Got a better fix?"

"Somewhere northwest and between 5 to 8 miles off the Bank is the best I can do at this point. There were only two survivors, a couple of Taino Indians—slaves—when the ship went down; and that was their best guess according to records. It's been looked for by numerous people but not found. I understand that at the moment you have no work. What do you say to letting me join you, as a trial, in a search for that ship?"

"We'll think about it," said Wayne.

Dinner came. They ordered wine. They ate. The talk became more of the chitchat kind. "We'll think about it," Wayne repeated after his fourth double-scotch, four glasses of wine and some disapproving frowns from his papa which he ignored. Looking at Dawton, he said, "Right, Kyle?"

Dawton's alcohol content was a close runner-up to his buddy's. "Yeah. Right." And raising his glass with a flourish, he said, "Here's to thinking about it!" And he knew that whether or not he decided to sell half his 40% ownership of Argos Salvage to her, he'd be thinking about Victoria Cooper for a long time.

She was, he realized with a stab of embarrassment, watching him keenly. But he saw no judgment in her stare, only interest. She said, "So what will you guys name the new ship?" Obviously she wasn't so presumptuous as to be thinking of herself as a partner yet and maybe she'd put the question that way to let them know it.

Several names were bandied between Wayne and Bill Cooper, none of them to Kyle's liking. "How about," he said, *"The Morgainne?"*

Everyone looked at him quizzically.

"A Brit sea goddess of old," he explained, trying to remember what he'd read and drunkenly aware he wanted Victoria to know he was not just a loot-lusting lout from Blowhole, Oregon. "From *Mari* and *Mara*," he expounded. "Two of the oldest names, oldest words, on this waterworld called Earth. Like Mama. Maerin, Marianne, Marian, Marianna, Marina, Maria, and Mor, a Celtic goddess of the sea. Mermaid . . . umm, Morgan le Fey—keeper of The Mysteries and Queen of Avalon, Isle of Women," he added, knowing that he was running on foolishly. *Also Goddess of Fate,* he remembered but did not say.

And the Fata Morgana, a strange sort of mirage visible just above the oceanic horizon.

No one said anything for a long moment, as if he'd been speaking in tongues. Then Victoria said, "I know I don't have a vote yet but I like it."

Wayne Chizzick raised his glass. "I like it too," he roared. "It sounds like *More Gain!*"

⤛⤜ ⤛⤜

In their hotel room that night, neither Dawton nor Chizzick had any trouble falling into a boozy sleep. But Dawton awoke in the wee hours with worries running amuck in his head: misgivings about having Victoria Cooper as a partner and what that might do to his and Wayne's friendship; worries about Argos going bankrupt and what he might do next in his life if it did. But most perplexing of all was his uneasiness about having known or felt the old U-boat was there before he found it. From childhood, he had had episodes of what seemed to be precognition or trans-temporal vision, most of which could have been illusion or the result of an overactive imagination—but a few of which became affirmed in reality. None, however, had led to anything as dire or hair-raising as the fight with the pirates who'd tried to take *Salvador*.

And as he pondered this fact, the surface worries suddenly ceased and the U-boat became a very different submarine. A modern one, much larger, not broken up but intact.

It shrank to a much smaller size but remained whole.

He lay still and wide awake and tried to discern more detail. But as if nothing more than a hallucination, an undersea *fata morgana*, it faded, leaving in its place a swirl of disturbed silt fraught with threat.

CHAPTER 3

New Mission

ON A DAY in late December under an overcast sky spitting snow, Captain-Lieutenant Anton Lepushin boarded the military version of a Yak-40 business jet at Severomorsk Air Base in northern Russia. Ordered to report to the Main Intelligence Directorate at the Moscow suburb of Khodynka, the narrow-faced but keen-eyed *Spetsnaz* officer sat in a back seat and wondered what was up. But having served in the Ministry for Internal Affairs, the Naval *Spetsnaz* and *Spetsgruppa*-Alpha, he was too experienced a special ops officer to wonder overly long.

The briefing would provide what was necessary to know.

Two Federation marines from brigade headquarters sat at each of the jet's two doors in the seven-meter-long cabin. Armed with Kalashnikovs, they were Lepushin's bodyguards. Despite the fact that he wore only the uniform of an ordinary naval officer, they looked at him when they braved a look at all with respect and deference, and perhaps a little fear—emotions usually felt by the regular military in the presence of Special Forces personnel. They would not know he was *Spetsnaz*, however, only that he was someone important enough to justify guards and a private jet.

Corruption and distrust being a way of life in Russia, so rife that many did not know the definition of either, one never knew who was foe or friend, in the military or out.

Lepushin too was armed, with an MP-443 Grach in a waist holster. Four years ago he'd been an officer in a topsecret Alpha Group force charged with ferreting out sleaze and mob elements within the Federation's military and intelligence units—a job that had a mortality rate approaching ninety percent. Since that time, he'd excelled as a reconnaissance-and-sabotage diver capturing or killing those involved in various kinds of maritime smuggling, piracy and other sea-related crimes. This work boasted a mortality rate similar to the first. Maybe someone in a high position he'd help put behind bars was trying prematurely to terminate his career. That possibility would be uppermost in his mind at the Main Directorate meeting.

As the Yak-40 rose above the subarctic landscape to achieve its cruising speed of 510 kilometers an hour, he thought briefly of his ex-wife now living in Sweden. This was a mental lapse that never failed to put him to sleep.

In a little over three hours, the jet was dropping toward Khodynka Airfield northwest of the Moscow Ring and just north of the GRU headquarters compound.

→═◑ ◐═←

"You are to locate and bring back a deserter, Captain-Lieutenant," said the Deputy Director of the Federal Security Service (successor to the KGB). He stood at the head of the long table, holding a wireless remote pointed at the screen at the front of the room.

A naval colonel and major in dress uniforms who'd accompanied Lepushin on the military helicopter from Khodynka here to the Center of Special Operations at Balashikha, another officer from the Security Service and two civilians all sat on the opposite side of the table. Lepushin knew the military men, none of whom had any reason to bear him a grudge. But during the introductions, the professions of the two civilians were not disclosed. As the briefing unfolded, they became easy to guess.

On the screen appeared a series of photos of a man in his mid-forties to early fifties, in various aspects of civilian dress and a few with him in a labcoat. Security photos, mostly, of the subject facing the camera, several with ID tags hanging from his neck or pinned to his shirt or suit jacket. "This is what he looked like before his desertion. What follows displays what he looks like at present."

The man had changed his face—the shape of his nose, his mouth, his brow, his hair and eye color. His hair was changed to a dark brown; his eyes to brown. And he now wore a beard and eyeglasses.

"His name, as you see in some of the photos, is Pyotr Telasnikov."

The civilian at the table who'd been introduced merely as Dr. Bukarov outlined the defector's background, profession, and accomplishments for the Federation.

Lepushin listened intently. He quickly understood why the GRU wanted Pyotr Telasnikov back. But the man's background and achievements stirred questions in Lepushin that exceeded his need-to-know.

"The stupid Americans do not realize what they have," said Dr. Bukarov, then glanced under heavy black eyebrows at the Deputy Director, obviously regretting having said something unnecessary.

The rough date of Telasnikov's defection four years before was provided; when and where he was first located by deep-cover Russian agents a year later; and when and where he'd moved soon afterward to be subsequently again located and his whereabouts reported to Moscow without his being aware he'd been found out.

"Yes, he was for a while protected by American agents," said the squat and balding DD. "We have thrice tried to grab him at risk of compromising our own agents and each time failed. We have a mole implanted where he is presently and we believe he is no longer under government protection."

On-screen followed more photos, these of a man taller and younger than Telasnikov, dressed in civilian clothes or labcoat. The name on his ID tag was at times Jacob, at others Yakov, Baturin. "A Canadian of Ukrainian origin, with a background in microbiology and nanotechnology similar to Telasnikov's, who came into the Russian embassy in Montreal one day and offered his services to Mother Russia. It took a while for us to assess him, develop his cover and find the right assignment for him."

Baturin also had had a change of face and identity.

Lepushin was told where these two men now worked. The DD pressed a button. A map of the northern Caribbean archipelago appeared on the screen. "We know from Baturin that unless their plans change he and Telasnikov will be in the northern Bahamas by January eleventh. Exactly where they will be and just how long they will be there is yet uncertain but at this point we are pretty sure he will be in this area." The DD moved his cursor to the indicated spot. "You will be told as soon as we know exactly where they are. It will be important that you move fast once we know. It will be of the utmost importance that you are nearby when we get the word."

"You will put together a team of special-operations divers," said the navy colonel. "You will be flown to Havana, there to be taken to a secret locale to go aboard a *Shchuka-B* codenamed *Opekun-681* that has been refitted for reconnaissance and surveillance."

"As soon as North Fleet command is able to make contact with it," inserted the Deputy Director.

The colonel resumed: "Its commander is Captain First-Rank Konstantin Sergeyevich Polivanov, its first officer Captain Second-Rank Isaak Kolotcha."

A series of photos followed of the two submariners, in dress and work uniforms.

Though Lepushin had never met him, he recognized Polivanov from his dossier, as he'd seen the dossiers of many naval commanders. Polivanov was a 22-year naval veteran who'd graduated from Kuznetsov Naval Academy in pre-*Perestroika* 1988. In Lepushin's investigations into corruption in the military, he knew a lot about the submariner. He knew that Polivanov was as clean as they came; loyal and devoted to Russia. He was also rumored to harbor a dislike for certain high-ranking personages in the Government, especially its president. In present company, Lepushin would keep that to himself, though any or all of the others in the room likely knew of such rumors. As for the military officers before him, he knew a lot about them also and they had to be aware of that. Though most in the Russian military maintained an apolitical stance, some were as potentially mutinous as many in the Federation's diverse populace were seditious. Lepushin's well-trained brotherhood was no exception. There were those in the *Spetsnaz* who still harbored a seething resentment for having been politically ill-used in coups d'état (unsuccessful or successful) during the breakup of the old Soviet Union.

On the screen had appeared the photo of a nuclear submarine of Russian fast-attack profile known as the *Shchuka* (or the NATO name *Akula)* with a

Spetsnaz minisub attached to the deck behind the conning tower; docked at one of the piers in the North Sea port of Murmansk.

The colonel said, "*O-681* is able to carry a *Spetsnaz* minisub on her back." The frame changed. "The special operations sub you saw in the previous photo had to be scuttled. Here, you see the new minisub *SZ-44*. It will be flown with you to Havana by cargo jet. A communication team will be at the intelligence facility at Lourdes. They will act as relay between Yakov Baturin, us, and you. Your messages will be relayed to us through the on-site encryption equipment in order to minimize the signal-intercept risk by American eavesdroppers."

Some more of what he'd already heard followed. Lepushin waited patiently while he ignored the unnecessary repetitions.

The colonel put his elbows on the table. "You were chosen for this mission," he said, "because of your experience and success in overcoming piracy in the recent past, particularly in regaining a pirated Russian merchant ship in the Black Sea last year through the use of a minisub similar to the *SZ-44*. Once the miniboat arrives at your place of rendezvous with *O-681*, you and your team will learn it thoroughly."

When Lepushin was finally allowed to speak, he said, "I would like to know the reason for an at-sea retrieval when one by land would be much less problematic. Would it not?"

"We have tried twice to retrieve him in the past—once when he was in Washington and once in Houston. We have reason to believe he will be easier to seize at sea. And you will have better flexibility as to when and how to take him. But *you* must be the judge of the when and how."

"Am I to use lethal force if necessary?"

"Only if absolutely necessary. You will be in waters patrolled by the American Navy and Coast Guard as well as the Bahamian Defence Force and on occasion vessels in the British Navy. It is imperative that you employ stealth at all times and avoid any kind of detection, let alone confrontation. We want Telasnikov back alive but only if you can get him without yourself, your team, or *Opekun-681* being compromised. If you are too much at risk in seizing him but can neutralize him instead, do so. If we cannot get him back, he is better off dead than remaining with the Americans. Though the U.S. Navy's Office of Naval Research let him go because he was not happy working there, someone in ONR might have a change of mind, realizing his real value, and want to exploit it. Were they to do so, he would immediately be under close security again and any chance of our getting him back would be seriously minimized."

Used to compartmentalized secrets, Lepushin said, "How much of this is Captain Polivanov and his second-in-command to know of the mission?"

"Only as much as is necessary for him to help you in its accomplishment. He has no need to know anything about Telasnikov's background or the reason we want him back. All Captain Polivanov needs to know is that Telasnikov is a loss that must be recovered."

"But you indicated that Captain Polivanov is not presently in Cuba, that you are not in contact with him—"

"That is correct," answered the colonel. "We do not know where he is just now. *O-681* was at Puerto Cabello for several months, its crew trying to train Venezuelan submariners. That, according to Capitan Polivanov, was an assignment of insurmountable obstacles, cultural and political. He has been on recon and surveillance patrol since October when he was missioned to lie off Guantanamo Bay and the U.S. submarine base on Andros Island to update our Fleets' sonic library of U.S. submarine signatures. We have not been able to make contact with him for two weeks. *O-681* has to be extremely quiet in those waters and Captain Polivanov has reported that his boat's anechoic skin is peeling, making her noisier and more vulnerable to adversarial sonar than one that never had it. It is very risky for Polivanov even to float a radio buoy because of all the maritime traffic in the region. Then there are CIA and NSA satellites, of course, passing over, monitoring all kinds of communication traffic."

"And *O-681* is all we have available for a mission so important?"

"I believe you know the state of our navy, Captain-Lieutenant," the colonel replied brusquely. "For the moment, *O-681* is the best boat for the mission."

"What if contact with Captain Polivanov is not regained, sir?"

"We have considered that possibility; considered that for some reason the *Shchuka-B* is lost at sea or, god forbid, has been captured by the Americans. But for now we must proceed in the belief we soon will make contact. When that occurs, you will immediately be told of it. You will be told what to do. Captain Polivanov will be told that once the two of you meet, he is to take orders from you as the mission requires. For that to be more acceptable to him, you will be given equal officer status. He will know you as Captain-First-Rank."

"And my past duties in Internal Investigations?"

"We do not believe he knows much about that."

"Is there any reason for me to think Captain Polivanov might be less than co-operative despite my equal-officer status and despite orders from the Directorate and Fleet?"

"Not that we are aware of," said the colonel. "Are you aware of any such reason, Captain-First-Rank Lepushin?"

"No. So I am to stand by at the place of rendezvous to wait for word from you that contact with him has been made, etcetera."

"If we have not made contact with him by December thirty-first, we will have to resort to an alternate plan, depending on the information we receive from Yakov Baturin. You will receive the details about that when it becomes necessary."

CHAPTER 4

A Distant Signal

IN ONLY A shorty wetsuit and with one tank of oxygen, Kyle Dawton was lower than he'd meant to go. The seabed here was lower than was indicated on the charts; a good twenty feet lower, if he remembered the chart depths correctly. More than twenty feet in some places. Or was it? His memory, his cognitive functions, were getting fuzzy.

What was that?

When he turned to look around, he saw nothing through his bubbles but low mounds of crumpled coral heads curiously blackened as if by soot. Sand, some of it also darkened. Fish swimming in and out of the scrambled outcrops. But he had an eerie sense that something or someone else was close by.

Sinbad lay above him, the only vessel on the surface within visual distance when he'd plunged into the water, leaving Ashley Dillet up there alone, sunbathing on *Sinbad's* bow deck in her birthday suit. Nice suit. Copper-colored skin gleaming with suntan cream he'd pleasurably applied. They'd been diving for the last couple of days after meeting at a scuba shop in Nassau. Diving and drinking and copulating like a couple of concupiscent eels—in and out of the water.

For his part, trying not to think of Victoria Cooper.

He looked at his depth gauge again. *Sinbad* lay 20 fathoms above when the distance should have been only 18 or less. He pondered that, his thought processes sluggish and dipping toward confusion. He'd dived thinking to go down only eighty feet or so, and followed a slope that went down much deeper. Why had he gone deeper? Something luring him?

Movement on his left made him turn again. At a depth of over a hundred feet, visibility was still Caribbean clear, though everything was bluish. Nonetheless, he raked the distance with his wristlights.

Again, nothing but fish and coral. But no, *something else. Coming at him out of the blue. Twenty, thirty meters away. People. Can't be. But here they came. Coming at* him. *Ragged clothes. No scuba gear on at all.*

They vanish.

Okay. Okay, calm down. Just the lingering images from that farcical movie he and Dillet watched on DVD in their Nassau hotel room before coming up here. Ghosts or zombies of departed buccaneers still in his head. That and the diving they'd done along the so-called Joulters Wall. That and too much partying. Shouldn't even be diving hungover and depleted. Breaking one of the cardinal rules for scuba, particularly at a depth in excess of fifty or sixty feet.

But what had disturbed the coral, the seabed here? And why didn't the depth-reading on his depthgauge agree with the depth recorded on the charts in *Sinbad's* cockpit? The discrepancy between the charts' depths and what *Sinbad's* depthsounder and sonar had recorded were what had urged him to dive here when, dulled and tired from too much *joie de vivre*, he should have stayed on the boat with Leyley.

Lowering depth . . . rising sea level because of melting glaciers, global warming . . . tongue of the ocean licking at the land . . . But lowering seabed making sea level rise? That didn't make any sense. Or did it? His foggy head wasn't making much sense of anything.

Something coming at him again. *A mermaid this time. Naked, beautiful. Victoria . . .* She morphs into a puff of smoke, a scattering of disturbed silt.

A stream of numbers began to flash in his mind's eye: 1, 12, 17, 27, and 1 again. Other numbers between them, dim, all of them fading. Tongue of a supernatural ocean licking at my ganglia. Getting silly. He looked at his gauges. *Yep, definitely time to go up.*

There she is. No, it's that horde of raggedy-assed ghosts. Coming at me.

Poof, they're gone.

And in the direction where they were, he sees something else. There on the sloping bottom amid the scattered coral. No turtle grass and not much sand. A vague shape, an outline, of what could be—a sunken ship! For a second, he has the sensation of being not under water or even on it but out in space somewhere, with a ghostship floating among the stars.

A galleon tossed in storm . . . waves 20 feet high or more, their troughs that deep . . . shrouds torn and tearing away . . . the mainmast broken and falling . . . men screaming . . . waves crashing like walls, like battering rams, over the main deck . . . ship listing far to port . . . breaking apart in the middle . . . men swept overboard . . . going over going down . . . down . . . down . . .

Shakes himself and realizes he's not only getting narced but cold. Looks again. Trains his lights on the seabed. Looks at his gauges. Seabed's about ten more feet down and maybe five times that distance from where he last checked his compass. On a slope toward darkness.

He heard a beeping. At first he thought it was the signal coming from his dive console, telling him it was time to ascend. But it sounded much more distant than that. Too weak. Off to the northeast. He listened, not breathing. Heard it again. Faint.

It turned into a bell. *Ding dong.*

Full fathom five thy father lies . . . of his bones are coral made . . .

You're much deeper than that, Dingdong . . .

The warning signal for him to ascend was now indeed emitting its rapid beep right in his ears.

Air low. Just enough left to decompress on the way up.

But at least he has the presence of mind and the discipline to obey the warning. And to look at his GPS. Presses its record button to mark and remember the location. Squirts gas into his buoyancy compensator. Begins to ascend. Pressure in his ears and voices in his bubbling head.

The wail of ghosts. No more flashing numbers. But that faint bell . . .

Sea-nymphs ringing my knell.

⊷▭◉ ◉▭⊷

He had just enough energy and strength left to haul himself out of the water, climb the dive ladder and shuck the scuba gear and wetsuit and sit there on the workboat's transom for a few minutes, clearing his head and sinuses.

And in clearing his head much of what he'd "seen" below began to fade into forgetfulness.

But his vision of a wreck remained. The inaccurate depths he'd encountered remained. He sat there trying to hold on to that until he saw a ship he'd not noticed before. Not the wreck below but one here on the surface. Maybe less than a mile to the east. Hadn't noticed it before because it hadn't been there. Or maybe it had. Maybe he'd been too preoccupied with making whoopee earlier to have noticed it. No, he had to have noticed it, large and close as it was. So it hadn't been there when he dived. In any case, there it was now. Some sort of research ship, it looked like. Close to 300 feet in length. About the size of *The Morgainne*. Coming toward *Sinbad*. Or so it seemed.

He got up and walked naked to the cockpit and found his shorts and the binoculars. Went out to the starboard rail and glassed the ship. Still lying in her altogether on the bow deck, Leyley Dillet said something but he didn't hear what it was and didn't respond.

The approaching ship had a low superstructure; a lot of heavy-duty equipment bristling the main deck: cranes, winches, generators, stacks of pipe and such. Due to its bow-on approach, he couldn't see what kind of stern it had. But he could see that it flew four flags: the U.S. national ensign and two designating the ship's organization, company or whatnot, neither of which Dawton recognized; and flying from the bow was the flag required of a ship in foreign waters, in this case the Bahamian courtesy flag that looked much like the red and white British flapper.

An empty helipad lay above the bow.

Two men stood forward outside the ship's bridge, which lay midships and towered over all the stuff on the deck, both with binocs trained on *Sinbad*, probably looking straight at him.

His forty-six-foot cabin-cruiser-turned-workboat was anchored bow and stern to the seabed. Having drunk of the devil juice addicting Wayne Chizzick in the Florida Keys' pirate fight, Dawton thought with a weird thrill of the rifle and shotgun stowed in a bench locker against the starboard bulkhead. In a drawer under the cockpit's control console was a Heckler and Koch MK23. But these guys watching him couldn't be pirates. Not on a ship like that. Just who or what they were remained to be determined. But in the determining, he didn't intend to be plowed under.

The ship's speed had to be between twenty and thirty knots. He was about to get on the radio and try to raise it but, closing the gap, it finally altered its dead-on course and veered to starboard so that it could come alongside *Sinbad's* port side. The name on its bow was *WildBore V.* No abbreviated prefix like RV (Research Vessel) or DSV (Diving Support Vessel) or anything else denoting its purpose. But he saw now that like *The Morgainne* it had a squarish stern with an A-frame for launching and retrieving submersibles or research and salvage robots.

"Yo, Leyley," he called forward. "Better get up and go below. Unless you want to lie there and give these guys a show and maybe get your bonny butt knocked overboard. These bastards are coming in close!"

Closer than the legal limit allowed.

Gathering her towel and sunbathing paraphernalia, Ashley Emma Dillet, allegedly of Freeport, Andros Town, South Palmetto Point, Cat Island, New Orleans and parts in-between, sashayed naked as a jaybird and none too hastily aft to the stern and, blowing him a kiss, finally to the ladder going down to the lower cabin.

Dawton turned his attention back to the approaching ship. He started *Sinbad's* outboards and turned her bow to face *WildBore.* A porpoise squaring off with a whale. He lifted an arm, swung his hand outward to tell those on her bridge to veer off.

One of the men standing outside the ship's bridge lifted a limp wave as if returning an indifferent greeting. *Checking you out, shrimp. What are you doing here?*

It was a mere forty or fifty yards away before *WildBore* began to turn. Its wave-wash soon slammed into *Sinbad's* port side with enough force to swamp the workboat's decks and almost capsize her—leaving *Sinbad* rolling like a cork in the ship's wake.

Kyle cursed and watched her go.

As the wash abated and *Sinbad* stabilized, he began to scan his surroundings to see if any other boat might be nearby to have witnessed the flagrant violation of maritime law.

To the south, dim in the distance, lay the largest and least explored island in the Bahamas, North Andros. At its visible tip was Morgan's Bluff Harbor, nine miles away.

Once a haven for seventeenth-century pirates and privateers like Henry Morgan, the Andros Group of three—separated by bights but often referred to collectively as Andros Island—was now a playground for other adventurers: yachters, sports fishermen and recreational divers (the 140-mile long Andros Barrier Reef was the third largest in the world), and folks on cruise ships. Though Andros had farms, tourist resorts, and the U.S. Navy's submarine base known as the Atlantic Undersea Test and Evaluation Center (AUTEC) on its east coast, much of it remained unexplored and underdeveloped. At the moment, nothing in its direction offered anything in the way of a witness as to what had just happened.

A small, scruffy little cay that was hardly more than a sandspit lay less than a mile to the west; to the west of that, rocks and shoals and to the west of them the string of rocky, uninhabited islets, covered with vegetation and surrounded by sand-shallows, called the Joulter Cays. "Joulter," he remembered reading somewhere, was an eighteenth or nineteenth century Irish word meaning fish-buyer that had through time devolved into an insult. Dawton felt insulted now, and jolted.

Nothing to the immediate north and east either, but the Tongue of the Ocean, known acronymically as TOTO; a deepwater trench with 6,000-foot depths that was a north-south extension of Great Bahama Canyon.

He saw no lighthouse anywhere.

No more ships or any other watercraft anywhere in any direction.

Why had the WildBorers come so close? Maybe just some jerks wanting to have some fun scaring a smaller craft? But somehow he thought the incident meant something more ominous. In fact, when he looked to see if *WildBore* was still departing, he saw that it was not. It was turning around and coming back!

Dawton thought of the guns again.

Leyley poked her head out of the cabin door below the cockpit. Still nude. "*Mwen anvi vonmi!* Everything in the cabin is a mess. I got thrown all over!"

Kyle replaced the binoculars and cranked *Sinbad*. Her three outboards roared to life.

"Eh," said Leyley, "we going?"

"Yeah. Those assholes are coming back."

"Can't you outrun a ship that big?"

"I can run circles around it." Kyle threw the glasses up. Saw the guys outside the bridge once more scoping him. He gave them the old highway salute.

To his surprise, the ship turned toward the northeast.

He slowed the engines.

Leyley wrapped herself around him. Arrggg," she said, "my hero. You shoot 'em with the bird!"

⋯▸▬◉ ◉▬◂⋯

He anchored *Sinbad* off a beach on South Joulter Cay that night. The lights of *WildBore V* were visible about two-and-a-half miles away where she hadn't moved for hours. It was curious that she was in the vicinity where he'd dived earlier in the day.

With the sun down and a breeze off the water, Leyley had finally put on sweatpants and a sweater. It was the first of January and the temperature at night here in the northern Bahamas could drop to the forties. Kyle had built a fire on the beach. She sat down beside him and looking at the fire said, "What else is bothering you? I don't think it is just that ship that almost ran us over. What else?"

He lay back on the blanket and looked at the stars and tried to think of what to say.

She poked him. "What did you find down there this afternoon? Atlantis?"

He tried to keep his face blank. "I saw a lusca."

She glared at him, dark eyes firelit and narrowed. Not about to be put off by any tale of a gigantic octopus.

"I know they say she hangs out in blue and black holes around Andros but this one is really huge. Big as a house. Could've come up from the TOTO deep. I'll bet that's what got all those planes and ships that have disappeared in the Triangle. Not a weird energy vortex or methane gas. No, it was a humongous lusca."

She swore. "Hey, you were down a long time." Her crisp Bahamian accent was more Brit than Creole. "How deep did you go? What did you see?"

He'd told her in Nassau that he was a salvage diver. "A treasure hunter?" she'd asked, her bare foot out of its sandal and climbing his leg under the table in the bar where they went for a drink.

"A dreamer," he'd answered.

"You saw something," she persisted now. "I can tell. Was it just more rocks, like the Bimini Road or those stone blocks off Cay Sal you told me about—or was it a real shipwreck, a treasure? Tell me!"

Having twice in his past incurred nitrogen narcosis when diving too deep and too long on air, having dived today to a depth and in a condition he should not have, Dawton didn't completely trust what he could remember, let alone his perceptions when down there. Some said suffering "the Rapture of the Deep" just once could make a diver susceptible to it again, at less and less depth. Others said you got used to it and eventually over it. It all depended on the individual diver. Then there were those seeming paranormal "spells" he'd had from time to time when he'd been nowhere near the sea. But had he really seen a sunken wreck, or part of one at least? Now on the surface, so tired he was hardly able to keep his eyes open, he wasn't so sure. "Saw ghosts," he muttered, suddenly remembering *that*.

"*Ghosts?*"

"Ghosts of pirates, like those we saw in the movie."

"Hey, come on."

"I saw a mermaid, too. Looked like you," he lied.

"So you're not going to tell me!"

Her insistent tone was becoming obnoxious. "I'm telling you."

"Okay," she said peevishly. "Okay, so did you catch her, this *manman-dlo?*"

"The what?"

"The mermaid!"

"Um."

"*Men wi!* If I let you make love to me again, will you tell me?"

"I've told you. And what's this '*let me* make love to you' crap? I think we've been going at it with equal give-and-take."

She lay down on the blanket, her mouth petulant; but she squirmed out of her sweats and put a leg over him. "I will curl your already curly hair. Come on."

Though her maneuvers awakened his indefatigable libido, there was no immediate arousal from below. Her hand moved over him, stroking and kissing muscles as hard as rope while *Zozo* refused to rise from the dead.

But depleted and thinking of Victoria, he was no longer interested. And he was yet under the influence of the deep. Then, looking into the fire, he had a glimpse not of Vic but of a dark-skinned woman walking along a broken seaside walkway, in her eyes the image of a shabby ship filled with desperate people and listing to one side as if leaking and about to go down.

The fire snapped and the vision vanished. He could hear the water lapping against the shore. Like a great tongue licking.

Tongue of the Ocean. Lapping over the unfound ruins of Atlantis. Lapping over longlost shipwrecks. And who knew what else?

Lapping in intervals like the beat of a great heart on this world where it was eat and be eaten. Like the beat of time itself slowly but inexorably chewing away at all.

Wooooo, said the ghosts he'd seen down there. *Look at us. Think of who we once were. Do you know? Do you have any idea?*

He heard a bell, distant. *Ding* . . . No. Not a bell. A beep. Not here on the beach but in his head—or somewhere. Knew he'd heard it before. Tried to remember when, where. Lost it.

Out of his intermittent memory he saw that streak of numbers again, like the series in a lottery ticket. But they were gone before he could grasp them distinctly.

Sinking toward slumber, he saw images he would not remember when conscious. Images of things so tiny they were not visible to ordinary vision. Images of miniscule mouths chewing, chewing . . . visions of dark slime like the excreta of some unknown bug species . . . turning to blood. And all of which became snarled with images of an unhappy man on a luxurious ship somewhere at sea.

⤙⬤ ⬤⤚

Next morning when he headed the workboat for Nassau, *WildBore V* lay exactly where it had the evening before.

Leyley was still in the sack and no doubt would be all the way back to Nassau. He was glad of that since she'd nagged unsuccessfully half the night to learn what he'd found. What had he found? Nothing. Nothing he could remember anyway . . . except . . .

He plucked the satphone from under the cockpit panel. Punched *The Morgainne's* data room number.

On the salvage ship waiting in Nassau Harbor, Tony Corro, answered. "Hey, Kyle! We thought you'd drowned somewhere, been abducted by aliens or something," said the information tech and believer in a host of extraterrestrial theories.

"Still on the planet, Tony. Something I want you to look up. Name of a ship. *WildBore Five.* That's Wild capital b-o-r-e, not Wild b-o-a-r."

"Yeah, okay, *WildBore Five.*"

It was still there to the north. Kyle cranked *Sinbad* up as high as its engines would go without cargo. At sixty knots it began to leave this northwest corner of TOTO behind.

The bow spray hit his face as the boat took the swells and he pondered what to tell Chiz and the rest on *The Morgainne*, but remembering what had happened the last time he found a sunken ship, Chiz especially. What had followed his finding the sunken U-boat wasn't fun. Somebody could have been killed. More than one somebodies. But that didn't mean something calamitous would happen again. In any case, Argos Salvage was in dire financial straits; after the failure to find the wreck off Cay Sal Victoria had researched, on the brink of going under.

"Something else," he said to Corro over the noise of the boat and the sea. He looked around the cockpit panel at the cabin door which was still closed. Put his mouth close to the phone's mike. Kept his voice as low as he could while keeping it strong enough for Corro to hear over the engine noise.

"Get Chiz on the horn. Off the Joulters—I may have found a wreck."

Maybe.

CHAPTER 5

The Boat

IN HIS PENTHOUSE office in the Uptown District of Houston, president and CEO of the JJ Oil Corporation James Jessup Harwood III sat at his desk looking out over the Galleria Towers and talking on the phone with the President of Neptune Boat Builders in Fort Lauderdale. "It's ready?" he said excitedly.

"Yessir. We've taken it out five times. Every wrinkle's been ironed out and every glitch fixed. You got the photos I sent?"

"I'm looking at them now." Harwood tilted his desk chair forward as he had another look. Spread over the desk was a number of glossy pictures, exterior and interior, of the new megayacht *Melanie Giselle Rose. Blue Bliss,* another luxury yacht similar in design and layout, was now a corporate boat harbored in Houston and used by JJ Oil employees for parties, vacation excursions and whatnot. But with four decks above the waterline and two below, the *Melanie Rose* was bigger, faster and more luxurious. At a price of 170 million USD, its white and silver lines radiated power, speed and affluence; with a sleek aerodynamic design tooled to cut through the worst of seas with a resolute and godlike ease. Registered in the tax haven of Panama, its home port too would be Houston. But for now . . ." She's a beaut. And the submarine?" (Another 36 million.)

"Yessir, *Blue Deep* is in her berth on Deck Four and ready to go."

So was Jim Harwood. He looked at the photos of the submarine. Almost half as long as the megayacht, it had a surface range of 1000 nautical miles and a submerged endurance of five hours at eight knots.

So thrilled he was shaking a little, he proceeded to make several more calls: the first and most important to his wife of forty-three years. "It's ready, honey."

"What's ready?"

"Your yacht! The *Melanie Giselle Rose!*"

Silence.

"Mel? Are you feeling all right?" He feared what she was thinking. He'd made so many promises through their long marriage, made them and reneged, lied, had affairs . . . but she'd fooled around on him too. "Mel?"

"I'm all right, J. J." Her tone was flat and tired, as if she expected another letdown. She said, "So when should your yacht be ready?"

"It's *your* yacht, Mel. We'll sail to the Bahamas, go deepsea fishing, celebrate your sixtieth—"

"Oh, *please.*"

J. J. tried to ignore her sarcasm and decided to end the conversation without allowing any more opportunity for more of the same. "We'll fly to Lauderdale in a week." He said flatly. When he hung up, he sat there irked by her lack of enthusiasm and her calling the *Melanie* "your yacht." *Sour.* She'd been sour for years. He had hoped the christening of the yacht in her name would sweeten things between them just a little. Then it occurred to him that he hadn't asked if a week would give her enough time to gather her usual crazy entourage for the trip. Just the kind of thing she'd accused him of so many times, thinking only of himself, giving orders, making the decisions without her having a say in them.

He called her back. She told him she'd be ready in a week and this time was the one to cut the conversation short and hang up before he had anything else to say.

Grumbling to himself, he called several friends and a few politicians to invite them along. Some wouldn't be able to make it. Most were appropriately grateful and eager to go. "Bring family, a friend or two if you like," he told them. "Plenty of room. Y'all come. It's the season for wahoo and mackerel and bonefish and—just put aside a few days for a whole bunch of fun sailing and partying and fishing and, you know, whatever. We'll have a helluva time!"

He would have called his kids and grandkids too but none of them had any love for the sea. Didn't give a hoot for the oil business either. And if the truth be told, he couldn't fault them there.

Still tired from the New Year's Eve party two nights ago, he was worn out from all the phone talk when he finally got around to calling his VP of Exploratory Operations, Eastern Division.

In his office one floor down, Woodrow Culpepper finally picked up after the fourth ring, as if he'd been sitting there at his desk, hesitating. And, like Melanie, he greeted the announcement of the yacht's "maiden voyage" with silence.

"You there, Woodrow?"

"Yessir."

"I assume you've got the day on your calendar."

"I'm mighty busy, J. J." And he launched into all the stuff he was busy with.

Harwood broke in irritably. "The trip's been planned since before Christmas, Woodrow! Give what you're doing to Alvin. He'll take care of it. As planned, you're to come along with Joseph Yord. You told me Yord has a lot of ideas about making offshore wells eco-friendly and he's trying one out on our Bahamian wells. I want to see what he's done there."

Culpepper's voice was suddenly tense. "We were just out there, Boss. Me and Dr. Yord. I sent you a report—"

"Oh? Guess I haven't gotten around to reading it." There was a lot he wasn't getting around to lately. His horses, his polo game, his hunting trips— and Mellie—were taking up all his time, most of the latter in goings-on he didn't care a damn about but after years of the marriage having gone south, he wanted to breathe new life into it, make amends. "What did it say?"

"Ridley Stukes is keeping a close eye on all six wells. You know, J. J., the Bahamas are a pretty scruffy locale. You oughta take your maiden voyage to someplace like Monte Carlo or Cannes or St. Tropez. Maybe Rio or Singapore. You know, like show off the boat in a really glamorous setting—I'll bet Mellie would like that."

Boat? Jim Harwood looked again at the array of photos. *Boat!?* He was so thrown off track he forgot what they'd been talking about.

"And you know I don't really enjoy the open ocean—"

"Woodrow?" Harwood shouted. "Like I said, this has been planned for weeks, with you and Yord along as part of the plan. Start packing. We're going to the Bahamas. We can go down in the new submarine to see the wellheads right up close! The two shallow ones anyway. I want to see them with you and Joe Yord along." He disconnected, irritated. His VP of the Eastern Division should have been overjoyed at being included, never mind his damned dislike of the sea. Hell's bells, the *Melanie Giselle Rose* was a long way from being a god-damned "boat!" She was a mid-sized luxury liner, a seaborne Waldorf-Astoria!

Culpepper had given him heartburn. He shoved an antacid down his throat, gulped water and tried to settle down.

His last call was to the Fort Lauderdale security outfit hired to guard the yacht, with whom he'd already made arrangements to provide a topnotch security team to be part of the crew. "Hell, these days there's just no telling what might come rolling in out of the blue."

"You got that right, Mr. Harwood," said the security sales rep. "But with these guys aboard your boat, you won't have a thing to worry about."

CHAPTER 6

In the Triangle

HE LEFT ASHLEY Dillet on Nassau's East Bay Street wharf. Miffed by what she called being dumped, she expanded on the matter by informing him that she was out of a job, destitute and needing taxi fare and whatever else he could spare. It occurred to Dawton that he'd paid for everything since meeting her. She'd so nagged him about what he'd done on his solo dive the day before that he had no wish to see her again in any case, and had ignored her repeated proposals in that vein. Belatedly aware that he'd fallen prey to an island trull, he nonetheless gave her most of the cash he had left and scrammed with a "Best of luck." She responded with, *"Ba bay, bouda fon!"*— the translation of which, he didn't think he needed.

Leaving Nassau Harbor, he almost ran into an approaching U.S. Coast Guard cutter. Not because he had his mind on Leyley but because he had it too much on that dim shape he saw at 20 fathoms.

Or thought he saw.

Saw the ship named WildBore V. No doubt about that.

He turned *Sinbad's* wheel and swung sharply to the right of the cutter. Trying to regain stability, he almost hit another boat—an old fifty-foot fishing trawler riding low in the water and jammed to the gunnels with people in ragtag clothes. Behind this trailed a Bahamas Defence Force escorter. He throttled down sharply. The Defence Force boat didn't look much better than the trawler. But though not always in agreement about drug and refugee interdiction, apparently the BDF and the USCG were working together today.

His speed slackened to a crawl as he passed the migrants' boat. Dark faces with sunken eyes stared at him. Mostly men but some women too. Hungry, desperate faces. He'd seen something like them just recently but could not remember where or when. Then he remembered: the young woman on a disheveled shoreline walkway, a crumbled and smoking city behind her. Her eyes and these eyes of the people here on the trawler clawed at him, his white skin, his—to them—rich and happy-go-lucky life.

Kyle Dawton was neither but he tried to smile. He waved. Some of them waved back. Some of them smiled. Most of them didn't respond at all. He wrenched his gaze away.

Now alongside the BDF patrol boat, he waved at the men on its deck. They watched him with stolid stares, without greeting. He might be a drug smuggler, a spy for human traffickers, anything. (But some in the BDF were known to drag their feet—or their propellers—when it came to cracking down on refugee and drug smuggling in Bahamian waters. Many Bahamians were sympathetic to either or both "enterprises" and by extension human trafficking, all of which contributed to the archipelago's economy. After all, the Bahamas had a centuries-long tradition of piracy, outlawry and smuggling of every kind.

Once past the BDF boat and the lighthouse at the end of Paradise Island, Dawton opened up the engines, wanting to put the crowded harbor with its palatial Hotel Atlantis, its opulent cruise ships, yachts and boatloads of busted poor behind. Running against a 14-knot wind out of the north-northwest, *Sinbad* took the sea swells at fifty knots.

The revamped *Morgainne* lay at anchor just north of Crystal Cay, gleaming blue-gray and white in the cloud-dappled sunlight; its decks, shops, winches, cranes, radome and superstructure a steel hosanna to the God of the Quest. But with nothing in her labs, lockers or storage bays in the way of recovered treasure from the deep.

Much had happened since that restaurant meeting in August: the unanimous agreement to Vic's becoming a third partner in Argos (despite Dawton's tangled emotions); the final work on *The Morgainne* and the ship's christening and sea trials; and with the signatory ink hardly dry on the new-partnership documents, Wayne's asking Victoria out for dinner and her tactful turndown (in Kyle's presence), and Wayne's subsequent funk which he'd tried unsuccessfully to hide. (Though the subject of Wayne's PTSD did not arise, Kyle was certain that

Victoria would not have gone into a partnership of any kind without knowing what she was getting into.)

Thus they had sailed in late October from Miami to Cay Sal and undergone over a month's futile hunt for the sunken privateer Victoria believed there. Ostensibly she had handled the disappointment like a seasoned archeologist but nonetheless accepted responsibility for the labor, time, money and energy spent. Kyle had tried to make light of it ("Hey, it's part of the game.") and so had Wayne in his way: "Get over it," he'd said, obviously still not over *her;* or his jealousy over the fact Kyle had often excluded him when talking to Vic; or the anxiety building in him over the threat of Argos going bankrupt. Having been rejected, Chiz had tried to find solace in telling Kyle that she was out to undermine their pursuit of riches with an archeological agenda, or she could be a saboteur for some unknown competitor, or a spy for the Argos investors, expected to report to her father and to Wayne's father and the rest of the Argos board as to how the company in general and Wayne in particular performed. Kyle had laughed. "How would all that bullshit square with her taking the blame for not finding the Cay Sal wreck?" When Wayne was assured by Admiral Curt, with whom he often quarreled yet trusted, that his suspicions were ludicrous, he more or less discarded them and looked for other reasons to think she was up to something troublesome. The admiral and Bill Cooper thought "Victoria and you boys" could work out any problem.

Kyle wasn't so sure.

Closing in on the 286-foot salvage ship, he throttled back and let the workboat glide the last fifty yards toward *Morgainne's* starboard side where the winch there would pull *Sinbad* up.

Part of the crew and staff lined the maindeck's starboard rail, Wayne and Victoria among them. With Vic was her five-member archeological team and with Wayne the two former fellow SEALs who'd signed on in September, Dan Clark and Rick Rivera.

In ten minutes, Kyle and the workboat were on deck where he received a warm welcome from all, excepting Chiz who looked on the verge of a fractious rant.

Victoria, hair pinned close to her head but some errant strands adorning the breeze, gave him a smile that seemed still shadowed by the Cay Sal failure, and a hug and a peck on the cheek that sent a hum to his toes. He hugged her back and everybody else, including Chizzick who could have been mistaken for a drugstore Indian.

"So you think you've found a wreck?" Chiz snapped—but with a hint of excitement and hope too. "We're set up in the conference room. We wanna hear about it. Let's go."

Everyone was aware of Chiz's mood and on the way to the conference room, the post-holiday chitchat was brief. African-American Dan Clark, cool and calm as fellow SEAL Chiz was splenetic, whispered in Kyle's ear with a chuckle, "He's missed you, man. That's all. He loves you like a brother."

With *The Morgainne* anchored off Nassau Harbor, running up bills and nowhere to go, those who'd wanted to go home during the Christmas and New Year's period had rotated four-day leaves while a skeleton crew stayed with the ship. With his own family in its usual state of episodic conflict and geographical displacement, Dawton had romped away his four days with Ashley Dillet, about which he had naught to say to his sea-mates but suspected her name would come up.

⊶⊜ ⊜⊷

In the conference room on the 01 deck, the salvage staff allowed Dawton center stage. Because of his satphone report, everyone already knew the location of his purported find. Tony Corro had laid out maps and set up a laptop and a presentation screen. From the long oak table, Dawton pecked the laptop's keys and showed them on a digital satellite map the place where he thought he'd seen the sunken wreck. Having marked the site on his GPS, he zoomed in on the small cay southwest of the site. "This is the nearest land. Just a knob—"

"Checked it out," said Chiz, at the head of the table. "Everything in the vicinity of the Joulters belongs to the Bahamian Commonwealth. No privately owned real estate anywhere around."

Sitting across from Kyle, Victoria said, "We've been trying to find any record of a ship having gone down at that location or anywhere else within a ten-mile radius."

"And?" said Kyle.

She gave him that less-than-happy smile. "So far, zip."

In the ensuing silence, Dawton could feel the doubts as well as the hopes hovering, not the least of which were his own.

Wanting details he hadn't given over the phone, Vic said, "How big was it? How much did you see?"

The expectation in her and all the other faces made him so want to be right. "Okay, I have to say this: When I was down there, I was sure I saw what looked like at least part of an old ship at the edge or the mouth of a canyon. It was dim, in the distance." *Felt a little narced. A little?* "I could've been seeing things." *I was. Ghosts and mermaids and . . .* "And I know what it will cost, what we'll gamble, by going up there and having a look. All that said, I believe something's down there." He avoided looking at Corro, who despite the fact he was familiar with Kyle's "hunches," would take wing if Kyle admitted what he was thinking: *I felt its presence before I saw it.* "It was too far away to see in any detail. The seabed went up and down but mostly sloped downward, and I was running out of air. We had only four tanks and they were all used up—"

"We?" said Chizzick, suddenly tense.

Kyle cursed his slip of tongue.

"Someone was with you?"

"I didn't spend four days alone, Wayne."

"A woman?"

Kyle said nothing but he gave his partner a look that was meant to tell him to back off.

Didn't work. "Did *she* see it?" Chiz persisted.

"No," retorted Dawton, becoming irritated himself. "She was sunbathing on the boat. And I said nothing to her about it." He grinned and tried for some levity. "But Leyley believes in voodoo, Chiz. She might divine it."

Everyone laughed except Chizzick. "*Lay-lay?*" he squawked.

"Leyley. L-e-y-l-e-y. A diminutive of the name Ashley," Kyle kept his voice even but he was bracing for a blowup.

"So we don't know her from anybody, Kyle. When you called to tell us—where were you? Was Chickypoo Voodoo with you?"

"She was asleep in the cabin."

"Where is she now?"

"I left her in Nassau. Relax. She's history and she knows nothing about it—"

"How did you meet her?"

"In a dive shop."

"What the hell was she doing when you went down to where you saw the wreck?"

"I told you. Sunbathing on the boat. I wanted to dive at that particular spot because the bottom depth on *Sinbad's* sonar was giving me numbers that didn't jibe with the charts. I wanted to go down and have a look at the seabed but I said nothing to her about any of that."

Victoria broke in, perhaps to relieve the tension building between the two. "How deep did you go?"

He looked at her and as usual enjoyed the view. "Over a hundred feet." Reluctantly taking his gaze off Victoria, he turned to marine geologist Rob Palmer down near the table's far end. "The seabed looked messed up, Rob. There was a lot of broken and scattered coral, exposed and cracked limestone. Much of the silt looked scrambled and pooled and black in the low places. Looked like everything had recently moved. And considering the discrepancy between the charts and the instrumentation—I'd say the bottom has sunk there and sunk more toward where I saw that dark shape that could be a wreck." He punched a key on the laptop, changing the image on the presentation screen. "As you can see, the charts say the bottom there varies from eighty to ninety feet. But according to my depthgauge and *Sinbad's* sonar, I was down from ninety to a hundred and sometimes deeper than that, I think." Actually he couldn't remember exactly how deep he'd gone. Forgetfulness as well as delusion could sometimes be a symptom of narcosis.

"One hundred and ten feet," said Nancy Coletti, Vic's assistant, "is still within recreational diving limits. But a microquake or subsidence, something like that, could have exposed the wreck, could explain why there's been no report, no sighting, of a wreck in that location." She looked at Kyle with an excited grin. "Till now."

Rob Palmer said in his professorial way, "The Bahamas region is one of the least seismically active in the world. But small seaquakes occur frequently all over the planet and many go undetected. As for subsidence, you can have that without any earthquake-energy release at all; above a hollow or unstable area, for example. Sinkholes, as you know, are all over the Caribbean."

Chizzick was squirming impatiently and Palmer got the message.

"Yeah!" said Tony Corro. "And who knows what's in them or what's going on down there! Maybe an alien subsea base causing microquakes. That kind of thing."

Accustomed to Corro's tangents, no one was currently in the mood to join in.

"But if it were a sinkhole that big—" Dawton answered the question before he asked it, "—so I guess there could be a hole under what appears to be seabed, on the verge of falling in." But he knew even as he said this that the seabed subsidence had another cause, though he could not say how he knew it or even guess what that cause might be. He looked at Corro again. "Have you found out anything more about that ship named *WildBore Five*? It passed by *Sinbad* too damned close. Looked like it could be a—"

"Yeah," said Tony. "It belongs to a company called Deepwater R and D out of Miami. Registered as a refitted offshore research vessel, formerly a drillship. Charged with checking out wellsites, working on wellheads, doing seismic work for possible wildcat sites. Deepwater R and D is a subsidiary of the big Texas company called JJ Oil."

"There's your answer," exclaimed their other marine geologist, Greg Kotalik. "That explains the subsidence. A microquake caused by removal of oil."

"Could be," said Palmer.

"Look into it," said Chizzick. "Find out if Nassau's allowing JJ Oil, or any other oil outfit, to mess with the seabed in that area. But do it without calling any attention to us." Chizzick's intent look swept around the table. "We don't have a permit for any salvaging in these waters yet and we don't need one unless or until we know for sure there's something to salvage. Everybody clear on that?"

As assents went around, Kyle for a second almost remembered something he hadn't mentioned. But it was gone, like a distant *ping*, before he could identify it.

"What?" said Chizzick, having seen his puzzled expression.

"I don't know. Something I'm forgetting. Can't . . . maybe it'll come back."

"Did you really see the wreck or did you just *feel* it being there?" said Wayne.

Kyle hesitated, again unsure if he wanted to broach this ambiguity in front of all present. But there it was, out of the bag. He bit the bullet. "Both." *I think.*

"Okay." Chizzick faced the rest. "I think everybody here knows our on-and-off record at finding sunken wrecks, including those of you who've joined us in recent months."

Kyle saw Vic cast her eyes downward and could almost hear her *Ouch!*

"In the four years we've been in business, we've found five. None of them off-the-charts profitable but, along with the ordinary salvage and rescue work, they made us enough money to stay afloat. Two were found through hunches, intuitive guesses if you like, by Kyle." Chizzick gave Tony Corro a look warning the pseudoscience buff not to go bananas. "One off the Yucatan and one off the well-combed Florida Keys. He's had four misses in the hunch department and, yeah, he didn't 'feel' anything when we were off Cay Sal looking for Coop's wreck, but the one off Yucatan made us a significant amount of money." (Victoria, Kyle noticed, was now being called Coop.) "That makes our checking out the Joulter area worth the gamble. If anybody disagrees or has a qualm of any kind, I want to hear it now."

Corro said, "The Joulters are in the Triangle. We're in it now, have been since we crossed north of Andros. Inexplicable things happen here."

Chiz turned to look at him pointblank. "Tony, you're an excellent IT guy, great with data, with computers, with research. And you can yak about your Bermuda Triangle crap all you want when you're with whoever wants to hear it. But that ain't me and in my opinion, it ain't a valid reason to vote for or against going to the Joulters. Okay?"

The chastised but good-natured Corro nodded and shrugged. "You bet, boss."

The silence that ensued made Kyle wonder if most, despite Chizzick's categorical dismissal, weren't thinking about what he'd just dismissed: the fabled "Devil's Triangle" that stretched from Bermuda to Florida and down the northern Bahama chain, where instrumentation allegedly went awry and ships and planes mysteriously vanished; where the so-called lost city of Atlantis was said to have sunk and UFO activity had been reputedly sighted; where strange mirages appeared and disappeared and time itself could go askew.

No one else had any comment. Chiz raised his hand. "Who's for going?"

All hands lifted.

Chiz got up and walked over to an intercom speaker in the port bulkhead. "Bridge, this is Wayne."

First Mate Buzz Franks answered. "Go ahead, sir."

"Let's get underway. Northwest heading for the Joulter Cays." Chiz gave Franks the coordinates logged on Kyle's underwater GPS.

"Roger," said Franks.

Chiz looked at the clock on the port bulkhead and then at the salvage staff. "Okay, we got calisthenics and hand-to-hand at fourteen hundred. Then we get ready for Lay-lay Bay!"

A few chuckles went around as the group dispersed. Kyle remained in his chair. Wayne had riled him before and he'd always shrugged it off, let it slide. But his restraint was wearing thin.

Passing him on her way out, Victoria put a hand on his back, making him forget about Wayne for the moment and his skin cells burn through his T-shirt to meet her touch.

"Sit a minute?" he said.

He was at the table's end. She took the chair at the corner to the left. He patted the hand that had warmed his back. "Vic, I know you're trying your best to move on but I think you're still pretty down about Cay Sal. Of course, it doesn't help when Wayne makes cracks—"

"I've had a look at the books. He has a right to be worried—"

"I know. And we're going to burn more money we don't have, risk all the usual, on the basis of another one of my 'hunches' which might not pan out. We're damn near desperate, could lose it all—"

"But like you told me when the Cay Sal hunt got us nothing, that's part of the game and the gamble. Tell me, why did you become a salvage diver?"

"Joined the Navy. Loved the sea. Liked diving."

"What did you like about it?"

"Going down to places that were mysterious and hidden. Looking for things thought lost. Uncovering stories, mysteries. I razz Tony sometimes about his Bermuda Triangle stuff but I believe there's a lot we don't know about, not just under the oceans but," he swept his hand through the air, "everywhere." He thought about what he was saying with a bit more depth and said, "Under the pursuit of adventure, the history hunt and the knowledge and treasure hunts, in the experiencing of any or all of these things, we're looking for hidden truths, I think; for deeper truths—about our world and about ourselves. Who we are. Where we came from. Where we might be going and why. I've thought about such things all my life. But . . . I think that just as we live on a world of oceans we also live within oceans unseen, only barely sensed, at times felt or heard by some, but for most of us no more graspable in the mind than water in the hand. They brush at our consciousness, though, like surf at a shore or whispers in the wind."

"That's beautiful. A poem?"

"Just an opinion." He grinned. "Or two. Anyway . . . I don't have any answers. How about you?"

She smiled and touched the hand that had touched hers. "Very much the same. Though I'm trained as a scientist who likes hard and irrefutable evidence, science in virtually all its fields continues to discover new things formerly regarded as theoretical, doubtful or unverifiable . . . or nonsense. My dream is yours: to discover something not known, not found before. Something that would increase our knowledge about ourselves, history, life . . . Hey, I find your so-called hunches fascinating. How do you explain them?"

"I can't." He was tempted to tell her more but decided to say simply, "I don't know what to make of them."

She still had her hand over his. "Kyle, I like you very much. I think, I hope, you feel the same about me. I want you to feel comfortable confiding in me. Please. You can trust me with whatever you want to talk about."

In other words, she knew he was holding something back. "I like you, too," he said. "I like you so much it scares the crap out of me, Vic. You're not like the women I've been with—the goodtime types, the party girls—ever since a failed relationship turned me into a wad of buzzard bait hanging from a seacliff. Pardon the comparison to Prometheus. But . . ."

"But we're in a precarious position."

"Umm, yeah, that. Wang Bang Wayne, bless his troubled spirit, could combust and catch the ship on fire if he thought we were 'carrying on' after you snubbed him. And we have this ship and a dive op to run, a treasure to find, riches to claim, mysteries to unravel . . . and so forth."

She smiled. "'And so forth' leaves a lot of wiggle room." She paused and he thought he saw in her eyes the hope that sometime in the near and discreet future they might do some wiggling. "But as much as I'm enjoying this, I'd better get down there to the workout. Are you coming?"

He shook his head. "I'm beat. Going to my cabin for a shower and nap. But maybe I'll come watch." *You especially.*

⋗▬◉ ◉▬⋖

Not long after the pirate attack off the Florida coast in June and two months before *The Morgainne's* christening, Wayne had lobbied his pop and the Argos board for permission to turn the company's salvage crew and staff into a crack security team. Kyle knew it was pointless to argue that they'd captured three of the pirates and chased the other three off. Having to rely on taking weapons from your attackers for use against them was not a good defense strategy.

Admiral Curt was able to acquire from an undisclosed source a small arsenal. They began a search for people who had military, preferably combat, backgrounds. The task proved not to be difficult. The ranks of unemployed were replete with veterans home from the conflicts in the Middle East, looking for new careers, willing to be retrained. Relying on the internet to get the word out, they had the crew and staff they wanted in a couple of months. By the time they'd left for Cay Sal, they had nine deepwater tech divers while every member of the staff and every crewmember were certified in basic scuba. In addition to Victoria and her archeological team that included two women, *The Morgainne* had a ship's crew of thirty-one and a salvage staff of research technicians, scientists and divers numbering eighteen. Four women in the crew and three in the salvage staff.

Chizzick, Clark, and Rivera all had seen combat in Iraq and/or Afghanistan. As had former Marines Eduardo Sanchez and Deck Chief Meg Latham. Though they rarely talked about their warfare experiences with anyone but themselves, they shared with the rest everything they knew about small arms and small-unit tactics above and below the water. A core group was formed of three teams headed by Chizzick, Clark, and Rivera. For good or ill, Kyle elected to be in Wayne's team. These nine came to be called the C Team after Chizzick's initial. And, said Dawton wryly, to encourage the fantasy of having teams A and B. And though he hated even the thought of another attack of any kind, he took part in the training with keen interest as almost every afternoon Wayne had all not on duty assemble at the fantail of the 01 deck for physical and martial-arts exercises; and at least once a week when at sea, target practice and the cleaning of weapons.

Dawton had showered and gotten into some clean shorts and a T-shirt and was out on the 02 deck watching today's grunt-and-groan session (mainly watching Vic who in her usual tankshirt and shorts wasn't grunting or groaning at all) when he heard the voice of Joe Fontana, *Morgainne's* chief cook, come over the PA: "Hey, galley here. We've got a stowaway!"

The galley was directly below the 01 deck. On his way down, Dawton could see several ships and smaller craft scattered about in the channel. He could also tell that the shoreline was a long way off. By the time he entered the galley, several others had arrived, including the muscular 220-pound Chizzick who had the scrawny stowaway by the front of his shirt and was pulling him outside toward the starboard rail.

A young Bahamian male obviously scared out of his wits.

"We found him in one of the storage lockers," said Fontana. "Cramming his gut to the gills."

Knowing what Wayne was about to do, Dawton yelled at him, "Wayne, wait a minute! It's got to be two miles or more to shore!"

Chizzick ignored him. The Bahamian was petrified, not struggling at all.

SEAL buddy Dan Clark said, "Wayne, hey, man, let's cool it, huh? We can hand him over to the Coast Guard."

Rivera said, "Yeah, hey, Wayne, let him go."

Others were coming from various parts of the ship. Kyle tried to free the stowaway from Chizzick's grip. With one hand, Chizzick knocked Dawton back against the bulkhead. Physically strong and in as good a shape as Chizzick, Dawton was nonetheless trying not to lose control himself. He noticed the round life preserver hanging from a hook to his left. He yanked it free just as Chizzick was about to hoist the Bahamian over the rail to sail out over the ship's frothing wake. Kyle slammed the air-filled preserver over Chizzick's head and jammed it down over his shoulders, breaking his hold on the stowaway and pinning his beefy arms to his sides.

Clark seized the Bahamian and pulled him to safety back in the galley. Rivera stood with Dawton as the entrapped Chizzick cursed Dawton and tried to get his hands under the preserver to push it up. But his torso filled the ring so tightly he could hardly move.

"Cool it!" Rivera shouted at him.

"Maybe," Kyle yelled, wiping blood from the cut on his lip from Chizzick's blow, "we should throw you overboard and see if *that* will cool you down!"

"Maybe you'd better get this goddamn thing off me before I tear *your* fucking head off!"

Members of crew and staff, Vic among them, were lined along the rail and more were coming. Together, Dawton and Rivera pulled the stumbling Chizzick inside the galley and closed the door.

Clark had taken the stowaway somewhere out of Chizzick's sight.

Dawton and Rivera pushed Chizzick down so that he could sit with his feet on a bench and his ass on its table. Dawton put his face close to his inflamed partner's. "Listen to me, old friend. We go back a way and we've had our ups and downs and I love you. I know you better than anybody else on *The Morgainne*. I know you've been through a lot of bad shit. I know you're brave, even kind when you want to be, but if you're going to come unraveled like this over nothing more than a starving stowaway—and another thing or two that's been shortening your fuse—"

Chizzick started yelling and Rivera looked as if he were about to put a fist in his face.

"—let me remind you," Dawton continued, "how many people are outside who saw what you were about to do. I've no stomach for betrayal and none of us want even a hint of discord, never mind mutiny! But I'm done with you and with Argos if you let yourself forget that maritime law says a stowaway is to be detained aboard the subject vessel until he or she can be handed over to the relevant authority!" Dawton took a breath. "As major owner of the company, you've technically got the ultimate say in all things Argos, all things that do not flout or circumvent prevailing laws of the sea or of humanity. But as regards *that*, you can be reported, turned in, arrested like anyone else. And don't forget this: barring a report to authorities, such misconduct can be reported to your pop the admiral!"

Chizzick had at last shut up. He sat there glaring at Dawton, wrapped in his straitjacket of a lifepreserver, breathing hard and smoldering, but Dawton's words had sunk in.

"You need to have one of those long and earnest talks with yourself, my friend," Kyle said. "Like the kind you've told me about in the past. You know the drill. You need to come in from the freaking wars, Chiz, as shrinks have told you. We ain't at war here. A starving stowaway is not going to blow up our ship!"

"We're in it," whispered Tony Corro later who stood with Kyle at the transom's starboard rail watching the sun go down. When Kyle didn't rise to the predictable bait, Tony thought he had to explain: "The Triangle," he said. "We're in it bigtime now."

CHAPTER 7

Contact

NEAR MIDNIGHT ON January 4, the Russian nuclear submarine *Opekun-681* rose to periscope depth 120 kilometers south of Cabo Beata, Hispaniola, at the northwest edge of the Venezuelan Basin. From horizon to horizon, nothing lay within either the observation- or the attack-scope's range.

The sonar supervisor reported no ominous acoustics within the kilometers-long reach of its passive-sonar complement.

When Captain Konstantyn Polivanov relayed through the Officer of the Watch that Radio should prepare for an outgoing message transmission, he sat down at his computer and had another look at the string of encrypted messages that had come in while he was in circumstances preventing a safe response. Almost every message had to do with an urgent order from the Main Intelligence Directorate in Moscow and/or Northern Fleet Headquarters at Severomorsk. In typically terse military vernacular, their gist ordered him to a small port on Cuba's southwest shore, thereby to pick up a special operations team headed by a *Spetsnaz* captain named Anton Lepushin. The mission would be under the *Spetsnaz* captain's command.

With a heavy sigh of disgruntlement, Polivanov pecked out his response.

RETURNING TO LA GUAIRA TO UNDERGO ELECTRICAL REPAIRS AFFECTING RADIO CIRCUITRY, ETC—WILL MAKE SECURE COMM FROM THERE.

He hoped the encoded message would get through despite *O-681's* electrical problems and U.S. intercept. Though he did not look forward to returning to La

Guaira, he looked forward even less to reentering the northern Caribbean for an undisclosed mission to be directed by a special ops officer he'd never met. But Polivanov knew of him, knew of his stint in Internal Affairs and more recently his heroism and leadership in overcoming pirates who'd seized a Russian merchant ship in the Black Sea.

Polivanov's original orders had been to debark for Kola Bay on January 8, there to debrief Command and submit the data gathered on U.S. ships and naval activity in the Caribbean region, undergo some badly needed repairs and upgrades for *O-681* and enjoy leave for his men and himself so they could go home to see their families. They had been away for two months—15 percent of the one-year enlistment for most of his volunteer crew—prowling the northern archipelago and before that overseeing exercises and drills with the Venezuelan navy while training its alleged submariners.

The Venezuelan navy, like the navy claimed by Cuba, was a lamentable joke. There were times when Konstantin Polivanov thought of the Russian navy in the same way.

The messages from Moscow and Severomorsk were no jokes. Nor, Polivanov was certain, would be *Spetsnaz* Captain Anton Lepushin.

⇥⊙ ⊙⇤

The sun had not yet risen when the Antonov 124 landed at Jose Martí International Airport in the Havana borough of Bayeros. The big airship having taxied to a stop on an apron at the runway's northwest end, newly but temporarily promoted Captain-First-Rank Anton Lepushin waited with his team of eight *Spetsnaz* operatives for the rear ramp to open.

They stood in the huge cargo bay in navy *Spetsnaz* battle dress uniforms with their gear, weapons and their midget submarine.

When the ramp was down, they stepped out to the tarmac. The humid temperature was eight degrees Celsius with a light but chill drizzle falling. Trained for and used to much harsher conditions, they ignored the rain.

A Ural 6x6 was waiting to take them to the Russian embassy compound. Having come in an aging ZIL limousine, the embassy liaison sent to greet them explained that the flatbed truck and crane required for offloading the minisub and transporting it to a hidden wharf west of the Gulf of Batabano would not arrive till next day. Meanwhile, Lepushin and his men could enjoy a night's stay at the embassy. He invited Lepushin into his car and the rest climbed into the Ural.

The liaison officer was the chatty sort. Lepushin said little as he watched the scenery go by, most of it agricultural, till they crossed over the Autopista Este-Oeste and entered the densely populated Cerro District.

Though yet kilometers away, the embassy's main building rose high above the palm-fringed streets and looked in the distance much like a giant robot without arms, vaguely human and vaguely of another world. Built by Alexander G. Rochegov during the Soviet era, Lepushin knew that even some Russians thought it one of the ugliest edifices in the Caribbean. Lepushin didn't care how it looked. Bureaucratic architecture was not one of his interests.

The liaison officer wanted to talk about friends he had in the Kremlin elite. Not caring much for the Kremlin elite himself, having that much in common with the submarine commander with whom he was supposed to rendezvous, Lepushin said nothing. By the end of the ride, he was more than ready to alight.

The mission required communication with Moscow and with the mole Yakov Baturin.

At the Lourdes spy base south of Havana next day, Lepushin went to the building designated in his orders and was shown a private room where he could send and receive encrypted messages. Despite the fact the exchange was deeply encrypted, what he read on the computer screen was couched in opaque text:

THE CONTACT REPORTS HE AND HIS CLIENT ARE STILL AT THEIR USUAL LOCATION BUT ARE ON SCHEDULE FOR THEIR TRIP. YOUR PICKUP VEHICLE HAS HAD TO RETURN TO THE SHOP FOR REPAIRS. TENTATIVELY WE HAVE A WEEK REMAINING FOR THE RENDEZVOUS. THE CONTACT AND THE PICKUP VEHICLE WILL KEEP US CURRENT WITH ALL DEVELOPMENTS. NO NEED TO CALL THE CONTACT AT THIS TIME. THAT IS ALL FOR NOW.

Lepushin signed off and, after having a good look at the encryption and communication equipment, met with his men by the truck waiting to take them to southwest coast.

"Headquarters has heard from the mole as to his and the defector's current whereabouts," he told them. "And contact with the *Shchuka* has been made. *Opekun-681*, however, has had to return to Caracas for repairs. Meanwhile, we will proceed to the southern port, stay fit, keep our weapons and equipment in good order, and learn *Saida* from stem to stern."

It took the *Spetsnaz* team the rest of the day to reach the shabby port where the midget submarine lay off a pier in a camouflaged cove. Though its classified military designation was *SZ-44*, it had been nicknamed the Russian word for pollock. Each man had his own *Saida* manual. Designed for naval rescue and *Spetsnaz* missions such as reconnaissance, capture and sabotage, she had two small viewports, one to the right and one to the left of the cockpit, and was painted a charcoal black. Below and to each side of the cockpit two retractable arms with claws at the ends could extend five meters outward for seizure or manipulation of exterior objects. Hatches above and below a central hyperbaric sphere allowed divers to leave and return. A rear transport compartment would hold gear and equipment. Twenty meters long and four in diameter, it displaced 55 tonnes and could dive to 1000 meters. Its size and shape were much like that of a Beaked whale, a common denizen in the Caribbean; but U.S. sonar operators were long inured to the "biologics" ruse, having used it for a long time themselves.

Inside *Saida* was a crate of amphibious rifles and pistols for both land and underwater use.

Three days after their Cuba arrival the GRU sent a message that "the pickup vehicle" had left "the garage" and if nothing else went wrong would be "at your location in four to five days."

"And the supplier and his client?" Lepushin sent back.

"The contact and his client are in the same place as was last reported but are scheduled to arrive at their planned location within a day."

Lepushin looked at the calendar page on his encrypted satellite phone. It was the 10th of January.

CHAPTER 8

Tsunami Warning

HAVING LEFT FORT Lauderdale the previous night, the *Melanie Giselle Rose* entered Nassau Harbor a little before ten in the morning on January 12. The gleaming 328-foot megayacht dwarfed everything else but the freighters, a few other luxury yachts approaching its size, and the cruise ships tethered to Prince George Wharf.

On board were its owner and his wife, with her garrulous entourage (the Nattering Nine, Jim Harwood called them) of personal secretary, financial advisor, beautician, dietician, masseuse, yoga instructor, workout coach and a couple of girlfriends. J. J. Harwood had along his aide and secretary, JJ Oil's Chief of Oil Operations who'd come just for the day, the VP of Eastern Exploratory Operations Woodrow Culpepper, and Dr. Joseph Yord and his scientific team; and for this leg of the trip a few old friends and relatives and some U.S. politicians and families; four helicopter pilots and a crew of thirty-four professional live-aboards trained and experienced in providing the owner and his guests the best in seagoing pleasures; and a team of fifteen security guards to make sure said pleasures were not interrupted or disturbed by any outside threat.

Wanting to celebrate the *Melanie's* maiden voyage and show everyone a good time, J. J. had entertained his guests through dinner the previous night. Not with boring stories about the running of a big oil company (or having others run it ever since he inherited it at age 28 with his heart then as now on horses, women, big game hunting, yachting and the sea) but with his knowledge of Caribbean exploration, long-ago sea battles, piracy and the Spanish Treasure Fleet. He also told them amusing stories about having caught with hook and line everything from octopus to goblin shark and was eager to show the others how to do the same. All of which his wife had heard a thousand times and halfway through it began to nod off.

He and Melanie had not slept in the same bed for over ten years. She did not stir from her bedroom in their suite on the topmost (the owner's) deck as he showered and dressed to go down to rejoin the guests, among whom were now four Cubans picked up in Nassau by the yacht's smaller helicopter.

In the next couple of hours, the Cubans were curried, cajoled, and treated to a lavish seafood lunch during which were discussed Cuban oil exploration, leases and concessions. J. J. would rather have talked about how the deepsea fishing was down there in those commie waters but today he listened and after lunch gave the newcomers a tour of the *Mellie Rose.*

Most were properly awestruck by the extravagant lounges and recreational areas, the splendid staterooms, dining rooms, cabins and such. The four Cubanos were mightily impressed with the yacht's state-of-the-art bridge with all its colorful instrumentation and security features. They were impressed most of all with the luxury submarine *Blue Deep* in her berth on the next-to-lowest deck. (They had glimpses of several of the security guards on duty fore and aft but J. J. did not point them out let alone introduce them.)

At 16:30, the Cubans and several other people had to return home and were flown back to New Providence on the 8-passenger chopper called *Big Bird.* But by the time the *Melanie Rose* departed Nassau Harbor that afternoon for the Berry Islands north of the Tongue, it was still a pleasure palace of almost ninety souls.

⊷≡◉ ◉≡⊶

As the dazzling yacht moved smoothly across the Northeast Providence Channel at a leisurely eight knots, the two remaining politicians aboard joined Harwood and Culpepper for cocktails in the owner's lounge on the topmost deck. Culpepper hadn't wanted to be included but J. J. insisted. Culpepper hadn't been very talkative since before they'd left Houston. He'd let others do the talking at lunch. And he'd tried to wiggle out of coming on the cruise to begin with.

With papers and maps having to do with sites in the Bahamas and off Cuba spread out on the table, the talk was at first about oil, a subject that was guaranteed to bore J. J. as much as Mellie was bored by his tales of the sea. But his lack of interest began to be replaced by curiosity as to why Culpepper, ever ready to toot his own horn even when there wasn't much to toot, remained silent. Come to think of it, Culpepper, who was responsible for them, hadn't been very talkative about the six JJO wellsites in the region for some time. And J. J. couldn't remember seeing any of the reports Culp claimed to have sent him. Fact was—a fact of which he was infrequently aware—he couldn't remember half of what was going on with JJ Oil anymore, if he ever did. But he felt there was something fishy going on with Culpepper and didn't think it had anything to do with what was being talked about.

A leggy stewardess in heels and short navy skirt he liked his female cocktail servers to wear brought drinks, turned on the flatscreen TV hanging from the starboard bulkhead, and charmingly departed.

The time was 16:51. The TV's sound was muted.

As the talk went around about the permits JJO had gotten in order to drill six wildcat wells in and near the Tongue of the Ocean, Culpepper just sat there looking at his goddamn feet.

"We found strong evidence of good deposits at those sites, didn't we Woodrow?"

Culpepper stirred. "Yeah." Then he muttered about the drilling that had proceeded in '08.

"But," said Harwood, "the Bahamians threw a halt to the leases in '09 after a blowout accident at a wildcat well out in the Tongue—drilled by a competing oil company. Now the heads of every one of our wells are capped. Right, Woodrow?"

Culpepper nodded. "We've sued for reopening 'em but that's still squat in litigation."

Harwood turned to Preston Slotter, the seventy-something Alabaman who served on the Senate Committee on Energy and Natural Resources and had heard all this before more than once. "We were hoping you could build a fire under somebody's butt, Preston."

"Working on it, J. J. So all you're doing now is just seeing that those wells stay capped?"

Harwood looked at Culpeper again.

Running an agitated hand over his brow as if to smooth out wrinkles, the VP said, "That's about it."

But J. J. could tell that wasn't all of it by a long shot. Though his interest in company and corporate matters had never been keen, though he'd given Culp free rein with JJO's Eastern Exploratory Division, his wonderment now as to what it was that Culp didn't want to talk about suffered another yank. He knew from Chief of Operations Alvin Plume that Culp had been spending more time of late with Joseph Yord and his reclusive team of scientists and engineers than with anyone else. As ordered, Yord and team had flown out with them to Lauderdale yesterday. Culp had sat with them in the rear of the Gulfstream with their heads together like a bunch of conspirators, hardly willing to give Boss J. J. the time of day. Vaguely, J. J. remembered Culpepper had hired Yord a year or so ago because the scientist had some ideas about how to make offshore wellsites more eco-friendly. Or something like that. And he remembered he'd told Culp he wanted Yord along on this trip to show and explain what he'd done or was doing with the Bahamian wells.

Melanie appeared with several women at the other end of the lounge. She waved and they sat down at a table as the stewardess approached to take their orders.

Harwood returned his attention to Culpepper. "Woodrow, call Dr. Yord up for a drink."

Culpepper took a quick gulp of his lime Perrier. "Dr. Yord took off for *WildBore Five* this morning in *Little Bird*, J. J. When you were still in your suite."

"He did?"

"Since we're near the Berries, he wanted to have another look at Well One . . . right away."

J. J. Harwood studied his VP as if he might see something not readily seeable behind Culp's thick eyeglasses.

"Who's this *Dr. Yord*?" asked Slotter.

"A JJO employee," answered Culpepper.

"I gathered that. But what's he do? What's he got to do with your wells out here?"

Beyond the senator's thinly haired dome of a head, the TV caught Harwood's eye. The screen showed a godawful number of ragtail-looking blacks running down a street with a building falling in the background. Dust and debris flying. The jumping, erratic video had to have been taken with one of those iPhone or iPad gizmos. J. J. pawed under the papers for the remote, found it, toggled the mute button.

". . . anniversary of the 2010 earthquake in Haiti," an offscreen commentator was saying.

Harwood realized they were watching a rerun of old news.

"Hell," said Slotter, "that was years ago. But god almighty, just look at that!"

Florida Congressman Roberto Delgado said, "Terrible disaster."

Under his breath, Culpepper muttered something, got up and departed the room.

J. J. Harwood stared at his back and said nothing. He looked at the TV again and for the moment forgot what he'd asked Culpepper to do because the earthquake footage suddenly inspired Slotter to indulge in a spluttering harangue about all the aid the U.S. had given Haiti that had gone down "that rathole. Damned pseudo-government's inept and rotten as those African countries they came from," said the once powerful member of the House Committee on Natural Resources Glad not one of the few black members in *The Melanie's* staff and crew were present, Harwood stared at the senator, who wasn't finished.

"And it's still a mess down there!" roared Slotter. "Those people have gotten millions in aid and they just keep wallowing in their own mess. Like Pat Robertson said, they made a pact with the devil way back. Help us free ourselves from the French and we'll serve you—"

"Oh Jesus Christ!" erupted one of the women at Melanie's table. "'Those people' have been kept down and made poor by such hypocritical fools as you!" She slammed her drink down, grabbed her handbag, and rose angrily from her chair. Harwood realized it was Delgado's good-looking niece, Sheri. "As for the aid they've gotten," she went on, "*that's* gone mostly into the pockets of the alleged aiders and politicians—American politicians included!" And with that, she left the room, leaving an atmosphere of shock and turbulence in her wake.

The look on Ernest Delgado's face indicated he thought the same as his niece with regards to evangelist Pat Robertson; as for including Slotter in some business dealings, maybe Congressman Delgado and J. J. Harwood, while perhaps not in a pact with the devil were in cahoots with a fool.

Thrown off for only a second or two, Slotter recommenced rattling on for another full minute till his face turned a hue that matched his bloodshot eyeballs.

Harwood had heard him spout off like this before. He found the remote and clicked the TV off. "Before you have a coronary, Preston," he explained. "Or give me one."

"Sorry, Preston," said Roberto Delgado, son of a Cuban who'd fled Cuba when Castro seized power. "Sheri's going through an ugly divorce."

Slotter mumbled something about "goddamn liberals" and finally shut up.

Jim Harwood liked his guests to be happy and have a good time on his yacht. He did not like discord; and he wondered what Sheri Delgado thought of *him*. JJ Oil had been profiting from deals with Haitian and Dominican oil interests even before the 2010 quake. Haitian oil reserves alone dwarfed Venezuela's. But closer to home were the wellsites here in the Bahamas. He wanted to talk to Culpepper about that. Where the hell had he gone?

Melanie and the rest at her table had departed. Having himelf lost his desire for social palaver, at least with Slotter present, J. J. Harwood went back up to the owner's deck. On his way, he suddenly remembered the discussion about Joseph Yord. But before he could follow up with Culpepper he was distracted by another clip on his private TV about the 2010 earthquake. Haiti, the Dominican Republic, Jamaica, Cuba, and the Bahamas had been under a tsunami watch. He thought about that, thought about undersea quakes that could happen and cause tsunamis out in the middle of any ocean in the world. The earthquakes of 2011 in Japan and 2004 in the Indian Ocean were both underwater quakes that caused horrific tsunamis. Off the island of Grenada to the south was an active undersea volcano that scientists warned could erupt anytime. If it did, it would cause a tsunami that could sweep across the Caribbean all the way to Florida.

Unsettled by the thought, he checked Melanie's suite. She wasn't there. He called the *Melanie's* bridge. Calling the chief steward, he learned she was out on the VIP patio with her friends.

He made another call, this one to Captain Mick Shelton who tried to assure him that there hadn't been any report of an undersea earthquake anywhere in the Caribbean for a long time."

But one could occur anytime and that possibility dogged J. J. Harwood into the evening.

Somehow, the old footage about the Haitian earthquake, his fears of a tsunami the report had spawned, Woodrow Culpepper's and Joseph Yord's puzzling and irritating behavior, Sheri Delgado's condemnation, all seemed snarled in the same crappy nest.

CHAPTER 9

Artifacts and Omens

RICK RIVERA'S MAGNETOMETER was pulsating. Its highpitched squeals could be heard easily by all four divers. Rick looked at its readout, turned and with index and middle fingers pointing at his eyes, then index finger pointing toward the target, signaled to the rest: *Look! Got something.*

Kyle Dawton gave the "okay" hand signal. His own mag not working properly and velcroed to his diving vest, he held the vacuum hose that was tethered to the line going up to the ship, ready for use.

Separated at no more than four-meter intervals, Vic and Ed Sanchez also signaled acknowledgement.

The mag was making too much noise to hear each other's voice through their throat mikes and, at 130 feet down, the underwater communication system didn't work at its best anyway. Kyle gestured for everyone to check instruments. Using open-circuit breathing with bladders fitted between wing-harness and tri-mix tanks, they'd been at depths between 90 to 130 feet for over an hour. But their gas supply was sufficient for a while longer at present depth, with time allowed for the necessary decompression stops on the ascent.

As Rick moved the mag around, sweeping its snout to find the direction where the signal was strongest, Kyle suddenly recalled the faint bell sound or maybe beeping he'd heard somewhere around here on New Year's Day.

Somewhere around here.

He'd heard no such sound since. But they were not in the same place . . .

If he only just now remembered that beeping, what else had he forgotten? And considering how little he remembered, how reliable was the memory? Maybe he'd been narced after all. Maybe he'd hallucinated. He was hungover, wasn't he? Having too much fun with Chickey Poo Voodoo? All this from Chizzick who had begun to think Dawton's sixth sense as faulty as the underwater GPS he'd used. Then there was Tony Corro: "We're in the Triangle, Kyle, where instruments go crazy." And maybe "hunches" too. In any case, he hadn't thought to record the coordinates in *Sinbad's* log. But no one disputed the fact that they were diving at depths 10 to 20 feet deeper than what was recorded on the charts. About *that*, he'd been right.

Ed and Vic were converging on Rick and Kyle, their lights aimed toward the target. Ed had the third magnetometer but for the last two days it had become like Kyle's, only marginally functional. Failing equipment, foul weather, and foul moods had been worsening for days. They were running out of money, patience, good humor, and faith in Dawton's hunches.

Rotating three teams of four divers each and diving around the clock for over a week, they'd scoured several areas, beginning with the coordinates recorded on Kyle's underwater GPS on New Year's Day. Keeping to depths that matched those Kyle remembered. But they'd found nothing in the way of any wreck. In each area, they'd repeatedly made square and circular searches, expanding outward, probing with sidescan sonar, with robot *Ogler's* sensors, and with the handheld cameras and magnetometers. As they pored over the images in *Morgainne's* photolab, they'd discerned nothing more than what they'd seen in their lights: a few objects which under scrutiny in the lab turned out to be mere litter and junk.

Rick's mag was pulsating more rapidly, picking up something near what could be a wall, dark and murky some ten meters away. Maybe the mouth of a cave.

Kyle had the impression he was nearing a hole in ordinary reality down here where ordinary reality to begin with was quite different from the one topside. So far, Dawton's "hunch radar" hadn't worked since New Year's Day. No visions, no inklings of any ghosts or any wreck.

But nearing the dark wall with the rest, taking slow and shallow breaths through his regulator, he felt it settle over him: *a chilling awareness that something terrible had happened here.*

A school of small red barbier darted in and out of his lightbeam and in colorful array vanished into an adjacent crevice like a lost wish. He looked up and around, making certain nothing was coming that might make of them a meal. Here along this fragmented deepwater reef they'd seen both shark and Great barracuda. Still well above the "Twilight Zone" between the upper sunlit waters and the abyssal depths of the Tongue, they should have been seeing on the seabed some stony reef-building corals giving way to the softer species—sea fans, sponges, polyps and such. There was little of that, not in its usual state anyway; just large chunks of crumbled coral and limestone amid sand and seagrass and silt pools that suggested recent disturbance.

Chief geologist Rob Palmer had yet to find an online report of any seismic movement in the region, recently or historically. But as he had said, miniquakes went undetected all the time.

Vic and Ed had turned their magnetometers off as Rick's rose in pitch. Goaded by its insistent tone, the four moved toward the cave. As their lights pushed away the darkness, it became clear that it was not a cave but a deep recess ragged and encrusted with algae and old coral, much of the latter lifeless.

Though fooled for days by their mags detecting only junk, the current pulsations of Rick's detector were nonetheless an electronic stimulus for hope.

The signal sounded musical. In fact, Kyle felt a little lightheaded.

Not good.

As they neared the recess, their lightbeams raked stone and coral, most of it a scrambled mess; some of it oddly blackened in spots as if blighted by leeches or some mysterious pestilence. In the lights, the black spots glistened jewel-like. In fuzzy fashion, Kyle remembered seeing this peculiarity before.

Holding the vacuum hose in his left hand, he thumbed his release valve with his right in order to drop a few more feet, then unsheathed his knife as he sank. A small ray rose from the shadows to Kyle's left and dashed into the blackness behind them. For a second, Kyle forgot what he was supposed to be doing. The mag's beeping brought him back.

Rick was touching one of those black spots staining the coral. His gloved finger came away with a sticky goo coating it. He smudged a finger of Kyle's glove with the stuff: it looked and felt viscous, like a globule from an oil spill.

Rick fanned his hand back and forth over a band of silt. Victoria and Eduardo were nearby, likewise examining the bottom. Kyle switched the suction hose on low power and began to lightly move it over the area Rick's mag pinpointed, sucking up silt and tiny coral fragments and a few of the oily blobs.

Ogler hovered nearby, tethered to *The Morgainne* above. In the ROV's shipboard control room, her operators had the divers on-camera, ready and waiting for any instructions.

Some small black bulges like rough stones the size of grapefruits began to appear as the silt and sand went up the lifter hose. Using the tip of his knife, Kyle began gently to pry one up. It was attached to what looked like a strand of rope—but it was too heavy for that. Maybe an encrusted chain. Too small for an anchor chain but a chain nonetheless. He gingerly raised the length of it till it ended in a crescent-shaped calcareous gob five to six inches wide.

Rick was also prying something loose. Kyle turned the hose Rick's way.

Vic and Ed were finding objects nearby, brushing them off, putting them back where they'd found them so that mapping and documenting could begin. Vic was taking photos. Over her phone, she told the ROV operators topside to move *Ogler* in closer. The ROV had stronger lights and video cameras than those the divers carried.

Kyle put the chain back as he'd found it.

Hopes rising, they began to put down stakes and with survey tape started laying out a grid so that each square could be photographed and sketched. Everything found and hauled up to the ship would be labeled with its identifying number in the grid.

They put the smaller things that might be artifacts in the mesh bags on their belts. The roughly round objects and some other items too encrusted to identify weighed more than the bags could hold. Kyle pulled closer the haul-up line and its larger basket. Everything would be later examined in the labs.

They kept sifting, taking pictures, extending the grid.

Anxious because of their accruing bottomtime and his growing wooziness, Kyle moved inside the recess, under its overhang. He probed quickly but gently with the knife. It struck something. He put his fingers into the silt and with Rick now operating the hose, felt and brought the object up. It was elongated and curved, a little over a meter long. Crusted over. But enough of its shape— the curvature and shape of hilt and handle—told him what it was. *A sword!* A cutlass maybe! He waved at the others and pointed. They looked and grinned through their faceplates.

Ogler's cameras purred and theirs flashed. Ed signaled having found something else. He pulled it up. Too covered with concretions and goo to tell what it was, he put it in his bag. The others began finding other small objects under the overhang.

Something huge and dark was passing over them. They froze. Vic turned her handlight on it. A *Rhincodon typus*. A slow-moving whale shark some 30 feet long and only ten feet overhead. Largest fish in the sea but a harmless filter feeder. It moved on.

They all breathed more easily.

Pointing at her dive console on her forearm, Victoria indicated they'd better ascend if they wanted to keep breathing at all.

Kyle put the sword into the haul-up basket and turned to have a last look at the recess where the lengthy section of limestone wall had crumbled, exposing the dark opening that looked now once again more like the mouth of a cave. And as he looked, it seemed to widen with the power of a lure both dreamy and ominous. All at once he began to see within it a glowing round stone rich with hieroglyphs, *a face in its center whose tongue stuck out . . . becoming a tongue of fire licking at huts in a jungle . . . people screaming and silhouettes hanging by the neck from trees . . . horses, mules and wagons waiting . . . then a storm at sea . . . people jumping from a sinking ship . . . the world heaving . . . cave growing . . .* sucking him in —

"Kyle? Kyle!" A hand grabbed his shoulder. It shook him, pulled him out of the recess—and back to the here-and-now. He became aware of the warning signal on his console.

He turned. Victoria was staring at him and making the sign to ascend. Rivera and Sanchez were already several yards above them. Unsettled by what he'd "seen," he began to follow her up the anchor line. But he couldn't resist one last return of his lights to the broken wall and that opening. No opening now. Just shadow. Exposed rock between broken coral heads.

Victoria was eight feet up the line before he realized she had stopped and was looking down, about to descend again to help him. He signaled that he was all right and resumed his ascent. The hallucination, his imagination gone wild, narcosis, whatever it was, gradually lost out to a burst of elation that stayed with him all the way to the top: *They'd found some artifacts! Maybe a debris trail! Maybe a wreck* down there somewhere after all!

But what kind? And in the muddle of the seafloor and the weird goo, where was it and what would be the challenges to salvage it?

⇥ ⇤

The rest of the dive team and others were there to greet them with cheers when they were raised on the dive platform by winch to the main deck. But as they shucked their diving gear in the dive room, though he appreciated the backslaps and hugs—even Chizzick hugged him—Kyle took only a cursory part in the excited chatter. And when they kept asking him how he did it, how'd he know artifacts were there, he said over and over again that he hadn't known. But he'd sensed a wreck in this vicinity. "Well," he said, "we haven't found a wreck yet, just some stuff that might or might not pan out to be worth something."

Victoria kept looking at him. Rick Rivera, who rarely missed anything amiss, watched them both. When Vic became aware of this, she took her eyes off Kyle and finished peeling down to her vest and leggings and went into the women's room to shower.

During the celebratory champagne and jubilation with crew and staff, Kyle tried his best to be social. Only Victoria and Rick continued to throw him curious and concerned looks and seemed to know he was keeping something to himself. But for now, the excitement and anticipation of the work ahead eclipsed everything else.

Kyle was relieved when Vic and her archeological team went below to the wetlab to begin the preliminary tasks of determining what they'd found and how much of it could be of historical and monetary value. The complete cleaning and conservation processes would take weeks, much of it to be deferred to Argos's main lab in Miami.

Kyle did not care to be alone for very long. He could not recall every detail of the dive or pin down the reason for his lingering disquiet, but kept telling himself it was natural to feel that something calamitous had happened in these waters. A debris field on the ocean floor was ample evidence of such, certainly. Was there any place in the world's seas that had not played host to some sort of calamity?

But these reasonings did not put to rest the disquiet. And considering some of the things he'd "seen" recently when undergoing a "spell," could the cause of the disquiet lie not in the past but in the near future?

When younger, he had tried meditation at times, even self-hypnosis, to see if he could venture deeper into the timeless dark; and in every attempt, when he reached that point, that portal where he might have taken the plunge, he pulled back, not knowing if or how he might return to accepted reality.

Crazy. He was crazier than Chizzick. And to escape himself he kept busy in the dive room preparing scuba gear and equipment for the next dive, or keeping up with what was going on in the labs and ROV room.

⊶⊷ ⊶⊷

Preliminary examination by microscope and chemical analysis of the samples of oily goo indicated an atomic variant of carbon and hydrogen but one with a new molecular configuration unfamiliar to geologist Rob Palmer or anyone else aboard who knew anything about hydrocarbons or crude oil.

Palmer had discovered that any JJ Oil activity in the Bahamian archipelago was not public. As for Argos Salvage, the fact that the salvors did not want any unwanted attention thrown their way required Palmer to provide a false name and alibi (just a curious tourist) to the bureaucrat in Nassau he'd spoken to over satellite phone. While the bureaucrat admitted that JJ Oil had several permits for oil exploration in the archipelago, those permits were currently under suspension. When asked if JJO had used at any of its sites the hydraulic fracturing of rock for the release of petroleum and natural gas into wellbores, the bureaucrat answered, "Absolutely not!" Palmer had asked where those sites were located. But by this time, Mr. B. must have suspected that Palmer was some sort of ecofreak out to sabotage oil wells and he refused to offer any more information. Thus their hope of finding anything out about the oil company's work here in the region came to nothing.

The goo would have to undergo more thorough analysis in Miami.

By afternoon, the drylab's x-ray machine had revealed that the sword was indeed a cutlass inside a scabbard composed of leather and wood. Though the latter materials were badly degraded, the sword's metal was in relatively good shape. Other objects brought up from the morning's dive turned out to be a string of beads, a lead musket ball, a roughly round stone of basketball size which, everyone agreed, was likely a ballast stone. And chains, leg irons, and iron wristlets.

Chizzick chose to focus on the latter items. Having dived that afternoon with Dive Team Three and too eager to hear the preliminary lab results of the morning dive to have taken a shower or brushed his hair, the thick black mat stuck up at odd angles, spiky as a bramble bush, and his eyes were fiery red. After turning the stowaway over to the Coast Guard, SEAL buds Clark and Rivera had had several private talks with Chiz. Admitting he'd made a fool of himself, he'd apologized to all aboard but his interactions with Kyle remained chilly and he continued to suffer episodes of irritability and depression.

"Maybe we've found the debris field of a goddamn slaver," he groused, looking at Kyle as if Kyle had purposefully lured them to an unprofitable find.

They were sitting at the long table in the wetlab with Clark, Cooper, Rivera, Diane Weitzman, Palmer and three of Vic's wetlab technicians. Being of mixed African-American lineage, Chief of Dive Ops Weitzman's attractive and expressive face gloomed over with thoughts of slave ships. Dan Clark, with more African blood, seemed indifferent and Kyle wondered if he'd ever taken much interest in his origins.

Wanting to dissipate Diane's funk and his own, Dawton offered this opinion: "Shackles were used on troublesome sailors as well as slaves."

"And," said Vic, perhaps wanting to mollify Chiz with the possibility they still could have found a debris field that could relinquish treasure, "slave ships coming from Africa to the Caribbean often had gold and ivory aboard. Not to mention personal items of wealth belonging to captain and crew."

Chizzick ran a hand over his rough-hewn mug and gave her a look that said not only did he not like her joining Dawton in any argument against him, he did not need to hear what he already knew, never mind his grumbling about a slaver wreck.

Kyle said, "We don't yet know what we've got."

This comment caused another long and questioning look from Victoria as if to say, *What did* you *see down there you're not talking about?*

The ROV room called. "*Ogler's* finding some interesting stuff," said Rob Palmer.

Wayne rogered the message and rose from the table with a brusque "I'm going to the ROV room."

Those in the diving staff who were done diving for the day followed and were soon crowding into the ROV control center to watch the high-definition monitors. Displayed on the array of screens were the feeds from *Ogler's* powerful lights and cameras.

Brad Shinley was acting as ROV pilot. Beside Shinley at the video controls, Rob Palmer pecked his computer keys while Shinley worked the joystick and his keyboard to advance the hovering robot slowly over the bottom. *Ogler's* haul-up basket (the third load of the day) was again full of various encrusted objects its arms and pincers, guided by Shinley, had picked up. Along what was increasingly looking like a debris trail under a layer of silt and calcium carbonate, lay more irregularities that suggested artifacts.

"Look at this," said Shinley. He used the joystick to move *Ogler* a few more feet forward and to lower its vacuum hose down to suck up the silt.

Through the mike at his console, Palmer updated the bridge on the movement Shinley was making with the ROV. Thrusters had to adjust the ship's position and stability to compensate.

On the monitors, other bumps and contours that looked unnatural were showing up in the recently disturbed silt and rock. The ROV's magnetometer was beeping furiously.

Something roughly round in shape but larger than shackle balls jutted from out of a jumble of broken coral and limestone. Shinley manipulated *Ogler's* arms and claws to pick up the encrusted item and put it in the basket. It could have been a bowl or pot but several in the room thought it might be something else. So did Dawton but he had grown uncomfortable with all the fuss over his hunch.

Shinley raised *Ogler* a couple of more feet and zoomed in her central camera. Other scattered and encrusted objects impossible to identify without bringing them up for cleaning appeared in the strong halogen lights.

"What's that," Wayne said, "that thing—" He leaned around Palmer and trained one of the cameras on what he was talking about: something protruding from what looked like a mat of rotted planking. "Pull that out, Brad."

Everyone held his breath as Shinley coaxed *Ogler* down through a school of mahogany snapper. The fish scattered. With *Ogler* only a meter above the seabed, Shinley used his console stick to extend the ROV's right arm and to drop its pincers.

Out of a nearby crevice rose a Caribbean Reef octopus, long arms stretching toward *Ogler.* The disturbed silt momentarily obscured the view on the monitors.

The beak in the mollusk's two-foot head snapped at the ROV's port skid. Changing color and texture, from blue to red, smooth to rough, its tentacles reached up toward the lights, the cameras, and into *Ogler's* guts: into tubing, cables, and electrical lines inside the titanium frame.

The monitors went blank.

"Goddammit!" exploded Chizzick.

Both Palmer and Shinley were punching keys and testing their sticks. No response from either console.

In the next hour, the deck crew had to haul the damaged ROV up to the transom with a squall threatening from the west. The octopus was hanging to the skids with several of its arms still in *Ogler's* internals. The overall conglomeration looked like some bizarre sea creature belched boiling from the deep.

Everyone left Chiz to rant at the ocean once the outraged animal was carefully removed and returned to its element and the ROV winched to her hangar for repair.

A half-hour later Dawton was at the aft rail of the 03 deck. The pleasant odors of dinner being prepared wafted up from the galley. In the ship's staff lounge, the celebration of the debris trail discovery was continuing.

The Morgainne was anchored with her bow to the north and her stern to the south. To the west, the squall had dissipated and the sun was going down beyond the cays, limning the ship's decks, her bays and shops and winches and cranes in soft tones of orange and red. To the south, some heaping mountains of cumulus were rolling upward in folds of light and dark gray over Andros Island. At the island's northern tip he could make out the faint outline of Morgan's Bluff Harbor. The similarity of the names of the salvage ship and the place named after the infamous pirate had been uneasily joked about by *Morgainne's* superstitious crew. A coincidence? An omen? An omen of what kind, good or bad?

Seabirds screeched and dove at a dark smear on the sea's surface some 200 yards to the west. Beyond, in the distance, lay the nondescript but discernible shore of the scrubby little islet he'd named Leyley Cay. And a little way to the north of it, just offshore of one of the larger Joulters, sat a boat. Without binoculars, Kyle could not tell just what kind but it looked to be no bigger than a medium-sized fishing cruiser. Small sailboats and motor cruisers came and went in these waters and there was no reason he should have taken any particular note of this one but he did. And could not say why.

Images from some TV footage earlier seen of the 2010 earthquake in Haiti flashed in his mind. His head jerked backward as if dodging a blow as he recalled the scenes that had flashed that night at the beach campfire with Ashley Dillet: of a young woman walking along a seaside path in whose eyes he'd seen a ragged ship canting as if it were about to sink. Only now he saw her running, horrified, an injured child in her arms, structures falling around her like those he'd seen on the news feeds, clouds of dust . . . wails of people injured, trapped —

"Want some company?"

Jolted anew, he turned. It was Victoria. He watched her approach and, uncertainly, gave her a smile and said, "Sure."

Her golden hair was down and freshly brushed whereas earlier she'd had it in a ponytail. Her eyes were a gleaming steel blue in the dwindling light, penetrating his core, stirring his heart as well as his blood. She held a thermos and two plastic cups which she put on the top of the rail. Opened the thermos. Poured its ice-laced contents into the two cups. "Cheers," she said, handing him a cup and raising the other to touch his.

They drank, each watching the other with unvoiced questions. "Umm," he said. "You make a fine daiquiri."

She turned to look at the sunset and stood close beside him, her hip brushing his. "A beautiful evening."

"Yeah."

"I'm sorry if I—you were deep in thought."

"It's okay. I was . . . just enjoying the view."

"It's not like you to go off alone when there's a party going on."

He laughed lightly. "I know."

She looked back out to sea and was quiet for a while, then pushed a shoulder against his and said, "Hey, we'll get *Ogler* fixed. And we found quite a few artifacts today in what has to be a debris trail. There's a wreck here. Maybe not exactly in the place you thought you saw it but . . . Kyle?"

"Um."

"Tell me, did you see or feel anything unusual today, when we were finding those things? You were very still for a while, looking at that wall, the recess."

Poor woman. She's partners with a combat junkie and a Woo World freak. He looked at those boiling red clouds to the south, trying to remember. Amnesia was associated with nitrogen narcosis. His memory of what he thought he'd seen in the darkness under the recess overhang was murky. He could recall feeling lightheaded but not quite dizzy or scared. He could clearly recall the objects they'd found, starting a grid map, Vic's touching him, then her looking down from the anchor line, starting to descend to help him. "Maybe I was a little narced."

"On trimix? That's not likely. But . . . maybe you should have Doc Pratt look you over."

"Yeah." He looked at the water below but, as if it could suck him into another reality just by looking at it, looked up again. Another look at her quickly returned him to the present.

She said, "I'll admit it's like narcosis to—it seemed you didn't want to come up. Or . . ."

Or?

"Like you were in an altered state. In any case, you scared me . . . and, going into an altered state down there, narced or whatever, I'm sure you know, could be disastrous if . . . I know we've been buddied up with others but I'd like to be with you from now on."

Altered state? How much was she fishing? How much had she guessed? Part of him wanted to confide in her and part of him didn't. He wasn't sure what her reaction would be and he didn't know what to make of his slides into Elsewhere and his fear that these episodic dissociations could become irreversible. She could very well be against his continuing to dive. He both liked and disliked the idea of their buddying up. In any case, he appreciated her concern if not her curiosity and couldn't think of a way to squirm free. And: *Maybe I need another pair of eyes. And another head?* "Okay," he said.

"I'll talk to Diane about us buddying up. I won't say anything about your . . . your concern about getting narced. But do promise me you'll talk to the doc about that."

Yeah, he thought uneasily. "Okay."

"Kyle, I know you've got a lot on your shoulders. We all do. But I know you're feeling a lot of pressure, that you feel our finding something here is on you more than anyone else."

"I'm the one who brought us here. It's on me that we save Argos from bankruptcy, that we—"

"That we're not on another fruitless search like the one I led off Cay Sal? Come on. What were you telling me just the other day about wreck-hunting being a crapshoot?"

"Um."

He had the feeling she wanted to say more but she didn't. Instead, she emptied her cup. "Okay. No more joy juice for me. I've a lot of work waiting in the lab." She kissed him lightly on the temple. "I'd kiss you on the mouth but I'm afraid I'd hurt that cut Wayne gave you."

He grinned. "He apologized for that."

She laughed. "In private, I guess."

"Yeah. Well, he has to keep up appearances."

She laughed again, patted his hand, turned and left.

He looked to the west again to keep from watching her go, the press of her lips still warm against his head, her words, her presence, still strong.

His eyes roamed the water to the horizon, wanting to think about something else.

They'd seen no sign of *WildBore V.* But he soon found that fishing cruiser. It had moved away from the cay and a little to the northwest. With the naked eye and in the fading light, it was just a dot.

Looking for some sort of menace—some sort of *diversion*—to take his mind off Victoria? But there were diversions, distractions, aplenty: some artifacts found, along with much evidence of a lowering seabed . . . mysterious goo . . . and in the past and future upon and under this secretive sea, people perishing because, figuratively or literally, the earth had cracked under their feet.

The ship's public address speakers blared. "Hey, listen up, everybody! This is Wayne. We just got a report from the ROV room. Before *Ogler* got attacked by that octopus, her starboard camera recorded what has to be a cannon!"

CHAPTER 10

Comrades

ON ITS COURSE from Caracas to Cuba, *O-681's* arrival had been further delayed by ship traffic through the Windward Passage, where U.S. Naval craft maintained a presence in the ongoing effort to suppress any leftist elements from taking over and joining other Latin American countries in the Communist mold. Never mind the fact that Mother Russia, struggling to recover from years of its own internal muddle, had all but abandoned the lot of them.

When *O-681* entered the small darkened harbor on the night of January 13, Captain First Rank Anton Lepushin and his men were coiled springs long past readiness for release. Nonetheless, they stood in the dark like mute statues beside their equipment on the wharf, watching the huge nuclear submarine rise to the surface. Two tugboats operating without lights began moving her in alongside the wharf where minisub *Saida* hung suspended by cables to the crane clutching it. As *O-681* was nudged in alongside the blacked-out wharf, the crane operator began swinging the minisub out over its docking clamps aft of the conning tower.

Two trucks with stores to be loaded onto the mothership waited near the crane. With *O-681* secured by rope fore and aft and the gangway extended, Captain Konstantin Polivanov and four other ship's officers descended in working uniforms from the tower and came ashore. The squat and overweight Polivanov returned the *Spetsnaz* team's salute and stood looking at the *SZ-44* commando craft. Lepushin saw in the captain's dour face a man who'd been at sea too long and was in the worst of wear for it. No stranger to Deep Submergence Rescue Vehicles, he no doubt had carried more than one attached to his submarine's aft escape trunk. Lepushin could tell the aging submariner saw even in the dark how much *Saida* had been modified for things other than rescue. Polivanov's greeting and invitation aboard *O-681* were gruff and formal. He said, "An extraordinary DSRV, Captain Lepushin. We are eager to learn of your mission."

Once in the submarine's control room, Lepushin got down to business, as far as he intended to go at this point. He unfurled a map he'd removed from a leather case slung over his shoulder. The map had a crooked red line drawn upon it. He pointed at the line. "This is the route we will take. And these," pointing at some figures jotted down at the edge of the map, "are the coordinates of our destination, subject to change. For now, plot your course for them. We must get there in all due haste."

Polivanov raised his eyes from the map. And he raised his voice enough for all the men at their various stations nearby to hear. "This is Captain Anton Lepushin. Being a *Spetsnaz* officer, he wears no insignia but his rank is equal to mine. He is the sole authority in matters pertaining to our new mission, yet to be disclosed." Polivanov was looking steadily at the *Spetsnaz* captain as he continued. "And I remain the sole authority in matters pertaining to the operation and security of *O-681*. The haste and success of your mission will be dictated by the latter."

Lepushin did not intend to set Polivanov straight in front of the men in the control room.

"Chief Petty Officer Byko," said Polivanov, "will show you to your quarters."

Lepushin made a curt bow of his head and turned to follow the indicated CPO.

The commandos were taken to bunks racked just outside the lockout chamber. Overhead, they could hear *Saida* being attached piggyback to the submarine's deck.

⋅⊷╺◉ ◉╸⊶⋅

For Konstantin Polivanov, both the route and destination spelled trouble, if not disaster. His crew was tired and longing for home. They'd been at sea for almost two months, had been prowling the Caribbean for weeks. Globally, tensions between U.S. and Russian submarines and the threat of a hostile encounter, ever present, were mounting.

After trying to sleep for a few hours, he called a meeting in the wardroom with Lepushin, their seconds-in-command, and *0-681's* one intelligence officer attending.

The superficial pleasantries deemed over with and the submarine underway, Lepushin wanted to know *0-681's* current speed, depth and course.

Polivanov pushed away his teacup and said, "We are at present 255 kilometers north of Havana, at a depth of 250 meters, doing from 35 to 40 kilometers per hour. We have been trying to dodge the sonar ranges of several American and Caribbean vessels. We are about halfway between the Florida Keys and the Bimini Islands."

"Good."

Polivanov decided to add, for Lepushin's enlightenment, "*0-681's* sonar-absorbent coating is peeling away. We could not revamp it in Venezuela or Cuba."

Lepushin said nothing to that.

"I'm sure you know that a minisub riding piggyback on a nuclear submarine slows her speed as well as causes flow-noise that will make her more detectable to other ships."

"Yes, Captain," said Lepushin, "I know that."

Polivanov got to the most pressing point. "I need to know more about your mission, sir. I was not given any information—"

"I will let you know what to do as the situation requires."

Anton Lepushin had a narrow face. His eyes in the low-lit wardroom were the color of the Barents Sea under an overcast. And like ex-KGB officer Vladimir Putin, Lepushin was a member of the security *elita* that had its roots in Lenin's secret state-security police, the *Cheka.* Before even meeting him, Polivanov, a career naval officer born in a small town in the Republic of Mordovia who privately despised the crafty yet dimwitted Putin and his ilk, knew he would not like Lepushin. "As captain of this ship, I have a right to know just what I am to expect and prepare for."

Lepushin looked at his watch. "We need to come to communication depth soon to receive updated instructions from Headquarters. I think it would be a good idea at that time for Headquarters to provide you as much clarification as it deems fit for now."

⊸═◉ ◉═⊶

"So what happened with our 'comrade's' comm to Headquarters?" asked Isaak Kolotcha, *O-681's* executive officer and second-in-command. The use of the old Soviet Union epithet for the *Spetsnaz* commander was delivered with sarcasm. Kolotcha and Polivanov were alone in the captain's tiny stateroom. Like Polivanov, Kolotcha came from a humble background and had never cared much for any resurrected version of the old Soviet elite. The two had long been trusting friends in matters political as well as personal.

Wanting to get some needed rest, Polivanov sat on the edge of his narrow bed, dropped a pill from a bottle into his hand and glowered at the water in the glass as if seeking a revelation. Ordinarily he slept all right but with *O-681* stealing through potentially hostile water and a Chekist *sraka* aboard to tell him what to do, his rest was seriously threatened. "The GRU is calling the shots, Isaak. As previously told, we can depend upon Comrade Lepushin sharing with us only what he wants us to know when he wants us to know it, nothing more, nothing less. But I'll be damned if I'll be the bastard's bootlick."

The tall and slender Kolotcha shrugged and moved to the stateroom's hatchway and stooped to go through it. He was a man who liked to see the brighter side of things, even in a fast-attack nuclear submarine 250 meters down in "someone else's ocean." He said, "Well, we are used to operating with scant information. And who wants to be in Severomorsk in January anyway?"

CHAPTER 11

Wellhead One

J. J. HARWOOD awoke and lay in his king-sized bed staring out at the view of the Caribbean. For a moment it looked as if a huge wave, stories high, was coming at him. He bolted from the bed and soon realized the sea was as calm as could be.

He peeked into Melanie's bedroom and saw that she was still asleep. He longed to crawl into bed with her but feared she would tell him to go away.

In his bathroom, he slammed down his daily throatchoker of vitamins and meds and suffered one of those morning squints at the body-length mirror. Though his pate was still crowned with an iron-gray mane, though he was as lean as a fencepost and he flattered himself that his eyes still burned with an adventurer's ardor, his skin resembled that of a plucked chicken. The mirror squint was never a good way to start the day.

At the navigational console adjacent to his desk in his office he saw from its positional graphic that the yacht was about a mile and a half northwest of Great Stirrup Cay in the Berries.

Near Block One.

He called Woodrow Culpepper who was down in the main salon. "Morning, Woodrow. Did you sleep well?"

"As well as I can on a boat, J. J. And you?"

Boat! "Fine. Tell me again, why did Joseph Yord go off to *WildBore Five* yesterday without—when I wanted the two of you along to look at the shallower wellheads in the submarine with *me*?"

Silence for a couple of seconds. Then: "We thought you were going fishing, J. J."

"I was. I am. I will! But first—you call *WildBore Five*. Tell Yord to get back here. We're close to Wellhead One. We're going down in *Blue Deep* to have a look at it. I want to see those rejuvenated coral beds you told me about."

"Yessir," Culp said quickly. "I'll call *WildBore Five*."

After disconnecting, Harwood called Cal McGinnis and told him he wanted to take *Blue Deep* to Wellhead One in an hour.

"Sure, sir," said the yacht's First Officer. "Conditions are favorable. We'll have her ready."

Leaving his office, Harwood looked in on Mellie again. She was awake and watching a report on some celebrity scandal. Having been a bad actor in too many soap operas of his own, Jim Harwood had no taste for his or anyone else's. But he still had a gnawing wish that he and Melanie could put the past behind them and resurrect what they'd had in the beginning. He said, "How did you sleep, Mel?"

"Okay," she said without looking at him.

"Was I a bore last night at dinner, going on about the sea and fishing and—?"

"No more than usual."

Stung but not enough to fight, he sighed and said, "I haven't had a chance to ask you—what did you think of Sheri Delgado spouting off at Senator Slotter the way she did?"

Melanie looked at him. No makeup on yet but on the brink of sixty, still plenty pretty. "I told her what I thought of it," she said. "I told her she was rude as hell and way out of line and she'll never be invited to do anything with us again. She'll be taken to Nassau along with her Uncle Roberto and the rest of those guests who have to get back to whatever they were doing. Frankly, I think we have too damned many people on board 'my' yacht."

"Oh. Okay." *Guess so*, thought Harwood. *Too many people and too many vexations*. "Well, I'm going down to tend to some business. Hope your mood improves. Another four days and it'll be your birthday. We'll—"

"So you keep reminding me. I'd just as soon forget it."

He ducked out and descended the stairs to the bridge deck, wishing for some private time with her, wanting to tell her he still loved her, wanting to know if she loved him at all anymore, and trying to ignore the ache in his knees despite his early pharmaceutical cocktail.

In the lounge on the VIP deck, Preston Slotter, Roberto Delgado, their wives, and several other guests whose names he could hardly remember, were having breakfast. Having drunk too much the evening before, Senator Slotter looked like he'd had trouble dressing himself. The fringe of thin hair below his bald head was a tangle and he was gulping a bloodymary as if he were nearly dead of thirst. The rest were confining their liquid intake this early to coffee and fruit juice.

"Hi, everybody," Harwood boomed, feigning an exuberance he did not feel. "This morning's agenda calls for a little excursion in the submarine." They'd all seen *Blue Deep* when he gave them the grand tour out of Fort Lauderdale. "Might not be back till after lunch."

Slotter's face had lost its color as if he were about to lose his breakfast. "Oh. Well, I don't know. I don't know how I'd feel in a submarine, down there, uh, I thought we were going fishing today."

"We will. Don't fret, Preston. When I mentioned going down in *Blue Deep*, I meant only myself and a few JJO staff. This dive won't include guests."

⇥ ⇤

By 11:00, Joseph Yord had not returned from *WildBore V.* According to Woodrow Culpepper, he was still down at Well One in *WBS-3*, a *WildBore V* maintenance submersible, with offshore-well maintenance chief Ridley Stukes. And Culpepper reported that *WildBore V* was having communications difficulty with *WBS-3* this morning and *WildBore's* captain wasn't sure if Yord had received the message to come up. Irritated and tired of waiting, Harwood stormed into Culpepper's office below the owner's deck. "We're going to Well One. *Now!*" Though he longed to take his guests down in *Blue Deep*, for now J. J. Harwood had a more pressing matter to attend to, though he could not say yet just what the matter might be.

Security Chief Marvin Quinn was charged with keeping *Blue Deep* ever ready for launch in the event of a pirate attack or some other calamity that would necessitate abandoning the yacht. And when Harwood did a dive in the luxury submarine, a security team of four in Quinn's unit was to go along. Headed by Quinn's second-in-command, they were the last to board and the least to be seen by the passengers once underway. The way Harwood had had its builder configure her, *Blue Deep* could comfortably accommodate up to sixteen people. On this dive, she took aboard only the boss, Culpepper, an aide each, the captain and first officer, one stewardess, one cook, and the security team.

In the control room in the submarine's nose, First Officer McGinnis took her down and headed for Wellhead One. Coffee was served in the observation lounge. Outside the big viewports the aquatic life streamed by.

"I've got this uneasiness, Woodrow," J. J. said from his barcalounger at the coffee table, "that something is not right with Well One."

On the other side of the table, Culpepper put his coffee cup down and did not respond.

"Well?"

"I'm a little queasy, J. J. Excuse me but I'd better go to the bathroom."

"The *head*, Woodrow. Take a seasick pill or stick one of those patches on your ass."

"They go behind the ear," muttered Culp, "and they make me drowsy . . . and make me have weird thoughts." He rose and quickly disappeared into the head at the aft end of the lounge.

Harwood was left with the aides, neither of whom admitted having any idea about what might be wrong at Well One. He zeroed in on Kenneth Murphy, Culpepper's guy. "So what's going on I'm not being told about, Ken?"

Murphy blinked at him. "I don't know, sir."

He wasn't acquainted with Murphy all that well. The young man could be one of those people who lied through his teeth and never showed the least sign of it.

Harwood turned to his own aide, Benny Kealing, who just shrugged.

"Find out!"

"Yessir," they chorused and moved off to another table on the far side of the lounge, opening their laptops as if therein lay the secret.

Harwood considered ordering them back but instead just looked out at the fish. At 200 feet down, they were nearing the area where JJ Oil geologists had probed the seafloor two years before and concluded from seismic and gravity analysis that significant hydrocarbon deposits lay at depths from 5,000 to 10,000 feet, many of them in limestone. But the extracting preliminaries had ceased when the Bahamians ordered all wells capped. Somewhere around the time that occurred, maybe a little earlier, Culpepper and Yord had flown to Nassau and boarded *WildBore V* to have a look at the six leased wellsites. J. J. remembered that. But he couldn't remember much else about that period except the fracas he and Melanie were going through over the fact both were having extramarital affairs. And he still hadn't gotten around to reading the report Culp gave him about his and Yord's trip out here only weeks ago. He couldn't remember where he'd put the report and hadn't thought to request another copy.

He was about to call Kealing back to ask him if he had a copy when McGinnis announced over the intercom that they were approaching the Well One site. J. J. got up and went to the starboard viewport and found himself looking out at a shelf of rock and deepsea coral lit by the sub's exterior floodlights. At a speed of two knots, *Blue Deep* moved quietly along and a little above the edge of the limestone wall that dropped below the shelf. First Officer McGinnis reduced speed as the sub slowly rounded a corner. J. J. could see the lights of the wellhead shelter coming into view. They were like lights in a fog. The water here was unusually dim. He could hear the station's homing signal despite the low thrum of the submarine.

As McGinnis brought *Blue Deep* to a stop and set the stabilization system to hold her steady, J. J. said over the intercom, "Why's the water so cloudy? We stirring all that stuff up?"

"Some of it, yes sir. And *WBS-3* was just down here."

There was no sign of the maintenance submersible, as if *WBS-3* had quickly departed upon hearing the approach of *Blue Deep*. "Where the hell is it now?"

"I'll call *WildBore*, sir."

The maintenance mothership was almost directly overhead. Nevertheless, McGinnis soon reported that he was not receiving a response to his calls up the comm line.

As Harwood pondered that, McGinnis trained *Blue Deep's* powerful starboard observation lights on the station. This was the first time J. J. had seen one of JJO's six wildcat wells here in the Bahamas up close and personal. At varying depths, deepwells Two, Four, Five and Six were accessible only by robot or manned submersible. Only Wells One here northeast of Andros Island and Three off the Joulters, lay within the depth range of *Blue Deep*.

He'd seen photos and drawings of all of them: the interiors of the shelters that housed the usual control modules, the wellhead "tree" assemblies of cables, cylinders, umbilicals and other equipment typical of a subsea wellhead. The exteriors were shaped like pyramids to deflect anchors, trawler boards and other crap that might descend from the surface to rake the seafloor and damage the site.

He noticed nothing about the shelter he hadn't seen from the photos except for the fact much of it was covered with coral. He hadn't seen any updates for a long time. Still coral free were the access doors and the big white signs with their red-letter warnings screwed to each side of the four-sided construction:

DANGER!—HIGH VOLTAGE!—KEEP OFF!
PROPERTY OF JJ OIL COMPANY, USA
VIOLATORS WILL BE PROSECUTED

J. J. called to aide Murphy, "Where's your boss?"

"I think he went below, sir, to his stateroom."

"Get him. I don't care how he's feeling. I want him up here."

"Yessir."

"Mac," Harwood said into the intercom, "Do a three-sixty around the site and tell me if you notice anything unusual—by eyeballing it or reading your readouts."

"Aye, sir," said McGinnis.

Culpepper returned with Murphy, looking worse than before.

"You able to talk?" J. J. asked him.

"Some. I guess."

"How did Well One's shelter get so covered with coral?"

Culpepper sighed and answered in a tired voice, as if put out for having to repeat something he'd told J. J. numerous times. "After Dr. Yord heard you reiterate at a meeting that you wanted our wells to be eco-friendly, we talked about it and I encouraged him to go ahead."

A meeting. There was a meeting—with Yord attending . . . actually presenting. What was that about? "Okay, I got no problem with that, as long as the wellheads can be properly maintained but—"

"Sir," said McGinnis through the intercom speaker, "parts of the seabed here and there near the wellhead have dropped from five to ten feet since our software and printed charts were last published. That's been in the last two years."

"What?" Harwood looked out the viewport. *"Where?"*

"It's okay, J. J.," Culp said quickly. "We know about that. The strata below the seafloor have been seismically tested and are solid. No sinkhole anywhere near the wellhead or the pipe."

"So why has the seabed sunk?"

"Don't know. Any number of things can cause changes in seabed levels—"

"But won't that affect the well?"

"No. It hasn't yet anyway. The seabed's being monitored by engineer Stukes, J. J. There's no leakage of oil or methane from the well. No gas bubble anywhere, no danger of a blowout." Culpepper's throat spasmed. He turned for the head again and with a choked voice said, "The integrity of the well is intact!"

Chapter 12

Mystery Ships

It took the better part of a blustery morning and the use of the heavy-duty A-frame crane at *Morgainne's* stern to pull the first cannon they'd found out of the sediment and transfer it to the heavy-duty sling needed to haul it up to the ship. Though the encrustation covering the gun obscured its original detail, it appeared to have its trunnion attached. The weight displayed on the digital readout in the crane's control station was well over two tons, a good indication it was of cast iron rather than bronze; a "24-pounder" in naval parlance, referring to the weight of the ball it had shot. A gun big enough to have required a sizeable ship.

Maybe they had found a slaver, maybe something else.

Working around the clock to bring up more artifacts, the rotating dive teams sifted and dug through sediment and disturbed coral along the debris trail at depths ranging from 130 to 170 feet.

For Dawton, the cave did not reappear under the limestone overhang. Nor had anything else appeared in the way of a vision or a plunge into that mirage-like realm that could so intrigue but threaten his grip on reality. Maybe it was the nonstop work and needed rests between that kept him "grounded." Doc Pratt had found no evidence of narcosis in his system but had cautioned him on his bottomtime limits and so on. He had to be experiencing some bubbles in his blood but they went away when he ascended at a safe rate, got proper rest and required surface time before a new dive. Kyle told the doc nothing about his visions or whatever they were. He told *no one* about them.

All he saw in place of the cave now as he worked with the rest, buddied up with Vic, was a terrace of crumbled limestone, fallen two to three more feet in the last two days, ruining much of that section of site-grid earlier laid down. No, sonar didn't hallucinate. Elsewhere, the seabed continued to show signs of additional subsidence when compared with earlier sonic readings and those recorded on the charts. Much of it sloped toward a depth of fifty fathoms and a dropoff to the Tongue. The deeper the debris trail went, the more difficult it would be to rescue whatever it might have left of value. In any case, the rate of the subsidence at this point was virtually impossible to calculate.

More of the oily goop was in evidence and much of the limestone was unusually flaky. Some of it crumbled in their hands, leaving a graphite-like residue on gloves that quickly dissipated in the water. Working in his lab on the main deck, geologist Rob Palmer had confirmed the preliminary analysis: the goo samples were indeed a variant of carbon and hydrogen with a new molecular configuration unfamiliar to him or anyone in his team. Identifying himself again as a curious tourist in a second call to Nassau, he'd talked to another government bureaucrat who would not admit to any JJ Oil activity in the Bahamas and, as did the one before, adamantly claimed there was certainly no fracking going on anywhere in the region by anyone. In fact, this one did demand to know if Palmer was some ecofreak saboteur. Palmer stuck to his phony tourist persona and clicked off.

For now, though, the objects they were finding along and just below the terrace overrode everything else. Despite lacking the use of their deepwater robot, they sifted and dug and vacuumed and uncovered and raised four 16 pounders, a swivel gun, more ballast stone, pieces of wooden casks, helmets, breastplates, a glut of musket balls, a rudder pin, an oarlock, iron fittings, nails, tools and loads of other small objects mixed with sand, limestone and shell detritus to be laid on deck for preliminary examination, then taken to the labs below where they would be protected for further cleansing and analyses.

But nothing had materialized in the way of a significant section of ship to tell them what kind of vessel had come apart here. Whatever it was, it had been ground down to fragments, no doubt by repeated storms and hurricanes, despite its depth. Thus far, the artifacts they'd found seemed planted by a mischievous hand only to whet their appetite, fire their enthusiasm, and keep them hanging.

The ongoing evidence of a sinking seabed didn't help. With the operation hobbled by lack of their ROV and repeated fruitless attempts to reach his father by phone, Chiz cursed and stomped the decks like peg-legged Ahab pacing *The Pequod*. He was in fact lame, having snagged a knee in a coral cleft and in trying to free himself ripped open his drysuit and cut the knee to the bone. Ahab aside, some aboard who'd felt his dictatorial sting had begun privately to refer to him by the name of another ship's captain of legendary repute.

"Hey, Cap'n Bligh," Kyle said where he found Wayne and Dan Clark below decks, cleaning weapons, "are you aware that you're giving some of the More-gainers migraines?"

The pieces of the disassembled Russian amphibious assault rifles acquired by the admiral the previous year made Dawton think of a viper's innards and he prayed silently they would never have to use them.

Chiz growled something. In addition to having hurt his knee, he'd fried his lungs by cutting his decompression stops too short on his way back to the surface. As a former SEAL, he was not living up to the rep. With a sore throat and sinuses clogged, his voice resembled the respirations of a pitbull on too short a leash.

Kyle said, "You know as well as I do that good morale makes for a good operation. Having fun cleaning guns?"

"Oh, fuck off, Dawton. This is therapy for me. Sit down here and help us." Chiz began to sneeze.

SEAL buddy Clark caught Kyle's eye, shrugged and chuckled.

A crate of firearms sat on the deck near Dawton's feet. "I'll take your first suggestion. I'll go fuck off. Meanwhile . . ." he grinned back at Clark whom he'd come to like a great deal, as he liked the third ex-SEAL in the dive team, Rick Rivera, "why don't you see if you can't work yourself into a laugh or two like Dan here. Be good for your condition."

Chizzick's sneezing and cursing continued. Clark handed him a hanky. "Blow," he said.

"Excuse me if I exit now," said Dawton. "Don't want to catch your cold—or your case of the chronic redass."

The sneezing stopped. Chizzick stared at him and Clark, blips of his synaptical squall flashing across his brow like those on a radar screen. He blew his nose into the hanky, sounding much like a foghorn. His scowl collapsed into a grin. He began to laugh at himself. Dawton and Clark laughed with him, happy at last, Kyle hoped, to have rammed some sunshine through the icecap.

⋯▶ ◀⋯

Late that night a huge anchor was found and brought up—and another not so big. Like the cannon, the size and shape of the anchors suggested a large vessel. At a depth of 210 feet lay three more cannon—demi-culverins—and the half-rotted remnants of much planking and some sizeable timbers, a length of which could be part of a mast and parts of what perhaps had been the forecastle; an encrusted flintlock pistol, another cutlass, other objects not so much of a lethal or martial nature—like a goblet that under its calcareous coating promised to be of gold.

The onboard labs were filling up, the concretized objects undergoing chemical baths in cleansing tubs and sinks and some, like the helmets and breastplates, beginning to tell them their find was likely of 16th or 17th century origin.

Speculations abounded as to what had been the mystery ship's fate and why it had not been discovered till now. When not resting between dives, Dawton joined Cooper and her team in continuing to research records of lost ships in the Caribbean, looking for any hint of one having gone down anywhere near the Joulter Cays. The worktable would be littered with notes, sketches, manuals, printouts and reference books. Photos and sketches of the debris field—with depth and location noted—were taped on the port bulkhead to show a graphic map of the grid. Vic and marine historian Skip Roberts pored over books and records in the ship's library, searched the internet and appropriate databases; had been on the phone with the National Association of Black Scuba Divers, an organization accredited with having done extensive research into sunken slave ships. Roberts offered: "In that four hundred-year history of the Atlantic slave trade, between the mid fourteen hundreds and eighteen hundreds, numerous ships went down, several of them slavers. But aside from the ones sunk in the Florida Keys and such noted tragedies as the *Whydah* that sank off Cape Cod, the *Adelaide* off Cuba and the *Trouvadore* in the Turks and Caicos, we haven't been able to come up with any record of any ship's sinking near the area off our little piece of nowhere called Leyley Cay."

Added Victoria, "Until we get one of the cannon completely cleaned, or uncover something else to identify the wreck, we'll remain ignorant of its origin."

Across Kyle Dawton's inner eye flitted an image of a piece of planking that bore the letters *T-r-o-u-v*. That was all. It vanished as fast as it appeared, as if flashed by a devilish hand.

But the fragment of a memory swirled up of a ship in storm, its masts breaking, sails in tatters . . . . He recalled the flotsam of several haunting dreams, at times awake and at times asleep, of smoke and the stench of burning flesh so powerful it nauseated . . . the wails of the dying violating a jungle night . . . dead and dying people hanging in trees, some burning as their village burned . . . some with hands or arms severed, some slain by sword and some by harquebus . . . a column of laden horses and mules moving through a jungle. A sixteenth sailing ship waiting in a port . . . the name Cabo Catoche out of the swirl . . . dissolving into a room on the ship where a black-robed priest sits writing at a small desk, having difficulty doing so as the ship is being tossed in storm . . . and another ship, a brigantine, is approaching and cries of fear rip through as an Indian slave enters the room with a raised ax . . . And all this mixed and confused with other stuff that contextually made no sense: like that place where smoke smears the sky but the scene is sunlit and the sun turns the foul and humid air into a rank cauldron where the dead are being pulled from rubble and left in the streets for the living to throw onto trucks bound for mass graves and incessant voices, frantic and woeful, rise and fall like the dirge of an abandoned race. And a large but listing steel trawler of 20th century vintage filled with blacks who, while not in chains or shackles, appeared to be crowded into cramped holds and watched by other blacks with guns . . . the big luxury yacht moving toward the trawler and a full-sized submarine lurking in the depths with a minisub on its back.

Alone in his cabin and at risk of sinking into a state from which he might not rise, he wrestled with trying to figure out what these things might mean, where they came from, if they were somehow valid or could be validated; trying to analyze, see more, organize them into some understandable chronology while wondering if they were nothing more than delusion and wondering if they had validity and why he was so bloody "blessed" in being their ignorant recipient.

He was rewarded with the vague memory of a dream of nights past in which he saw long tentacles descending into a black hole at the edge of the debris field. A giant octopus covered with goo, mad, confused, dragging treasure and *Morgainne's* divers with it down into a vortex. The legendary lusca he'd kidded Leyley about. In the dream, the monster had become a great tongue licking at the rim of the hole, eating the limestone . . . with the limestone turning to goo and the goo to blood.

⋆≡◉ ◉≡⋆

Without authorization, the Argos Company salvors risked fine and imprisonment in bringing up any artifacts from their find. Wayne had called Nassau to report the debris-trail discovery and initiate the preliminary paperwork via satellite phone for the permit, with a faxed assurance that as soon as his father the admiral could be reached—Papa Curt having inopportunely gone off hunting in a remote part of Alaska with some of his old Navy buds—he would fly to Nassau to facilitate and complete the process. The mere mention of Curtis Chizzick's name was enough to gain *The Morgainne* a go-ahead from the Bahamians.

The next night, Admiral Curt at last returned his son's call from Fairbanks. Wayne ordered the senior staff into the conference room. After hearing a summary of what they'd found thus far, Curt said he'd be at the Bahamian ministry in a day.

Ogler needed a couple of parts that had to be flown from Miami to be picked up in Nassau as well.

The need to get samples of the goo and some of the artifacts to the Miami lab where they could be more thoroughly processed was also pressing. Victoria said, "If we don't want to take *The Morgainne* in yet, away from the wrecksite, we need to use *Sinbad* to take in what we can. The engravings and identifying stamps on the cannons are impossible to determine completely under the kind of cleansing we're able to do aboard ship. We need to get at least one of them to Miami asap. One of the sixteen-pounders with the foundry name and date on the end of its trunnion will give us a lead to the wreck's provenance."

Establishing provenance was crucial to any historical or archaeological discovery. But proving it cut two ways: lack of such proof could lessen the value of anything found while proof could attract others who, though they had nothing to do with the work, the risk, the investment or knowledge of a wreck's location or fate or the restoration of any part of it or of anything it carried, could use confirmed origin to justify a claim of ownership of either or both the transporting vessel and the goods under transport. Some of such claims had been ruled justified by courts; some had not.

Feeling a growing need to get off the ship for a while, as if running from himself, Dawton said, "*Sinbad* can make it to Nassau with a full load in a couple of hours. Be back aboard ship by evening, depending on how things go at customs and the airport."

"They're going to go without a hitch," assured the admiral. "My flight will take over eight hours. Whoever goes with *Sinbad* should plan for an overnight stay in Nassau. I'll buy dinner and deal with the redtape next day."

Chief of dive operations Diane Weitzman had the say as to who would go. Kyle reminded her that he, Vic, and Dan Clark had logged too much bottomtime to be diving for the next couple of days. "One of the ROV techs needs to go with us to deal with what's needed for *Ogler.*"

Diane agreed. When Chiz said he wanted to go, Diane vetoed the idea, never mind the fact Wayne owned controlling interest in Argos Salvage. "No, you're staying here. The doc's told me and he's told you that if you don't take care of that knee, you won't ever dive again. As for your cold, you need to go to bed and stay there till you're over it or somebody will be taking *you* to Nassau for treatment of strep or pneumonia. Aside from that, none of us want to catch what you've got."

About to protest, Wayne succumbed to another sneezing fit as everyone jerked their heads aside and he covered his face.

On the way to his cabin to pack for the trip and for some reason recalling the day he'd been with Leyley in *Sinbad* and was almost capsized by *WildBore V,* Dawton scanned the surrounding sea. Fortunately, he stayed in the present. But he had the creeps. He did not want to go tripping off again into a state that only teased his reason and threatened his sanity. But something was close, a looming threat of some kind. He sensed it but could not perceive what it was.

He went forward to the bridge for an update on what craft were in view. There were four in visual range, several more on sonar.

Several orange buoys with their flags flapping ringed the dive site.

The Joulter Cays were popular with anglers after bonefish and tarpon. And *The Morgainne* and its activities were subject to scrutiny by them and by various passing vessels between New Providence, North Andros and the Berry Islands. Thus far, the salvors had been lucky. If the word spread that they'd found treasure, however overblown that word might be, the place would swarm with gapers; some of whom would try to breach the dive perimeter for closer looks or try to grab what they could for themselves. Regarded by some as looters anyway, treasure hunters were free game for those wanting to take their "loot." The thought of anyone trying to take what the Argos divers had thus far found or might find in the future didn't do Kyle's mental state any good. Mixed with his apprehensions about Argos regaining financial stability were the uncertainties about his state of mind and usefulness as a diver. His credibility to the crew and to himself as a dependable member of the dive team and as a wreck finder was on the line and needed to be validated. Most of all, as he'd told Vic, he wanted a find that would save Argos. And once found, he would fight tooth and nail to keep it.

What he could scope at the moment with binoculars were a sailboat a good ten miles to the southeast on an ostensible heading for New Providence; another just north of Andros; a small fishing boat near an estuary in the Joulters; and that cabin cruiser he'd noticed before, two miles to the east with a couple of guys in the flying bridge, one in the fishing chair and, deepsea fishing pole out with something on the line, reeling it in. The boat had an inflatable raft with an outboard motor tied to the stern. Kyle had noticed the cruiser in almost the same spot the previous day.

But *WildBore V* had not reappeared. Why had it come so threateningly close to *Sinbad* when he was here with Ashley Dillet?

CHAPTER 13

Pirates Again

OUT OF SIGHT in the cabin of the cruiser, Ashley Dillet watched *The Morgainne* with a high-powered telescope poked through a window slit. Having overheard Kyle Dawton say over his satphone on New Year's Day that he may have found a sunken wreck, she had learned from a friend at the Bahamian Maritime Ministry the name of his salvage company and its ship. Leyley had then recruited five toughs she knew, one of them the owner of the cruiser, who would join her in seeing if *The Morgainne* had found anything. Three of her team were with her in the cabin, one using binoculars, while the two up in the flying bridge pretended to fish and were now actually hauling something in.

For more than a week, they had been watching the salvage ship off the Joulters, moving the cruiser to a new position every day or going over the horizon and returning from another direction to prevent suspicion from the salvors that they were being so watched.

When Ashley and gang first laid eyes on *The Morgainne*, it was unsettling. The size of the ship exceeded their expectations. Then they observed members of the crew, Kyle Dawton often among them, engaged in target practice with automatic weapons and doing calisthenics and close-quarter combat drills on the afterdeck when they weren't bringing up various clumpy and obscure items in mesh bags and baskets.

Leyley and her boys began to argue. Three wanted to up-anchor and go home. Though outgunned and outmanned, Leyley and the others thought they could sneak aboard the ship and take hostages enough to force the salvors to give up what they'd plundered. But the would-be pirates weren't sure what they'd seen coming up so far was worth the risk and wouldn't waiting longer mean added booty? So they had mulled and argued and drank and smoked and waited to see if something was raised of certain high value.

Argument and mulling temporarily ceased when they began to watch the salvors load the workboat Leyley remembered was named *Sinbad*—about the same size as their cruiser—with various plastic and aluminum containers. Some objects glinted and shined enticingly through the plastic.

With rising excitement, they watched the workboat being lowered to the water by winch, with only a few people aboard it. Among them, Kyle Dawton!

They were taking treasure somewhere! Maybe to a hiding place in the Joulters, maybe to the Berries, maybe to Andros. Leyley and team watched and waited and drank some more, argued some more, and at last decided to act.

⊷▣ ▣⊶

With Dan Clark, Victoria and ROV-tech Rupert Minns aboard, Dawton manned *Sinbad's* wheel and they took off for Nassau at 08:25 with a load of artifacts, including one of the smaller cannons wrapped in a protective shroud. Barring any unwelcome happenstance, *Sinbad's* three powerful outboards would have her cargo in Nassau Harbor before noon. With arrangements for transport of the artifacts via jet to Miami already made by satphone and Admiral Curt on his way to deal with the Bahamians, they would return to *The Morgainne* next morning. Or such was the plan.

The forty-six foot *Sinbad* was ten miles away from *Morgainne*, out in the Tongue and cutting through the swells at thirty knots when Dan Clark, moving up beside Kyle with binocs, pointed at a boat approaching them off the port bow. Kyle instantly recognized the fishing cruiser he'd seen earlier. It was barreling down on them.

As they watched, the cruiser swerved to the right, directly in *Sinbad's* path a scant fifty yards away.

Kyle turned the wheel, changing his course sharply northeast. As he did, the cruiser made a U-turn.

What the fuck! Another pirate attack? Two in half a year? Not possible!

He increased his speed and began to leave the cruiser behind. But it was pulling its ten or twelve-foot skiff, a rigid-hulled inflatable like a Zodiac. People were jumping from the cruiser into the inflatable. Three, four, five, six—each of them wearing lifejackets and clutching assault rifles or submachine guns to their chests.

"They're armed," Clark shouted over the noise of engines and bowsplash.

Not another boat or ship in sight anywhere.

Clark was pulling guns out of a sidebench storage locker. Two assault rifles, a Mossberg 12-gauge and a 9mm Glock.

Well, the Bahama Islands had a hoary history as havens for thieves and cut-throats of every sort who had enjoyed its coves and shantytown hideaways for years. But as Kyle had noticed this particular cruiser long before now, he also had the weird suspicion that someone in it related personally to him.

He throttled up to the max, hitting the swells at thirty-plus knots. The last thing in the world he wanted was another shootout with pirates but with *Sinbad's* heavy load of artifacts, he knew she could do no more.

Vic was at the VHF set, pressing the button that would automatically send *Sinbad's* identity to the Maritime Mobile Service and, through the boat's GPS re-ceiver, their position. But she got no immediate response. Switching to Channel 16 and turning the volume up and the squelch down, she said. "Mayday, Mayday, Mayday!" She verbally gave *Sinbad's* identity and repeated it twice, gave their GPS location and bearing and said, "We are being attacked by armed pirates and require immediate assistance!"

The 25-watt set's maximum range was no more than five nautical miles at sea level. They were six times that from Nassau.

And the skiff with its large outboard was gaining on them.

"I'll take the shotgun," he heard Vic yell.

Clark handed it over. Yessiree, old SEAL Dan Clark had the Glock in his waistband, one rifle in his hands and the other slung across his chest. "One of these is yours," he said to Kyle, "if needed."

"Maybe they just want to race," Kyle joked. But no one laughed. He took the proffered gun and tried to think of another way out of this. He looked at Victoria. He had seen her shoot and she was good. Shooting at inanimate targets like biodegradable party balloons floating off *The Morgainne.* "Vic," he said, "I sure would feel better if you'd go below." He looked at Rupert Minns who, like the rest of *Morgainne's* staff and crew had been trained by Chizzick and his ex-SEAL buds in close-quarter combat, was nonetheless not a good shooter. "You too, Rupe."

Minns nodded and complied. Victoria didn't. Instead, she shoved a pistol into the front of Kyle's belt and let her hand linger ever so briefly there before pulling it away; then stood to the portside of the cockpit with the Mossberg, her eyes hidden by sunglasses.

Steely. Beautiful. . . . immortal too, I hope.

Clark moved aft to stand in plain sight amid the cargo secured to the open deck. Having to hold on to the starboard rail as *Sinbad* ripped and bucked through the chop, he raised his rifle so their pursuers could plainly see it and maybe be dissuaded. But they kept coming.

There was no response to Vic's Mayday call.

Kyle pulled his satphone from its pouch on his belt and punched the button for a signal. The battery meter said the freaking battery was low! No signal.

The skiff was now about fifty yards off *Sinbad's* starboard side and closing. Kyle considered turning and running right over the skiff at risk of being riddled by bullets.

The six people aboard it were clad in black wetsuits with hoods that covered their lower faces. The *ninja* look. One of them in the skiff's bow stood, submachine gun raised, and jerked his flattened hand across his neck. *Cut your throat? No, cut your engines.*

One of the ninjas was shorter, slighter and more curvaceous than the one in the bow. Had a familiar look in the tight wetsuit. He couldn't believe it. "Leyley?" he shouted.

"I can blow that thing to shit," said Clark.

Certain that it was Leyley on the skiff, he said, "Maybe we can talk them into going home."

Clark said, "Hey, man, I like your sense of humor. I like *you.* I'd like to see you keep making us all laugh. And I'd like to see you keep breathing."

Kyle throttled down.

Both craft bobbed over the swells with occupants ready, as they say in combat parlance, to engage. "Leyley?" he shouted again.

She didn't answer but he could tell he'd hit the mark. *Nice.* "*You were down a long time,*" she'd said that day he'd surfaced after seeing what he thought was a wreck. "*How deep did you go? What did you see? You saw something.*" So she and her little party had been watching the *Morgainne* for how long? Watching them dive, lower *Ogler,* pull up artifacts . . .

"You are thieves!" she finally yelled back. "You are taking Bahamian treasure! We are Bahamians! It belongs to us!"

"We are taking your boat!" the man in the bow yelled with more directness and less nonsense.

Minns had come up out of the cabin but was keeping his head below the top of the gunwale. "I can run the boat," he whispered. "I'll keep down. So you can shoot!"

"Take it," Kyle said to him, "and take off."

Minns squatted between the cockpit's two seats, grabbed the bottom of the wheel and reached up for the throttle.

Kyle looked at Cooper and Clark who were watching the pirates. "Get down and hold on!" he shouted at them.

Sinbad roared forward.

Bullets hit the cockpit glass, sending shards over him and Minns. As Kyle moved on all fours out to the afterdeck, Clark said to him, "What the fuck are you going to do?"

"Just stay down!" He knew if he explained to Clark what he was going to do, the former SEAL would think him nuts. And maybe he was. He just couldn't bring himself to killing or even wounding a woman he'd made love to if he could find a way out of it. Out of the pirates' sight at portside, reaching to grab a cleat, he pulled the pistol from his belt, dropped it on the deck and hurled himself over the gunnel. As soon as he hit the water, he pulled his dive-knife from its sheath.

Beneath *Sinbad's* wake, he swam underwater toward the skiff. It too was moving again, resuming the chase. As he came alongside it, he reached but missed the first tow ring he grabbed for but snagged the second. The ring was at waterline. Holding on to it as he jabbed the knife into the skiff's portside buoyancy tube, he was able to remain hidden under the sliding water. The attention of those aboard the craft was on the fleeing *Sinbad*.

He cut a foot-long gash in the tube. Still holding onto the tow ring, he reached to where he could jab the knife into the skiff's bottom. Many inflatables had plywood bottoms but this one's was, like the buoyancy tube, made of tough resistant material the sharply honed knife blade could penetrate. Once having made the cut, he pushed away, let go the skiff and dove quickly deeper lest the propeller of its racing outboard take his head off.

Treading water in the skiff's wake, he watched its slashed port tube deflate and the port side begin to sink. Its heavy motor canted to port and dragged the rest of the craft to a crawl. The six on board were scrambling to hang on to the still inflated starboard tube. Less than a hundred yards to the west, Kyle kept his head down so they wouldn't see him. When he felt a swell, he would rise with it and have a look.

A quarter mile east, *Sinbad* was turning back, making a wide arc to maintain a good distance from the skiff. He heard the popping noises of automatic weapons fired by Leyley's gang. But the skiff was listing and bobbing around and they were having to cling with one hand to its starboard tube. Their shooting was a haphazard indulgence in fury with little possibility of a bullet striking the workboat.

Bobbing himself, Kyle realized his friends might have a difficult time seeing him. If he tried to catch their attention—jumping above the swells and waving—those on the raft might see him. And he was very much in range of their weapons.

So would *Sinbad* be if Minns tried to pick him up where he was.

He ducked under the water and began swimming fast toward the workboat. Every few yards he surfaced to find it, then plunged again. When he thought somebody on *Sinbad* might be able to see him, he thrust himself above the water as much as he could, waved both arms, and dropped. On one of his leaps, he saw that *Sinbad* was coming back.

Looking west, he saw that he had increased his distance from the skiff by another fifty yards or so. The skiff looked as if it were going around in circles and sinking. Maybe in their wild shooting, they'd blown a hole in the good tube.

In any case, at least for now they were too busy just trying to stay afloat to be looking for him.

Sinbad was coming fast. Only she wasn't coming toward *him*. Whoever was now at the wheel was heading the workboat straight for the skiff, or what was left of it.

He thrust himself upward again, waving—*hey, hey, I'm HERE!*—and falling back. On another leap, he saw Minns at *Sinbad's* starboard rail waving at him. So they knew where he was. So who was at the wheel and why were they headed straight for the skiff?

Those of the pirates who could still shoot while clinging to their wreck were now doing so with a new desperation. But *Sinbad's* bow was riding too high in the water for many of the rounds to hit her cockpit. The fiberglass bow was taking most of the incoming rounds.

Kyle heard the impact when the workboat struck what was left of the skiff. There was only a slight and brief decrease in *Sinbad's* forward momentum as it tore through its target. Kyle had glimpses of pirates and pieces of skiff scattering to either side of *Sinbad* as the propellers of the workboat's three engines slashed broadside through the inflatable's shorn tubes and hull, missing its engine by inches.

Coughing and spitting, Kyle heard the workboat's engines throttle down. It was turning toward him. Minns was at the stern ladder, watching him, yelling, ready to help him up.

Once aboard, he saw that Vic was at the wheel. And Dan Clark was lying sprawled amid the precious cargo with his AR-15 clutched against his chest and an egg-sized lump on his forehead. He was groaning. Minns and Dawton called out his name. Kyle looked for a container of water he could throw on Clark's face. But Clark was coming around. "What the hell . . ."

"You lost your footing," said Minns. "Your head hit the gunnel."

"Hooyah," said Clark, using the SEAL battle cry. "Don't tell Wayne . . ."

"Hey, you lost your balance in a bucking boat?" said Kyle with a fraternal grin and a shake of his head. "But I won't tell him you're human!"

"We just got a call from the Coast Guard," Vic yelled from the cockpit as she steered into a wide circle back to the west. "They got our Mayday and are on the way!"

Kyle looked back to see the tattered skiff turning in the sea. Leyley and her buds were clinging to what was left of the stern.

The skiff's motor, still attached, was spinning them around in a way that made him think of the doomed crew of the *Pequod* going down with Moby Dick.

CHAPTER 14

Moving Target

THREE HUNDRED METERS down, on the Tongue of the Ocean's east side, *Opekun-681* lay under a cliff to avoid sonar detection. Twelve kilometers to the north lay New Providence Island whose capitol was Nassau; and thirty kilometers to the southwest, on the Tongue's opposite shore at North Andros, lay the U.S. Navy's Atlantic Undersea Test and Evaluation Center.

Two SSNs—American fast-attack nuclear submarines—were too close for comfort, one less than ten kilometers southeast of *O-681's* position; at a depth of 200 meters and coming from AUTEC on a northeast heading and a bearing of 20 degrees. The other SSN was farther west but nonetheless on a similar course and coming at a faster rate of speed.

Not exactly coming *Opekun's* way but that could change in a heartbeat.

Heartbeats on *O-681* had undergone frequent quickening since leaving Cuba. U.S. Navy activity in the Caribbean was busier than usual. From Cuba north through the Florida Straits and all the way east to the New Providence Channel and southeast down into the Tongue, Captain Konstantin Polivanov and his crew had been under constant fear of detection. "Comrade" Captain Anton Lepushin, however, seemed too little perturbed by the possibility. Whether his irritating sangfroid was a result of overconfidence in his undisclosed mission or just plain stupidity, Polivanov wasn't sure. In any case, the maritime activity had made communication with Moscow and Severomorsk difficult despite the Lourdes relay. And what communicating there had been was kept secret by Lepushin.

"We will proceed to these coordinates," he'd said, pointing at a location northeast of the Berry Islands on map and chart. "With all due haste." But after a second communication with Moscow several hours later, he'd pointed to a new destination 300 more kilometers south, at the end of the Tongue.

At both sites, *O-681's* passive sonar had picked up a low-frequency signal in the range of 38 to 50 kilohertz at a pulse rate of about ten per second coming from a source over a thousand meters down. A depth no submarine and few submersibles could reach. To *O-681's* sonar chief, the beeping signals sounded much like the homing signal of a deepwater oil well.

At neither site was there any undersea or surface ship anywhere close to *O-681*.

A third comm with HQ told Lepushin to order the submarine back north, back up the Tongue, to a location northeast of North Andros Island. And that's where they'd been going when the American SSNs out of AUTEC forced them to lie low along the edge of Great Bahama Bank.

Captain Polivanov was at his station in the conn, mulling all this, when the *Spetsnaz* officer entered the control room.

"We must move," he said. "The target could be gone again if we—"

As badly as he wanted to hear more, Polivanov put a finger to his lips, signaling silence. He pointed at the console screen before him. In its center was the nearest U.S. sub.

Frustration and anger were in Lepushin's eyes but he displayed neither emotion otherwise. And as Polivanov ordered, the *Spetsnaz* officer remained silent. Silence to a disgruntled Polivanov was, in fact, Lepushin's modus operandi.

The computer provided the identifying data: The nearest SSN was in the "Virginia class," the newest of U.S. fast-attack boats. Location, speed, sonic signature, and other data were displayed at the screen's edges. The image of the American sub was computer-drawn from a databank of U.S. ships, superimposed on the screen by the program that converted the sonar data to 3D imagery. Some of this data was new, the painstaking result of *O-681's* earlier reconnaissance.

The *Shchuka-B* boat had only the minimum of its life-support mechanisms running. But the nearest SSN was sending out active sonar pulses, obviously having no fear in giving itself away; perhaps engaging in tests. But these were friendly waters for Americans. Not so for Russians.

With much of *the Shchuka's* anti-sonar coating having peeled away in the last several months, the cliff she was near might conceal her shape and it might not. Significant improvements in sonar systems were ongoing, especially for the damned Americans.

They waited.

Polivanov's mouth was dry. He took a drink from a water bottle. He didn't want to contemplate what might happen if they were detected. Peacetime rules of engagement notwithstanding, *O-681* was prowling a region jointly protected by American, British, and Bahamian forces. The latter might be laughable but the first two were not.

The foremost SSN's heading was now more toward the northeast, away from *O-681's* vicinity.

Polivanov said to the current watch officer in a voice hardly above a whisper, "Get underway as soon as it's safe to do so."

"Aye, Captain.

"Chief of the Boat, tell First-Officer Kolotcha to come to the wardroom."

"Aye, sir."

It was not good for Polivanov's crew to know friction existed between him and Lepushin, though by now they had to be aware of it.

He said to the *Spetsnaz* officer, "Let us go to the wardroom, Captain."

Once inside the wardroom and having closed the door, before sitting down, Polivanov repeated the word Lepushin had used when Polivanov shut him down. "Target, Captain? What exactly is the *target*? Are we going to attack an American ship?"

Captain-Second-Rank Kolotcha entered, looking a bit disheveled from having been just awakened.

"No," said Lepushin, sitting down without invitation. Indeed, the invitation for the other two men to sit came from him. "Have a seat, gentlemen."

When Polivanov and Kolotcha were seated, Polivanov at his rightful place at the head of the table, Lepushin said, "I apologize for not being able to fully inform you of our mission but as I've told you, I am under orders to withhold that information until it is certain that we are about to retrieve our prey. The information is highly sensitive and fluid. At this point, that is all I can tell you, short of telling you where to go. I will admit that thus far we seem to have been on a fool's errand but the messages from command, relayed through Lourdes, Cuba, have been in one case late and in the other a mistake; but we must act on faith that the information will eventually be accurate and we will be at the right place at the right time for the strike."

"'Target,'" grunted Polivanov. "'Prey.' 'Strike.' Forgive me, Captain, but these are crumbs and they are not to my liking."

"Your objections are noted, Captain Polivanov," Lepushin said rather ominously. "I am sorry, but I am under orders—"

"The GRU doesn't trust the boat's captain with any more information than that?"

"At the moment, that is correct. As I said, the situation is fluid and Moscow does not want me to share information until or unless it is necessary."

Polivanov looked the *Spetsnaz* officer in the eye and said, "I know of your background in Internal Affairs, Captain Lepushin. A background that has to have created many enemies. And I am sure you know of my opinion of our current president and his cabal. Is it not possible that someone on high has set us both up for failure, for disaster? To get rid of us?"

Lepushin was taken aback but tried not to show it. He conjured outrage to hide his unsettling surprise. "At the cost of a *Shchuka-B* and all her men? At the cost of a crack *Spetsnaz* team? At the cost of the international embarrassment Russia would suffer? That is a preposterous idea, Captain Polivanov. And also treasonous."

"Yes. As preposterous as the fear and distrust and betrayals—of which you are no doubt well acquainted—eating at the very bones of the State. We both know there are elements in our country in positions high and low that care for nothing but themselves."

"Unlike every other country in the world, Captain?" Lepushin ground his jaw and tried not to think of the arrests he'd made in ridding Russia of the rot to which Polivanov referred.

Polivanov was not going to quit. "We are both aware of the endemic suspicions and duplicities—not to mention incipient insurgence—festering among some in our military and intelligence units. We are in someone else's ocean and

I wonder if this 'fool's errand' we are on could be designed by someone in the GRU who bears you a grudge and would just as soon see you terminated, yes, even at the expense of a *Shchuka-B* and its crew."

Lepushin said, "That is a very dangerous idea, Captain. And one not at all for discussion."

In the charged silence, Kolotcha sought to defuse it with what he meant to be a joke. "Are we missioned then to find and seize evidence of a new U.S. weapon?"

Lepushin let go a sigh. "I will tell you this: We are missioned to retrieve a new weapon that was ours and will be again, thanks to our succeeding in our mission."

Hating to beg and compounding his vexation with ire, Polivanov said with a growl, "Can you at least tell us, Captain, something about those signals we picked up at the two locations where we might assume the 'target,' the 'prey,' was supposed to be but was not?"

"No, Captain Polivanov. Not at this time."

⤞═◉ ◉═⤝

Later, alone with his men in their cramped quarters adjacent to the submarine's lockout chamber, Anton Lepushin maintained the same disciplined demeanor he displayed in the presence of Polivanov and Kolotcha and their submariners. But privately he could sympathize with the irritation and concerns, even suspicions, of the *Shchuka's* commander. And it wasn't the first time Lepushin was nagged by the possibility someone had sent him on a foredoomed mission, unbelievable as that might seem. Barring that, given the best-case scenario he could come up with, he could not help but wonder if those in command knew what the hell they were doing.

CHAPTER 15

A Cruise Gone Sour

IN THE BRIDGE of *The Melanie Rose*, Captain Mick Shelton stood before the central console, having been summoned by First Officer Cal McGinnis. Displayed on the console's main sonar screen was the fuzzy image of a submarine lying near a cliff at a depth of 825 feet.

"Must be one of ours out of AUTEC," said Shelton. "Not the first one we've seen in the last week."

"That would be my guess too," McGinnis responded. "But it kind of bugs me the way it's just squatting there so damn still."

"No telling what those guys are up to."

"Think we should call AUTEC, or Nassau?"

"Nah," said Shelton. "Last time we did that we were politely told to mind our own business. Courtesy of the U.S. Navy. Remember?"

"Yep."

⋅⊷⊜ ⊜⊶⋅

In the night, the yacht had moved south to lie off Whale Cay in the southern Berries, out where the dropoff from the flats and reefs was steep. But pressing phone calls in trying to track down Joseph Yord had prevented Jim Harwood's going out in the catamaran with his guests to fish. Yord had slipped away again slick as a whistle while JJ Oil's VP of Eastern Operations lay in his stateroom claiming to be too seasick to talk—a claim damned dubious, in Jim Harwood's mind, considering the generally calm seas.

Harwood himself had had little sleep, forget peace of mind, since learning of the lowered seabed around Wellsite One. He was troubled by fears of a leaking wellpipe, a gas bubble forming in a strata pocket that could cause a blowout and create a tsunami born not from a distant earthquake but a methane explosion at one of his own sites. In addition, he had had to deal with a number of less ominous yet bothersome obligations: like seeing off guests who had to get back to jobs and other commitments, among them the Delgados and among *them* Ernie Delgado's niece who hadn't said much to anyone since lambasting Preston Slotter. She seemed to have been stewing ever since.

"Did you have a good time?" Harwood had asked her as they gathered in the main lounge to depart for Nassau on *Big Bird*. Sheri Delgado had turned on him like a rattler: "Frankly, you make me sick. You and all the rest of your fatcat kind who've gotten filthy rich off ordinary, hardworking people you rip off every day, every second, with high gas prices—high prices on everything made from oil—so you can make your yearly billions!" (Congressman Delgado was by now trying to hush her and pull her out of the lounge but she shook him off.) "Have you any idea what poor people all over the world are going through? Have you ever had a thought about it? If you did, would you even care?" She slapped a sheet of paper in his hand. "I made some calculations. Your sumptuous yacht burns enough fuel in one day to feed a starving village in Sudan for a year! What have you ever done to help anybody—" Till at last her uncle, having apologized to Harwood repeatedly, was able to get her out of the lounge and to the helipad where the Sikorsky-76 was starting up.

Dumbstruck, J. J. Harwood had backed off with his chest tightening as if stabbed; and for the rest of the day he kept seeing a tsunami of the world's downtrodden and destitute rolling toward the *Melanie Rose,* a great wall of human misery coming to engulf the unfeeling oil tycoon and everything else aboard his opulent yacht. Delgado's headstrong and unruly niece obviously had an ax to grind and an emotional problem to go along with it. But no matter how he tried to shake the incident off, what she'd said had hurt and it had cast a pall over what was supposed to be a fun-filled cruise and celebration of wife Melanie's sixtieth birthday which was tomorrow. Preparations throughout the yacht were underway. But along with everything else going on, Sheri Delgado's diatribe kept chewing at him.

After *Big Bird* left with its load of passengers, he'd called Ridley Stukes, chief engineer of wellhead maintenance on *WildBore V.*

"We're in Nassau Harbor, sir," said Stukes. "For resupply."

"I want to talk to Joseph Yord. Culpepper said he's with you."

"Oh. Dr. Yord had to fly back to Houston."

"WHAT?" J. J. had shouted at Stukes over the satphone. *"Why?"*

"To examine some samples he took of the seabed at Wells One and Three."

Flabbergasted, Harwood said, "I thought he'd already done that! I've been down to Well One. Why is the goddamn seabed sinking around Well One, Ridley?"

"I don't know, sir."

"Does Yord know?"

"He's working on it. That's all I know."

"And what about Well Three?"

"Yessir."

"Yessir, *what?*"

"The seabed has sunk some there too."

"Why?"

"That's out of my expertise, sir."

"Shit," said Harwood, and clicked off.

When he called corporate headquarters, he was told that "Dr. Yord" was not in his office or his lab at the moment.

"You get him on his satellite phone," Harwood barked, "and tell him to call me. Now!"

When Yord finally called back, Harwood said bluntly, "Have you done anything at Wells One or Three to have caused the seabed to sink?"

"We're looking into that, Mr. Harwood."

"Well, what the hell could you have done to have caused something like that?"

"At this point, we don't know."

"Who's this 'we' you keep talking about?"

"Myself and my team, sir."

Harwood suddenly remembered what Yord's team was called. The MITERS. From the acronym MITE. But he couldn't remember what the acronym stood for. Jesus, he just wanted to go fishing.

"We have taken specimens of the surrounding seafloor material at Well One," Yord was saying, "and we examined them as best we can on *WildBore Five*. But we had to get them here to the Houston lab for a better breakdown."

Breakdown. That's what you're giving me! "I thought you had already done that!"

"We're doing it again, sir. It's needed."

"But what could you have done to have caused—"

"We do not yet know that. It could be something unrelated to either well-site, a result of natural causes, something we know nothing about at this point and have no control over."

By the time Harwood clicked off, his suspicion that he—THE BOSS!—was being given the runaround again had pushed him near the boiling point. He hadn't learned a goddamn thing!

⊸▬◉ ◉▬◈⊸

The sun had set and the Caribbean sky was bejeweled with stars. Outside the *Melanie Rose's* bridge, former Delta Force Captain and combat veteran Marvin Quinn glassed the sea. The moon would not rise till an hour before dawn and would be only a sliver at that. It would be a dark night but for the stars and the lights of other vessels.

He saw several, two to the north, three to the east, one to the south, at diverse distances from *The Melanie Rose*. Two were containers, one possibly a tanker. The others were smaller but big enough to be called ships. As he watched, one of these seemed to be coming toward them. But he soon realized it was moving northward.

Had he wished it was coming toward *Melanie Rose* with malevolent intent?

Quinn had been warned by a fellow Delta Force officer who'd tried a stint working for a maritime security outfit after being discharged from the Army.

"If you're looking for a rush, forget it," the friend had told him. "You'll die of boredom."

As usual, he could hear the noises of the owner and his wife and guests having dinner in the VIP dining room. He could smell the appetizing aromas wafting up and tried to ignore his rumbling stomach. Neither he nor any of his men on the evening watch had eaten yet. Over his handradio, he called quietly for the quarter-hourly security check and listened to the reports from his men posted in different parts of the yacht.

All was well on *The Melanie Rose*. The yacht was equipped with short- and long-range radar, with sonar, with acoustic blasters and water cannons. Closed-circuit TVs and alarm systems throughout the ship were connected to a bank of monitors six high and ten wide in the security suite's own room behind the wheelhouse. And there was Quinn's crack security team. J. J. Harwood could afford all the security he wanted and Marvin Quinn intended to give him the best.

He glassed the sea again. His eye caught something as he was moving the binocs slowly from east to west. He stopped, swung the glasses back to the spot. But whatever he'd seen was no longer there.

Continuing his scan, he finally lowered the binocs only after returning twice to the place where he thought he'd picked up an irregularity. Maybe a big fish jumping from the water, or a whale. He could see disturbed phosphorescence out there. Like the phosphorescence roiling in the wake of the yacht.

Could have even been a submarine. *Ours surely*, thought the security captain. Unable to be picked up on the yacht's sonar? *Sure*. Subs had so much stealth equipment on them now they could sneak into a fortified littoral without detection. Or so he'd heard.

Lights spilled out over the water on all sides from all four decks.

Dark night, bright craft.

Captain Quinn did not like so much illumination.

⋆⇒ ⇐⋆

At the head of the long lavish dinner table, J. J. Harwood was still trying to be a man who matched his yacht but too many other things were on his mind.

Culpepper still claimed to be sick and was not present. The mystery of the low-ered seafloor around Well One and the slipperiness of Dr. Joseph Yord nagged. So did his having been verbally flogged by Sheri Delgado. Then wife Mellie had told him just before dinner that she missed Houston, missed the kids and grandkids, didn't care for the *Mellie's* maiden cruise in the Bahamas and wanted to go home.

Caught by several of the guests who'd fished that day, wahoo, mackerel, bonefish and snapper had been prepared for the munificent meal, including vari-ous and sundry side dishes.

Having heaped his plate and now gorging himself, Senator Preston Slotter raised his wineglass and, buttery jowls aquiver as he chomped, delivered with a laugh one of those bromides typical of some in the fatcat class to which Ms. Delgado had consigned James Jessup Harwood:

"I wonder what the poor people are eating tonight!"

CHAPTER 16

Crowded Waters

TWO DAYS WERE spent seeing to workboat *Sinbad's* repair, identifying Ashley Dillet and her boys when they were brought in by the Coast Guard, answering questions by investigators, obtaining the required Abandoned Wreck Permit and going through the other red-tape rigmarole for the artifacts to be transported by air to Miami, all of which was made easier by Admiral Chizzick's arrival and clout. Dawton was still a little amazed that Leyley Dillet had eavesdropped when he told Tony Corro over the satphone on the day after New Year's *"I may have found a wreck."* Thus she'd gotten together a ragtag gang of Bahamian misfits and been watching *The Morgainne* and its dive operation days before they actually began to bring up artifacts.

Poor Leyley. Though laws against piracy had been in the books since the Middle Ages, they were not internationally defined and codified until the Geneva Convention of the High Seas in 1958 and the UN Convention on the Law of the Sea in 1982. Piracy's current resurgence off places such as Somalia and the Indian subcontinent left maritime authorities with little inclination toward leniency. This was especially true in regions that derived a large part of their revenue from seagoing commerce, not to mention the tourist trade. An activity associated with Bahamian history as much as slavery or the raising of cotton and sugarcane, maritime piracy under Bahamian law—which being a member of the British Commonwealth derived its laws from the UK—had been a capital crime since the 17th century. Leyley and her buds could be in jail for months and no judge was likely to be lenient when it came to sentencing—unless he was corrupt and the defendants somehow managed to scrape up enough pounds to buy him off. Not likely. He felt a little sorry for Ashley Dillet. With her looks, she could have chosen a much more sensible career.

Leaving Nassau Harbor with himself at the workboat's wheel, Dawton saw a ship he'd seen before: the one that had almost capsized him and Dillet. *WildBore V.* It lay alongside the crowded wharf on the north side of Potter's Cay. When Dawton recapped to his companions his earlier acquaintance with the offshore research vessel, they all eyed it with keen curiosity, passing binoculars back and forth. *WildBore V* was an ORV registered out of Miami, Tony Corro had said. Owned by Deepwater R&D, a subsidiary of JJ Oil. They saw only a few deckhands on board the presently observed ship, going about ordinary business.

So what exactly was *WildBore V's* business off the Joulters to have wanted to swamp *Sinbad* New Year's Day? They'd seen no evidence of any oil-related activity in the area. No oil platform or drillship on the surface anyway.

A spray of saltwater coming over *Sinbad's* side hit him in the face.

What about *under* the surface?

Victoria was close by in the workboat's stern, golden hair flying and eyes hidden behind her wraparound Raybans. Still burning in his heart and his loins was the memory of the way she looked the previous evening when they had dinner with Admiral Chizzick. She'd worn a shortskirted dress, a lowcut blouse and black pearl necklace and earrings that made him want to gawk like an adolescent while the admiral talked about how he'd mitigated the bureaucratic hurdles related to the salvage permit and the investigation into Leyley and gang.

But something else was trying to make its way into these thoughts.

A beeping. "Hey, guys," Kyle called, "I just remembered something."

The three others moved closer. Vic entered the cockpit, a space big enough for two to occupy without having to touch but with the sway of the boat, she leaned close against him.

He tried to focus on what he meant to say. Not yet out of the harbor and *Sinbad's* outboards throttled down, it was easy to talk. "I heard a beeping signal when I was off Leyley Cay—sorry for the name Wayne gave it. Sorry I met her. Yet it was my going to the Joulters with her that put us onto that debris trail. That irony aside, I haven't heard that pulsation since. Maybe when we checked out that area, we weren't close enough, or the underwater sound currents were different—and oh yeah, my GPS was fritzing that day—but I'll bet it was a well-head locator, a homing signal. There's an oil operation of some kind going on somewhere around there. And I'll bet it has something to do with *WildBore V* and that gooey stuff we've been finding—"

"And maybe the lowered seabed," said Vic.

⋯⊷═◉ ◉═⊶⋯

Woodrow Culpepper lay abed in his stateroom on the VIP deck, still feigning *mal de mer.* He was in fact a bit sick but not from the sea. At least Ridley Stukes had been able to clean up or hide the percolations around Wellheads One and Three and straighten their shelters before J. J. saw them. But the truth could not be forestalled forever.

His phone buzzed. Fearing it was Harwood, he didn't bother looking at the caller ID and made ready to sound sick as a dog and punched the talk button. "Yaaahh?"

"Mr. Culpepper, this is Ridley Stukes. We're twenty miles out of Nassau Harbor.

We were on our way to Block Two but—Do you remember me telling you about a forty- to fifty-foot powerboat named *Sinbad* I saw in Block Three on New Year's Day?"

Culpepper sat up in the bed. "Yes?"

"We went up pretty close to it to have a look but saw just a couple on board. The gal wasn't wearing a stitch so we figured it was just a recreational boat. But we saw it leaving Nassau Harbor this morning. So after we got underway for Block Two, I decided to see where it was going. It was out of our radar range by then but just acting on suspicion, we swung northwest. We had it on radar and tracked it to Block Three. There's a ship there, apparently anchored. About the size of *WildBore V,* maybe a little longer. The powerboat was winched aboard the ship."

"So they're inside the Block Three perimeter!?"

"Yessir. That's what I said. We're not in visual range, not close enough to see her name or what flags she's flying. We could call Nassau—"

"No. I don't want the Bahamians snooping around Well Three. How close?"

"How close are we to the ship in question, sir, or how close is it to the well?"

"How close is it to the wellsite?"

"About four hundred meters."

Culpepper's gut clenched. "How close are you to that unidentified ship?"

"Ten point eight miles, sir. We can move in closer if you want. Or send the chopper—"

"Wait. No. Yes. I want you to get close enough to identify it. Flag, name, anything you can get. But don't . . . just . . . don't go too close to them or they'll want to know—don't get too close to the wellsite either. We don't want to call their attention to that. Just watch them, see if you can figure out what kind of ship it is and what they're doing there—"

"If we get close enough to see what they're doing, we'll be identifiable too. But what can we do anyway about a ship in any of the blocks, Mr. Culpepper? The wells are capped, the permits suspended. And even if they weren't, they allow JJ Oil only the mineral rights—"

"Quit telling me crap I already know! Find out what that ship is and get back to me!"

Culpepper jabbed the disconnect button. He missed the old phones whose receivers you could bang into their cradles or throw at a wall with vented fury. He lay there in a fettle, aware he had to calm down in order to think straight. But what if those in that unidentified ship discovered the lowering seabed and leached hydrocarbon deposits? Maybe they already had!

The well in Block Three, like Block One, had been "seeded" by Joseph Yord's MITE team but Stukes knew nothing about that. Very few people did. Those who didn't included J. J. Harwood. Culpepper wanted to take one of the yacht's copters to Block Three to have a look at this mystery ship himself but how could he explain to J. J. his reason for doing so without once again incurring a lot of questions about Joseph Yord? He'd already lied, misled, evaded and diverted till he was a nervous wreck. Until this trip, Boss Harwood had in general taken little interest in what Culpepper had been doing with JJO's Eastern Offshore Division. If Culpepper's vexations continued to mount here in this godforsaken place, he might succumb to something much worse than feigned seasickness. He rued the day he let himself be persuaded by officers from the U.S. Navy to hire Dr. Joseph P. Yord. He punched Yord's private number.

The microphysicist answered immediately. "Yes, Mr. Culpepper?"

"Where are you? What are you doing?"

"I'm in the photo lab at Corporate Headquarters, looking at the data from Sites One and Three and working on the reversal. I have to be here—"

"Your *team* can work on the reversal! Goddammit, this is the age of sat-phones, computers, iPhones, iPads and a whole of other i-shit. You can work on the reversal *here*! You get back here. Bring along Greaves if you need somebody with you from the MITE team. But you are going to have to explain to the boss yourself, in person, what's going on. I can't stonewall him anymore, can't keep fielding his goddamn questions alone! Do you hear me?"

"Yes, Mr. Culpepper." Yord's pronunciation of Woodrow's last name always came out sounding like "Kilpeppah." Though the scientist's well-vetted background indicated he'd been born and raised in California, he often uttered other words, phrases, that sounded a little odd; but, hell, in this day and age weird accents were commonplace all over.

Woodrow turned to his laptop and looked again at the latest video Ridley Stukes had taken of Wellsite Three. Stukes had tidied it up the way he had Wellsite One. The situation at both was similar but judging from the video, they looked in decent shape.

⇥ ⇤

On *The Morgainne* that evening, Kyle was about to join Victoria for dinner in the staff's mess when the bridge reported it had found a beeping signal in the area 400 yards northeast of *Morgainne's* position and the debris trail, at a depth of 240 feet. The signal was weak and inconsistent. Listening to it over the hydrophone link, Kyle could not say for certain if it was the one he'd heard on New Year's Day.

"I'll bet it is," Victoria said. "And if it is, the wreck you sensed couldn't be far away."

Sensed? Kyle noted her use of that word. But not since her questioning that followed his "episodes" at the overhang and their finding the debris field had she tried to probe him further. *Sensed? Hunched?* Haunted by the events of recent days, not the least of which were his episodic trips into Streamland and what he'd seen in the "streams," he knew Victoria's point about the proximity of a wreck to the wellhead signal was worth considering.

In addition to monitoring the wellhead signal and scanning the seabed for a wreck nearby, the *Morgainne's* bridge was also watching a sizeable ship seven miles to the east-southeast. Picked up on radar from 15 miles out, it had been on an undeviating course for the Joulters at a speed of twelve knots until it stopped at its current position and had not moved in the last hour.

Together, Kyle and Victoria went up to the bridge. (Quarantined by Diane Weitzman and Doc Pratt, senior partner Wayne was still confined to his cabin.) From outside the bridge, they raked the ship with binoculars, seeing little deck or visible bridge activity, till the last of the day's light was gone. Kyle was certain that it was the offshore research vessel *WildBore V.*

"They're watching us," said Vic.

Dawton had the feeling there was more than just *WildBore* watching them.

"Like they're afraid we're going to find something they don't want known," added Victoria.

⊷⊶ ⊷⊶

After struggling with disquiet and indecision through half the night, Woodrow Culpepper had decided by 0200 on Sunday morning to order the *Melanie Rose* south while the boss was still asleep and damn the consequences if he didn't like it. First Mate Cal McInnis had the watch and questioned the order. Technically, Culpepper was out of line. Though he was a JJO VP with these Eastern Division waters within his responsibility, the boss was The Boss and the *Melanie Rose* was his happytime boat, not a ship under JJ Oil operations. But Culpepper was gambling that Joseph Yord's return from Houston would make J. J. forget everything else. Only thing was, when the boss heard what Yord had to say, he might come undone—with a lot of the undone-ness flying Woodrow's way. "We've got an emergency, Cal," Culpepper told McInnis. "The boss is asleep and I don't want to wake him. I'm making the decision to move."

Culp wanted to get as close to Block Three as possible short of coming within visual range of the mystery ship.

By 0645, Ridley Stukes had identified it and called Culpepper. "It's a salvage ship with the name of *The Morgainne*. Belongs to a company called Argos Salvage. Based in Miami. They're a quarter mile inside the west boundary of the block. To judge from what we've observed from six miles away, they're involved in some sort of salvage operation."

"Treasure hunters?"

"Maybe."

"But you don't know what they've found?"

"Guy I talked to at the Maritime Ministry couldn't or wouldn't talk about that."

Culpepper thought of how much J. J. liked to go on about sunken ships and the like and had a passing idea that maybe the boss could be diverted from sticking his nose into Yord's work by getting him to stick his nose into that salvage operation. But Culpepper feared that might be a ploy that would only backfire.

"Okay. You back off, Ridley. Move *WildBore* out of range of their visuals. Right now! Go back up to Well One and make sure everything's still okay up there, or stable anyway, then give me a report."

Stukes did not immediately respond. Then he said, "Well One's okay. Maybe I should stay here to observe that *Morgainne* operation, make sure her divers aren't going to damage Wellhead Three."

"Why the hell would they do that?"

"I don't know. They could hate oil operations, be, um, ecoterrorists or something."

"Oh, bullshit, Ridley. You get up to Well One and stay there till I order you otherwise!"

"Yessir."

At dawn, the yacht was three and a quarter miles from the edge of Block Three and about six from the salvor. Thanks to the Bahamians' tightfistedness, Block 3 was only three miles wide and four long. In any case, after having to cap all the Bahamian wells, JJO hadn't been allowed to leave any sort of markers at any of the blocks to indicate claims to them. JJO *had* no claims to them at present!

With those treasure hunters inside Block Three and only 400 yards from its wellsite, they could be diving and digging and groping their effing way right to it. A *MITE* site! Peering through binoculars out a rain-lashed bridge window, Culpepper at last had momentary sight of the salvor. He could see some of the red buoys marking their dive perimeter. He ordered the yacht's captain to stop and stabilize the craft. Once the yacht had stopped and her thrusters were holding her in place, Culpepper could see *The Morgainne* better with the naval glasses. It was still too far away to make out finer detail but close enough for activity to be seen here and there on its three upper decks. He thought he could make out four divers on a dive platform being boomed out over the water by winch and an ROV about to be lowered from a heavy-duty A-frame crane at the stern.

Culpepper thought of Marvin Quinn and his security force. Maybe he could use them in some way to scare off the treasure hunters. He called down to aide Ken Murphy and told him to get online and find out everything he could about Argos Salvage and its ship *The Morgainne.*

He heard *Big Bird* coming in from having picked up Yord in Nassau. Maybe the helicopter's racket would wake J. J. and maybe it wouldn't. Having swilled a barrel of booze and bombarded his guests with bullcrap half the night, the boss would hopefully not make his increasingly nosy presence known no sooner than noon. Culpepper didn't know if he wanted him awake before that or not. Maybe not. The situation with Wells One and Three had Culpepper so rattled he was having absurd fantasies of J. J. not waking at all. Ever again.

He rushed down to the main deck and aft to meet Yord on the Sikorsky 76's helipad.

Wearing a suit and refusing to let a steward take his bags, Dr. Joseph P. Yord looked as ill as Culpepper felt when he stepped down from *Big Bird's* passenger cabin. Close behind, his assistant Don Greaves kept ducking his head as if he were about to be decapitated by the chopper's cycling-down rotor blades.

"Since I've had to come all the way back out here again," Yord shouted peevishly over the copter's noise, "I want to take some more samples from the seafloor around Well Three."

"I've sent *WildBore Five* back to Well One!" Culpepper exploded. "I thought you had enough samples from Well Three!"

Yord just stared at him. Greaves said nothing, hadn't even proffered a greeting to the VP of Exploration, Eastern Division. Greaves never had much to say about anything, come to think of it. As for decisions, Woodrow Culpepper was about to make another that could send J. J. Harwood into the stratosphere—and Woodrow Culpepper packing.

On their way to the VIP deck, Culpepper swallowed his fear of going down in *Blue Deep* and said, "We'll use the yacht's submarine. It's equipped with all sorts of crap, including a hose that can suck up stuff big as coral and rocks. You can have McGinnis take samples with that. And I want to see Well Three for myself. Before the boss wakes up and starts asking more questions!"

But Culpepper would soon suffer another jolt. At 09:40 when *Blue Deep* was about to be launched, he learned that only two security guards would accompany him and Yord and Greaves on the luxury sub.

"Fish poisoning," answered Dr. Nantz in the foyer of the infirmary where Culpepper went to find out why half the yacht's security force, including its team leader Marvin Quinn, were sick; along with them a significant number of the yacht's staff and crew. Nantz explained that he had only a half hour ago found the source of the illness by examining what had yet to be eaten of the previous day's catch. "The mackerel was the culprit."

"What about the boss, his wife—"

"They're still sleeping. But the chief steward said they didn't eat the mackerel."

As Culpepper had not. He hated fish of any kind.

The two security guards with them on the submarine hadn't eaten the mackerel either. But for christ's sake, *half the security team sick?* Culpepper had regarded all the security business for the *Melanie Rose* as a bunch of silliness stemming from J. J.'s wanting to play the part of a sea-going emperor. But hating the sea as he did, and almost paranoid about all the things that could go wrong while on it—or under it as was now the case in his going down in the submarine—Woodrow Culpepper took this weakening of Quinn and his team as woeful news.

He badly needed some news of the good kind. But as soon as *Blue Deep* reached a depth of 200 feet and Pilot Cal McInnis leveled it off at five knots and proceeded toward Well Three as per Culpepper's instructions, the VP of Eastern Exploration stood with his face glued to a viewport on the observation deck, sometimes on the port side, sometimes on the starboard, eyes raking the sea bottom with mounting dread.

CHAPTER 17

The Wreck

BEFORE TURNING IN the previous evening, Dawton and Cooper had listened repeatedly to the beeping signal through *Morgainne's* hydrophones. Its detectable strength came and went. Sonar continued to search for any sign of a wreck in the vicinity but found nothing definite. Not having dived since their trip to Nassau, Victoria and Kyle made preparations to take *Sinbad* to the signal's coordinates and dive to find its source while *Morgainne* would stay in its current position over the debris field.

With Wayne out of quarantine but advised to refrain from diving for another day, and with half the rotating dive team in need of rest, four who were fresh were descending to work the debris field with *Ogler* this morning.

The debris-field grid had been extended. More artifacts had been found, including more cannon. The size of several of the guns and their trunnions suggested a galleon but nothing yet had been found or cleaned well enough to substantiate identity or origin. Lab examination of what they'd taken to Nassau for transport to Miami could span a period of days to months.

⊸⊨⊙ ⊙⊫⊸

Submarine *Blue Deep* was headed due west. Perpendicular to its course was a zigzagging limestone shelf. Under *Blue Deep's* multiple observation lights, Woodrow Culpepper saw the ordinary sandflats, limestone and silt begin to turn a mottled color as they crossed over the shelf. Toward the north and the south, the checkered trail disappeared into the murk. Toward the west and the wellhead, it grew wider. In a stupefied state, Culpepper listened to what he'd heard before.

Joseph Yord stood next to Culpepper at the viewport, with his usual dead-pan expression. "As I have said," Yord went on in his careful and precise way, as if his words were steps through a minefield, "we cannot yet be certain what has gone wrong but it seems they have eaten their way through the steel casing of both Wells One and Three and are breaking down the underlying material around the wellheads. We are still analyzing the samples thus far taken from the sites. At Well One the seabed-lowering does not seem quite as severe. But we will know more when we have full analysis."

"But how could this be happening?"

"We do not yet know, Mr. Culpepper," said Yord patiently.

Culpepper's aide, Ken Murphy, stood at the next viewport aft, video camera ready to take footage of the wellsite, as Culp had ordered. The ever silent Don Greaves stood on the deck's opposite side, fidgeting with something in his pants' side pocket.

The submarine continued toward Wellhead Three with a low drone and efficiency that only added to Culpepper's sense of forthcoming doom. "You don't *yet* know? You don't *know* yet? Don't tell me that! Tell me what the fuck you are going to do about it! Don't just stand there like a goddamn statue. Say something that will make me believe this can be fixed and pronto!"

Dr. Joseph Yord said nothing.

⋅⊷▭◉ ◉▭⊶⋅

Cooper and Dawton had left the ship in the workboat with a pilot and a dive assistant. From *Sinbad's* yawing transom, they'd dropped into the sea with cameras and four cylinders apiece of trimix. Seasoned to deep-diving techniques, their descent rate was relatively fast.

They heard the signal long before they reached the bottom. But once on the bottom, they failed to pick it up again. Kyle suggested they move eastward, the direction in which they'd heard it on the descent.

They were down a long time, searching, before they heard it again. They soon began to see lights—and the dim shape of a . . .

Seasoned diver and all that aside, Kyle again feared he was becoming bub-bleheaded and hallucinating. He looked at Vic and pressed his talk button. "Do you see a *pyramid*?"

"Yes," she answered. "Looks fuzzy but it's definitely pyramid-shaped."

Pyramids were, of course, part of the Bermuda Triangle and Lost Atlantis lore. But this one didn't look any larger than an ROV shed. He couldn't re-member seeing any lights around here on New Year's Day. Maybe because of the uneven terrain or maybe the lights weren't working then or maybe he hadn't looked their way or . . .

"And look there toward the east!" said Vic.

He turned and saw a cluster of stronger lights before he heard the low thrum of the submarine's power plant. Maybe a hundred yards away but curiously com-ing in a broadside approach.

They dropped to the edge of a crumbling dead coral bank only a few yards above and north of the lit-up pyramid. They turned off their helmet and hand lights and breathed slowly, shallowly, to lessen their bubbles, and watched the oncoming sub. If it were military, it would be as dark as the deep—unless it was some sort of craft used for special research. But one fitted with powerful outside observation lights and glass portals almost as big as a garage door?

The low noise of its engines soon drowned out the pyramid's beeping.

A row of smaller portholes lay along a deck below the larger ones. At the for-ward end of that upper deck was a group of smaller ports and a large one in the nose. The latter would have to be the control room. Though it was yet hard to tell, Kyle judged the boat to be well over a hundred feet long. Coming at about five knots.

He was soon able to make out people standing in two of the large viewports on what would be the observation deck. The combined illumination from both inte-rior and exterior lights clearly revealed two people standing before each glass. Men. Looking out, looking toward the pyramid. In the sub's looming lights, the pyramid's size became more distinct: maybe about eight-foot square. No, not anywhere big enough to fit into any Lost Atlantis scenario but the right size for a wellhead shelter.

⋯⊨◉ ◉⊨⋯

Fifty yards from the wellhead, *Blue Deep's* engines stopped and soon were reversed.

Culpepper gaped at the wellhead housing. And suddenly realized the submarine was turning around.

Cal McInnis said over the intercom, "Mr. Culpepper, I just received a call from Mr. Harwood. He's awake now and he told me to return you to the yacht at once."

The submarine began turning back to the east.

What? How? McInnis must have the goddamn radio buoy up!

"I need more samples!" Yord cried.

Culpepper ignored him. The boss was awake and knew the supposedly seasick Woodrow had taken the submarine down. He cursed under his breath; tried to see through binocs the seabed around the site and what Yord had described and proven with photographs: the dark seabed several feet lower than when the wellhead was put in place, the leach pools covered, the shelter itself still upright.

Yord was looking at him. Greaves and Murphy were looking at him. The question he thought he saw in all their troubled eyes was the same one pounding in his brain: *What are you going to tell Mr. Harwood?* Culpepper almost bellowed it aloud. *What are WE going to tell the owner of JJ Oil!?*

<hr />

For a few seconds Dawton and Cooper watched the sub withdraw before their attention leapt back to the pyramid. They moved up over the coral bank and down toward the bizarre object. As they went, they frequently threw glances to the east and saw the sub's lights dimming in the distance.

They turned on their own lights and circled the pyramid, taking photos of the structure and the seafloor around it. The pyramid's wooly appearance proved to be the result of new coral growth. The beeping came from a small transmitter near its steel door, which was devoid of any polyps as if made of some anti-coral material. On the door was a sign identifying the thing as the property of JJ Oil.

Kyle had seen wellhead shelters before but never one shaped like a pyramid. He began to probe around it with his diving knife. Vic did the same on the other side.

As they'd seen in other places, the seabed had been disturbed here but in this case, he saw no evidence of any oily goo—until he turned over some of the chunks of limestone near the shelter's base. He now realized the rocks that had covered the goo here had been purposely laid over it. To hide it. The possibility that they were looking at the result of a leaking wellhead—or the preliminary signs of a blowout—made the surrounding sea feel as if itself were a stifling goo from which there was no escape.

A strange panic hit Dawton, as if this were the first time he'd ever been submerged, let alone this deep. It was for certain the first time he'd ever had such a sensation and this fact alone stunned him.

But his fear began to feel remote—or otherworldly. As if it did not belong to him. Eerie tendrils wormed their way into his awareness that had nothing to do with his immediate surroundings. *Except they were of the sea. A sea in storm. This sea. A ship upon it . . . two . . . three . . . far apart, lost from each other in the storm. Sails ripping apart, masts snapping like twigs and men blown like pieces of canvas overboard . . . all going down . . .*

He felt something pulling on his arm. He turned. *Victoria.* She was pointing. He looked, saw in the faint light-swath of the receding submarine a canyon cleft in a coral shelf to the southeast. A shelf that looked recently crumbled in places, and streaked here and there with glimmering sludge. A little to the north, at the edge of what they could see of the canyon, lay something darker than the surrounding terrain. It looked to be artificial but not anything related to a modern underwater oil operation. From their perspective, it was easy to see how the passing submarine had missed seeing it because of the contours that lay south of its path.

As the sub's illumination faded and the gloom closed in, they trained their handlights in the anomaly's direction. But they were too far away for their light-beams to reach it.

They swam toward it. The closer they came to it the more it began to look like part of an old ship lying precariously near the top of the steep canyon slope.

A wreck mostly intact. *Maybe.*

Kyle suddenly thought he sensed something else; something, long, ominous. Back to the south.

He whirled around, searching with the beam of his handlight. Whatever it was, it lay beyond the power of the beam to reach it. He would have asked Vic if she "sensed" it too but distrusted his own faculties. And he did not want her to think him delusional whether he was or wasn't.

Lapping at his inner depths was memory of images incurred recently, among them those ghosts of three weeks before when diving here. Like the fragmented footage from an uncanny video stream the memory became that of the sailing ships he'd seen a moment ago and earlier, tossed in storm, separated, doomed. And as they faded, the lopsided trawler of rusted steel appeared.

Vanished.

He heard a beeping close by. On his wrist.

A face suddenly appeared before him. Big blue eyes in a diving helmet. A mermaid in a drysuit. Beautiful bod obscured by tanks and hoses and loose neoprene . . . so beautiful she had to be alien. Maybe she came out of the pyramid. "You okay," she said.

"Yeah." *No.*

She pointed at her dive console. It was not beeping.

For a moment, he was confused. "Yeah," he said, "let's call up . . . tell them to move *Morg*—" he looked at his own console hanging from his vest and forgot why he looked at it.

"Kyle," she said, "*Sinbad's* up there, not the ship. We're not on a tether and not connected by phone. Our bottomtime's up and you're losing it. We've got to ascend."

Bottomtime up . . . already? Where had the time gone. His sense of it was screwy. *But . . . a wreck . . . there . . .*

Why was his console beeping and hers wasn't? Because he usually used up his gas supply quicker than she did! Yeah! But . . . *A wreck?* Elation, confusion, curiosity swirled with a worsening dreamstate that made him mentally drift.

She pulled on his vest, raising him.

He fought off her grasp.

She stared at him in alarm. Gripped a strap of his vest. "Kyle, listen to me! Talk to me. Who am I? What are we doing here?"

Okay, okay. Yoohoo, Dawton, come back. "Me Neptune and you Morgana, Queen of the Deep. Say something nice."

Though he'd never heard her talk this way before, he would realize later that her fear for him explained the salty language. "I'm going to drag your ass to the surface if I have to grab you by the balls to do it."

Wow. Sure, baby. Whatever you say. Follow you anywhere . . .

⋆⊨◉ ◎⊨⋆

They radioed from *Sinbad* their location and the ship was moved there to pick them up. When back on *The* Morgainne, cheers and backslaps and hugs accompanied them to the dive room: They had seen the wreck, or *a* wreck! They had yet to determine if it was the one Dawton thought he saw on New Year's Day or some other.

Despite the morning's windy conditions, the ROV crew dropped *Ogler* to the site and she was sending up fascinating visuals. The dive room soon emptied of the celebrants as they moved to other parts of the ship to view the feeds from the robot.

Alone at last, Dawton and Cooper helped each other out of their drysuits. Peeling him down to his Thinsulate underwear, Vic said, "Kyle?"

"Yeah.

"How are you feeling?"

"Okay."

"You were slow to respond when—"

"I know. I'm okay now." But he was not.

"That other ocean?" she said, sweat beading her face as she pulled out of the lower part of her suit.

He felt his hand trying to hold on to water and the water slipping through. This initiated the inexplicable glimpse of a lattice through which he might pass as through a curtain—or in which he might become entangled as in a net.

"Kyle?"

Wanting familiar reality, he assured himself that he was sitting on the bench between the cylinder racks looking at Victoria in her Thinsulate. And she was now straddling his waist as she sat and took his face between her hands. Her face—beautiful as ever with strands of her golden hair wild and whirled after the removal of her hood—was creased with unease. "Are you here?"

"Umm."

"I think you were a bit out of it when we had to come up—and when we came aboard and were talking about the wreck to the others. No one else seemed to notice but . . . weren't you?"

"I'm back now. With you sitting on me like this, I'm very much back."

"Don't joke."

"I'm not joking."

"But it's not narcosis. Doc Pratt said you—"

"Yeah. No bubbles in my bloodstream when he checked me out. But that was after coming up. And though I passed the neurological test, maybe there are some bubbles in my head that eludes his expertise." But he didn't want to go any further than that. In any case, she had a good point. Contrary to his earlier suspicion that it was usually at depth when he had his visions, the ones he'd been having of late kept intruding when he was in shallower water or even on the surface.

"Did you see . . . what did you see down there besides that wreck?"

"I . . . I'm losing what . . . not remembering." She had said something to him before they started up, something demanding, strong, yet loving, enticing. What was it? "Tell you what," he said. "Put your mouth to mine and breathe into me *your* memory."

She gave him a concerned yet willing smile and leaned in to do it. Then the dive team that had been working the debris field began to come in. She got up from his legs, patted his cheek and said, "See you topside." She turned and, gathering her gear, moved to the women's locker room.

→〰◉ ◉〰←

"Good morning, all." In Miami, Admiral Curt's authoritative voice came through the speaker on the table in front of *The Morgainne's* main conference room. Son Wayne, self-freed from quarantine and claiming to be over his cold, had called to tell his father what they'd found. After those on the morning dive had been checked over by Doc Pratt, he'd called a lunch meeting and begun it by announcing that the admiral was online and receiving the same photo-and-video feeds they were watching on the big screen hung from the room's forward bulkhead.

After the room responded to the admiral's greeting, Wayne followed up with what he'd told his father over the phone: "That submarine that was approaching the wellhead shelter when Kyle and Victoria were down there was launched from a floating Taj Mahal presently lying six miles to the northeast of us, named *Melanie Giselle Rose*. We looked up its registry. Launched just two weeks ago. It belongs to one James Jessup Harwood the Third."

Said the admiral, "Have you tried to raise *The Melanie*?"

"Not yet," answered Wayne. "But with your concurrence, we will."

"Yes, do so."

After Wayne relayed the admiral's request to the bridge, the admiral resumed: "On Friday, when I firmed up the Abandoned Wreck permit, I talked with the authorities in Nassau about JJ Oil and what it was doing in the Bahamas. It has six wildcat wells in the Northern Caribbean. But the permits for those wells were for mineral rights only and were suspended over a year ago when the Bahamians shut down all wildcat operations because of a blowout by another oil company."

Kyle sat at the front table with Victoria and Wayne, having trouble concentrating on what was being said, mind wanting to drift into a different current.

"JJ Oil has, however, been allowed to leave the wellheads in place, as long as the company provides appropriate safety maintenance pending reinstatement of the permits. Each wellsite is within what's called a Block some two to three square miles in size. The debris field and the wreck Kyle and Victoria found this morning is in Block Three. When I acquired the wreck permit on Friday, I said nothing to the Bahamians about the oily gunk or the lowered seabed but after receiving your report this morning on the condition of the wellhead near the wrecksite, I called JJ Oil headquarters to inquire about that. It being Sunday, I wasn't able to reach either receptionist or secretary. I left voicemail emphasizing the gravity of the situation at our wrecksites and our concern about their environment; but have received no reply. If my secretary is successful in tracking down Mr. Harwood's private satphone number and we have him online, I'll patch you in. Hopefully we will receive a reply soon. So . . . carry on with the meeting."

Wayne nodded for Victoria to proceed.

Focusing on *her* helped Kyle stay where he was supposed to be.

Operating the computer on the table, she began displaying on-screen the photos she and Kyle had taken of the JJO pyramid. Several of the crew in the room who'd worked on offshore-oil related jobs affirmed that the pyramid looked like a capped wellhead shelter, shaped that way to protect the head from seafloor trawling.

Greg Kotalik in the ROV room called down to say that the realtime video-streams from *Ogler* were coming in.

"Send them down to us," Wayne told him.

The feed was soon duplicated on the video screen. Manipulated by Kotalik, *Ogler* hovered at a depth of 220 feet, her two anterior cameras panning the wreck and its surrounding terrain and sending high-resolution video images up through the fiber-optics cable.

The wreck lay at a depth of 230 feet, sticking out of the sand like the half-buried bones of a sleeping enigma. Its battered and mangled decks lay at the edge of a canyon that plunged out of the limestone shelf toward the Tongue. Parts of the slope and the old coral terraces above looked as if they had recently crumbled and rolled down the canyon wall. The dropoff swallowed the beams of the ROV's lights.

Canted twenty degrees to port but mostly upright, with her bow smashed into the canyon's slope and her stern crumpled where her name should have been inscribed, her beam span from midships to stern and sterncastle was wide enough to be that of a galleon. The feed revealed a ragged doll's-house arrangement of the partly crushed sterncastle and the deck of the captain's cabin; below that, a broken and scrambled web of other rooms disappearing into darkness. Upper corroded remnants of what was likely the whipstaff steering gear and hinged rudder were faintly visible above the muck.

As Kyle watched, its upper timbers, truncated masts and spars, seemed to become hung here and there with dark goo, which looked much like the "rusticles" draping sunken steel ships, the term having been coined by explorer Robert Ballard who found the *Titanic* in 1986. Looking like mineral icicles, rusticles were the eerie waste product of microbes eating *Titanic's* iron. But the old ship atop the canyon was made of wood. Then, in staring at the illusory rusticles, Kyle began to see them as the shredded sails of a wooden ship—one of the ships he'd envisioned before, on the surface of the sea and torn by violent storm and sinking.

He tried to hold on, feeling as if *he* were about to sink.

"You okay, Kyle?" Chizzick's voice.

Kyle rallied and looked over at him. "Yeah. Just a little tired, I guess." He felt Victoria's hand touch his thigh under the table and tried to focus on the video again.

Maybe to get Wayne's mind off Kyle, Vic voiced something they all could surmise: "Sand and silt washed toward the Joulters in repeated past storm surges could have buried and kept the ship hidden for hundreds of years."

Depth-data coming in from *The Morgainne's* sonar reads had revealed recent subsidence here. When Chizzick told Kotalik to move *Ogler* around the wreck and zoom-in her forward cameras on the surrounding seabed at the canyon's edge, they saw several dark trails through the scrambled limestone that led back south toward the wellhead. Moving one of *Ogler's* arms in to remove a sample from a trail confirmed it to be of the same oily goo they'd encountered at the debris field and which Victoria and Dawton had uncovered and photographed around the wellhead shelter.

Chizzick was swearing under his breath. He called up to the bridge. "You guys got ahold of that yacht yet?" The reply was negative. "I'm going to take *Sinbad* over and find out what they're doing here and what's going on with that goo and—"

The lordly voice of the admiral broke in. "Maybe just a radio call will get us some answers. We need to play things carefully. Don't want them to know too much about what we're doing and they're bound to ask questions about us when we start asking ours. So . . . meanwhile, good show."

⤙⊜⊜⤚

Checked over by Doc Pratt and given the okay by Dive Master Diane, Wayne joined the afternoon team to the wrecksite.

Kyle was lying on the bed in his cabin with the door open despite an occasional gust of wind blowing in rain when Victoria knocked on the outside jamb. He sat up. All he wore was a pair of boxer shorts but she'd seen him that way plenty of times.

She stepped in and sat down in the chair in front of his small desk and said, "Talk to me."

"Babuk adoom inner splipf," he joked.

"Please. Listen. I'd stay here with you all night if you'd feel better about telling me what you think you can't."

"That is a very tempting proposition. But . . ." He patted her knee. "It's not that I don't trust you, Vic. It's that I don't trust what I—what I'm dealing with. I don't know enough about it, can't make enough sense of it, to talk about." *And if I told you about it, you'd want me to stop diving. Maybe.* "Anyway, we're both tired, need to get some rest. But thanks for the offer. I'd dearly like to take you up on an all-nighter of any kind but for now . . . thanks for listening."

"I want to be more than a listener, Kyle. I hope you understand that." She stood and leaned down close. "Here's that mouth-to-mouth that got interrupted in the dive room." She put her hands to each side of his face and kissed him, long and deeply. Then she pulled away, turned and walked out, leaving him aflame.

Alone again, his thoughts darted here and there edgy as fish fearing a predator. Recent events had allowed little mental drifting; and exhaustion at the end of each day allowed nothing but the deepest sleep. But now his restlessness pushed him out to the rail where he stared at the sea and began to recall bits and pieces not of the past but of what felt to be the present or immediate future. Alternately doubting and believing the validity of these mind's-eye blips, he saw some things he'd seen before and some he had not. The beeping from the wellhead pyramid, like a warning, insinuated itself into his consciousness, pulsating in time with the beat of his heart, his pulsating blood.

Back in his room, he was dropping into that twilight zone between wakefulness and sleep's first stage when a mélange of disturbing thoughtforms began moving out of the gloom: that rusting, listing trawler he'd previously vizzed, leaking from a gash in its keel incurred crossing the Great Bahama Bank, the pumps that had tried to dispel the seawater coming in no longer working, its cargo of duped refugees beginning to panic and gunmen telling them to jump overboard into a sea roiling with sharks and then something lying low in the depths. Not the wreck on the brink of the canyon dropoff . . . no, that long low submarine shape larger and longer than the one he and Vic saw at the wellsite. No windows. No sound . . .

CHAPTER 18

Watchers

SHORTLY AFTER DAWN on Sunday, at Anton Lepushin's order, *Opekun-681* had risen in a keen wind and roiling seas to the surface, twelve kilometers southeast of the Joulter Cays. From the bridge atop the conning tower, Lepushin and Captain Polivanov tried to scan with their binoculars the circumambient horizon. The wind and the seas made this difficult but Lepushin finally found the large luxury yacht he was looking for. It lay twelve kilometers to the north-northeast and through the glasses he determined with patience that it had four decks above the waterline and that the name emblazoned on its bow was *The Melanie Giselle Rose*.

"That is the vessel we've been looking for," he said.

Studying the yacht keenly, Polivanov said, "We have been looking for a pleasure boat? A pleasure boat the size of a ship?"

Lepushin answered, "What I said, Captain."

Fourteen kilometers to the southwest, very near the Joulters, another craft lay at rest. Its length, multi-deck superstructure, deck profiles and A-frame wench in the stern suggested an offshore oil ship or a salvage vessel. The name on its bow was *The Morgainne*.

Both the yacht and the salvor were flying U.S. flags.

Sonic signatures of a robot submersible periodically lowered and raised from *The Morgainne* suggested the activity of a salvor. Maybe those aboard her had found a sunken ship of the Spanish Treasure Fleet. Beleaguered by days-old tension and stress, Lepushin fancifully entertained the idea of forgetting Pyotr Telasnikov, of moving closer to the salvor to see what it had found and, if indeed a trove of riches, of taking it and himself defecting. He almost laughed out loud at the vagary, then wondered if his sanity were becoming as questionable as that of those who'd sent him here.

Hearing the distant noise of a helicopter to the northeast, he searched the sky and found it on an approach toward the yacht. As he and Polivanov watched, the copter banked and came downward to the swaying helipad aft of the yacht's second deck. Lepushin strained to keep the copter in sight but realized its passenger door was on the side he could not see. Due to that and the sea swells, the distance and the drizzle, he could not tell who alighted but was certain he saw at least four people move from the craft into the yacht's interior.

"If we can see them, they can see us," grumbled Polivanov. "If they look hard enough. We must submerge."

Lepushin wiped saltspray from his face and said, "The wind, the wave action, will degrade both their radar and sonar, as it has degraded ours. But . . . all right, take her down to periscope depth, Captain. But I must watch that yacht."

"In these seas, you will see *nothing*."

"Take her down to periscope depth, please, Captain."

Polivanov gave the *Spetsnaz* officer one brief look of anger and descended the ladderway. Lepushin quickly followed as if Polivanov might order the hatch shut before Lepushin could drop through.

They'd been from northeast of the Berry Islands all the way to the southern region of the Tongue and were now back in its northern end with Lepushin saying only that he was acting on his most recent communication from Moscow. Frustration had been mounting with nerves on edge and discipline among the submariners strained.

Lepushin could sense the uneasiness among his own team. By the time he entered the control room on Polivanov's heels, his mind was made up.

He went to the periscope platform where Polivanov was overseeing the dive. Lepushin waited for the necessary orders and acknowledgments to cease and, pulling a waterproof pouch from inside his coat, removed from it several photographs and said to the acting officer-of-the-deck, "These are photos of the man we are looking for—before and after his face alteration—and our agent who is with him. I want you or someone you designate to keep watch on the yacht to the southwest at two-three-one degrees. If you see either of these men on that yacht, notify me at once."

Every man within hearing distance was hanging on every word. Until now they'd not had an inkling they were "looking for" someone.

Lepushin said to Polivanov, "If you will come with me to the wardroom, Captain. And summon your executive officer to join us."

Lepushin called for his own second-in-command. Once the four were alone in the wardroom and seated at its table, Lepushin said bluntly, "Communication with Moscow through a relay team in Cuba has not been reliable. It has been slow and sporadic. I will no longer wait for Moscow to tell me when it is time to inform you of our mission, gentlemen. We are after a defector. Our man who is with him and is supposed to provide me with information as to his whereabouts may have been compromised, maybe captured, and could now be undergoing interrogation by American agents. Every attempt I've made to message Moscow in the last several hours has received no reply. The last communication I received from GRU Headquarters said that by today the defector would be aboard that American luxury yacht to the northeast of us."

The table before them tilted slightly back and forth with the yaw of the sub in the agitated sea. Konstantin Polivanov stared at the *Spetsnaz* officer as if the sturdy steel beneath their feet were cracking; perhaps thinking his worst fear was now confirmed: He had aboard his boat a minion of madmen who could get them all killed or at the least caught and captured by the U.S. Navy.

"I will admit to you," said Lepushin, "that the more I have lived with it the less I have come to like this mission. But I have my orders and we all know the consequences if we do not carry them out."

Nothing more had been said about "the fool's errand" Lepushin might be on, the possible setup for them both to fail and either die or be captured for it. But it hung in the air between them like an odiferous fog. A fog, Lepushin knew, that had been there from the start.

Polivanov retorted, "Why wasn't this defector snatched when he was on land, where it would have been a hell of a lot easier?"

"I asked the same question, Captain. I was told that was tried. Three times. The last time, the snatch team was almost caught. They had to abort."

"If you have lost contact with both the mole and the GRU, I suggest *we* abort."

"You do not know the importance of retrieving this man," Lepushin countered. "If there is a reason for me to continue to believe in this mission, difficult or crazy as it may seem to be, that reason lies in that importance."

Captain-Second-Rank Kolotcha inserted, "Is this defector the secret weapon we talked about, Captain Lepushin?"

"Yes."

"We are listening, Captain," said Polivanov.

The *Spetsnaz* commander had decided to tell these officers more than he had to, hoping for better cooperation. "I am sure you are aware of the fact that the United States and Russia, despite the ENMOD treaty endorsed by both in the seventies, have been for some time covertly engaged in projects related to what is euphemistically referred to as environmental modification. The acronym ENMOD, however, can apply to anything and everything from cloud-seeding and exfoliation, such as the Americans employed in Vietnam, to tectonic and weather warfare or the meddling with electromagnetic energy and the use of the ionosphere as an electromagnetic gun—or using the upper atmosphere to create a vast electrojet antenna for communication with submarines. Projects like the High Altitude Auroral Research Project known as HAARP—"

"Or the Sura Ionospheric Heating Facility near Nizhniy Novgorod," interrupted Polivanov skeptically. "Are you saying our defector—"

"As you might guess," resumed Lepushin, irritated by the interruption, "our defector has a background in work much less exposed or debated, but no less important to Russia's defense. The man is a genius, I was told. Just before he defected, he was supposed to have been on the brink of a nanotechnological breakthrough that would have given us a tremendous edge. I suggest you consider what it would mean if the Americans gain that edge. Or perhaps worse, what having that edge could mean if someone else were to have it. Like Israel. Or elements in Chechnya or Georgia or Ukraine . . . You, Captain Polivanov, are in fact on record as having damned to hell some of our military and intelligence officers and retirees who have sold on the blackmarket Russian arms and technology to buyers of questionable backgrounds. Imagine what such an edge—"

"If this defector is such a genius," Polivanov interrupted again, "what's he doing out here on a luxury yacht in the northern Bahamas? Why isn't he at Los Alamos or Lawrence Livermore or the Office of Naval Research?"

"The CIA took him in, of course, when he defected. After they interrogated and vetted him and decided he was not a Russian agent, they sent him to the Office of Naval Research. Our information is spotty and questionable regarding his time at ONR. But apparently he was not happy there and he was not adding much to what they already knew. So they let him go to the private sector, at his request. The parting was less than amiable. Telasnikov did not want to work in weapons-research anymore. He wanted to work in environmental improvement instead of environmental manipulation for the military. The CIA allegedly did not deem him worth the continued expense of keeping him under protection or surveillance. He went to work for a Houston-based oil company named JJ Oil. The yacht out there is owned by JJ Oil's owner. In a matter of months, the GRU was able to infiltrate the big oil company with one of their agents. At JJ Oil, this mole finagled a position as assistant to Telasnikov. Telasnikov's alleged inimical parting with ONR and his alleged dislike for military research and the fact he is working for JJ Oil now—none of this means he isn't also working for one of those American entities you mentioned that are engaged in weapons research, or some other entity that contracts with the U.S. military. His parting with ONR and CIA could be a ruse, a cover, though we have had no corroboration of this from our mole. That said, let me emphasize that he is a very important individual to the Federation and we are missioned to seize and take him back. I am acting on the last best information received which is that he should by now be on board that yacht."

"So how do we—or you and your team—how will you take him and get him to Khodynka? How will you do that without alerting the U.S. Coast Guard and Navy to our presence here?"

"I will admit that will be difficult, but not impossible, if I lack further communication from the mole who is supposed to be with him, or lack any further word from the Intelligence Directorate. I have considered several—"

The voice of the officer-of-the-deck came over the bulkhead speaker, "Wardroom, this is the OoD: Captain, we have a vessel bearing one-one-seven degrees . . . estimated range six thousand meters, course one-three-four, speed four knots."

Polivanov pressed the transmit button. "This is the captain. Identification?"

"A civilian ship, sir. We are trying to determine . . . sea conditions are making it difficult but . . . sonar reports that it sounds like it's running on one engine and . . . it looks . . . wait one . . . I think it may be a fishing trawler, sir. And it seems to be listing badly."

"Well," said Polivanov, "we do not want to be seen even by a crippled fishing trawler."

"Aye, sir."

Rising from his chair, Polivanov punched the main-circuit button. "All stations, prepare to dive to depth. Officer-of-the-deck, set depth at three hundred meters, steer course ninety degrees at slow speed."

"Preparing to dive, aye, Captain. Depth three hundred, course ninety . . ."

Alone in his quarters later, Anton Lepushin stared up at the darkness over his bunk.

What exactly was Telasnikov doing for JJ Oil? Lepushin was told at Khodynka that the scientist had been working at Dubna north of Moscow as a molecular engineer in environmental warfare when he defected. Whatever he was doing here in the Bahamas did not technically fall into the realm of Anton Lepushin's business. His business was to capture and haul him back to Russia where he would be pressed into the sort of work he was doing before he defected. But the very idea of meddling with the planetary environment, whatever its particular component—atmospheric, biologic, oceanic—seemed the stuff of Doomsday and Lepushin didn't like it.

CHAPTER 19

Borebots

HAVING STAYED UP late drinking too much and trying to entertain his guests with tales of pirates and the Spanish Main with a gusto he no longer felt, J. J. Harwood did not get out of bed until almost ten on Sunday morning. It was Mellie's birthday! She was not in her suite. In the next hour he learned enough to make him want to go back to sleep, perhaps, for eternity.

His aide Ben Kealing told him that Joseph Yord had arrived and he and Woodrow Culpepper had gone down to Well Three in submarine *Blue Deep*. Trying to stifle his irritation that he'd not been awakened when Yord arrived, he ordered their return immediately.

Through the plate-glass window in his office he could see some land to the north. Things didn't look the same as the day before. "Where are we?"

"We're about four and a half miles southwest of Chub Cay, sir. Mr. Culpepper told Captain Shelton to move to this locale in the night."

"So we're close to Block Three."

"Yessir. Less than four miles from its eastern perimeter, sir. And there's something else."

"*What?*"

Kealing spoke in a hurried and worried voice. "Dr. Nantz called from the infirmary a couple of hours ago. About half the security team's sick, Captain Quinn included. Some of the yacht's staff and crew too. Senator Slotter is in bad shape and we might have to fly him to Nassau. I've spoken to Commander Quinn. As you can imagine, he is very upset and anxious that he and some of his men won't be able to stand their posts."

"Sick with what?" Harwood blurted.

"Ciguatera," said Kealing. "Fish poisoning caused from eating fish contaminated by toxic reef algae—"

"Yes, yes, I've heard of it. Didn't the cook examine the fish?"

"The toxin has neither smell nor taste, sir. And the poison can't be cooked away."

"Were all the fish contaminated?"

"Just the mackerel. Nantz said the disease can come on quickly or not so quickly, so there may be some more who come down with it."

Jim Harwood couldn't remember if he'd eaten any mackerel or not but other than the hangover, he felt all right. So far. "How long are the effects?"

"Like the severity of the disease, the effects can vary between individuals. Nantz has some medication that may help and he sent *Little Bird* to Nassau for more. Meanwhile, he's ordered those affected to get some rest and remain as comfortable as possible till the initial symptoms abate and he can see how they respond to the medication."

"How long will that take?"

"It depends on the patient. The initial symptoms can last up to two weeks in some cases. It depends on how much of the toxin you have in your system and how you respond to the medicine. It's too early to tell if anyone will have to be flown to Nassau or Miami."

J. J. suddenly remembered again that it was Mellie's birthday. "What about Mellie? Where is she? It's her birthday, for chrissake! All the preparations, all the—"

"Mellie's all right, sir. She went out early with those wanting to fish. That was before Nantz knew what he was dealing with. But we called the catamaran and told her. A couple of people who went out weren't feeling well but not badly enough to come in yet. Most said they hadn't eaten any of the mackerel. Mellie said that whatever they caught today, they'd throw back. Her bunch just wanted to fish."

Ten minutes later the bridge called to report having sighted a listing trawler three miles to the northeast. "On a northwest heading," said Captain Mick Shelton, "but moving very slowly in a sort of zigzag pattern. Not the usual straightforward way a trawler would move. We can't see the bridge very well because of the list, which is to starboard. Its port side is to us. Can't see much of the stern either. We've tried to raise it but received no answer. We've called the Coast Guard but all their craft are tied up elsewhere right now."

Back in his suite for his pills, J. J. went out to the sundeck with his binoculars and, rocked by the wind, finally found the trawler. It looked as askew as he felt. And as he looked, he thought he saw the sea churning a little way aft of it. He could not tell what was causing the disturbance but the vessel wasn't moving fast enough to make much of a wake. He went back inside to the intercom mike. "Keep trying to raise that trawler. It sure as hell looks like it's in distress."

"Yes, sir. Mr. Culpepper and Dr. Yord are coming in. And sir?"

"What?"

"The salvage ship about six miles to the west of us, identifying itself as *The Morgainne*, has been trying to raise us but Mr. Culpepper told us not to respond."

"Never mind what Culpepper said! Answer that ship's calls."

⊷▬◉ ◉▬⊷

Upon entering the theater room adjacent to J. J.'s office, Woodrow Culpepper began instantly to babble. "Dr. Yord wanted to take more samples at Well Three—"

"Why did you tell the bridge not to respond to that ship to the west of us?" J. J. demanded from the front of the room as Yord quickly opened his briefcase, pulled out his laptop and handed it to Greaves.

Culpepper said, "Ah—it's sitting now a mere three- to four-hundred yards north of the wellsite."

"So what's it doing?"

"They're treasure hunters, trespassing on Block Three."

"Trespassing? How in hell can they be trespassing when we only have the mineral rights to the block and even those are suspended—"

"They're bound to have noticed the change in the depth of the seafloor and want to know why —"

"Me too!" Harwood looked at Yord and Greaves. "What the hell's going on?"

Culpepper said, "We're working on it—"

"That's what you keep telling me. What—" J. J. took a breath, let it out, his mouth tasting foul as a sewer despite his having brushed his teeth and gargled mouthwash. "You said the wells are intact. Didn't you?"

"Yessir."

"Are they?"

"We're no longer sure."

"ARE WE IN DANGER OF A BLOWOUT, CULPEPPER!?"

Woodrow looked at Yord who was looking at the viewing screen which was as blank as his face. "We don't think so, J. J. Do we, Joseph? The pressure readings continue to indicate no problem with—"

"You mind telling me just what the hell's going on, then, that I don't know about?" J. J. cast his baleful gaze at all three. Yord and Greaves were at the presentation table, fumbling with their stuff.

Culpepper was again the one who answered: "J. J., you know oil exploration in these carbonate banks has a history of spotty success with the old procedures. And with drilling suspended out here and our mineral rights in bureaucratic limbo, we decided to try a new technique, undisclosed to the Bahamians—"

"And to *me*!" J. J. roared.

"— in two of the wells. So if you'll let me—you see, Wells One and Three—in those two, just those two, we tried a procedure that was successfully tested in the lab and in the ocean environment—"

"Successfully tested *where*?"

"In the Gulf of Mexico."

"Strictly under *your* supervision?"

Culpepper swallowed and squeaked, "Yessir!."

"When was this going on?"

"Two to three years ago."

"Why wasn't I told about it?"

"We kept it under wraps because we did not know yet what we had, if it was going to work. Didn't want to bother you with it till—It was still experimental,

J. J., and you were busy with your horses, your trips and—and there was the danger of corporate espionage—"

"I'm not a goddamn spy in my own corporation, Woodrow! And you didn't want to *bother me with it*? I should have been the first told, consulted, *asked* if I wanted you to go forward with it! Not told about it *after the fact!*"

"Yessir. But . . . look, I've been taking care of everything while you—while you—"

"Never mind that! What *new procedure*?"

Culpepper looked at Yord. With a sigh, Yord began to speak. "Mr. Harwood, to begin with, we used nanosensors to detect oil deposits at a 15,000-foot depth through multilayers of limestone and dolostone—"

"Nanosensors? What the hell are *they*?"

"Very small—infinitesimal—molecularly engineered sensors that can transfer data from the nano realm to the macroscopic—the world we all live in. Nanosensors occur in nature—in biological or chemical form, for example—and in recent years, nanotechnology has been advancing in the creation of nanotools for various uses."

Nanotech: One of the numerous things that had popped up in recent years that J. J. had a hard time, as Culpepper put it, wrapping his head around. Involving stuff so tiny you couldn't wrap anything at all around it, let alone your head. The idea of wrapping one's head around anything just now worsened his hangover.

As Dr. Joseph Yord rattled on and, sitting at the laptop, sidekick Greaves began to run a presentation program with text and graphics that was supposed to augment what was being said, J. J. had a sudden memory of Yord—what in blazes was he, a microbiologist, a microphysicist?—having given a presentation at corporate headquarters in Houston months ago. Here J. J. was seeing it again. He stared at the subject heading and saw PETROPHYSICS AND NANOTECHNOLOGICAL APPLICATIONS IN THE OIL AND GAS INDUSTRY.

He recalled a meeting with corporate officers and board members in which Culp and Yord gave this same razzle-dazzle presentation with graphics of molecules bonded together in structures looking like rolled-up chicken wire. They liked playing with the word a*lchemy*, applying it to cutting-edge chemistry. Stuff on the nanoscale. Invisible, undetectable, except through instruments like electron or atomic-force microscopes. The employment of laser beams, micro-electro-mechanical systems . . . . He hardly read the industry rags anymore but knew that nanotech had been bandied about in the oil and gas business since 2006. It was supposed to offer all sorts of benefits in extracting oil not extractable under the old way. Supposed to be beneficial to the environment as well. J. J. had given his approval. He'd done a lot of that in recent years, approved things he really didn't understand and relegated to vice presidents and managers. No, this was hardly the first time in recent years he'd felt engineering, let alone science and technology, was passing him by. Not that he'd ever quite gotten on to it to begin with. And Culpepper had told him more than once that he was averse to change.

Culpepper was saying, "The two MITE stations were experimental or exploratory probes preparatory to drilling, J. J."

MITE. He glared at Greaves' screen. Saw: *Molecular Intelligence Technology and Engineering.*

Yord said, "It was when we were working with oil remediation, with microbes that eat crude, that we came upon a way to engineer an allotrope of carbon that extracts oil and gas from limestone, Mr. Harwood."

Culpepper broke in anxiously, "You know, J. J., there are bacteria that, ah, 'eat' metal as well as oil. And a number of companies have been working on micro-robots, borebots—"

"Borebots?" J. J. was trying to get his bearings. "You engineered a *micro robot* that eats *rock?*"

"Leaches oil from porous limestone," said Yord. "We engineered 'borebots' to work in swarms, guided by pre-programmed electromagnetic fields from the wellhead stations, monitored periodically by AUV or manned submersible that—"

Culpepper again broke in, "Stukes and the monitoring crew know only that they are monitoring the EM and other reads, J. J. They don't know what for."

"Once the borebots reach deposits," Yord continued, "they switch or reassemble their molecular architecture to separate oil from water, stone, etcetera—"

"Wells one and three were the only ones inserted with TOTO-Twelve, J. J.," said Culpepper.

"TOTO-Twelve?"

"The name we gave the borebot," said Yord.

As Yord talked on and Culpepper interrupted and Greaves's presentation moved from one thing to another, J. J.'s head pounded and he had an unsettling tightening in his chest as he listened and stared at stuff about nanotubes, bucky-balls and fullerenes till his brain was numb. But he was beginning to remember that Yord had come to work for JJO after having spent some time at the Office of Naval Research. A genius, he was supposed to be. An experimenter, a pioneer in microphysics, nanotech and molecular biology.

Why had he left the ONR?

He'd felt too constrained, he'd said, too limited by government rules and regs. Don Greaves was an assistant to Yord. Culpepper had hired them to be part of a group of JJO scientists trying to improve a naturally occurring bacterium, according to the text J. J. now stared at on the presentation screen, known as *Alcanivorax borkumensis*, a microscopic critter that fed on crude oil. It had been found in oceans the world over but especially in areas where oil spills had occurred. Improving a microbe that turned crude, low-grade oil into a useable and marketable source of energy had interested, even excited, J. J. But in the throes of another threatening divorce from Mellie, he'd forgotten all this.

Yord was saying, "In addition to extracting oil from limestone, the allotrope leaves a beneficial and commercially viable byproduct that is similar in composition to a carbon nanobud. A hybrid that will have practical applications in microelectronics—"

"But if One and Three are being monitored—you think the *WildBore* crew can't tell that the seabed is going down?" J. J. exclaimed. "They're bound to know something's screwed up. And those treasure hunters—if the thing's sinking the seabed, they're bound to notice *that*!"

"That," said Yord, "we are studying. From the start, the big challenge was how to direct and contain TOTO-12. A composite well cylinder was created that kept the borebot within the cylinder's seal down to where the limestone layers rich in oil and natural gas should be. But it seems something has gone wrong with the containment factor. This did not happen in the Gulf."

"The containment factor," J. J. muttered. "If that is true . . ."

"Results from samples taken at the two sites have been analyzed and show evidence of TOTO-12 boring through the wells' containment walls in places, eating some areas of limestone and turning that into the allotrope. The molecular structure of the resulting material is much thinner, smaller, than sand or limestone. It is less compact than the natural seabed. But its oily material can be mined—"

"I don't give a damn about that! Can you get it under control? Can you stop the leaking?"

"As Mr. Culpepper has said, we are working on a remedy. We are making some progress in Houston. I was busy with that when I was again ordered back out here. I am in constant communication with my lab. We are running computer analyses, modification models—"

"ARE WE IN DANGER OF A BLOWOUT?"

A nervous tic had appeared on the left side of Yord's thin mouth that looked like it was trying to pull his lips shut. "As Mr. Culpepper tried to tell you, sir, the pressure in the wells is stable. We have yet to determine how TOTO-12 is migrating from the casing before we can say there is any danger of a catastrophic event."

Catastrophic . . . Rip Van Winkle Harwood had been sleeping while the world slipped onto some strange track toward an unknown but decidedly bizarre outcome. *In his own lifetime!*

J. J. heard the intercom buzz and said into the intercom speaker, "What?"

"Mr. Harwood," replied Captain Shelton, "you wanted us to keep an eye on that listing trawler to the northeast."

"Yes?"

"It's less than a mile away now. We still have not been able to raise it. It doesn't respond either to our radio calls or lamp Morse. It's listing worse and we can see what looks like a lot of shark activity around it. They dumped a lot of fish earlier. We can make out an expanding blood trail but dead fish wouldn't make such a large trail."

CHAPTER 20

The Trawler

KYLE DAWTON HAD dozed fitfully and finally come fully awake after swimming up though a phantasmagoria of troubling images—a sea of time it seemed, with currents of the remote past and near future—that had besieged his attempt to rest. Nausea threatening and mind trying to clear, he staggered around for some shoes and a shirt, knowing that Chizzick's dive team had to be at the wrecksite by now. Putting on the clothes, he blundered down to the ROV room.

Victoria was there, not able to rest any better than he. Indeed, about a third of the dive staff filled the room as all eyes watched the video screens and computer monitors. Sitting at the control console, Greg Kotalik and Rob Palmer were manipulating *Ogler*. Those immediately behind the operators stepped aside to give Dawton a place next to Cooper.

As Kyle's eyes moved from *Ogler's* screens to the camera feeds coming in from the individual divers, he was able to shake the storm from which he'd awakened.

While Nancy Coletti and Skip Roberts were shining their lights into the mangled rooms exposed at the wreck's stern, Chizzick and Brad Shinley were moving gingerly over the shambles midships.

Chizzick spoke up. "It looks like the deteriorating seabed could have exposed the wreck but at the same time, whatever is making the seabed sink could undermine what's left of this shelf and the whole thing could fall into the canyon."

Palmer was training *Ogler's* front cameras over the upper part. "A lot of it looks pretty well preserved. Must have been partially buried—Hey, what's that—there behind you, Wayne?" He zoomed *Ogler's* forward port camera on something glinting under debris.

Chizzick and Shinley turned and moved to it. Carefully they began to brush and sift through to the shiny object. Shinley at last extracted it. Rubbing it clean, it glowed like an irrefutable promise: a belt buckle made of gold, with part of the leather belt still clinging to it.

For the next several minutes those in the ROV room watched with mounting excitement as Coletti and Roberts joined Chizzick and Shinley and, moving away debris, found the corner of a chest under some half-rotted planking. The weight of the encrusted planks made the chest hard to pull free. The chest itself was obviously heavy. When they'd worked it gingerly out from under the planking, they knew it would have to be hauled up in a strong basket or sling. They would open it later in the ship's lab under controlled conditions.

They found what could be a partly crusted-over skull and, moving deeper into the wreck, Chizzick found more bones. He tried not to disturb them, honoring at least for now what was, among other things, a graveyard here.

Shining his light on what he was talking about, Shinley said, "The lack of encrustation here and there, like places on this chest and skull, could be explained by its having been buried."

The divers were putting what they could easily extract into baskets. Chizzick was securing the chest to the haul-up line when the voice of Captain Jon Nielsen called down from *The Morgainne's* bridge.

Dawton pushed the button that enabled Wayne to hear what was about to be said and then spoke into the intercom. "Yeah, Cap'n. Dawton here."

Nielsen replied, "There's a fishing trawler seven miles to the northeast that's in trouble."

Of all the stupid luck! But a trawler. Didn't I see . . . "Where's that big yacht?"

"Much closer to it than we are. Less than a mile."

"Are you in contact with it?"

"Affirmative—finally. I've just talked to *The Melanie Rose's* captain. Captain Shelton said they're watching the trawler too. It's listing badly but hasn't transmitted any distress signal and is not responding to their attempts to contact it. Shelton says they can't see much; just the port side of the hull because it's listing away from them. And they can't hear anything because the wind's from the northwest. They did see a lot of fish go into the water early this morning, presumably to get rid of the weight. The water around it's churning with sharks."

"Has *The Melanie* called the Coast Guard?"

"Affirmative. Coast Guard and the BDF. But they're both spread thin and you know how long it might take them to get here."

The U.S. Coast Guard could be dealing with any number of problems and the Bahamian Defense Force would be of questionable merit even if they arrived within the hour.

Wayne's voice came up from the wrecksite. "Hey, we got what could be a freaking bonanza hanging on a cliff that could give way any minute and a leaking wellhead that could blow. So we've got work to do right here with our resources already taxed to the max."

After Kyle did not respond, Nielsen said, "Roger, sir."

"I'm going up to the bridge," Kyle said to no one in particular.

Vic followed. From inside the bridge's control room, they each snagged a pair of binoculars, went out to the starboard rail and found both the yacht and the trawler off to the northeast. Little was visible of the trawler but the portside of the hull and a sliver of the ship's meager superstructure.

Kyle went back into the control room and to the communication console where he took the mike from radioman Pete Wilson. "*Melanie Rose*, this is Kyle Dawton on *The Morgainne*. I would like to speak to your captain, please."

"This is Captain Shelton," soon came the reply.

"Are you prepared to rescue people from that trawler?"

"I know the protocol, Mr. Dawton, but can't make that decision alone. The yacht's owner has been informed about the trawler and we are awaiting his decision."

"But do you think you guys can handle a rescue by yourselves if it comes to that?"

"We have a lot of lifeboats and two helicopters—and a catamaran. But if we need additional help, we'll call you."

Kyle was of two minds when he heard this answer: relieved that maybe *The Morgainne* would be spared having to take part in a rescue but afraid something much worse was about to occur. "Okay," he said uncertainly.

When he handed the mike back to Wilson, dive ops chief Weitzman's voice came over the intercom: "Bridge, this is Diane. Kyle? Victoria?" Obviously she was in the dive center, looking at its video monitor of the bridge.

"Yes?" said Dawton.

"You two need to rest. The way things are going there's no telling what might happen next."

⊶≡◉ ◉≡⊷

Having wandered a quarter mile east of *The Melanie Rose*, her fishing catamaran *Catchum* rolled in choppy swells. A younger friend of Mellie Harwood's named Danielle was strapped into the fighting chair, a red windbreaker snugged around her bikini. The wavesplash had been coming in over the stern. Everyone on the diving platform was clad in wetgear, lit with alcohol and having a whooping good time.

Danielle shrieked.

At the rail, Mellie's masseur, Clyde Bustus, saw her line go taut. Two deckhands were on each side of the line, ready with grippers and net to help haul in whatever Danielle had hooked.

The line dropped dramatically.

Feet planted firmly on the footrest, Danielle worked at the reel till she could no longer turn it.

Bustus moved to the chair. "Let me in there." He reached to release the straps holding her in. The line suddenly sprang up as if the fish had gotten free of the hook. But the line did not slacken completely.

Danielle tried again to reel in her catch.

Clyde Bustus moved over to her side and put a hand over hers to help. He could feel the weight still on the hook. But whatever remained caught wasn't fighting. With his hand over Danielle's, he helped her work the reel, carefully bringing it in.

The boat's stern did an abrupt dip. A wave slammed in over the deck. Drenched and batting away seawater from his eyes, Bustus could not see what they were trying to pull in.

But the deckhands did. The one with the net had dropped it to the deck. Both were frozen. They looked at Clyde as if to ask him what they should do. Clyde didn't understand their looks. "Pull it in, pull it in," he shouted at them.

They did as told. Using their grippers, they soon had it over the rail and into the boat.

At first, Clyde thought it was nothing more than a big tangle of seaweed, or some weird creature he'd never before seen. Then screams and howls began to burst from those on the platform and in the cocktail lounge forward. Clyde heard Danielle's sharp intake of breath, then a gasped, "Oh my god!"

On *Catchum's* swimming deck lay part of a human corpse. All that was left were the mangled head, shoulders, ribs, hips and the remainder of a thigh. The other leg and both arms were gone. The fact that it had been too heavy for Danielle to haul in at first could be explained by the likelihood of a pretty large fish, probably a shark, having been attached to it before letting go.

The blood running from it indicated a fresh kill.

At the forward edge of the fishing platform, Mellie collapsed but her yoga instructor and her physical therapist caught her before she hit the deck.

Danielle had her face in Clyde's chest, moaning and sobbing and clawing at her fishing harness. Clyde got her loose. She sprang from the chair and ran forward into the lounge, banging into a petrified steward, knocking over things and wailing as she went.

Without thinking, Bustus waved at the two men at the rail as if they were to blame. "Throw it back!" he shouted. "Throw it back for chrissake!"

⊶═◉ ◉═⊷

After those who went fishing were back aboard the yacht and J. J. Harwood heard what had happened on the catamaran, he rushed to the infirmary where

Mellie, Danielle and several other guests were being treated for shock. Mellie was asleep, sedated by Dr. Nantz. Having learned half his security force was sick, having listened to Yord's explanation of TOTO-12, having heard Captain Shelton's report on the trawler, and then hearing what Clyde Bustus told him about Danielle catching the corpse, J. J. Harwood needed sedating himself.

But he went up to the bridge where he stood with Shelton glassing the distant trawler. It was still listing too badly to starboard for them to see anything but the port side, which rose well above its normal waterline. The frothy swells around the ship were red with gore and Harwood spotted the fins and fangs of sharks. The corpse Danielle had caught had to have been carried toward the catamaran by a shark. The man must have fallen overboard . . .

"We called the Coast Guard again," said Captain Shelton, "and were told a cutter had been dispatched from Nassau and unless something happened to delay its arrival or alter its course, it should be here within the hour."

J. J. was not only mindful of the age-old maritime law requiring one vessel going to the aid of one in distress but also still smarting from Sheri Delgado's scorn. He ordered Shelton to up-anchor and move toward the trawler and, while doing so, to launch the yacht's lifeboats and the two helicopters for a rescue.

"Jesus, J. J., I don't think that's a good idea!" Culpepper was abruptly there outside the bridge. "We've already got enough problems," he said. "I don't think Melanie will think it's a good idea either. If we take those people on, there's no telling what—"

"So what would you have me do, let them drown? We're the closest vessel. We've got to save them, Woodrow!"

"Captain Quinn won't think it's a good idea either," Culpepper shouted over the wind. "Especially with him and over half his security force disabled!"

⊷⊨◉ ◉⊨⊷

In the sick ward of the infirmary, Marvin Quinn's handradio buzzed. He opened his eyes and tried to wake up. Raised a shaking hand from under the blanket. He was cold and shivering. A little while ago, he'd been hot and sweating. A little while ago? He wasn't sure how long ago he'd been hot. He looked at the radio in his hand and for a second did not know what to do with it. The mental fog parted a little. It was a handheld squad radio. PRC-126. Frequency range, 30 to 79.95 MHz. Ten Channels . . . But what was he doing with it? Where was he? He looked around. Saw several other men lying on single beds, one tossing back and forth, the others apparently asleep. Men who were part of a unit under his command. What command? What the hell was the matter with him? Was he wounded? Concussed?

The radio buzzed again. He put it to his mouth. "Quinn here . . ." The present slammed back. He was on the megayacht *Melanie Giselle Rose*. He was in charge of its security unit. His callsign was . . ." Bluewave One . . . here. Bluewave One Actual." His voice was thick and rasping.

"Bluewave Two Actual," said Lieutenant Ed Ricco, Quinn's second-in-command.

"Are you able to talk, Marv?"

"Go ahead."

"We got a problem. What appears to be a fishing trawler is going down off to the northeast. Coast Guard and the BDF are supposed to be on the way but the boss has ordered a rescue."

Quinn tried to sit up. "Okay. Okay, I'll . . . I'm getting up. I'll . . . l. . ." Quinn lay back down, feeling too weak and fuzzy-headed to focus on any one thing for long.

Ricco was talking.

Sick. He'd gotten sick. These other men here in this room, his men . . . all sick . . . having eaten contaminated fish. That's what Ricco was saying.

Need to do something. So sleepy . . .

CHAPTER 21

The Rescue

DESPITE THE DIVE chief's order to get some rest, both Dawton and Cooper were on the *Morgainne's* bridge with the captain and first mate, standing in the sporadic drizzle trying to watch across six miles of choppy sea the yacht *Melanie Rose* launch rescue craft, including a sizeable catamaran and two helicopters. They could not see the trawler because the yacht lay in the way. And the trawler could be sinking fast.

The drizzle was a veil that threatened to part and pull Dawton into that "inner ocean." As part of his awareness fought it while another part wanted to succumb, he concentrated hard on watching what he could through the binoculars.

South of where the trawler should be people were in the water, thrashing desperately to keep afloat. It was hard to tell but none seemed to be wearing lifejackets. Most were disappearing beneath the waves. The dorsal fins and snouts of sharks studded and churned the bloody froth.

Dawton went inside the bridge and aft to the radio room to see if *Morgainne's* radioman was getting any updates from the *Melanie Rose*.

No, he was told. At the moment, the yacht was not responding to calls.

⋆⟫⊜ ⊜⟪⋆

On *The Melanie Rose*, the scene that soon unfolded was one of bedlam. As those in the lifeboats coming from the trawler began to clamber up the accommodation ladders—some falling out of the rafts into the sea to be pulled out half-drowned or shark-bitten—members of the yachts' crew helped them aboard.

Obeying J. J. Harwood's orders, members of the medical staff were seeing to those who needed immediate aid.

Culpepper, Yord, and Greaves had fled to their staterooms and no doubt locked their doors, leaving Harwood and aide Ben Kealing to watch from the helipad on the lounge deck the palatial yacht filling up with ragtag people from the rafts. Actually, all they could see was the main deck's open transom one deck below the helipad. And as Harwood watched, he began to realize that not all were exactly ragtag. Scattered here and there were several men wearing life vests or life jackets under which they wore coats whose tails extended below their waists. They weren't milling around, looking terrified and lost like the rest, but were standoffish, raking their surroundings with watchful eyes and trying to hide their determined faces with visored caps or the rims of bush hats. They held travel bags whereas most of the others did not. Now and then, one would incline his head into the collar of his coat. And just as J. J. Harwood realized how often he'd seen that peculiar nod and where, he saw a guard from the yacht's security force approach one of them with his submachine gun readied.

The big man he approached did not submit to the guard's demands but quickly pushed the muzzle of the guard's weapon to the side and thrust his body forward as he pulled from under his coat what had to be a knife. The guard's gun fired wildly as he went down. Bullets struck people close by. The packed transom erupted in screams and yells. The other *Melanie* guards posted in this part of the yacht, a mere three or four in number, tried to see through the thickening crowd what they were up against. And J. J. Harwood stood frozen to the rail overlooking the scene, his mind reeling and unable to believe what he'd just witnessed.

My god, what have I done!

Aide Benny Kealing grabbed him by the arm. "These bastards are hijacking the yacht, sir! We've got to get to the saferoom!"

"The bridge," Harwood gasped. "We've got to warn the bridge, send out a Mayday. And Melanie—all the people in the infirmary. We've got to get them!" Still fighting disbelief, he heard more guns firing, some from below and some above.

Then he heard the upper deck explode.

⟜▣ ▣⟞

Kyle had left Vic on *The Morgainne's* bridge and returned to the ROV room when the voice of First Mate Buzz Franks came over the intercom speaker: "All hands, this is the bridge. We have finally had a report from the *Melanie Rose*. The yacht's captain just called and said the firing of guns was audible below the bridge deck and he had a report from the chief steward that some of the people from the trawler are armed and have killed several of the yacht's security guards. They are hijacking the yacht, taking hostages. His transmission was abruptly cut off and we can no longer raise him. We're calling the Coast Guard again and the Bahamian—wait—I think—the bridge of the yacht has just been blown!"

Kyle grabbed binoculars and rushed out to the rail to see the yacht's bridge, its radome and communication masts all going up in pieces spinning in smoke.

The smaller of the yacht's two helicopters was returning from the trawler. No doubt, seeing the bridge go up, the pilot veered off but, twenty or thirty feet short of its helipad, was shot out of the sky by what had to have been a rocket propelled grenade.

Kyle went back inside the ROV room and grabbed the ship-to-diver phone from Palmer, keyed it and repeated what Franks had told them and reported what he had just seen. He waited a few seconds. "Wayne, did you copy?"

No answer.

"Wayne?"

"I copied," at last came the reply.

The irony of this unwelcome turn of events wasn't lost on Dawton. He said, "Man, I don't want to abort or jeopardize the salvage operation any more than you do but if we don't do anything to help those people, *we'll* be a hostage to what happens to them for the rest of our days." *Jesus, I'm trying to convince* Wayne Chizzick *to fight?* "If we don't do something—whatever we find here, salvage here, will have blood on it." *Not ours, I hope.* "It will be *cursed,*" he emphasized melodramatically. *But then, considering the wreck's precarious perch on the edge of the abyss, the sinking seabed, and now* this, *maybe it already is.*

Victoria had come in and was watching him keenly.

"Congratulations, Kyle," Chizzick finally shot back. "You've just talked us into a shootout. But okay. Every diver down here's a member of the C Team. Tell every C Team member topside to get everything ready. *Morgainne* will stay over the wrecksite though. Get *Sinbad* ready for launch. Get me all the info you can on that yacht, what's going on and so forth."

"I'll call the maritime phone network. Somebody on that thing must have a satphone that's working."

"Hope you're right. We're going to need all the intel we can get. Coming up."

⋗▰◉ ◉▰⋖

In the quarantine ward of *Melanie Rose's* infirmary, Captain Marvin Quinn had awakened at the distant noise of automatic-weapons fire. Shaking with chills and sweating, he'd tried to rise from the cot, reaching in the air for his weapons but falling instead from the cot to the deck.

The other guards in the infirmary wing too were struggling to control their bodies, make them function as they should. They were having little more success than their leader, and some less. They resembled a grim scene from a ghoulish movie about the awakening dead. Only they weren't fully waking. Vaguely Quinn feared that soon they would indeed all be dead.

Hearing more gunfire on the deck above, he was up again, reaching, groping in his debilitating fog for his M5, when the door burst open. He had a hand on the weapon and was turning to use it when the darkfaced men coming in saw the security uniforms hanging from racks, the weapons, the sick guards lying on their cots or who, like Quinn, were on the floor readying feebly to defend themselves as the slaughter of them all began.

⋗▰◉ ◉▰⋖

Harwood and Kealing were in the lounge atrium, almost to the infirmary, when an able member of Quinn's team burst through a side door. The guard's face was streaked with sweat and a trickle of blood running down the side of his head where a bullet had grazed it. He spoke between quick haggard breaths. "This way, sir!" he barked as he gestured toward the place in the atrium's bulkhead where the saferoom elevator was concealed. "Hurry!"

J. J. said, "We have to get Mellie—"

"I have to get *you* on the elevator, sir! Then we'll get your wife and the others."

The first escape route would have been to *Little Bird* where it should have been sitting on its helipad up on the owner's deck but *Little Bird*, the guard informed J. J., had been blown out of the sky. *Big Bird* had not returned from the trawler and the last communication they'd had from its crew was that it was beating off refugees from the last sliver of the trawler's deck that was still above water.

"What—who are these people?" J. J. said as they began to descend in the elevator.

"Pirates, hijackers, among the refugees, sir. Caught us unawares, half of us sick, spread thin—they're trying to take over the yacht—"

An explosion reverberated from below.

"Are Mellie, the guests, the crew—"

"I don't have that information at the moment, sir."

The lift stopped.

The guard jabbed the down button but the lift didn't respond. The deck numbers above the doors were no longer lit. The guard hit the down button again. Instead of going down, the doors opened. Harwood recognized the hidden anteroom of the main deck. The wall in front of the lift doors had been blown partially away and was smoking.

"Get down!" the guard whispered.

As Harwood and Kealing dropped to the elevator's floor, entangling themselves in each other's arms and legs in the confined space, the guard sprang out with his rifle up.

The sudden gunfire was deafening. It sounded as if deck, walls, and ceiling were being ripped apart. Lying on the floor with his hands covering his ears, J. J. mentally struggled with his helplessness. In a remote part of him rarely plumbed, he was finding argument with Sheri Delgado who'd never given him a chance to defend his fatcat greediness: *I wanted to do the right thing, Sheri. I wanted to help, save people!*

The shooting stopped.

He heard yammering in a Caribbean tongue.

Two armed black men appeared in the elevator doorway in camouflage dungarees. They poked the ends of their submachine guns in the backs of Harwood and Kealing and ordered them to their feet in broken English spattered with Kryol.

⊸━● ●━⊷

On *The Morgainne*, Dawton kept busy and focused on helping Clark, Rivera and Ed Sanchez supervise and prepare for the trip to the yacht. Checking the bags of underwater weapons that fired steel bolts instead of bullets, he thought of how many times they'd trained in their use, not wanting to believe that someday they'd use them.

He'd had no luck reaching anyone on *The Melanie Rose* by satphone, no luck reaching the yacht's catamaran or its larger helicopter. His guess was that both craft had been taken over by members of the hijacking gang.

Chizzick's last report was that he and his dive team were halfway to the surface.

Two pirate attacks in less than a year, Dawton thought ruefully, *and now this? Wreck and wrecksite threatened since the getgo. The Devil Sea, all right. Why not a hostile UFO attack or an alien sea base full of bloodsucking fiends who'd push the wreck over the abyssal rim or a methane explosion strong enough to blow it and* The Morgainne *to bits; or a rogue wave big enough to . . . but no, it's more freaking pirates—or hijackers or human traffickers who'd lost their faux trawler! So yeah, congratulations, Dawton. What we do or don't do here will be with us the rest of our lives—and that might not be for long. Why didn't your Woo World powers foresee this?*

Maybe they had. Just not in the grim detail that was unfolding in reality.

His onrushing thoughts, he knew, were simply trying to keep his mind off his worriment and fear but they were about to pull him under again, out of the reality that had to be dealt with. He needed to be thinking tactically like Rivera and Clark and Sanchez who were giving what they were about to do strict military direction.

Crew members were bustling about. C Teamers were putting guns, knives, grenades and diving gear into the big workboat.

The idea of waiting till nightfall to approach the yacht, of diving from *Sinbad* and sneaking aboard under darkness, had been bandied about. But the hijackers, in control of the yacht, would likely take off before then and how many yachters and refugees would die in the meantime?

Kyle was still looking over things when Victoria suddenly appeared beside him. "You shouldn't go," she said. "You need to rest. What if the team has to dive for some reason? What if you have to dive deep and you . . . ?" She didn't finish.

He looked at her earnest and lovely face, glistening with wet from the drizzle. *Sure want to see that face again.* "I'll be all right." He managed what was probably a sickly grin. Victoria said nothing.

He wanted to hold her, tell her how harrowed and scared and angry he was. Angry that they had to deal with this, put themselves and what they'd found so far, *The Morgainne* itself, in harm's way. But all he said was, "We shouldn't have to dive, Vic. We'll board the yacht from *Sinbad*. If we can't get up ladder or transom, we'll use grappling hooks and line."

"I'm going too, then."

"Vic—"

"I've trained just like you and the rest. You know how well I can shoot."

Yeah, better than me. "No. You and Diane will be the only divers left with *The Morgainne* and the wreck. We need you to run things here."

The argument was suspended with the arrival of Chizzick's dive team and their being lifted on the divers' platform from the water. Chizzick was the first on deck. They could hear him barking orders into his handradio as Clark and Sanchez moved to help him shuck his scuba gear.

Kyle looked at Vic. "I'm sorry but I have to go and you have to stay. I'm sure Wayne will agree."

"But Wayne doesn't know what I know."

"What do you know?"

"That you have lapses of being present, lapses of—"

"I'll be all right, Vic. I swear."

She sighed. "So you think I wouldn't tell him if it meant saving your life?"

"You think I'm gonna let you risk yours?"

She turned away but just before she did, he caught the glint of tears.

The face-off left him feeling like crap but he resumed his task with the gear for *Sinbad's* launch.

An image of that long black sub lying on the seabed floated up again. He felt its lurking presence, its waiting . . . but for what?

Where? Why?

Despite his fear of losing the present, he tried to see the thing better.

And it vanished.

CHAPTER 22

Hostages

ANTON LEPUSHIN HAD ordered a hesitant Captain Polivanov to move *0-681* to within 1800 meters south of *The Melanie Rose* and to surface. Lepushin was gambling that what had developed with the sinking trawler and the yacht's rescue effort would provide enough distraction for *0-681* to escape notice. There was still no word from Yakov Baturin as to his and Telasnikov's exact whereabouts. Having established contact with the Cuban relay station, Lepushin had sent another request for an update from Moscow but received no reply.

With his binoculars trained on *The Melanie* he still saw no sign of Pytor Telasnikov. But the yacht's helicopters suggested how Telasnikov could have arrived aboard *The Melanie*, or left it for that matter.

He had been watching the yacht for so long his arms were going numb. And he had a headache trying to suppress his frustration with seeing no sign of his quarry. What he'd seen thus far wasn't Telasnikov but a scene of crazed calamity on *The Melanie Rose*.

⊷⊨⊚ ⊚⊨⊷

Captain Konstantin Polivanov was close by in the tower's narrow space, feeling as if he were adrift in a nightmare. By now he was in a perpetually wavering state, trying mentally and emotionally to walk the brink between two decisions: do everything Lepushin ordered or arrest the *svoloch* and tie him to a *Shkval* torpedo for launch. But wasn't the need to retrieve a goddamn genius who knew how to wreck the environment important not only to Mother Russia's continued survival but to her need to regain power and prestige on the world stage in the name of Czar Putin? *Der'mo*!

He looked at the *Spetsnaz* officer and said, "It seems your American yacht has taken on some bad agents, Captain. That trawler was obviously a human trafficking vessel. I hate to be repetitive but perhaps we should abandon your mission and its hopelessly elusive object and get the hell out of these crazy waters and go home."

Lepushin said nothing. Nor did he look at Polivanov.

A head came up above the tower hatch. "Sir, we have had a response to your message!"

Lepushin brushed by Polivanov to reach the hatch and the ladder. Soon in the radio room, he read the reply from Moscow. When Polivanov came in, Lepushin said, "Our mole, Colonel Yakov Baturin, reports that he and Telasnikov have been herded along with other people in the yacht to a bay on the vessel's fourth deck that holds a civilian submarine! We've got to move, Captain—and prepare the *SZ-44* for launch!"

⇥▬◉ ◉▬⇤

Prodded and daunted by the armed black men, James Harwood and his aide had been taken down to *Blue Deep's* berth where they were forced into the submarine along with a host of others. It would not have been difficult for the thugs to find *Blue Deep*. Like the layout and specifications of *The Melanie Rose*, such information pertaining to the luxury submarine was posted in any number of places throughout the yacht. Harwood figured they were taking the sub to escape anyone coming to rescue *The Melanie*. And aboard *Blue Deep* they would have an untold number of bargaining chips or shields in the form of human hostages.

As he searched for his wife, he saw in the crowd the yacht's captain, his first mate and navigator, other officers, and members of the yacht's staff, as well as its guests and a number of refugees rescued from the trawler. Captain Mick Shelton had been beaten and was bleeding in the face. Along with his navigator and first officer, he was moved at gunpoint forward toward the submarine's nose where the control station was located. Harwood was relieved to see Mellie with several of her friends and a few other guests in a huddle on *Blue Deep's* first deck. He also spotted Culpepper, Yord and Greaves. He did not see Senator Slotter or his wife but for the moment his concern was for Mellie.

Her masseur and Dr. Nantz were holding her up. She seemed lethargic and disoriented but conscious. Reaching her, he wrapped his arms around her and said, "Thank god you're okay. I was so worried."

She moaned something he couldn't hear over the noise. He noticed the accusing stares from crew and guests, as if he were to blame for their horrific predicament.

"Mel, I'm so sorry that this, that I—but I—"

"You people!" bawled a bull-throated voice from someone who'd joined the thugs watching the group. Harwood saw that it was the big black who'd knifed the security guard in the transom. He was carrying a submachine gun and wearing a baseball cap, a radio headset and a bloody sleeveless shirt. And sure enough he was holding one of *Blue Deep's* plastic-covered layouts. His English had a southern Afro-American accent. "I am Maxime Jalabert. I was born and raised in Little Miami! I joined the U. S. Army and served in Special Forces and was sent to Haiti to fight the insurgents trying to overthrow Jean-Bertrand Aristide. But I decided to leave all that bullshit and apply the skills I learned in Special Forces to become an entrepreneur!" He laughed. "I have made a guess from the way you are dressed, your jewelry, the way you act and so forth, that you are VIPs. We have confiscated all phones, iPads and any other thing you might use for communication. We are going down in this very cool submarine and out to the Northwest Providence Channel. There we will come up to communication depth and you will provide the information necessary for us to call the people with whom we will arrange your ransom. You saw your captain's face? That is the way any of you will look if you refuse to identify yourselves. One by one, do it now! You first!" He pointed at Joseph Yord who quickly and shakily complied.

And so it went, one by one. When it came J. J. Harwood's turn, he simply said, "I am the owner of the yacht and this submarine."

"Hah!" said Maxime Jalabert. "I thought so."

Harwood said, "The submarine cannot take so many people. It is designed to hold only twenty-four passengers and a crew of eight. Just thirty-two people in all!"

"Designed for *luxury* for that many," the thug snapped back. "It will hold more, much more. Isn't that right? Tell the truth or we will beat it out of you."

"The truth is we do not know how many it will hold. Thirty-two is the maximum for luxury accommodations, yes. Forty-eight is the maximum for excursions—"

"That means it will hold more! But never mind that. What is that ship to the west?"

For a moment, Harwood did not know what ship the bastard meant.

Culpepper blurted, "A salvage ship named *The Morgainne*. They're treasure hunters! We've seen them bringing up all kinds of things, gold, jewels—"

"Why would it have launched a boat that's coming toward the yacht?"

"I don't' know," said Culp.

"I think you're a lying sack of shit, Mr. Culpepper!" With the butt of his gun, Jalabert knocked Culp to his knees and turned to his gunmen. "Take all these *very important persons* up to the bridge! I'm going to the control center to kick things in the ass."

The two gunmen leveled their rifles at the Americans.

As they followed the one in the lead up the stairs, Harwood heard a series of horrible explosions deep in the yacht. They shook the submarine. His heart pounded and his gut convulsed. "What . . . what have you done?"

No one answered as they were herded at gunpoint up to the submarine's narrow bridge, a space only sixty feet long and eighteen wide and a quarter of that taken up by its control room. It had a few lounge chairs, a couple of small tables, where in normal times passengers or crew could enjoy looking out at the undersea world.

Harwood could feel his fine submarine lurch, which sickened him further. He realized *Blue Deep* was moving down its ramp to the sea.

⤙⬤⬤⬤⤚

With his head down and one hand holding an AR-15, Kyle Dawton kept his eyes on the upper decks of *The Melanie Rose*. They had no idea just what the hijackers possessed beyond small arms and RPGs. Chiz had to be thinking about all possibilities, like a good *warfighter.* But the hijackers firing small arms alone from the yacht's upper decks could drill *Sinbad* full of holes along with her buckaroo occupants.

The megayacht's bridge still smoked. Coming upon her midships, *Sinbad* pilot Rupert Minns began to circle the yacht by steering toward her bow. The others kept low in the open area behind the workboat's cockpit, like a bunch of Marines about to hit a beachhead. Only they weren't wearing helmets or jungle camouflage. They were more like frogmen, wearing wetsuits in case they had to don scuba gear and hit the water.

Why didn't one of his unsettling visions—or whatever they were—kick in, burn through the needed grip on "reality" and tell him what lay ahead? Maybe he didn't want to know.

With the workboat doing thirty to forty knots, it was around the yacht's bow in less than a minute and then, as planned, racing back toward the stern. *Sinbad* drew no fire. They saw no one on any of the decks. But halfway to the stern, they heard several explosions deep inside the yacht.

On Chizzick's order, Minns turned *Sinbad* farther out and away from *Melanie Rose,* and cut the engines. They listened but heard no more explosions. They heard no gunfire. The decks remained eerily empty. Then a low hydraulic whine carried across the water from the yacht's stern.

"Holy crapola," said Dan Clark who'd risen from his crouch just behind Dawton. "Look what's coming out of the stern."

Through binoculars they watched the sleek submarine move along a tracked ramp, bow foremost, out of its berth in the stern of the yacht's fourth deck. All those aboard *Sinbad* took it in. They had seen luxury submarines of various shapes and sizes but never one as big and sleek and stylish as this.

Except for Dawton and Cooper. "That's the sub Vic and I saw at the wellhead," said Kyle. *But not the one I've been seeing lying on the seafloor.*

"The goddamn hijackers are taking that thing down to escape the Coast Guard or anyone else coming after them," said Chizzick.

Like us, thought Dawton.

All eyes scoured the civilian sub's every exterior feature with the perplexing prospect of having to take it. Its detail was much more discernible than when he and Vic watched it at the wellhead. He saw that it was close to 150 feet long, with a bridge almost a third that length and below the bridge two decks, the uppermost of these arrayed with the large observation windows Kyle remembered. The bow of the observation deck held what looked like the forward control room for subsurface operation, some of the instrumentation visible through its mostly glass nose. And as the stern came into view before sliding into the water, they saw a dorsal hatch that maybe provided access to a diver-lockout chamber. The nine C-Team morgainners studied this latter item with keen and crucial interest.

Some people were entering the forward control room, three men in yacht-officer uniforms, one of them bloodied—and behind these, two men in green cammies holding guns on the first three.

The sub was soon totally in the water and dropping under the waves.

"Look at the yacht!" said Dan Clark.

Like the already sunken trawler, *The Melanie Rose* was sinking as well. The detonations heard minutes ago had to have been charges set to blow holes in her hull.

People were appearing on her previously empty decks, some wearing life-jackets, some trying to get at lifeboats and ring buoys. Some were obviously refugees, others members of the yacht's crew and staff left out of submarine *Blue Deep's* escape, likely many of them gladly so, even if they had to deal with abandoning a doomed ship.

Under a leaden sky still spitting rain, the bow of the magnificent megayacht had begun to slant below its waterline. Kyle raised *The Morgainne's* bridge on his handradio. He told Captain Nielsen what was taking place and to send lifeboats to rescue those left on the gravely wounded *Melanie Rose.*

CHAPTER 23

Give Us Joseph Yord

With *O-681* having dropped to a depth of 16 meters and moved to 600 meters south of *The Melanie Rose*, Captains Polivanov and Lepushin stood at her two periscopes, eyes worn and bleary yet still riveted by what they'd been watching.

Minutes ago, *O-681's* sonar had recorded the explosions deep in the luxury yacht. The noise had carried through the underwater medium like a rapid sequence of torpedo strikes. Soon afterward, sonar had also detected the sound of a sizeable craft being launched from the yacht's stern. Repositioning *O-681*, the two captains had watched through the periscopes the civilian submarine go into the sea. Then the single workboat that had come from the salvage ship *Morgainne* to the west had reached the *Rose* and circled it.

"Multiple small surface craft launching from the salvor, sir," said the senior sonar operator now. He called out the boats' bearing, heading, speed, and distance from *O-681*, and their acoustic signatures: single engine inflatable lifeboats about a kilometer northwest of *681's* position and heading east toward the sinking yacht.

The Morgainne itself was remaining where it had been since the Russians arrived in these waters. Not about to leave its treasure site, Lepushin supposed.

Constant sonar reads confirmed what the two Russian captains had absorbed visually. But now their sonar team was trying to separate the sound of the unidentified civilian sub—presently at a depth of ten meters, diving and turning east at a speed of ten knots—from the noises made by *The Morgainne's* lifeboats.

Lepushin stood back from the command scope, rubbed his neck and looked over at Polivanov. "The hijackers, pirates, whatever they are, have blown holes in the yacht and are taking that recreation submarine east for the Northeast Providence Channel—to escape detection. According to the message received from Colonel Baturin, they have the yacht's owner and others from the yacht aboard. And Pytor Telasnikov."

Polivanov said nothing.

Lepushin went to the captain's station and grabbed the mike and called the airlock. "Is the *SZ-44* ready?"

"Yes, Captain," came the reply from his second-in-command.

Lepushin moved back to the periscopes.

Polivanov whispered so no one else in the control room would hear: "Captain, is your intention to board that civilian submarine?"

"Not if I can avoid it. We will come up under it. You will follow us but stay at a safe distance. I will demand that Telasnikov—Joseph Yord—be put in the sub's airlock, with Colonel Baturin, of course. If the hijackers refuse to give him up, I will threaten to sink them. The civilian boat will no doubt exceed the speed of the *SZ-44*. If they try to outrun us, I will return to *0-681* and we will then pursue and overtake them and we will send them to hell. My orders are to take Telasnikov out if I cannot bring him back."

"And Colonel Baturin?"

Lepushin did not answer the obvious.

Polivanov said, "Captain, you are tired like the rest of us. You have not slept and have been under much stress."

"I am in efficient condition. As are my men." Lepushin picked up the intercom mike. "*Spetsnaz* team, this is your captain. Prepare to board the minisub."

Konstantin Polivanov stood there trying to think of something else to say, aware of his submariners in the control room staring at him. This time Polivanov spoke loudly enough for his men to hear. "Before you launch the *SZ-44*, there is something you must understand, Captain Lepushin. If for any reason *Opekun-681* is in danger of being found out or captured by the Americans, we will have to abort and steal away, no matter where you are or what is happening to you. We have been treading a razor's edge ever since you and your strange mission came aboard but one defector—and you and your *Spetsnaz* team—are not worth the loss of a Russian nuclear submarine and its crew. Is that understood?"

"If you desert me, Captain Polivanov, you will answer for it in Moscow." Lepushin turned away and moved for the aft hatchway and the lockout chamber, leaving the control room as quiet as a crypt.

Acting Officer of the Deck Kolotcha looked at the men sitting, standing, in shock. "Attend to your stations," he shouted at them. "We will get through this just fine!"

But his usually cheerful voice had an edge they'd not heard before.

⋄⊨⋑ ⊜⊨⋖

One of the two hijackers left to guard the people in *The Melanie's* bridge was in contact by radio with his commander. From the fragmentary one-sided remarks J. J. heard, some of them in English and some in Kryol, he deduced that "Colonel" Maxime Jalabert had ordered Captain Mick Shelton to take *Blue Deep* down to a depth of sixty meters and proceed at maximum submerged speed due east where lay an island a few miles off the southeast end of the Great Abaco chain. Shelton had argued that if they dived to that depth, they would not be able to ascend because of the weight of so many people aboard the submarine. Harwood had no idea just how many comprised that number but assumed his beloved luxury sub was packed throughout. Jalabert had finally agreed to maintaining a depth of twenty meters.

Holding his weeping and terrified wife close, number one hostage James Jessup Harwood tried to think of something he could do to stop what had already gone, he feared, past any possible point of deliverance. The two hijacker guards posted at each end of the room watched him keenly. One was near enough to knock him down if he were suspected of a wrong move.

He heard shooting below, at first desultory but increasing in intensity.

⋄⊨⋑ ⊜⊨⋖

Rupert Minns had positioned *Sinbad* above the spot where they'd last seen the pleasure submarine below the surface. As the workboat heaved in the swells, the divers pulled on scuba gear and peered through the wind and rain at the chop.

Dan Clark was applying camouflage grease paint to Kyle's face as Chizzick talked to *The Morgainne*. "*Morg's* having a problem pinpointing the sub because of the lifeboat noise." He handed the satphone to Minns and said, "We'll have to stay in contact by wire down there. If we don't find the sub right away, we'll have to rely on you to relay its position once *Morg's* found it again."

Darkening Dan's face as Dan had darkened his, Kyle wished Chizzick would refer to their ship by its full name. *"Morg"* did not sound auspicious.

"But remember, we're going down covertly," Chizzick said to Minns. "We'll have to communicate with muted Morse."

"Copy that," said Minns.

Dawton looked over the others again. All of them blackfaced now. Yes, they'd volunteered a long time ago for something like this. He could tell by their eyes which ones were itching for it and which ones weren't. He was definitely a member of the latter bunch. And it wasn't just a "fight" they were going into.

The Morgainne's eight lifeboats were moving past them now, slowing down as they neared the crippled yacht.

Chiz said to those in *Sinbad*: "Check each other over again. Once we find the sub, we'll have to keep back from being seen by the people inside. I'll guide us. Maybe they'll have the interior lights on and we'll be able to have a look at them but—maybe we can latch on to the top of the bridge in positions where they won't be able to see us through the windows. Or maybe we can make our way back to the diver lockout and see if we can open its hatch. If we can't do that, maybe we'll trash the propeller. That'll force them to blow ballast and return to the surface. That happens, we reconnoiter, maybe blow the upper windows open to make sure they can't take the sub down again. Maybe we can get into the airlock then. But we'll have to get a fix on what we're faced with before we act. Got it?"

The team chorused affirmation.

Whole lotta maybes, thought Dawton. A new apprehension had been eating at him since seeing *Blue Deep* go down. As he'd told Victoria, he hadn't thought they would have to dive but now had no idea how deep they might have to go.

What if he went into one of his altered states? He could endanger not only himself but whoever in the team might be relying on him at the moment.

Faces were soon all that were exposed, thanks to the hooded wetsuits. Soon faces were covered by diving helmets. Soon everything about them would be covered by the sea.

The rain had quit and the clouds were breaking up as sunlight broke through them and the morgainners dropped into the water. Bobbing with neutral buoyancy, they assembled in an inverted V formation with Chizzick at the point, Ricardo Rivera on his immediate right rear and Dawton on his left. Dan Clark and Ed Sanchez were in the formation's two tails with Brad Shinley between Dawton and Clark.

Chiz gave the signal to descend. Releasing air from their wing bladders in unison, they dropped. Equipped with closed-circuit rebreathers, they would produce no bubbles. A nylon line kept them grouped but separated at five-foot intervals.

Blue Deep was already down a good 70 feet but they quickly located its lights. Whoever was in charge of having seized the submarine perhaps was weighing the risk of being seen from above against the need to see what was going on below, both outside the sub and inside it.

The lights helped the divers find her but would also expose them once they drew near. If she descended to her maximum depth, they wouldn't be able to catch it at all. They'd have to give up the chase or croak from not only diving too fast but too deep.

But suddenly she stopped. They heard a great *whoosh* as her ballast tanks ejected water. Slowly she began to come back up—right toward them.

Chizzick motioned for the team to inflate their suits. They began to rise at a rate that kept them beyond the reach of *Blue Deep's* lights.

Back up at about sixty feet, the submarine leveled off and stayed there. Her exterior lights went out but her interior lights and the penetration of sunlight at this shallow depth revealed the submarine and the undersea environment well enough.

The C- team dropped to a point that was level with her bridge—outside the area lit by its interior lights yet close enough for the divers to see inside. To allow for more freedom of individual movement, Chizzick motioned to detach from the line holding them together.

Then the sub's interior lights went out.

⋅⇥⊙ ⊙⊨⋅⇤

From the radio chatter, J. J. Harwood knew a gunfight had broken out on the second deck of *Blue Deep*. The hijackers had quelled a revolt by both *The Melanie's* crew and some of the refugees. How any of the captives had gotten hold of guns, Harwood could not imagine.

Shortly after the revolt was quelled, Maxime Jalabert had ordered Captain Shelton to extinguish the outside lights. Soon after that, he'd ordered the interior lights out. The low-intensity blue lights along the bottoms of the bulkheads still burned and here in the bridge the control room forward glowed with its small instrument lights and computer screens.

Jalabert's big head appeared in the ladder well and rose as did the rest of him as he climbed the last few steps. In the low light, Harwood could see that his shirt was torn open and bloody and a wound in his left shoulder had a compress bandage over it. The dim floor lights cast his rough features in enraged brutality. With his submachine gun draping his chest like a malevolent talisman, he resembled some African warlord about to lay waste another village of helpless victims. He turned on a flashlight to rake the occupants in the room. Twenty or so, according to Harwood's estimate. All standing. Nauseated, bewildered and petrified.

"Ahh," he said, "is everyone comfortable? Would anyone like refreshments?" He laughed angrily, winced, and then looked at Harwood. He beamed his light at Mellie. "The two of you should bring at least a billion in ransom. Yes?" He turned the flashlight on the rest. "And who else among your little party here could be as important, as rich, or almost so, or more so?" He lowered the flashlight. "But we must get well away from where we sunk your kingly yacht. Then, when it is safe, we will surface so that we can communicate transfers into several bank accounts of the offshore kind." Jalabert laughed again. "But listen now. If I don't get complete cooperation, I will begin sending one of you out this submarine's escape hatch each time we suffer any sort of resistance or trickery. I rule the roost now! And I am what's to come, Mr.

J. J. Harwood. I am a pointman for the pathetic horde that's storming your gates and will have you for breakfast! Do I make myself clear?" He put his big hand under Mellie's chin, bent down and thrust his face close to hers. "Do I make myself clear?"

"You leave her alone!" shouted Harwood.

Jalabert hit him in the face.

Knocked down in a chair, blood jetted from Harwood's nose and upper lip. Jalabert laughed again. "You talk to me, you white fuck, you say 'sir' and 'please' and 'mercy' and 'please, may I lick your ass' and such like."

But the bastard straightened up with a grunt of pain—so close, Harwood could see the strain, the fear, in his eyes; and realized at that moment that Maxime Jalabert had taken himself much farther than he'd ever intended to go with his captive refugees.

⋄▸▮◉ ◉▮◂⋄

Watching through the windows of *Blue Deep's* bridge at a distance of thirty yards, the *Morgainne* divers had seen a tall man with gray hair knocked to the deck by an armed but wounded gorilla waving a flashlight. Though they couldn't hear what he said, they'd watched him talk and could tell by his body language he was obviously the leader of the gang that had taken over *The Melanie Rose* and now its submarine.

Wayne Chizzick signaled for the team to drop another twenty feet so that they could see through the big forward observation ports along the starboard side of the two lower decks. They saw bluish but shadowy forms crammed together like cattle in a livestock truck. A few had flashlights and were waving them about. These men were armed and watching the rest. Kyle saw a few whites among the dark-skinned refugees, several of the former in yacht uniform, huddled near one of the ports.

But his attention quickly shifted when he sensed something else coming up from a lower depth to the south. At first, he saw only a dark fish-like shape. But the nearer it drew to *Blue Deep* the more distinct it became. *Another freaking submarine!* But this one was much smaller than *Blue Deep*. About sixty or sixty-five feet in length, Kyle judged. About eight in diameter. Unmarked and totally black, with a hatch at its top and a small port on each side of its bow. But if ports, they were either lidded or the interior of the craft was completely dark. Below the ports were twin bulges that might house extendable arms of the kind used to dig or claw or pull. Altogether, it looked like a military minisub.

He signaled to the others but they too had heard and seen it.

So where was its host, its mothership? *That long ship at rest on the seabed?*

Somewhere down there in the gloom?

Chizzick signaled for the team to move over to the other side of *Blue Deep* and up above it so that they could keep the minisub in sight.

As they ascended some thirty feet, the minisub closed the distance and came to a stop bow-on and a mere ten feet from *Blue Deep's* starboard side, at an observation window midships.

Some of the people inside *Blue Deep* were pointing and gaping at it.

A loud voice broke through the water and over the noises made by the two crafts' thrusters and engines: "ATTENTION, YOU IN THE SUBMARINE *BLUE DEEP!*"

The voice came from an exterior loudspeaker embedded in the minisub's nose. The strength and clarity of the speaker indicated state-of-the-art underwater communication. The voice had an accent—European, maybe Slavic—but the English was clear.

"YOU HAVE ABOARD YOUR BOAT ONE JOSEPH P. YORD. WE HAVE NO INTENTION OF HARMING ANYONE IF YOU PUT MR. YORD IN YOUR SCUBA CHAMBER FOR HIS EXTRACTION. OTHERWISE, WE WLL SMASH ONE OF YOUR LARGE WINDOWS AND YOU WILL SINK TO YOUR DEATHS!"

CHAPTER 24

The Entry

IN *BLUE DEEP'S* bridge, Culpepper, Yord and Greaves lunged toward the port windows. J. J. Harwood sprang from the chair he'd been knocked into and did the same.

The hijacker guard nearest them watched and nervously fingered his weapon.

They saw a black minisub lying out there, bow-on to a window on the deck immediately below.

"No!" yipped a distraught Culpepper.

Standing near him, the usually stoic face of Joseph Yord was pale and stricken. The scientist staggered backward and fell into a chair.

Harwood could not believe what he'd heard broadcast. He could not believe anything that had happened since he'd ordered those in the sinking trawler rescued. *What the hell was coming next?* "What's *this* about, Joseph?" he asked Yord.

The scientist did not answer.

"Joe?" said Culpepper, who apparently did not know what to make of it either.

Maxime Jalabert bowled his way to Yord. "What's this about?" he roared. "Who is that out there? Why do they want you?"

"I don't know," Yord said weakly, unconvincingly. "That is the answer to all of your questions."

"You'll give me better answers, the right answers, or I'll start making you wish you had!" Jalabert looked at Culpepper and grabbed him by the throat. "Starting with *you*!"

Culpepper gagged and coughed and began to yammer, trying to think as fast as he could: "Doctor Yord is a scientist, an employee who works for me, us, JJ

Oil—he made a mistake and created—he created a situation that undermines—threatens a wellhead near here that could—it will explode if he does not fix—correct the situation—if that happens the well will blow and oil will fill this ocean and the oil will get into the inner workings of this submarine and you—we'll all go down! He has to—we have to keep him so he can—"

"Shut up," said Jalabert. His eyes were darting from Yord to Culpepper and back to Yord again. Apparently he did not know whether to believe what Culpepper had just said or not but finally, rather quickly, he seemed to believe it. "He should bring a good price then."

The voice from the minisub said, "THE DROPOFF TO THE ABYSS IS NEARBY WHERE THE OCEAN'S DEPTH IS OVER ONE THOUSAND METERS. WE WILL RAM YOU, SHOVE YOU, BREAK YOUR WINDOWS AND YOU WILL GO DOWN LIKE A ROCK. YOU HAVE TEN SECONDS TO RESPOND TO MY DEMAND!"

Maxime Jalabert deliberated only a second more. He looked out, looked down at the black minisub out there and said, "Does this submarine have outside speakers like that guy does?"

No one said anything.

Jalabert grabbed Culpepper by the shirtfront and repeated the question in a louder voice.

The quaking Culpepper stammered a *"Yes."*

"Where?"

"There!" Culpepper pointed toward the cockpit.

The hijacker grabbed him and pulled him forward. "Show me!"

Culpepper pointed. Jalabert pulled the outside speaker mike from its hook and pushed its transmit button. "Hey, ASSHOLE!" he said, "you with the funny accent in the little black subby wubby. Who the fuck are you?"

"WE ARE MEMBERS OF A GLOBAL ORGANIZATION COMMITTED TO RIGHTING WRONGS DONE TO THE SEA."

"Hah!" laughed Jalabert without mirth. "Why you want Joseph Yord?"

"THAT IS NONE OF YOUR BUSINESS."

"What will you pay for him?"

"I WILL NOT BARGAIN OR HAGGLE WITH YOU IN ANY WAY. YOU WILL BRING YOUR BOAT UP TO A DEPTH OF TEN METERS. YOU WILL PUT MR. YORD IN A SCUBA SUIT AND PUT HIM IN YOUR DIVING AIRLOCK ALONE AND OPEN THE LOCKOUT HATCH SO THAT HE CAN LEAVE YOUR BOAT AND ENTER OURS. YOU WILL LEAVE NO ONE IN THE AIRLOCK BUT MR. YORD. YOU WILL TRY NO TRICKS. YOU WILL DO THIS IMMEDIATELY OR DIE!"

"Hey, get this! I just learned this Mr. Joseph Yord has to fix a wellhead before it blows up or we'll *all* go under. You got that?"

Silence from the minisub. Then: "NO MORE TALK. LET US HAVE HIM AND WE WILL LET YOU GO. OTHERWISE, DIE."

They heard the minisub's propeller sputter to life. The ominous craft emptied some of its ballast and started to rise straight for the window where Jalabert stood. "Okay!" he barked into the microphone. "Okay! All right! You can have the sonofabitch! BACK OFF!"

The minisub slowed and stopped.

Overcome by frustration and fear for them all, J. J. Harwood reached to attack Jalabert. He was flattened by a blow to the head with the near guard's rifle. The guard proceeded to beat him senseless with the butt of the gun. Mellie threw herself over J. J. at risk of her own life.

Jalabert told the guard to desist and backhanded Mellie to the deck. Turning to the mike in the bulkhead, Jalabert said, "Hey! We are bringing Joseph Yord to the airlock."

"You can't do this!" yelled Culpepper as the beaten and bloody Harwood, hardly knowing what he was doing, tried to shield and comfort Mellie.

Culpepper made a gasping noise. "I have an idea! Whoever they are—maybe they don't know what Joseph looks like. Even if they do—in a scuba suit, in the flooded dive chamber, they wouldn't know the difference—like they won't know it's him or not till they have whoever we—we could put a substitute in the dive chamber is what I'm saying. They won't know who it is till he's on their boat and by then, we could be off and—*Blue Deep* has to be faster than that smaller sub—we could get away!"

"They wouldn't know the difference if I put *you* in a scuba suit in the flooded airlock!" said Jalabert.

Culpepper blanched and was silent.

"Who are you anyway?"

"I am a division chief for JJ Oil," Culp answered in a weak voice.

"Okay. You must be worth a few million. Huh? Guess we'll keep you."

Jalabert looked at Yord again and then cast his protuberant eyes over the other whites in the room. He looked at the guard forward near the control niche. "Get a white from below, an ordinary crewman the same size as Dr. Yord here. Get him in a scuba suit and put his ass in the dive chamber and do it quick."

The man started down the ladderway.

Jalabert said into the speaker: "Hey, fuckwad, we're giving you Joseph Yord!"

J. J. Harwood pulled a sobbing Mellie closer. It had been a very long time since he'd held her so close. Overwhelmed by the fact she'd thrown herself over him to save him, he was on the verge of tears. They had shown each other so little love or even compassion for such a long time . . . and now as he felt her heart beating against his, it was hard to tell which of these tempos of a tenuous mortality beat faster.

⊷═◑ ◑═⊷

The *Morgainne* dive team was back at *Blue Deep's* windowless stern, keeping out of sight of those in the black minisub and trying to make sense of the exchange heard over the hydrophones between it and the civilian sub. They now had a confirmation of sorts to speculations about the sinking seabed. But a confirmation that hatched a hive of new questions. This was no time to ponder them, however, and in Kyle Dawton's case, no time to slip into the haunts.

While the mysterious minisub withdrew from the middle of *Blue Deep* to turn aft, the C Team quickly located the pleasure sub's escape trunk. The diver lockin/lockout-chamber would be inside immediately beneath the hatch. It would take some minutes for the guy named Joseph Yord to suit up and enter the airlock, then for the lock to be flooded to equalize the pressure in the chamber with that outside. In the interim, at risk of being seen by the approaching mini-sub and on Chizzick's order, Dawton and Clark worked hurriedly to see if they could open the hatch while Chiz clicked Morse, inaudible outside his headset, over his underwater phone. He told Minns on *Sinbad* about the minisub and its demand for Yord.

Minns sent one short beep, one longer, and a short one again—R for roger.

The effort to open the hatch from outside proved futile without the proper tool. Only when Yord was readied to leave *Blue Deep* would the chamber's inside locking mechanism be released. Chizzick waved an arm to get everyone's attention. He pointed upward and gave the sign to ascend ten feet on *Blue Deep's* port side in hopes of remaining out of sight of the minisub as it neared the stern opposite.

⋅→⊨◉ ◉⊨←⋅

Konstantin Polivanov and Isaak Kolotcha stood at *O-681's* command station, their slick faces gleaming haggard and pallid in the control room's low light. The room was deathly quiet but Polivanov could clearly hear the blood pulsing through heart and vein, his breath coursing in and out. He thought he could even hear new beads of sweat popping like miniscule eruptions out of his skin.

The vocalizations between Lepushin and whoever was acting as spokesman on the civilian submarine had been recorded on *O-681's* passive sonar and processed into understandable voice.

Kolotcha said in a hushed tone, "So this Joseph Yord is Pyotr Telasnikov, the expert in environmental-modification weaponry? Working for an oil company?"

Kolotcha was obviously having a hard time believing any of it.

Polivanov could not say exactly what he believed of this bizarre *putanitsa*. But his mind was made up: he would stick to his warning to Lepushin.

⋅→⊨◉ ◉⊨←⋅

J. J. Harwood sat with his head in his hands beside his wife, his blood-soaked handkerchief on a knee. He heard Maxime Jalabert talking into his throat-mike.

Apparently Jalabert's men had found one of *The Melanie Rose's* prep chefs, to be clad in a scuba suit and put in the dive chamber as a surrogate for Joseph Yord. The real Yord was still here on the bridge, looking very close to meltdown.

"Does the lockout chamber have a window and inside lights?" Jalabert was saying into his mike. "Can you see inside it?"

Harwood could not hear the answer but knew the chamber did.

"After putting the guy in the chamber, flood it and open the escape hatch. "Let those fuckheads from the minisub get into the chamber to snatch their bait, then shut the hatch on them and lock it. I'm on my way there."

⋅→▰ ▰←⋅

Half as long as *Blue Deep*, the black minisub now lay off the larger craft's tail at the same level as the latter's airlock hatch. While the minisub's stabilizing system emitted a low hum, it remained dark. But occasional illumination from inside *Blue Deep* exposed it in sporadic and shadowy detail.

Neutrally buoyant twelve feet above, the nine Americans hovered quietly. They were visible in the daylight coming from the surface at their shallow depth but the sun had gone behind cloud again. In any case, the men in the minisub would have to exit their craft and look upward to discover them there.

For Kyle Dawton, this hanging in silent suspension would ordinarily have risked a drop into that stream wherein he might get lost amid the cave-like maze of phantasms. But the greater external danger eclipsed any such slide.

He heard a metallic groan come from under the minisub's belly. The sound of its ventral hatch opening maybe. This guess was quickly confirmed by the sudden appearance of a diver moving out from under the craft. Then another. Commando-garbed.

Chiz signaled for the team to descend again, to use *Blue Deep's* port side for concealment. He designated two to move back behind the minisub to take out its propeller.

A third frogman came out of the minisub's underside. Then a fourth. And any lingering doubt that these *righters of wrongs done to the sea* meant lethal business was negated by the fact that all four wielded assault rifles with long magazines—underwater weapons maybe as good as or better than the ASM-DT rifles and the chunky HK P11 pistols the morgainners now carried. The five-cylinder HKs had only a range of about thirty feet and the ASM-DTs no more than a hundred.

They watched the foremost of the unknown quartet reach *Blue Deep's* escape hatch. The guy began banging on the hatch with his rifle butt and yelling through an underwater phone in his helmet. The morgainners were too far away to hear his words clearly but they could guess what he was saying.

One of his buddies behind him who was scanning the surrounding water with a strong handlight turned it in the direction of the *Morgainne* divers. The beam struck them.

Spotted!

At the top of the lockout, the three frogmen raised their weapons.

The C Team divers were already spreading and their guns too were readied.

The hatch over the lockout chamber began to open.

When it came to a battle, former SEAL Chizzick believed in giving before he got and was the first to fire. At the same time the rest with him began shooting, the two morgainners at the minisub's stern fired bolts into its propeller assembly.

Caught by surprise and no doubt thinking they were in a crossfire, the frogs began to fire at those above and at those to the rear of their sub.

The spray of steel bolts from overhead deterred the man at the hatch from entering the dive chamber. Hit, he writhed backward with a ribbon of blood curling out his chest. Another grappled with the airhose that had been shot loose from his tank as the tank spewed gas with a force that spun him off *Blue Deep*.

The minisub's damaged propeller screeched to life as, stabilizing thrusters now off, the craft began to pull away from *Blue Deep* even as the frogs scrambled to get under its belly and back inside.

With adrenalin ripping through his blood, Dawton had turned on his handlight as he fired at the minisub's bow ports. The ports were so small most of his bolts missed their targets but at lease one struck glass. Seawater spewed into the pilot's station. Dawton could see sparks flying in the cockpit as the minisub turned and wobbled off toward the southwest with one last frogman still hanging from outside its ventral hatch. Then it veered more directly south as if the effort to ruin its propeller had also damaged its rudder and the pilot was having difficulty steering it. Bolts that had penetrated the port glass could have also hit the cockpit's control panel, its wiring, anything.

But who the hell were they? Whoever they were, they were military. And that minisub belonged to a much bigger submarine. It had to be lurking not far away. Another fear swept over him: what if those in the minisub learned the location of the canyon wreck and out of vengeance kill the divers at the site, destroy the wreck, attack *The Morgainne*?

Chizzick was reassembling the team over *Blue Deep's* now opened escape hatch that went down into her dive chamber. Kyle pushed these new fears aside so he could replace them with the more immediate one back in his face.

⋅→▣⊚ ⊚▤◄⋅

J. J. Harwood heard muffled gunfire back at the submarine's stern. His chair was near the forward guard outside the bridge's small control room. The guard had no earbuds or throat-mike but was using a handradio instead. Harwood could hear what was being said by Jalabert. The thug was halfway to the engine room and dive chamber when he'd heard the gunfire. He was asking a man named Baptiste, whom Harwood knew by now was inside the engine room, "What's going on?"

"I don't know, Colonel," came Baptiste's reply. "A fight outside, up above—right outside the dive chamber."

"Who—"

"I don't *know*, Colonel! We can't see out there from here in the engine room."

"Is that prep chef still in there, with the chamber flooded?"

"*Wi.*"

"Could somebody have come into the chamber?"

"Nossir. I'm looking in the chamber window. Nobody in there but the prep chef in his scuba suit."

"Did you find the control panel back there?"

"*Wi.*"

"It should have switches for the lights. Find the one for the exterior lights and turn them on."

The firing had ceased but Harwood could hear something screeching and banging like out-of-whack metal hitting metal. The noise soon receded.

⟶⊨⊙ ⊙⊨⟵

Anton Lepushin lay on the wet floor outside *SZ-44's* airlock. Midshipman Dmitri Ghukov, the chief medic in the *Spetsnaz* team, frantically tried to examine his commander's wound. The 5.66mm steel dart had cut through Lepushin's upper thigh but exited.

Water was pouring in through a damaged port forward.

"I think the bastard was firing an ASM-DT, sir!" said Ghukov.

Wounded by a Russian amphibious assault rifle! The bitter irony wasn't lost on Lepushin; but he had neither time nor inclination even to curse it.

Three of his men were trying to stanch the port leak while pilot and copilot tried to get the minisub under control. It seemed to be veering this way and that. Lepushin was about to call for a casualty report when the pilot yelled:

"We are taking on too much water, sir!"

Groaning and gritting his teeth against the pain, Lepushin had Ghukov help him up to walk the few splashy steps forward to the bow. Reaching the cockpit, he bent down. The cracked port was partly plugged with improvised material and strong water-resistant tape. It was still leaking, however. He looked at the drenched control console. "Get us turned! Get us back to the *Shchuka!*"

"I'm trying, sir!" said the pilot, "but the propeller is damaged."

Shchuka O-681 lay 600 meters to the south. Assuming Polivanov had not moved her.

⟶⊨⊙ ⊙⊨⟵

"*Chërt voz'mí!*" muttered *Kapitan* Polivanov as he stood before his sonar screens with headphones clamped to his ears. The sonar chief relayed the *SZ-44's* weaving course. The midget sub was veering away from the bearing that would take it to *O-681*.

Polivanov had heard the gunfire, saw it on the sonar reads. Something had gone terribly wrong and the *SZ-44* had had to turn tail. Apparently it had somehow been crippled in the firefight. That was the only explanation for its zigzagging and lurching path wayward toward the Joulter Cays.

Into waters too shallow for *O-681* to go to retrieve it.

Isaak Kolotcha was standing nearby. "We will have to send a rescue team in a couple of inflatables. Yes?"

"We will move west as far as we can," said Polivanov as he removed the phones and swiped a tired hand over his face. "We will wait until nightfall. But unless we reestablish radio contact or they are able to send us some sort of signal, it will be impossible to find them."

⊷▬◉ ◉▬⊶

When *Blue Deep's* exterior lights came on, Dawton and Chizzick were exposed but clinging close over the opened lockout chamber. The rest of the team hovered near in a ring around the two partners, their weapons at the ready. Here at *Blue Deep's* stern, they could not be seen by anyone looking out her side windows forward of the engine room. The engine room itself had no windows.

Not one of the morgainners had incurred a wound from the minisub's frogmen but the hijackers remained inside *Blue Deep* and Dawton was sure the fun had only begun.

The dive chamber was spherical, about six feet in diameter, and filled with seawater. Lights were on inside it. They could see one violently shaking man in scuba gear discharging a cloud of bubbles and clinging to the chamber's rail; looking up at the divers with eyes that seemed to be leaping out of his diving mask.

The chamber was not big enough to accommodate more than four men at a time in scuba gear. With the terrified guy who was already in there, that meant for the moment only three of the C Team could enter. Then the chamber would have to be emptied of water and filled with air so that they could enter the engine room. Likely into an ambush.

Pointing to himself, Dawton and Clark, Chizzick indicated who was to go in the first group. He spoke softly through his throat mike to tell Rivera, Palmer and Kotalik to move forward to the bridge and check the situation there. "After having a look at what's going on in there, if you think it useful to make yourselves known to those inside, do so. Ed, Brad and Skip—come in after the lock's flooded again and the hatch reopens. With the chamber as small as it is, the filling-and-emptying cycle should be short."

Through the hatch, Chizzick dropped feet first, legs tucked closely together to keep his footfins from hitting the rim of the hatchway.

About to enter, Dawton threw a last look back at where he'd seen the black minisub floundering off on its crazy course. He saw nothing in that direction but dark ocean. But as he looked, he felt again the pull toward that inner sea in which he might flounder, where he did not want to go, could not dare go at this crucial moment.

CHAPTER 25

Trapped

HAVING ENTERED THE diver-lockout chamber and closed the escape hatch behind Chizzick and Clark, Dawton dropped with them to the chamber bottom where the lone man in scuba gear clung to the rail. As Chizzick and Clark gave him a brief once over, Dawton quickly studied the interior control panel to determine how to flush the seawater out and replace it with air. He'd been in similar chambers before and the control buttons weren't hard to figure out. He punched the required sequence.

A small window next to the panel looked out on the semi-lit engine room. For the moment, he could see no one out there. Clark found the inside light switch and turned the chamber's light off. A little of the engine room's low light came in through the chamber window.

As the spherical lockout emptied the last of the water and began filling with air, the three morgainners removed their masks and motioned for the guy at the rail to do the same. When he did, he began instantly to speak shakily. "Who are you?" he said.

Chizzick answered, "We are from the salvage ship *Morgainne*."

"Oh yes, the treasure hunters. The ship to the west, the—"

Chizzick put a finger to his lips and whispered, "Tone it down and slow down. What's your name?"

"Terry Atkins. I'm a prep cook on the *Melanie Rose*," and thus followed a rushed narrative as to how he'd ended up in the dive chamber. "I don't even know how to use this stuff," he said plaintively, fumbling with his mask and hoses as if they were the appendages of some creature sucking at his veins. "I am claustrophobic too. I was going crazy in here—"

"What's the situation on *Blue Deep*?"

Atkins didn't know much. He did know the location of the *Melanie's* crew on the first deck forward. But he had no idea how many "pirates" had overrun the yacht and now taken over its submarine.

"Hello," murmured Dan Clark. He was looking at a face looking in at them from the engine room.

·→═◉ ◉═←·

In *Blue Deep's* bridge, J. J. Harwood heard the forward guard's radio hiss and crackle. The voice of Maxime Jalabert, broken up with grunts and heavy breathing, was saying to his men scattered throughout the sub:

"Listen up! Baptiste just reported that scuba divers have come into the dive chamber from outside! They have to be some of those we heard shooting outside. They turned off the light inside the chamber but Baptiste thinks there are three!" Then Jalabert addressed the man in the engine room directly. "What the hell, Baptiste? Where were you? What were you doing? It takes time for an airlock to empty and fill—"

"I was . . . I had to take a leak, Colonel. I'm worn out—"

"You had a man with you. Where is he?"

"He went back into the main part of the sub for some additional ammo—"

"We have unknown divers in the dive chamber while both of you deserted your post? Next time piss in your pants! You listen to me, you idiot . . . you plant your ass at that chamber and keep it there. Why didn't you override their flushing the lockout?"

"I couldn't figure out how to do that from outside the chamber. I—"

"Can you figure out how to flood it again?"

"I don't know . . . I don't think so."

"Can you lock them in?"

"I don't know. I'm looking at the control panel out here but there's so much shit—"

"I'm coming! You get ready to ambush whoever might come out of that chamber. Use your knife. We don't want anything in that engine room damaged. You understand, Baptiste?"

"Yeah, Colonel."

"I'm coming with a couple of men. You get ready!"

The guard near Harwood cut in. "Colonel, Seguin here. In the bridge. There are scuba divers right here, right outside the bridge! I can see them!"

James Harwood looked up. He saw three divers outside. Two at the port glass and one at the starboard. They had swum in close, plainly wanting to see what was going on inside and plainly wanting to be seen by the guards as well as the hostages.

As most of the latter cried out with hope, pointing, yelling as if the divers might hear them, the thug at the rear of the room aimed his rifle at the two divers on the port side.

"Don't be a fool!" shouted the guard called Seguin. "One shot will break the glass and we'll be flooded!"

"How many divers at the bridge?" Jalabert rasped through the radio.

"Three," answered Seguin.

Jalabert swore. "How can divers keep up with—but we don't seem to be moving. Pajaud?"

"Yessir, still in the nose, in the control room."

"Are we moving?"

"Not much. Submarine cap'n says the submarine is too overloaded."

Jalabert said, "Baptiste?"

"Yessir?"

"I'm sending Robion to help you back there. I have to go to the control room and find out what's going on. You figure out how to keep those divers in the lockout chamber or how to kill them without hurting anything in that chamber or in the engine room! You understand?"

"Yessir."

The guard closest to where Harwood sat had his eyes on the glass bridge dome. The three divers who'd hovered outside had disappeared. Harwood knew how to shoot a gun, had hunted big game in the American West, in Africa, India . . . and for a wild split-second he thought of wrenching the guard's rifle from his grasp. But right after that thought came fear he would fail. In his fear and hopelessness, he turned to Culpepper who was sitting with Yord. But Culpepper looked sicker than ever. Harwood looked at Yord as if the scientist might know something to do. But he looked as bad as Culpepper. Harwood directed his question at Yord. "That guy in the minisub—who was he?"

"I don't know," answered the scientist—too quickly.

Yord's assistant, Don Greaves, sat as if he longed to be catapulted from his chair into another world.

Harwood pressed Yord. "But he knew you, knew *of* you at least. He knew about—he knew something about what you do. He said—"

"I know what he said. I don't know what he knows or thinks he knows."

A bald-faced lie, thought Harwood. Overcome by a burst of rage, he sprang with his hands reaching for Yord's throat.

⊷⊷⊚ ⊚⊷⊷

Kyle Dawton could see through the dive-chamber's window the low-lit but gleaming assemblage of turbo-diesels, generators, gear housing, coolant and oil lines, gauges, circuit boxes—and one sweating gunman at the outside control board, talking into his throat-mike, pecking at keys, glancing fearfully at the chamber window.

Chizzick pulled a gas grenade from his side pouch. "Put your masks back on and turn on your tanks," he said.

Dawton helped Atkins get ready, though the cook plainly did not know what they were about to do.

Clark hit the button sequence that would empty the chamber of air and reflood it with water.

Chizzick pulled the pin from his gas bomb. "Now," he said with a nod.

Clark opened the hatch to the engine room just wide enough for Chizzick to toss out the grenade.

⊷⊷⊚ ⊚⊷⊷

Once again, Jim Harwood sat beaten into submission in the chair closest to the cockpit with Melanie covering him as if he might try to move again. He listened numbly to the radio chatter over the guard Seguin's radio. Another revolt had broken out below decks. The submarine's emergency alarm began to howl. Harwood could hardly hear over the noise it made but caught something about one of the Haitians having shot at "a fugee" and caused bullets to hit a window.

Harwood heard the angry voice of Jalabert but could not make out what was said. Then the voice of First Officer Cal McInnis came over the submarine's PA system. "Attention, attention! We have water coming into the lounge on the second deck! Engineers are on their way there. Make a path for them!"

⊶▄◑ ◑▄⊷

The engine room was fogged with tear gas spewed from the thrown canister. Now out of the refilling dive chamber but wearing their diving masks for protection against the gas, the first three in the C-team could hear the alarm circuit going off. With weapons up, they cautiously made their way toward the only two hijackers they could see in the room. The gunmen were coughing and choking and groping blind for their guns. But as Chizzick and Clark sprang with swift gunbutt blows to their heads, they were quickly down and out.

The divers took the hijackers' automatic weapons with long magazines, their spare ammo and headsets. "Put your underwater guns here near the lockout, out of sight but easy to get to," Chiz shouted over the pulsing alarm.

In the blurry ambience Dawton felt as if he were about to plunge down that preternatural path that could lead anywhere. Out of the lingering mist something only partly formed seemed to appear, vaguely demonic. A laughing head with dim yet fierce red eyes glaring at him. He wrenched himself free of the vision by helping Dan Clark drag the hijackers to the starboard bulkhead where they secured their limbs with duct tape to some steel pipes.

The sound of seawater rushing into the dive chamber ceased. The display on the chamber's outside panel indicated it was fully reflooded. Chizzick punched the button that would open the upper escape hatch for the three divers remaining outside to enter.

The three inside the engine room kept their masks and tanks on, hoping the sub's filtration system would have the air clean enough to breathe comfortably by the time the outside three entered the chamber and it was flushed and refilled with air.

The main circuit alarm suddenly stopped. Dawton pressed his confiscated set of earbuds to his ears and listened to Haitian voices yakking back and forth about some of the refugees and crewmembers of *The Melanie Rose* having tried to overcome their captors. One of the big observation ports had been hit by bullets. Water was coming in. Crewmembers were trying to plug the leak and pump water from the second deck down to a ballast tank.

Sanchez, Roberts and Shinley stepped out of the air-filled dive chamber into the engine room.

The six morgainners began removing their masks and tanks. The submarine's air-filter system had "scrubbed" most of the tear gas. What remained burned their eyes and nostrils but not enough to debilitate. Intending to move forward into the passageway to the main part of the sub, they were all putting their diving gear to each side of the dive-chamber's door so they could recover the stuff in case they had to retreat back into the chamber when a noise forward made them turn, weapons raised.

The hatch between the engine room and the main part of the sub had swung all the way open. In the ill-lit opening stood a hijacker with an assault rifle.

As the *Morgainne* six jumped for cover, he opened up. Bullets struck metal and rubber and plastic and as Dawton landed behind the portside engine, he thought he heard the rending of flesh and bone. From his concealment, he fired. Someone to the left of him also let go a burst.

The gunman fell backward in the passageway and did not move.

Dawton felt the faint but lingering traces of teargas in the air cling to the sweat on his face, the mucous in his nostrils. He could hear the noises forward in the submarine: people crying out, howling with pain, angry voices giving orders; the splashing of feet in ankle-deep water. He could hear the breathing of the others in the engine room. Though the overhead lights in the room were off, small foot-level lights and the lights on instrument panels remained lit. He could see things, the machinery and the equipment, the overhead, his fellow divers, the two Haitian gunmen taped to the pipes; all of it with an unusual clarity. Not one of his visions. Juiced instead with the same elixir that ran in Chizzick, in Clark and Rivera and Sanchez, he guessed. He'd felt this juice before when Leyley and her boys tried to seize *Sinbad*, and months before that, when pirates tried to take the *Salvador* off Florida.

Dan Clark moved to a better firing position forward of the engines and closer to the hatchway on its port side. On the starboard side, Brad Shinley did the same.

They waited tensely, crouched behind machinery and watching the forward hatchway which was partly closed, watching for any sign of regaining consciousness in the two Haitians trussed to the pipes. One was moaning and moving a little but not much.

Dawton heard the drip of a punctured fuel or oil line. Maybe more than one. And he heard some ragged breathing across the aisle between the machinery and peered around the portside engine. "Who's hit?"

Sanchez answered from the starboard side. "Wayne."

Another hijacker appeared in the hatchway, holding a female refugee as a shield. But the man was so big his head towered unprotected over the woman. "Who are you in there?" he bawled. "What the fuck do you want? Identify yourself!"

He got no answer. But Dawton recognized the voice of the one who'd addressed the minisub.

"Throw down your weapons and surrender! Do what I tell you or this woman and more like her will die! Including the owner of this submarine and the big yacht!"

Dan Clark pulled a dummy grenade from a side pouch, pulled its pin and tossed it to the foot of the hatchway.

The man leapt back, falling backward over the hatchway threshold with the woman on top of him, his submachine gun firing blindly into the engine room as he scrambled back up and withdrew.

"Everybody watch that hatchway," Dawton said, as if they weren't doing that already. He crawled over to the starboard side and pulled his firstaid kit from his belt. The deck was greasy with blood and diesel fuel leaking from a nearby fuel line.

Chizzick half lay, half sat behind the engine there, bleeding in his right leg.

"Not good," said Sanchez, who was looking it over. "Hit in the right knee, calf and foot. Won't be able to swim."

"I'll swim if I have to," Chizzick muttered through teeth grinding in pain. And the pain forced him down.

Kyle put his flashlight on the leg. Sanchez was right. The knee looked shattered.

Sanchez was wounded too, bleeding on the side of his jaw. "Just a nick," he said when Kyle put his flashlight on it.

With frequent glances at the forward hatchway, the two began dressing Chizzick's wounds.

The moaning Haitian taped to the pipes was becoming conscious. Skip Roberts, who was nearest him, muttered something about "you sonsofbitches fucking up our treasure hunt" and hit him over the head with his rifle, putting him out again.

Their dilemma didn't seem to be much better than that of the sonsofbitches. They were in effect trapped in a stalemate. They could still escape back out through the lockout chamber but that would leave the sonsofbitches in possession of the submarine. Meanwhile, the only way the sonsofbitches could get at them was through that one forward hatchway.

They could don their masks and tanks again and throw a gas grenade into the passageway but then what? Go charging into that four-foot-wide space with guns blazing at anything that moved?

Chizzick cursed his bad luck.

Dawton batted his eyelids over stinging eyes and stifled the need to cough. "No whining," he said as he finished wrapping the knee. "We love this shit, don't we? Bite the bullet." Amazed that he could muster any humor at a time like this, even of the gallows kind, he said, "I'm going to see if I can't find a way to get us in a bigger mess."

He moved at a crouch forward amid the transmission boxes, fuel and water pipes, electrical conduits, gauges, looking for something—as if indurate machinery might offer a clue as to their next best move.

Tiny lights aglow on the room's master control board against the starboard bulkhead led him to it. Nestled as it was behind larger and tougher equipment, it had escaped damage.

He saw on the panel readouts nothing that indicated the sub was moving. It in fact felt motionless and he realized the engines here in the engine room were not engaged. Moving or not, the boat's electrical power was the source of everything from oxygen to illumination. "Shit," he whispered, seeing what he wished was not true.

From a few feet forward, Brad Shinley said, "What?"

Staring at the control board, Dawton answered the question loud enough for all to hear. "Like we heard over the PA . . . boat's leaking in the second deck lounge. Losing oxygen and pressure too, as well as taking in water."

This news was greeted with a heavy silence but for Chiz's irregular breathing.

Dawton scrutinized the board once again, looking for a switch, a button that would tell him he might be able to raise the sub from back here. He found a row of switches labeled BALLAST TANKS. But his hope that the submarine could rise by blowing its ballast hit bottom when he saw that every tank had already been emptied.

CHAPTER 26

Sinking

"OUR DEPTH IS sixty-nine feet and dropping," Kyle said, looking at the gauges in the control panel. "Oxygen content throughout the boat is down twenty percent and water continues to come in. We can bug back out through the dive chamber or we can stay here and fight. Maybe fight our way through to the sub's control room . . ." The thought petered out, cancelled by its own stupidity.

"The bastards know the boat's sinking just like we do," said Chizzick who was lying in four or five inches of saltwater and blood. "They probably know there's scuba gear in here and the only way out is through us. We hunker here and kill them as they come through that hatchway,"

"As we sink? Anyway, you're wounded," Kyle told him, "and you'll have to be carried out. So you don't get a vote."

"I can shoot, goddammit."

"You still don't get a vote." Kyle looked at the others.

"The bottom here is almost two thousand feet deep," said Dan Clark. "Even if we stop every one of the hijackers, we'll still have to bug out or sink in this thing."

Yes, thought Dawton, *that's the happy truth. So why not leave?* "There's also the risk that minisub will find our divers and the canyon wreck. What's it going to be?"

He had his answer before he wanted it.

From the forward hatchway crawled somebody. A desperate hijacker, then another immediately behind, both suddenly firing wildly. The morgainners opened up with their odd assortment of weapons. In shooting from their concealment, they gave away their positions but tried to take out their attackers before they advanced more than a few feet. As several more jumped into the room, the noise of the gunfire and its ricocheting bullets was deafening in the confined space.

A couple of the scuba tanks not stowed out of harm's way were hit. One flew spewing gas and threatening to hit somebody till the dive-chamber wall stopped it. The other, near Skip Roberts, spun around and around till he kicked it over. The regulator hanging off a third was shattered. Bullets whizzed, banged and clanged.

On their respective sides of the aisle, Sanchez and Roberts were hit. Trying to get to a better firing position away from the control board, Dawton saw Sanchez crumple. With Clark and Shinley still firing at the forward hatchway, he leapt behind the starboard engine beside which Chizzick and Sanchez lay. He pulled Ed Sanchez behind the engine and tried to cover Wayne.

Something hit him in the back, either a ricocheting round or a piece of flying metal. He had no time to give it any attention as he joined in keeping up a concentrated fire at the hatchway with the SKS carbine he'd taken from Chizzick.

The initial exchange of fire was soon over. The air smelled of bullet propellant, blood, fear and sweat. The hijackers they'd duct-taped to the pipes between the port engine and bulkhead were now still, no doubt riddled by the wild firing from their fellow thugs.

The relative quiet was punctured with the sounds of humming or harrowed machinery, leaking pipes, heavily breathing men, bodies shifting, low groaning and grunting. Kyle had checked Wayne to make certain he was relatively okay and was moving back to have a look at Sanchez when a loud slam of something outside, hard and heavy, reverberated through the submarine's pressure hull. It sounded near the stern. Hearing other thumps, some scraping noises forward along the length of the vessel, his first thought was that the sub had hit an undersea wall or terrace. But then he heard the muffled sound of engine noise overhead, as if it could be coming from the surface.

Another burst of gunfire from the forward hatchway area sent bullets his way and jerked his attention back to the fight. He started to return fire in the direction of the burst but the SKS let go one round and quit, its magazine empty. Having reloaded, the others were firing, however, even Chizzick who had risen beside Kyle and was using a pistol to shoot under the forward tanks and equipment at vague shapes lying less than ten feet away.

Flaming insanity. Deal with it or croak. Probably gonna croak anyway.

This second exchange could not have lasted for more than half a minute. When it stopped, he heard the scraping and thumping noises overhead again and wondered what could be going on outside the sub. Could the three C Team divers who were still outside be trying to do something he couldn't guess or imagine? Had that minisub come back to at last make good its threat to crash windows? The noises didn't fit that.

Suddenly the room tilted toward starboard, sliding Dawton and the others over the slick deck and up against unforgiving surfaces. Chiz had fallen back down and Kyle grabbed him to keep him from rolling.

Their loose scuba tanks and other gear clattered and crashed around them.

Out of the hatchway came another hijacker, firing as madly as the others before. Another followed. And another. Their guns were again silenced by the divers' fire but this time, because of the rolling submarine, not so easily.

Enough bodies now lay in the small space between the hatchway and the machinery to provide cover for any Haitians left. One or two might have escaped a lethal hit and could be lying there amid their dead or wounded brethren like snakes waiting for the right moment to strike.

The submarine rolled again, this time back toward port, so severely Dawton and the rest were almost thrown upside down. The scuba tanks that hadn't fallen before fell now. One hit the release button on an air jacket, spun and slammed hard into Skip Robert's knee.

Whatever the cause of the rolling chaos, several more hijackers decided to use it to cover their entry.

In the semi-dark, Dawton fumbled with a third magazine. The other divers were firing despite the rolling sub. The two or three hijackers who'd tried to enter this time dropped in the pile just inside the hatchway.

"Give me that SKS," said Chizzick as he grabbed the edge of the engine's hood to pull himself up.

"You lie back down and be quiet," said Dawton.

Another gunman fired from the hatchway.

Dawton pulled Chizzick down and ducked. The bullets from the hatchway kept coming. He fell over Chizzick to protect him with his own body. *So this is it, old salt. See you on the other side . . .*

He heard curses and gasps across the walkway between the engines.

The sub tilted again to starboard. Dawton, with Chizzick beneath him, was catapulted up and over the engine and other machinery forward into the heap of bodies fronting the room. On the way, Kyle's head struck something hard before he landed atop the pile, hands flailing to find Chizzick and the SKS he'd lost.

⋅⊷▶ ◀◉⋅

He regained consciousness with rain pelting his face. He looked up and saw the eyes of Victoria close to his.

"Kyle?" she said. "Do you know who I am?"

"Aphrodite. The Foam-Born."

She smiled. "Be serious. You've had a bad blow to the head and I'm checking you for concussion."

"Umm."

She was wearing a rainjacket, its hood over her head. God, she was beautiful, damp tangled hair hanging out of the hood, a streak of oil or grease across her cheek; her lower lip bleeding and a bleeding scratch on her forehead; eyes wide and swimming with concern and fear. With *love?* He was alive and he appreciated what he was seeing as never before. "What happened to you?" he said.

"Do you know who I am?" she repeated.

"Venus. Inanna. Rhiannon—"

"Do you know where you are?"

The wind howled. The deck rolled. His brain seemed awash in a black sea that seemed ready to sink him. He looked up and around, realized he was lying in a sling suspended from a side winch. He saw that he was near the stern of *The Morgainne.* Beyond the ship's A-frame crane that stood over the transom, lolling in the swells, was submarine *Blue Deep*. Another ship lay on the far side of the sub. The *WildBore V* ORV. Cables hung suspended from the cranes of both it and *The Morgainne*, holding the sub between them. Lifeboats surrounded *Blue Deep* and were taking aboard people from her.

Nearby were two Coast Guard ships and a U.S. Navy destroyer.

He heard familiar voices. "Chiz," he said to Vic. "Sanchez . . . Clark . . . where are they? The rest—?"

"Be still," she answered. "We've got all of you out and everyone's okay. Alive anyway."

Morgainne crewmen lifted him out of the sling onto a stretcher and carried him into a very crowded and busy maindeck infirmary. Victoria helped slide him onto one of the beds. Chizzick and Sanchez, Shinley, Roberts and Clark, were all there, all of them wounded and lying down and being seen to by Doc Pratt and his two nurses.

Victoria wiped Kyle's face with a warm cloth. It came away bloody. He closed his eyes against the ache in his head; felt the faint pressure of a cotton swab she held against his brow and the sting of its antiseptic.

He said, "So the Coast Guard, the Navy, got us up?"

"No. With the help of the JJ Oil ship, *we* got you up as they were arriving. Also in response to our Mayday, several civilian craft showed up but were shooed off by the Navy."

"How did you get us up?"

She began opening his dive suit. "We were picking up some stuff through sonar and hydrophone—heard the gunfire outside *Blue Deep*, had that minisub on sonar. We heard shooting inside the Harwood sub—we feared you guys were in bad trouble. We heard *Blue Deep* was sinking. We couldn't just sit at the wrecksite. We left a workboat there and with *WildBore V* having come, we—Diane and I got the idea that maybe we could raise *Blue Deep* with *Morgainne's* A-frame crane and the crane on *WildBore*—"

"You—"

"Don't talk. Listen." She unzipped his dive suit down to his underwear and said, "Turn over on your side.

When he did, he felt the stickiness between his skin and the suit. Victoria let go a low whistle. "Bad cut on your back," she said. "Don't think it's a bullet wound though. I'll get a nurse, see how soon the doc can—"

"So *WildBore*—"

One of the nurses came over. Victoria helped her pull his underwear down so that she could put a needle in a buttock. Stripping him all the way down, Victoria and the nurse looked him over and the nurse concluded the cut in the left side of his head and the slice in his back were all he'd incurred in the way of flesh wounds. Embedded in his back was a piece of metal that could be pulled out and the wound stitched.

Victoria said, "We coordinated with *WildBore* and the three in the C Team who were outside *Blue Deep*, got slings under *Blue Deep* and around the sides. At first, the sub rolled a lot, back and forth—we thought we were losing her. But we finally got it rightly balanced—"

"You were—"

"Diane and I and the other divers outside and several divers from *WildBore* got everything connected and stabilized."

As she went on, he felt the drug beginning to take effect and thought about the risk Vic and the rest, the slingers, had taken in connecting cables and hooks around a submerged vessel. Very dangerous work. With the help of crane barge and tugboat, he and Chiz had taken part in raising two sunken ships in the past. On one of those jobs, cables had snapped and a winch come loose. Several in the dive team came close to being killed or at the least seriously injured.

He closed his eyes. Said, "But how—the sub was sinking. All those people on board and . . . the weight . . . the ballast tanks were empty . . ."

"*Blue Deep's* captain fixed the glitch in the ballast-tank sensors that was giving wrong feedback. The tanks weren't empty. He was able to clear them after several of us showed ourselves outside the glass of *Blue Deep's* control room and we signaled that *Blue Deep* was being slung and raised. By emptying the ballast—" She saw that he was fading fast. "Short version, we finally got it up to the surface."

Trying to remember what had happened, he said, "That minisub outside *Blue Deep* . . . where'd it go?"

"Okay, be quiet now," the nurse said, appearing beside Vic. "Dr. Pratt is coming over to have a look at you."

Victoria leaned down, her hands and jacket smeared with his blood and, pressing her chest to his, kissed him on the mouth. "We lost it on sonar."

⋆⇢⊨◎ ◎⊨⇠⋆

Fighting the leaks in the forward port, the *SZ-44* pilots finally regained control enough to nose the minisub toward the nearest coast. Two men worked with sealant to stanch the leaks and two more worked the pumps to rid the *SZ-44* of the excess water. They were two kilometers out and at a depth of 20 meters when Lepushin ordered the pilot to find a place to hide it on the seabed until nightfall.

The copilot emptied what was left of the ballast and the pilot settled the craft up against a limestone terrace, hoping it would be undetectable by sonar and virtually invisible to divers' or a submersible's lights.

A check of his men determined that one was dead. Lepushin was the only one wounded. The team's chief medical officer cleaned and dressed his thigh wound.

Having repaired most of the damage to the leaking ports, checking the pumps and hastily going through a troubleshooting sequence with the controls and mechanisms, pilot Oleshuk said. "I think we can fix everything."

"The propeller? The rudder?"

"Yes. We should have the necessary spare parts."

"Can it be repaired where we sit?"

"Maybe, Captain."

There was little point in trying to return to *O-681*. Lepushin no longer knew her location and in any case had scant hope of Captain Polivanov trying to find and rescue them. Not with so many Americans in the area.

He did not realize just how many had arrived until after being helped into an undamaged wetsuit and making it in to the shore of the nearest cay. With a man on each side to help him swim and then limp to a tree-fringed knoll, he saw through binoculars all the craft knotted around the now surfaced *Blue Deep*. Along with the salvage ship *Morgainne* and an oil ORV with the name of *WildBore V* on its prow, lay two U.S. Coast Guard cutters and a United States guided-missile destroyer of the Arleigh Burke class.

Lepushin and his team were beat up and abandoned. His rage against those who'd fought him off *Blue Deep* knew no bounds.

CHAPTER 27

Disclosures

On the night of *Blue Deep's* rescue, the critically wounded were medevac'd by the U.S. Coast Guard to Nassau where they were flown by jet to a trauma center in Miami. Among them were Wayne Chizzick and Ed Sanchez, both of whom would have to undergo emergency surgery. A Navy doctor from the on-site destroyer boarded *The Morgainne* to treat the less serious injuries, Kyle's among them.

The metal that hit his back had chipped out a small piece of his scapula and required onboard surgery to replace it with a synthetic bone graft made from coral. The old line from *The Tempest* floated up out of memory: *Of his bones are coral made . . .*

A potted plant in a corner of the infirmary's recovery room looked as droopy as he felt. In his opioid gaze, it swayed like a ship in a gale. Morphed into a palm at the edge of a shore.

The palm sinks, becomes a wreck, a ghostship of slave-day vintage whose timbers are like bones through which could be seen an undersea plain of sand. The sand grows coral and the colorful coral brightens into stars . . . beneath which lies jungle. Those timbers are suddenly crawling with goo that is not oily black but blood red that turns into zombies holding automatic weapons, moving through her empty viscous rooms as the ship tosses and a minisub crashes into it, knocking her to pieces . . . and under the falling ruin, timbers burn . . . timbers no longer of bone but of thatch . . . people hanging from them or from trees . . . black night, bright fire . . . a disc shining in a wagon, reflecting the firelight, two dark-robed priests arguing over it, one wanting it destroyed as a pagan idol, a Devil Stone, the other wanting to take it to Spain . . . the cries from captured Indian slaves when asked what it was, where it originated: Huehuetque! Huehuetque! De Los Viejos! From the Old Ones, the Ancient Ones, people of whom were spoken with awe and veneration and mystery. The disc being taken in the wagon through jungle to be put aboard a ship, a galleon, on the coast; and the ship in storm with other ships, going down . . . the disc spinning down into a sea, an Ocean of Time that moves in a realm beyond ordinary reach, the disc itself a symbol of Time and Time's cyclic, circular nature . . . with a ghastly face in the middle, its tongue hanging out . . . Tongue of Time, Tongue of the Ocean, some realm beyond ordinary reach . . .

He rose back to the here-and-now, dazed and once again wondering if he could be diagnosed as delusional—or demented. How much of this stuff was nutty and how much had validity? And if it had validity, what kind? If it had validity, why, how, was Kyle Edward Dawton from Backwater, Oregon able to receive it?

What if he could sink deep enough . . . or go out far enough—would he see where that black minisub went?

Where did it go? he asked The Darkness.

And felt on the brink of a plunge from which he might not return.

⤐▬◉ ◉▬⤏

On the second day after surgery he was helped back to his cabin on the 03 deck. In his post-op stupor, a sea-nymph rang his bell.

"Kyle?"

He opened his eyes.

Victoria stood over him in a tank shirt and shorts, holding a travel mug and a medical kit. "How are you feeling?"

"Much better, with you to look at."

She smiled. "I brought you some coffee. Can you sit up so I can look at your incision? The medical staff is so busy."

She sat down on the edge of his single bed and helped him sit up. As she scrutinized the surgical wound and redressed it, she told him some things he hadn't heard.

The rescue flotilla from *The Morgainne* had saved the refugees left on *The Melanie Rose*. The yacht itself had not sunk. Activated by emergency sensors, it had automatically sealed the section on the bottom deck where the hull had been punctured by a volley of concentrated RPG rounds. The mechanics and engineers from both *The Melanie Rose* and *The Morgainne*, had plugged the hole blown into the yacht's hull and repaired *Blue Deep* well enough to get both vessels by Monday morning to the New Providence harbor for repairs.

She told him that dive teams were bringing up salvage of historical value. Kyle was glad to receive this news but aware that it was his "hunch" about a wreck that had lured them into peril and harm. And with the mystery of that minisub and its mothership still unresolved, the peril remained.

Vic said, "Admiral Curt has come from Nassau. Do you feel up to seeing him?"

Already in the doorway, dressed in slacks and polo, the admiral entered. He looked travel-worn and harried, his finely chiseled face almost as gray as his hair. He was carrying a thick briefcase. His greeting was sympathetic but brief, as Kyle's was numb. Kyle invited him to take the small room's one chair at the desk next to the bed. The admiral sat. Put the briefcase on the floor. And said, "I'm sorry this isn't exactly a social visit. But I do want to say right off that, though you won't be getting any medals, you're heroes for what you did." Looking at Victoria who still sat on the edge of the bed, he added, "You two and the rest of the C Team and everybody on *The Morgainne*. I'm proud of you. And sorry for your wounds. Glad you're alive. But I've got some things to tell you that you're not going to like any more than I do." Curt opened his briefcase and began pulling out papers. "I've just come from a meeting at the U.S. Embassy in Nassau with some Coast Guard and Navy brass. Have to talk to you two and the rest of the staff and crew before any investigators do."

Kyle bristled at the mention of investigators.

Admiral Curt said, "I'll be seeing Wayne and Ed at the University of Miami Hospital tonight. How alert are you, Kyle?"

"Alert enough." *I hope.*

Curt Chizzick explained that the Nassau-based investigation had begun that afternoon. Coast Guard Operations Bahamas, Turks and Caicos (OPBAT) learned that the communication centers in both Nassau and Miami had been hacked into. The hacking had confused and delayed the arrival of a Coast Guard rescue. Distress calls from *The Morgainne* and several other vessels in the area that had become aware of the megayacht's plight were jammed or rerouted to thwart reception at OPBAT, the Bahamian Navy's HQ, and any other maritime agency in the region. The gunmen who'd seized *The Melanie Rose* and then *Blue Deep*, several of whom confessed under interrogation, were a gang of human traffickers working for a global syndicate. They'd duped the shipload of refugees into believing the latter were being taken to Miami when in fact they were to be dumped at a remote spot off Little Abaco or Biscayne Bay, there to be secretly sold like cattle, like slaves of old, to a buyer posing as a transporter of "various goods." Efforts were underway to track down said buyer and destroy the global trafficking ring.

Curt waved the papers in his hand. "In case you forget anything, I've printed off what you are to say and not say to the investigators. And I have NDA's for you to sign."

Non-disclosure agreements. Kyle inwardly groaned as the admiral told them that they had to comply or their plug would be pulled from any further work in the region. For good. This did not set well with Kyle nor, he could tell, with Victoria. Kyle said, "This can't have anything to do with those hijackers—traffickers. It has to do with that unmarked military minisub we tangled with, doesn't it? What that guy in it said . . . his wanting that Joseph Yord—"

"Right," said Curt, cutting him off. "And we are not to talk about any of that."

But Victoria said, "So whoever was in that minisub struck at the time they did because those inside it thought the distraction caused by the hijackers offered a good opportunity for them to nab him?"

The admiral nodded cautiously. "They had no interest in you or the traffickers or any of that. You had the bad luck to have gotten yourself in the middle of something that had nothing to do with your wrecksites and salvage operation. You just got in the way."

"So who's Yord?" said Kyle. "Why did they want him so much?"

Curt took a breath and exhaled slowly.

In the silence, Kyle pressed further: "I think we have a right to know what's going on in the waters around us. Don't you, Admiral?"

"Okay. You guys deserve something of an explanation, I know . . . but I'm limited in how much I can tell you and what I am about to tell you is not to be repeated to anyone by either of you. Understood?"

Their nods of compliance were dutiful but unenthusiastic.

The admiral thought for a moment. He took another breath and said, "Look, I respect your position. But I'm afraid you're going to have to respect that of the powers-that-be also; yes, without even knowing why or what it is. In any case, stick to your work as salvors. Unless something happens to get in the way of that, you might make enough to get Argos out of the red, pay me and the other investors off, and have the money to go hunting lost wrecks elsewhere. But remember these NDAs are binding for life."

That sobering comment and the tone in which it was delivered confirmed that Curtis Chizzick was as unhappy with the NDA and secrecy business as were Vic and Kyle; and maybe unhappy as well with what he'd learned that he could not talk about.

Kyle said, "You were going to tell us—"

"Okay," said the admiral. "Joseph Yord is a scientist who defected from another country several years ago. He's been with JJ Oil for the last two or so. In short, he's supposedly brilliant and that other country wants him back. We believe those commandos in that minisub were missioned to take him back."

"Defected?" said Kyle. "Another country . . . Russia?"

"That's classified," said Curt. "What I just told you is *classified.*"

Kyle moved a little and grunted, "Yord isn't his real name then, is it?"

The admiral's voice now had its own agitated tone. "I realize you will have a lot of questions about this but I can't answer them and you are not to ask them of anybody. Not only because this is classified information but because, speaking for myself, I simply do not know much. Being retired, I'm no longer in 'the need to know.' And even if I weren't retired, I couldn't tell you—"

"So where did you get what information you have?" Kyle said.

"Aren't you listening? I can't answer that." Though the admiral had been a deskjock at the Pentagon for the last three years of his active service—and that was over four years ago—and was no longer "in the need to know," he obviously still had intel and Pentagon contacts. In fact, he was now acting as an intel liaison, never mind any claim he might make to the contrary.

"Joseph Yord found a way to pull oil, or an oil component, out of limestone," Kyle said flatly, heedless of the admiral's tone. "On some kind of microscopic scale."

Curt Chizzick was quiet for several beats, then said, "I can see how you might have come up with that. "But . . . look, I can't prevent you from speculating. But obviously I've got to remind you again that you are not to talk about any of this to anyone. It's spelled out in these NDAs. As I've already said in so many words, we have no choice about this. Either we cooperate or the Navy will see that Argos's salvage permit down here is revoked, that the salvage of both debris field and wreck is terminated and *The Morgainne* leaves the Bahamas, forbidden to enter Bahamian waters from now till hell freezes. As long as you guys tend to your own business—"

"Got it, sir," Kyle said. "I think we can agree to remaining quiet about what we know and ignorant about what we don't know and sticking to our business, but not knowing if the bottom's literally about to drop out from under us or blow up in our faces promises a lot of distraction."

"Unfortunately, you're going to have to live with that."

"How did the ones in the minisub know Yord was in *Blue Deep*? How did they—"

"Kyle," said the admiral, "enough."

Kyle tried to let go the subject of Joseph Yord for the moment. But the secrecy business had eaten through his painkiller fog like Yord's invention maybe ate at limestone; only in Kyle's case the result was bile. With caffeine and irritation being part of the mix, he said, "Do you know if they've found that minisub? We shot the hell out of it, knocked out a port. Messed up its propeller. That minisub had to have come from a mothership, had to have piggybacked—"

"The Navy and Coast guard are looking for both—with submarines, submersibles and divers. Anything you guys might see related to it—or anything else unusual—is to be reported to me or to several specified members in the Office of Naval Intelligence mentioned in the NDAs. You will be given a special frequency for use in the event you need immediate help."

Dawton said, "So we're sitting ducks if that minisub *didn't* sink, is still out there somewhere, hellbent on getting the defector back and wiping out anyone who gets in the way."

"You are to keep your eyes peeled."

"So what's JJ Oil going to do about the goo and the sinking seabed? Are we allowed to know *that*?"

"Not exactly. But since JJ Oil will be working not far from your salvage areas, I'll tell you this: it will start cleaning up the wellhead near the wreck and outward, in circles, as soon as it gets the go-ahead from the Navy. You will see, by the way, that in addition to the NDAs you're to sign with the Navy, you will also sign similar agreements with JJ Oil, drafted by its lawyers."

Kyle's audible groan derived from his mental effort to absorb all he was hearing, especially the news that *Morgainne's* salvage operation would have underwater oilworkers in its midst. "What does 'cleaning up' mean in this case? What will it do to the wrecksite and the debris field?"

"I was told by J. J. Harwood that neither will be harmed by the remedial operation."

Dawton was skeptical. "How are they going to prevent that and still 'remedy' the goo at those sites?"

"I don't know. And that is the truth."

"But the remedial op is supposed to reverse what Yord has done?'"

The admiral regarded Kyle with a warning silence and waved the papers again like they comprised a magic wand that would make all these questions go away.

It didn't work. "So where is Yord now? Is he going to be part of the remedial op?"

"I can't tell you that either." Curt passed the papers across to them and said, "The NDAs make it clear that you are to tell the investigators only about your fight with the traffickers who tried to take the yacht and its submarine. You are to say nothing about that unmarked minisub or what was said from it. And incidentally, J. J. Harwood, his wife, his guests, his staff and crew have all signed Navy NDAs."

"What," said Vic, "have the Bahamians been told, or the Coast Guard for that matter?"

"Not much," said Curt.

Kyle said, "So how is the Navy, or whoever's behind this secrecy business—how are they going to keep the deaths—the people who were killed or seriously wounded by the traffickers—how are they going to keep all *that* secret?"

"They have people working on it. Now, I've told you all I can and probably too much."

"And I guess your knowing more than we do, you've got more to think about."

Admiral Curt sat there regarding Dawton with a wooden face, perhaps not wanting to think about all he had to think about.

Vic said, "May we ask a question that has nothing to do with what is under official obscurity?"

Curt sighed again. "Try me."

"What has been done with the refugees?"

"They've been turned over to the Coast Guard for return to Port-au-Prince." Curt closed the lid on his attaché case. "According to J. J. Harwood—and you'll see in the NDAs that you are not allowed to discuss any of this with him or anyone else—the leader was killed by one of the female Haitians. Scuttlebutt has it that he'd tried to rape her on the voyage from Haiti but one of the other Haitian males stopped him.

Kyle said, "What did she look like?"

"I don't know," said Curt. And with that, he rose and bid them good luck.

"Why did you ask what she looked like?" Vic said after the admiral left.

"Curiosity, I guess." But he had seen her: a young Haitian woman walking a disheveled waterfront, a smoking city at her back and . . . in the harbor, ships and boats mangled and tossed.

The familiar bosun's-whistle recording broke over PA speakers throughout the ship. The voice of Diane Weitzman came on. "Listen up! We've just had a report from the team at the wreck. Part of the stern has fallen down the dropoff and the rest of the sterncastle has collapsed. We have divers hurt and ascending! Retrieval team, look alive!"

CHAPTER 28

Marooned

For 76 hours *O-681* had lain fifteen kilometers south of the Berry Islands and fifteen east of the Joulters, monitoring by sonar and periscope the increasing US and Bahamian naval presence in the northwest Tongue. As Konstantin Polivanov had feared, Anton Lepushin had stirred up a hornet's nest.

Polivanov had no idea where the *Spetsnaz* officer was or the shape he and his men were in. Nor had he received any response from GRU Headquarters, Moscow via Lourdes.

In the early morning of the third day, with *O-681* lying at a 200-meter depth, his sonar supervisor reported the unmistakable acoustic signature of a U.S. destroyer 3000 meters to the north with its active sonar probing the seabed and coming their way.

Polivanov gave the orders to dive to an increased depth of 400 meters and to withdraw east on a stealthy course for the Providence Channel.

His wrinkled face was glazed with perspiration in the control room's low-intensity light. His voice was a gruff rumble when he told his second-in-command, "Unless we receive orders directing us otherwise, we are returning to Cuba."

Isaak Kolotcha nodded, agreeable as always.

But they were facing a harrying game of evasion with a destroyer that might detect them any minute and soon be on their tail. Polivanov figured it was only a matter of time before an American submarine or two, up from AUTEC or wherever, would join the hunt.

Compliments of Captain Anton Lepushin.

⊷⊨⊜ ⊜⊨⊷

The night they'd snuck ashore on the scrubby cay, Lepushin ordered four of his best men, two of whom spoke English, south to Andros Island, knowing the Joulters region would soon swarm with Navy and Coast Guard units. Lepushin and his two remaining men hid in a cave under a limestone terrace, venturing out only when a lull in the search effort permitted, and meticulously covering their tracks each time they did. Not only did they have to avoid being seen by flyovers and onshore search teams but also excursionists or fishermen who came to the tidal flats to fish and party while Lepushin and his men hid like rats in the brush or the cave, drank rainwater and ate birds, bugs, and lizards.

But the efforts to find them became furtive and desultory. It was Lepushin's guess that those behind the search operation did not want to attract unwelcome attention. Likely, the word put out to the media and the public was that the Navy and Coast Guard were carrying out a training exercise; an exercise that had petered out in less than a week. Lepushin suspected he and his men were finally assumed sunk and dead in their disabled *SZ-44*.

One swam out to check on it. The minisub had not been discovered or disturbed where it still lay hidden under the reef overhang offshore. The underwater weapons were cached inside it, their limited range virtually useless on land. Having used their intra-team radios only when necessary, those devices still had plenty of battery power left. But the radio in the minisub was ruined, as was Lepushin's satellite phone. The *Spetsnaz* captain had no way of contacting Konstantin Polivanov, no way of receiving any messages from Yakov Baturin or the liaison in Lourdes or GRU headquarters in Moscow.

His single source of intelligence lay in what he could observe through binoculars from a bush-covered limestone knoll above the cave, to which he was helped by a man on each side bearing much of his weight. The rifle bolt that penetrated his thigh had torn only muscle before it exited. Though cleaned and dressed by the team's medic, the wound still hurt like hell.

From the knoll, he saw several vessels out in the Tongue. It took him a while to put things together. While at it, he saw the one U.S. Navy destroyer still on-site leave, heading south toward where Lepushin and his men had last left *0-681*. Within hours, the last two Coast Guard boats had also headed in that direction at full speed, which made Lepushin fear that Captain Polivanov's boat had been spotted and the chase for it was on.

All that remained were the salvage ship *Morgainne*, the oil ship *WildBore V*, and the big yacht *Melanie Rose*. As he watched, the latter up-anchored and turned southeast, toward Nassau. Lepushin did not know what had happened to the civilian submarine *Blue Deep*. Maybe it had sunk. Maybe it had been raised by *The Morgainne* and *WildBore V*, both of which, especially working together, could have raised the sub and seen to its reberthing inside *The Melanie*.

By next day, *WildBore V* had also departed, on the same course as *The Melanie*. In another day, the oil ship returned with another ship much like it bearing the name *WildBore II*, both loaded with canisters the size of 150 liters or more, cryptically labeled TOTO-12X3. The canisters were stacked and trussed in the sterns where the ships' deep-submergence vehicles received a load of them and were launched by A-frame crane every few hours, around the clock.

One of the DSVs had been transferred to *The Morgainne*. While *WildBore II* eventually moved off to the north, *Morgainne* and *WildBore V* remained about 300 meters apart to the northeast of South Joulter. While the salvor cycled divers and submersibles from ship to divesite, *WildBore V* lowered and raised her DSVs with similar frequency in the area of the JJO wellhead, whose homing signal submarine *O-681* detected days ago. But because of the oil ship's deck profile and all the equipment cluttering it, Lepushin was rarely able to see who entered or exited her deep-submergence boats.

In the next few days, various helicopters and Navy craft came and departed, their activity centered on *The Morgainne*. It was impossible for him to guess what they were about.

Not once had he seen Pyotr Telasnikov, on oil ship or salvor. Telasnikov could have been transferred from *Blue Deep* to the destroyer here earlier, whisked away by agents from the Office of Naval Intelligence. Without having any word from Yakov Baturin, Lepushin had no idea where Telasnikov might be. Nor did he care very much by this time. Thanks to those who were going to pay for it, he was certain he had lost his first quarry but now had another.

What had happened to those scuba divers who'd attacked Lepushin and his men at the stern of *Blue Deep*? Had they entered the sub and fought the hijackers, overcome them? Judging from all he saw off the cay, the hijackers had been defeated, were likely taken away to Nassau. If so, had all those divers survived the fight? A few? More than that?

In a psychological sense, the pain of the thigh wound had spread through his blood with a white-hot fury that would not be assuaged until he had satisfied himself that every remaining bastard in that dive team was dead. And he'd begun to nurse a notion, a desire, he'd dismissed days earlier as absurd. But the more he seethed, the more he liked it. For two reasons: his hatred and rage for them and a longing for what he suspected they'd found. Observing from the knoll, he'd seen them bringing up *treasure*! Objects were too far away and too corroded for him to discern detail. Nonetheless, he was convinced they had found a legendary sunken galleon full of gold, silver, jewels, and other precious artifacts. And he began to ponder how to take it all.

On the fifth day, the four he'd sent south to Andros returned in the middle of the night. On the night they'd left they had come upon a camp up an estuary occupied by four men and two women. The man on guard had been taken out easily and the rest killed as they slept. Their fifteen-meter motoryacht was tethered nearby and inside Lepushin's men found bags of money, heroin and cocaine. Once underway for Andros in the yacht, they tied the contraband to the bodies, slit the bodies open and, with jokes about drug-crazed sharks, dumped it all overboard. In a couple of towns down the Andros coast, they were able to procure supplies, fuel, equipment, and material for *Saida's* repair.

CHAPTER 29

Intruder

THROUGH THE ACRYLIC bubble of the former JJ Oil submersible he'd nicknamed *Wallbanger*, Kyle Dawton had a clear view of the wreck and the four divers moving through its scrambled and encrusted interior. He had spent the last two days clearing away the collapsed sterncastle with the submersible's long arms and claws. Using the thrusters to maintain position, he now kept *Wallbanger* five yards from the edge of what was left of the stern and ten feet above the canyon's north slope. The JJO deep-sea craft had been given to Argos Salvage by James Harwood in appreciation for the morgainners' rescue of his submarine and yacht. Admiral Chizzick was at the moment in Houston, becoming better acquainted with Harwood and his wife and talking them into making a sizeable monetary investment in Argos.

Dawton had operated research and salvage submersibles in the past but *Wallbanger* was state-of-the-art. Having been trained by a JJO pilot and a technician, he'd soon mastered her operation. Having mastered it, he was on his own: The oil ships *WildBore V* and *WildBore II*, the latter having arrived two days ago from the Gulf of Mexico and now gone north to another JJO wellsite, had no one to spare in the way of a copilot.

Working 24/7 with a banged-up and worn-out diving crew that was missing two of its best divers in Wayne Chizzick and Ed Sanchez, knowing that any minute the rest of the wreck could collapse or fall down the dropoff and with it the very salvation of Argos Salvage, Inc., they were pushing abilities and equipment to unprecedented limits. Everything they found was treated with the greatest care. Thus no one in Victoria's archeological team had raised any protest as to the way anything was removed from the site and handled on *The*

Morgainne. Victoria herself and the other divers presently inside the wreck where neither ROV *Ogler* nor *Wallbanger* could go were on their second dive of the day and despite disclaimers to the contrary, had to be exhausted.

Two members of Victoria's archaeological team were working in the wreck midships while Victoria and Rick Rivera were at the exposed and partly fallen-away stern. *Ogler* hovered nearby to provide with strong lights and cameras an overview for the two forward while Kyle's craft at the rear of the wreck did the same for Vic and Rivera. Whenever the divers needed a large piece of wreckage removed they judged of no salvable value, the signal was given Dawton to move in with the claws. His still-healing scapular wound consigned him to nothing more strenuous.

He watched Vic move deeper into what was left of the stern. Her exquisite shape was obscured by tanks, mask, hood and drysuit. All four divers were laden with back- and side-mounted cylinders as well as underwater rifles and archeological tools. In the two days he'd spent recovering aboard *The Morgainne*, Vic had seen to his every comfort and need when she was not busy in the labs or on a dive or resting for the next one.

The morgainners treated him like a hero. He didn't feel like a hero. And with those who'd taken more hits than he, like Chizzick and Sanchez who were still in the Miami hospital, he included them in every toast. With a bullet wound near the heart, Sanchez had come close to checking out. Kyle was on the phone daily with Wayne who was recuperating pretty well.

He could hear the faint but distinctive whirr of the JJO submersibles through *Wallbanger's* hydrophones. The last report from *The Morgainne's* bridge, in communication with *Wallbanger* via cable-linked floating antenna, placed the nearest JJO craft at 360 yards to the southwest. The other was farther to the east. In the nearest one's expanding circle around the wellhead, its distance from the wrecksite was decreasing by the hour. Instructed to keep to their salvage work, the morgainners could only guess from what little communication they had with *WildBore V,* what they observed from *Morgainne's* bridge, and the reads from sonar, that the two JJO DSVs were performing some sort of spraying operation; likely an attempt to destroy or alter whatever was eating certain materials in the seabed environment and producing the goo.

Righting a wrong done to the sea?

Though the samples they'd sent to Miami had gleaned confirmation that the goo was hydrocarbonic in content, it had properties that yet defied analysis.

The distant noise made by the DSVs not only complicated the salvage job but interfered with *Morgainne's* picking up the sonic signature of a hostile minisub were it to come into their midst. Maybe it had crashed, sunk, all within drowned. But what if that was not the case? Maybe its unknown occupants were still lurking about, biding their time for a new attempt to seize Joseph Yord. Why did they want him? Why were they willing to kill, to risk their own lives, to get him? Who were they? Along with worries about seabed stability, the danger of the wreck falling off the precipice, and the secrecy business, these questions hung with the weight of an imminent storm.

While James Harwood had hired two security ships that were on their way from Miami, U.S. Navy and Coast Guard craft were supposed to be scouring the region far and wide but had reported no sighting of any military minisub. The destroyer that had come days ago had taken off to the south without explanation.

As the Navy and Coast Guard investigators came and went, vacationers and fishermen called Nassau wanting to know what was going on off the Joulters. But the true nature of the activity remained disguised and concealed from onlookers and media. For their individual reasons, Argos Salvage, JJ Oil, ex-admiral Curtis Chizzick, and the US and Bahamian Navies all connived to keep the minisub incident and the demand for Joseph Yord under wraps.

Dawton had thought a lot about those NDAs they'd all had to sign. Agreements not to disclose the truth. Why? And what exactly was the truth?

He'd thought a lot about death too; how close it had come for the morgainners; how it had come to many of the refugees and some of *The Melanie Rose's* crew; how close death was there always and for all. But it moved across his mental sandflat not as the Grim Reaper with rancid breath and icy fingers wrapped round a scythe, but as a portal into that unknown ocean; an ocean not unlike the one he was familiar with: rich with beauty, mystery, darkness, discovery, and threat. Beckoning and warning, enticing and shunning, it lapped at his waking and sleeping dreams like a tongue ready to devour or expel. On its waves and in its currents, he saw indecipherable things; but of those that were to whatever degree fathomable, one recurred and remained: that of a gaunt but laughing captain welcoming him aboard a ship made of wind, holding a shining disc on which he was ordered to write in blood: *Forget the truth.*

In a lull in the noise made by the distant JJO DSV, he heard a thud from within the wreck. *Pay attention to the divers.* He looked but couldn't see much. "Everybody all right," he said into his mike.

One by one, the divers rogered. All were okay.

⋆▸═▪ ▪═◂⋆

Captain Anton Lepushin sat behind *Saida's* pilot and copilot, in a drysuit with his diving gear and tanks at his feet, like his men who were crammed into the passenger compartment forward of the lockout chamber. He watched them as the *SZ-44* crawled away from its concealment off South Joulter. They knew, or at the least suspected, that *0-681* was on the run, in effect had deserted them. Even Lepushin now thought any attempt to capture the defector hopeless, suicidal, as Captain Polivanov had feared from the start. Lepushin still lacked communication with Baturin, Lourdes or Moscow. He and his men seemed to have been deserted by all.

But emboldened by the success of the four who'd killed the smugglers and seized their motoryacht, he said, "If by chance we see Pyotr Telasnikov, we will take him. Hopefully, Baturin will be with him and help us do it, will act when he knows we are about to strike. If we can't take Telasnikov, we will take him out. Baturin included if necessary."

Lepushin shifted to a more comfortable position in the narrow seat. "Telasnikov aside, we will lie off the treasure hunters' wrecksite until the time is right for us to capture the divers working there. From them, we will learn their ship's layout, their watch routine, the number of their crew, the arms they have—and where their treasure is being stored. Then we will seize their ship. We will first take the bridge, then the rest. You know the procedure. We will take the ship to Cuba. We will sell it and its treasure on the black market. Any questions?"

Though he saw doubt on faces, no one said anything. Maybe they thought the plan too preposterous for question or comment. They were all skilled in ship seizure and, like Lepushin, two in the team had had hands-on experience in the rescue of a merchant vessel taken by pirates. But they knew *The Morgainne* could still have trained combatants aboard or among the divers at the wrecksite. Maybe some of his men thought Lepushin mad. And maybe he was. He hadn't been before this mission but now . . . maybe Polivanov was right: the days of tension and frustration had taken their toll. Lepushin added grudgingly, "If for whatever reason we have to withdraw, we will go south to Andros Island and find one of its many hidden coves where we will recover and reassess our circumstances."

The disbelief on the men's faces deepened. Several had wives, children, back home.

"They surprised us before," Lepushin asserted. "They won't surprise us again! Say it!" he shouted at them, angered at his own doubt. "We are *Spetsnaz*! We will do this!"

Dutifully, they repeated the mantra.

⊷═ ═⊶

Kyle watched the video feeds as the divers worked. With the wreck leaning precariously on the canyon slope, the debris field had been put on hold. Having undergone as much cleansing and conservation as possible in the onboard labs before transfer to Miami, relics rich in historical value had been salvaged from that site but nothing in the way of a ship's name; and no treasure of the kind they all dreamed. The chest Wayne found before the trawler debacle had been partly cleaned and opened and its contents examined. A sealed case made of silver contained a sheaf of letters written to a captain named Rodrigo Sanabria and translated by Victoria. The letters bore *Cabo Catoche, Nueva España* as their destination but contained no mention of a ship's name or anything else that would shed light on what they had found. The letters were from Sanabria's wife and provided no information at all about him or her but for the ongoing complaints that she was woefully tired of being wedded to an "edge-of-the-world explorer" with five children to take care of and an endless stream of bill collectors at her door.

The letters told them nothing at all about the ship's cargo, crew or purpose. No trace of a ship's log or journal had been found.

But *Cabo Catoche* . . . . Kyle tried to remember where he'd come across that name before. And seemingly out of nowhere it came to him, that *fata morgana* of images swirling in out of the dark: *a ship in storm, masts breaking, sails ripping apart . . . and ripping open a veil behind which lay that jungle village where people hung from trees or burned alive . . . two priests arguing over the butchery and a round "devil stone" in a wagon, one wanting to destroy it, the other wanting to save it . . . .*

He was sliding with the knot in his stomach revolting against the scene, against the stench of burning bodies; his mind sinking into a sea he feared he could not maneuver, over which he would have no control.

The timer on the instrument panel beeped. He stared at its digital readout for a second, not knowing what it was. The present kicked in. The divers had been on-site for almost an hour. He looked through the glass of the cockpit and tried to concentrate on them.

Occasional fish darted across the submersible's light beams. Still down in the stern of the wreck, Victoria and Rick threw frequent looks up and around to make sure their equipment ran no risk of snare or entanglement. Though much wreckage had been cleared away, a great deal of jumbled and encrusted timber remained in the reaches beneath them. Removal of anything from its shambles was delicate and nerve-wracking work.

The noise of the nearest JJO submersible was growing louder, whirring, hissing, grinding in the phones as silt stirred from its sprayers began to come toward the wrecksite.

A wave of lethargy swept over Dawton, an internal parallel to the silt that was sweeping over the wrecksite. Seemingly out of it came a horde of gibbering ghosts. The streams of time intermingled in confusing array, weaving a shroud that undulated in tantalizing denseness.

He rallied, shook his head to clear it, concentrated. Saw that Victoria and Rick were working their way through what was left of the captain's cabin and downward.

Linked to the divers' headphones, Kyle said through his mike, "You guys be careful in there." The advice was unnecessary but needed to vent his tension.

"Copy that," Vic said. Turning from the port side, her magnetometer began to beep. Its readout indicated a strong source below the shattered planking. Rivera began carefully to pull loose a few half-rotted boards and clumps of debris in search of anything worth taking out to *Ogler's* bucket. Victoria dropped through the hole to the next deck level. Pieces of the floor of the captain's cabin now lay dangerously overhead. Heart pounding, Kyle was about to order her out of there when she said, "Hey."

On the screen in *Wallbanger's* console that streamed Vic's camera feed, Kyle saw bones. Parts of a skeleton maybe. Partly encrusted. Bones and skulls had been found here in the wreck and in the debris field, and left where they were found or removed to an onsite container where they would be safe from harm and not interfere with the salvage work.

Disturbed detritus floated up to obscure the video feed and Vic's vision. She waited, letting the water clear.

Kyle could see skeletal remains lying in the mishmash of rubble.

Rivera moved down to Vic's level to be near her.

"You see this?" said Vic, waving her hand to clear what she could of silt from a roundish shape. She trained her headlamp directly on it. "I think we have the head here." She began brushing and picking away goo, crust and sediment without damaging what she was trying to uncover. A human skull began unmistakably to reveal itself. Eyes, nostril holes, mouth were full of silt but with a brush and small narrow trowel, Vic carefully extracted as much of that as she could. She worked with a studied reverence. "There's a lateral crack across the cranium."

Kyle saw the crack in the video image. *He saw an ax coming down to strike the skull. One of the empty eye sockets pulled him in like a vortex and suddenly he was outside the submersible's cockpit, out in the wreck with the divers but not in diving gear; suspended beside Vic ghostlike and staring not at the skull but into the black shambles below. They opened up on an abyss where he saw that colorful circular stone seen before—in the wagon by the two priests, now on the deck of the cabin where sat the priest at the table, writing in a diary when his ship was in storm —*

The sound of Victoria's magnetometer penetrated. He was back in *Wallbanger's* bubble trying to gather his wits.

Neither skull nor bone was making the mag go crazy. He saw on the video screen that amid the human remains were other objects that looked much heavier. Objects that had to contain or be made of metal; not immediately identifiable. One, however, was not so encrusted. Its shape suggested something about the size of a shoe box and in Vic's headlight, through a gap in its dark coating, gleamed a hint of gold.

The voice of First Officer Buzz Franks broke into the comm link. "We're receiving some seismic reads of seabed disturbance 105 yards north-northeast of the wellhead. That's 250 yards southeast of the debris field and 210 south-southeast from where we are over the wreck in the canyon. We called *WildBore Five*. *WildBore's* captain admitted picking up the same seismic signals, though he denied having an explanation or any certainty as to their cause."

"At what depth is that disturbance?" Kyle said.

"From 300 to 320 feet."

"What's the seabed depth there?"

"Between 260 and 270."

So the disturbance was shallow. Kyle raised geologist Rob Palmer in the ROV room. "What do you think, Rob?"

"I don't know. Maybe some of that seabed subsidence we've recorded since day one. Only in this case, it's apparently more active."

"Too close for comfort," said Kyle. "Keep monitoring it to see if it gets any stronger—or closer to the wrecksite." Irritated and worried about this new complication, Kyle addressed the divers. "Be ready for immediate ascent if necessary."

"Copy," came the reply from each diver, beginning with Vic.

In minutes, Buzz Franks came on again. A second submerged craft had been detected coming from the southwest, moving on a course toward the nearest JJO submersible. Franks had called *WildBore V* to ask if they had launched another DSV. The answer was negative and *WildBore* too had detected the intruder. "Sonar," said Franks, "paints it as cigar-shaped and over sixty feet long."

The JJO deepsea crafts were oval in shape and did not exceed fifty feet.

"We're beginning to pick up an odd propeller noise," added Franks.

The divers had to have heard this exchange.

A sudden cloud of sediment enveloped the wrecksite, obscuring Kyle's visual field and obscuring the camera feeds. "Vic! Time to get out of there!"

CHAPTER 30

Wrecking Ball

THE SPETSNAZ PILOTS kept the minisub close to the bottom of the seabed. At depths from 70 to 75 meters, this was not easy with both interior and exterior lights off. The sunlight filtering down from the surface was weak and did not allow a speed exceeding four knots. Though the *SZ-44's* propeller had begun to rattle despite its repair, Lepushin hoped the oil DSV up ahead was making enough noise with its sprayers to blanket detection from sonar sweeps by the American surface vessels. The sealant around the damaged viewport was holding, however; even at a depth of almost seven atmospheres.

The oil submersible was moving in a south-southeast direction—toward *Saida*.

When within fifty meters of it, Lepushin told the pilot to halt the minisub's movement and hug the seabed to wait for the DSV to pass.

Through *Saida's* nose viewports, he could see its lights. As it moved at only one knot, the reason the deepsea workboat was making so much noise became more obvious. But the composition of the cloudy substance jetting from its belly sprayers was impossible to determine.

Lepushin recalled the canisters he saw on *WildBore V's* deck: *TOTO-12X3*. Whatever *that* was.

Not only were the craft's exterior lights ablaze, so were its interiors. He saw through the disturbed silt the name *WBS-3* inscribed in red on its flank as it followed a rough gully a meter wide and a half meter deep that looked newly formed. The oil craft was egg-shaped, less than twenty meters long and about six wide, painted a bright yellow. Her cockpit was an acrylic bubble with a 300-degree view and her manipulator arms were extended several meters forward with claws holding receptacles that were scooping up rock and sand from the gully's bottom and sides. Lepushin had occasional glimpses of two men in the seats behind the two DSV pilots, both of them peering out through the rear of the bubble and consulting handheld gadgetry.

Using *Saida's* navigation screen, the *Spetsnaz* pilot reckoned *WBS-3* to be a little over sixty meters south of the JJ Oil wellhead. And 240 meters or so southeast of the treasure-hunters' divesite. As the JJO craft came to within 20 meters of *Saida*, it dipped a little deeper in the gully. Below the *Spetsnaz* craft now, the four men in the cockpit could be seen more clearly. The two behind the pilots were instantly recognized by Lepushin. *Pyotr Telasnikov and Yakov Baturin!*

Having relinquished his capture of Telasnikov, Lepushin had to make an instant change of plan. Inured to snap decisions required in combat, he rekindled his initial purpose and, pointing out the prey to his pilots, said, "Follow that DSV. Get above it. Make ready to seize and stop it with the forward claws." He turned to face his extraction team and said, "Everyone get ready." He called out the names of three. "You will exit with me to take them. The rest are to remain aboard *Saida* as backup and be ready to help bring them in."

Saida's airlock could accommodate only two at a time. As the first two men prepared to enter the chamber, *WBS-3* began turning back to the north as it moved behind a low knoll.

"Wait," Lepushin told the men about to enter the lock.

The oil boat's lights soon reappeared beyond the knoll, rising a little to follow the erratic course of the gully. Then it dropped in depth again as the gully abruptly deepened. This new course would take it closer to a position below *WildBore V* and, farther to the southeast, *The Morgainne.*

"Extend the arms and accelerate!" said Lepushin to the pilots. "We've got to seize them before they get any closer to the two surface ships!"

The pilot powered up and jerked his control lever back. Stirring a cloud of silt, *Saida* rose sluggishly from the seabed. At its maximum speed of six knots, it moved upward and forward at what seemed like a snail's crawl to overtake the DSV.

The propeller began to rattle worse, then to whine, and finally intermittently to screech. Lepushin stiffened. He turned to look at the mechanic behind him.

Though the man had repaired the rudder all right, the same could not be said of the propeller. Lepushin wanted to curse him roundly but he'd probably done the best he could with the equipment he'd had.

While the noise of the oil sub, its spray and the silt it disturbed, might protect them from being spotted visually, the propeller noise could give them away. They were forced to act.

⋄⊨⊚ ⊚⊨⋄

Inside *WBS-3*, pilot and copilot heard an approaching clamor that cut through the noise made by their craft's ventral sprayers. The copilot shut the sprayers down. The strange noise was part screech and part rattle. They looked out their bubble in an attempt to find the source. So did the two men seated behind them.

The unidentified craft came within range of the JJO boat's outside lights. The four inside saw two mechanical arms sliding out from beneath the intruder's bow with claws opened at the ends and surging straight for their boat. Instantly, the pilot throttled up and jerked the stick aft and to port in an attempt to escape not only the attacker's claws but the confines of the gully. *WBS-3* slammed into the gully's right slope so hard it knocked its four passengers sideways. Their safety belts held but the pilot's head hit the glass. Badly stunned, he sagged in his seat.

The frightened copilot began frantically to take over the controls and ascend as *WBS-3* scraped its starboard side and then its belly against the gully's slope.

Behind the pilot seats, the two scientists yelled needless orders at the copilot. The one called Joseph Yord was close to hysterics, as if he knew who was in the closing craft and that they were after him in particular.

And suddenly the man he knew only as Donald Greaves, a microbiologist who'd come to work for him at JJ Oil over a year ago, now had a pistol in his hand and was pointing it at him.

"Stop!" Greaves told the copilot as *WSB-3* at last cleared the gully.

The copilot was too busy trying to regain his sense of direction, trying to pull the unconscious pilot to the side so that he could see the navigation instruments, to pay immediate attention to such an insane demand.

"Stop the submersible," Greaves yelled, "or I will kill you!"

Pyotr Telasnikov aka Joseph Yord was not a violent or aggressive man and at present was scared stiff. Nevertheless, he saw that Greaves's attention was momentarily on the copilot. Telasnikov knew that if he did not move at once, he likely would not get a second chance. He lunged for the pistol. Though restrained by his seatbelt, his hands were able to reach Greaves's wrist and shove the gun down.

Aware of the struggle between the two behind him and still trying to pull the pilot aside and evade the claws of the minisub, the copilot had *WSB-3* swinging wildly to port, to starboard and back to port again, unwittingly on a general ascent toward the southeast.

⊷⊨⊙ ⊙⊨⊷

Having expected the JJO boat to make for its mothership, Lepushin was surprised when it veered off in a southeasterly direction. Then, with the silt subsiding, he caught glimpses of what was going on in its cockpit: the copilot trying to pull the pilot up and, behind him, Telasnikov and Baturin in a violent struggle. Lepushin's guess was that mole Baturin, seeing the minisub and guessing rightly who was in it, had pulled a gun on Telasnikov.

"Lock on!" he told his copilot who was operating *Saida's* arms. "Lock on to them!"

"I am trying, Captain!"

The *Spetsnaz* team was rocked back and forth as the pilots tried to grab the oil submersible. Looking forward over the backs of his pilots, Lepushin tried to read the instrument panel. He'd memorized the coordinates of the JJO wellhead and the position of *WildBore V.* The JJO ship lay to the east and he had a good idea just when *WBS-3* missed the opportunity to ascend to her. Maybe because of what was taking place inside his craft and maybe in his desperate attempt to evade the commando sub, the man at the oil submersible's controls was zigzagging off any understandable course, accelerating in convulsive spurts that kept the sluggish minisub at bay but often scraping the seabed and filling the surrounding water again with a dense haze of silt. Though it was difficult to tell, Lepushin thought he had glimpses of the seabed giving way where *WBS-3* struck it.

Through the newly swimming silt, Lepushin no longer could see the submersible's cockpit very well, or what was happening between Telasnikov and Baturin. But in the banging, swerving, chase, at moments when visibility improved, he began to see dim lights beyond *WBS-3*'s corona.

At last, *Saida's* copilot was able to close one of her claws over an aft section of the oil submersible's port skid.

Hearing the clang of metal to metal and feeling the sudden drag, *WBS-3's* copilot jerked his craft to the left and right, up and down, in an attempt to break free. Crashing against the seabed again, he finally did. The oil boat shot away from under the minisub and, losing the latter's pull, surged forward anew.

Lepushin saw that the distant lights were spaced enough to suggest they were those of another submersible. North of it were several smaller lights, swinging oddly about like old-fashioned lanterns in the wind; moving in and out of a jumbled maze that alternately obscured them and let their beams break through. The treasure hunters! Inside a sunken wreck!

The salvage ship had to be above that divesite. Having wandered closer to her than to *WildBore V* in his efforts to evade *Saida*, the oil submersible's copilot was now on an ascending course for *The Morgainne!*

Lepushin stared at the divers' lights, tempted once again to forget Telasnikov and alter course for the wreck. But he thought it better to let the divers do their work; bring up more treasure to *The Morgainne* so that the *Spetsnaz* team could later take it.

Still climbing, *WBS-3* had slowed. Maybe because of the fight in the submersible's cockpit. *Saida's* pilot pushed his craft close behind as he shoved both claws into the oil boat's stern above its propeller cowling.

"Drag her down!" Lepushin shouted, strapping on his diving gear, readying his diving helmet and weapons. "Smash her into the seabed and we'll take him!" He turned to the men behind. "Make ready to open the airlock!"

But in *Saida's* effort to pull the submersible downward and the latter's desperate attempt to break loose, both craft were veering in the direction of the wrecksite.

⇥⊙ ⊙⇤

"Vic!" Kyle yelled, straining against his seatbelt as if he might catapult himself through the submersible's bubble the way he saw himself doing minutes ago. "Did you copy my last?"

"Copy," he heard her say through the console speaker, over the noise of the nearing subs.

"I've got it! I've got that gold box!"

He looked over at her monitor. Some of the silt had momentarily cleared in and around the wreck. She was holding the object and it looked much too heavy for her mesh bag which was already full. "Get out of there!" he rasped.

"Copy. Coming up!"

But whereas Rivera was out of the cavity, Vic was having difficulty holding on to her prize while trying to maneuver upward. Turning, she snagged her left side-cylinder in a cleft. Kyle pushed against his seatbelt. "Vic!"

Rivera moved back into the hole to free her. One of the divers forward said, "We're on our way back there!"

Another cloud of silt rose from the east, obscuring everything. He heard the growing drones of the two approaching subs, and a faintly erratic whine. It sounded like the hated minisub's damaged propeller, in an attempt to drag *WBS-3* down, was spinning in reverse. As the murk partly cleared again, he saw that the two craft were much closer. Through the swirling sediment, the forward lights of the JJO boat swept the wrecksite.

It began flashing an SOS as the pilot tried to ascend and at the same time shake loose of the minisub. The latter was hanging from the oil boat's stern. Kyle could see its propeller spinning counterclockwise within its cowling rim. Despite the bullets and bolts they'd put into it, it was performing well enough to pull the JJO boat down. Why *WBS-3* had wandered so far east of the spray site was puzzling. Maybe its erratic route was at least partly due to its effort to elude the minisub and in doing that, it had wandered closer to *The Morgainne* than to *WildBore V.*

With the JJO boat trying to climb, the minisub's drag was swinging both craft toward the divesite with the implacable aim of a wrecking ball.

CHAPTER 31

Welcome Aboard

THROUGH THE STARBOARD viewport, Lepushin and his pilots saw an oil boat roar out of the gloom at the wrecksite. It leapt at them at full throttle. "Brace yourselves!" he bellowed.

With its blunt nose, the assaulting craft struck the minisub's extended arms, crashed over them and veered away. The sudden drop in depth told Lepushin that their hold on *WBS-3* was broken. Freed from *Saida's* grip, *WBS-3* surged upward. Knocked off course and having lost the oil boat's weight, minisub *Saida* dropped and slammed hard against the edge of the canyon's mouth.

"Get that *svoloch*!" Lepushin shouted. "Smash it, smash it!"

Fighting to raise and stabilize *Saida*, her pilot wrested his sluggish craft away from the canyon's edge and thrust it toward the designated target.

--- ⊙ ⊙ ---

In Kyle Dawton's front floodlights, through the churning debris of disturbed seabed, appeared the black snout of the minisub. It was rising and angling for *Wallbanger*. He had no time to think about it, no time to repeat his order for the divers to leave the wreck and ascend.

With all the engine noise, they likely would not have heard him anyway. But only fifteen yards away, they had to see what was taking place between him and the commando boat.

Sweat streaking his brow, mouth dry and gut knotted, he revved *Wallbanger's* power and surged forward through the swimming murk.

He'd seen the specs. *Wallbanger* weighed eighteen tons. If the sleek minisub were comparable to the undersea commando boats Kyle had seen while in the Navy, its weight had to lie in the sixty-ton range. He was a shark attacking an orca.

Approaching it, he swerved left just before impact to avoid damage to *Wallbanger's* nose and cockpit. Her starboard side slammed against the port side of the minisub, knocking it off course but not far. *Wallbanger* rolled under the impact, throwing him willy-nilly against the restraining seat straps.

Hanging upside down in his seat and bleeding from a cut in the forehead, Kyle fought to regain control of the craft as it fell dangerously toward the canyon wall. The bubble hit rock. Unable to see anything, he nonetheless reversed engines and steered to clear the wall.

Out over the canyon, he got the *Banger* upright. Rocked dizzily in his seat and wracked by fear for the divers, he rose again to find the minisub. The debris cloud caused by the previous clash threw the beams of Kyle's floods back at him. But through infrequent breaks in the cloud he saw the dim outline of the minisub. It was closer to the wreck than before. And it seemed to be stuck with one of its mangled front arms caught in the seabed.

Kyle throttled up and roared toward it, angling to the right to come around and knock it away from the wrecksite. But as he neared, the sub broke loose and caromed to the left. He grazed it, tried to slow his momentum and turn, but the tail of *Banger* raked the wreck midships. Old timbers crashed in upon *Banger*. The water exploded with debris so thick he could see nothing in any direction he turned in the bubble. Heart sinking with the thought he could have killed a *Morgainne* diver or all four of them, he had no choice but to throttle up and tear lose of the shambles.

When he broke free, he ascended several yards above the murk. Through the blood and sweat coursing down his face, he searched anxiously for any sign of the divers' lights but could see nothing through the debris haze. He grabbed the console mike. "Vic, do you copy?"

No answer.

"*Morgainne*, this is Dawton. Do you copy?"

No answer.

He had to have hit and severed the divesite's tether cable. All of Kyle's monitors were now blank and he had no way to communicate except by hydrophone with the divers or *The Morgainne*. He had no hope of that.

He turned *Banger* to find the minisub. Could not locate it anywhere around him.

The spinning debris finally thinned enough for him to see down to the wreck. Or what was left of it. What he could see told him that much of it had caved in and slid farther down the canyon's slope where it had come to rest at the edge of a gaping black hole that he couldn't recall having seen there before.

Searching again the sea above the wrecksite, he saw a diver's light flashing Morse some eighty feet above the wreck. *We are okay.*

He breathed a little easier—then saw that a crack had appeared in the top of his bubble. Water was trickling through.

Another break in the debris swirl told him the minisub had leveled off to the east, veered back and was now coming at him. He levered the stick to throw *Wallbanger* into an evasive turn. He throttled up.

The minisub swept near. Its claws at the end of their crooked extenders snapped at *Banger's* stern but missed.

Gaining separation, Dawton barreled blindly through the roiling gloom. Zings of pain in his back burned holes in his concentration. He thrust upward, then back to the east, intermittently wondering if he was still in the "real" world or some other.

Against the swirling darkness he located the black minisub. Its nose was now pointed toward the surface, damaged forward arms still extended. Damaged they might be but they could no doubt smash into and skewer or crush the divers who were ascending toward *Morgainne*!

He throttled up again. Closing the distance between himself and the minisub, he realized the closer he got that it was hardly moving. The screech and rattle of its propeller cut through the noise of *Wallbanger's* engines.

Kyle looked at the control panel. He saw the switches for *Wallbanger's* stern arms.

He punched buttons. The panel graphic indicated the arms were extending. He angled upward for the minisub which now seemed to be falling toward him.

He roared past it and throttled down and put the *Banger* in reverse and turned on its rear floodlights. On the cockpit panel's rearview monitor, he saw the minisub's arms. They were much smaller and much shorter than those of the oil DSV. *Banger's* arms could be extended over the middle of the commando craft if he could achieve the right position.

The minisub was still losing speed, enough to require Kyle to struggle with the throttle while he punched the sequence that would extend *Banger's* arms to the max and open their claws. Swerving sideways to place *Banger* perpendicular to his prey and having to rely on the monitor's screen, he tried to clamp them down, one over the minisub's ventral hatch and one over its belly.

Missed. Tried and missed again.

The minisub was falling faster than he could keep beside it.

He increased his reverse speed and caught up. Once he was able to move *Banger's* stern to within ten feet of the minisub's middle, he closed the claws again. This time, while missing the ventral hatch, he snagged the dorsal.

Kyle shoved the gear stick back into forward.

The one claw held well enough for him finally to slam the other over the dorsal hatch. Bigger than *Banger* though it was, the minisub was now clamped like a bug between pincers.

⊷⊶⊙ ⊙⊷⊶

"We are caught!" said the *SZ-44* pilot. "They are pulling us up! But I think it is a good thing, Captain. We were losing power, dropping!"

Lepushin strained against his harness to see through the small viewports. The JJO submersible's aft floodlights prevented his being able to see much but he could make out the two arms jutting from each side of its stern. *"Chto za huy!* They are pulling us to our doom, you fool!" he shouted at the pilot. "Break their hold! We will abandon the boat!"

"We can't, sir," retorted the copilot. "The escape hatches are clamped down—"

"You don't know that!"

"The instruments indicate —"

"Break their hold!" Lepushin repeated, issuing a command made pointless by rage and fear.

The pilot hesitated and then tried to do something with the controls.

A horrific rattle and shriek told them that the propulsion motor and propeller were coming apart.

⟶▷● ●◁⟵

By the time *WBS-3* breached the surface twenty yards off *The Morgainne's* stern, the heavy-duty A-frame had been tilted out to grab, lift and haul her in. Fortunately, the wind was light and the swells shallow. In his control station above the 02 deck, the A-frame operator listened to deck chief Meg Latham guide him in and soon had the JJO boat lying on the maindeck's wide transom. Deckhands were there and quickly pulling its four passengers out: the unconscious pilot, the distressed copilot, and two other men, one of whom was shot in the chest and bleeding badly. The other held the pistol used and was too distraught to surrender it. He also carried a briefcase and a daypack.

"I'm Joseph Yord," he yelled. "I had to do it. It was him or me! You've got to hide me, protect me!"

Having been forbidden to ask any questions about this guy, no one had any idea why Yord had to be helped but Latham ordered some nearby crewmen to take him and the other three men to the infirmary.

⟶▷● ●◁⟵

Wallbanger rose at last to the surface, her nose up but her stern and the snagged minisub still submerged. From the leaking bubble, Kyle saw *Morgainne's* A-frame crane swing out over *Banger*. He worked the submersible under the lowering hooks and clamps. The A-frame was 25 feet wide and 30 feet high. Its lift capacity was 60 tons. The combined weight of minisub and submersible was well over that. But he had confidence *The Morgainne's* deck crew knew what to do.

In confirmation, hands were rolling supporting mobile winches to the transom to position them on each side of the A-frame's base.

Four *Morgainne* crewmembers armed and in scuba gear jumped into the water to either side of the minisub. Four others crouched at the transom's port and starboard rails with rifles ready. Several more jumped to *Banger's* side decks to connect the haul-up cables to her lift-rings.

Aching in every quarter, Kyle unsnapped his seatbelt, forced the oil boat's bubble loose and raised it. His feet were calf-deep in bloody water.

Standing at the edge of the transom, a crewman said over his hand radio, "Haul us up, Meg!"

Rising with the submersible, Kyle saw that its twin, *WBS-3*, lay in the water off to *Morgainne's* starboard side. He wondered where its occupants were but was sure the morgainners had taken them to an appropriate place.

Deck chief Latham was in the A-frame's control station. Kyle could hear the A-frame's engine and mechanisms whirr and groan. As *Wallbanger* rose above the water and the crane began swinging the craft in toward the transom, those on deck began to see the minisub breaching the waves but still in the oil boat's clutches.

Meg Latham was raising the cables as fast as they would go and at the same time swinging the crane forward. Cables connected to the side winches aided in the lifting and steadying of *Banger*. With the submersible swinging in, crane and winches dragged it closer to the transom.

Deckhands at the mobile winches rushed to fasten cabled hooks to the tow-rings in the nose of the oil boat. The winches roared, pulling the craft farther aloft and inward. The combined weight of the *Banger* and minisub had lowered the already low transom several feet closer to the waterline.

Latham transmitted, "Kyle, I'm afraid the crane is going to break! I see steel bending and bolts popping out!"

Still standing inside *Banger's* cockpit, Kyle said into his mike, "Pull me up far enough to get the minisub on deck."

A few more yards and the minisub was on the transom far enough to let *Wallbanger* go. Kyle tried to release the claws holding the minisub. Pushing buttons and pulling levers, he said, into the mike, "Not getting any response. Claws aren't releasing!"

Something cracked in the crane's upper starboard arm. Hanging from the crane above the minisub, *Banger* sagged abruptly on the starboard side. Both claws at last tore away from the minisub. Cables on the port side snapped. *Banger* came crashing down sideways but on top of the commando boat. The minisub's two nose viewports popped out. Neither was big enough to allow an exit by those inside. And their two escape hatches were now sealed between *Wallbanger* and *The Morgainne's* deck.

Kyle had to scramble down the sides of the two craft. On the way, he looked into one of the minisub's open viewports. He saw the pilot and copilot but wasn't able to see much else. Both men stared at him as if he were something from a ghoulish nightmare.

"Welcome aboard!" he said loudly enough for those on *The Morgainne* to hear.

The cry was repeated and became a chorus among all the hands on deck.

—◦═◉ ◉═◦—

Lepushin heard too and silently emitted a curse. *Chyort voz'mi! We are screwed.*

He was certain that he and his men would be tortured, imprisoned, perhaps never to return to Russia. All for what had been a doomed mission from the start—while Captains Polivanov and Kolotcha were most likely sitting somewhere in Havana, maybe on the beach; sipping cuba libres and hoping never to hear from *Spetsnaz* officer Anton Lepushin again.

CHAPTER 32

Threats Old and New

HAVING RANGED MILES to the south in their hunt for the minisub's mothership, a Coast Guard cutter, a Navy destroyer and submarine were on their way back to the divesite in answer to *The Morgainne's* summons.

WildBore V was now anchored a hundred yards north of the salvor.

Meg Latham told Kyle about the four men who'd been in *WBS-3*. "They're in the infirmary. One was shot by a guy claiming to be Joseph Yord. Yord's about to come apart. Jesus, Kyle, from the looks of you, you could stand some medical attention yourself."

"What about Vic and—"

"They're okay. They came up fast so Diane ordered them into the hyperbaric chamber. But they're okay."

Leaving Meg to oversee the holding of the minisub to the transom, Kyle called for Dan Clark and Rob Palmer, both of whom were armed, to join him as he rushed for the infirmary. "I want to talk to this guy Yord before the Navy gets here."

In the infirmary, Kyle found the unconscious *WBS-3* pilot and the badly bleeding man who'd told Doc Pratt that his name was Donald Greaves. The bearded figure who'd identified himself as Joseph Yord sat in a chair in the corner, waiting to be looked at. His pallor contrasted sharply with his longish dark hair and his hands holding his briefcase and daypack were shaking. Though he did not look physically wounded or injured, he was obviously traumatized.

Doc Pratt and his nurse and a couple of crew volunteers were busy with the bleeder.

"Is he going to make it?" Kyle asked.

"Doubtful," said the laconic Pratt who took a cursory look at the cuts on Kyle's head. "Need to clean those up."

"I want everything on him in the way of information, identification," Kyle said, ignoring his head wounds for the moment.

Yord had relinquished the pistol which lay on a shelf nearby. Kyle grabbed it.

Dan Clark knew what was wanted without having to be told. "Let's have those," he said to Yord, indicating briefcase and knapsack.

Yord clutched both against his midriff. "The—these are mine," he stammered. "They are—they belong to me and n-n-no one else. You wouldn't be able to read anything in them. They're—"

The former SEAL leaned in and put his hand around Yord's throat and squeezed. The scientist gagged and let go his baggage. Palmer took the pack and briefcase and Clark released Yord's throat. Yord coughed and heaved to get his breath.

When the spasms subsided, Kyle pointed over at the man called Greaves. Bone weary and a little woozy, yet burning to get to the bottom of the mystery of Mr. Joseph Yord, Kyle said, "Who is the guy you shot?"

Yord stared at him, stark fear in his eyes.

"We gave him an injection to settle him down," said Pratt. "He may cease to respond."

"Looks alive enough to me," Dawton muttered. He put his face close to Yord's.

"Hey, you in there? You hear me?"

Yord spoke, voice shaking. "You've got to sink them, the men in that submarine. I've told the captain of this ship. Sink them now!"

"Why?" said Dawton.

No answer.

Kyle had noticed the faint trace of a Slavic accent. He recalled the guess he'd made when Admiral Curt brought the non-disclosure agreements to be signed. "You're a Russian defector, right?"

Yord jerked his head back. "How did you learn that?"

"Just a guess."

"On what grounds?"

"No grounds. Came out of the blue."

Yord obviously did not believe this off-the-wall answer. *But if Dawton knew he was a Russian defector*.... "Yes," Yord admitted, hanging his head, then yanking it back up and finding something to say that might protect him. "I—I've worked for the U.S. Navy . . . Office of Naval Research . . ."

"And those men in that minisub are Russian commandos sent to take you back to Putin Land?"

Yord just stared at him.

"So how did you come to be hired by JJ Oil? Is working for JJO a cover?"

No answer.

"What have you been doing for JJO? You were down there with the spraying operation. Has the lowering of the seabed in the Well Three area here got anything to do with your work?"

"I can't answer these questions!"

"I think you already have." Dawton felt that he was closing in. "I'll make another guess: When you turned yourself into the U.S. Embassy wherever you were when you left Russia, the CIA snatched you up, right? They had their way with you and decided your expertise could be best used by ONR. But for whatever reason, you didn't stay there. You left ONR and went to work for JJ Oil. But somehow a mole got into the picture. A mole working for Mama Russ. Is that guy over there a Russian mole?"

"He is dead," said Doc Pratt, sounding irritated and on the verge of telling Kyle to leave the room.

Kyle said, "Am I warm, Mr. Yord, or whatever your real name is? Hot? You, if you don't mind me saying so, look a little sweaty. Don't worry. We're not going to throw you to those wolves out there in their miniboat. They'll be turned over to one of the U.S. Navy ships about to arrive. I guess you will too. But you should feel like you're with friends, right?"

At last Yord found his tongue again. "They had me working on a nanotech weapon at Dubna."

Dawton hadn't a clue as to where or what "Dubna" was. *"They?"*

"Moscow! They had me working on an environmental weapon. I didn't like that kind of work. I wanted to do something good for the marine environment! I wanted to—"

"By lowering the seabed, making it unstable? How? What?"

"But you treasure hunters—had it not been for my work, you would not have found that sunken ship!"

"Oh? Hey, we've speculated about that. If it's true, well—one of the many ironies of life, I guess. But, that's a bit off track. Anyway, I find the prospects and potentials of your 'work' fascinating and scary as hell. Do you care to explain just how your work might have exposed our wreck?"

"No! I can't!"

"Did you invent something, like an artificial microbe or—something that can pull oil from limestone?"

Yord gawked with surprise again, and guilt; but said nothing.

Looking at him, having listened to his plaintive and anguished voice, Kyle felt sorry for the scientist. "Hey, he said, "I can imagine what it would be like to have one's talent and passion, one's reason for being, perverted by doing work he loathed."

"Kyle," said Doc Pratt, "if you want anything left of him to question by you or the Navy, we need to look him over before he collapses. As for you—you don't look so good yourself. Have one of the nurses look you over, then go to your cabin and get some rest."

⋅⇥⧳ ⧲⇤⋅

That afternoon a party of armed sailors boarded *Morgainne* and took Joseph Yord to a nearby U. S. destroyer. A Navy salvage ship that had also arrived dealt with the Russian minisub, hauling it up to her fantail and letting it sit there while another team of sailors held rifles on the craft and several technicians went to work cutting open the squashed dorsal hatch with blowtorches. Those on *The Morgainne* would never learn what was done with Joseph Yord or the Russian snatch team sent to retrieve him.

Based upon what little Kyle had been able to scan and understand of Joe Yord's notes and papers before the Navy whisked him away, and based on Argos lab analysis, the goo had been the byproduct of an engineered "micro robot" called TOTO-12, designed to pull oil from limestone. Agents from ONR, breathing down their necks, ordered the Argos lab staff to keep their analyses a secret. Like everyone else involved, the lab staff had signed NDAs. To expose the micro-robot invention would raise the question of its less benign potentials— who created it, how and why, the creator's background, and so on. So questions about Yord would remain; and for Argos probably never be answered.

Yord's notes indicated that a deep seismic or tectonic disturbance near Well One had ruptured its casing and caused Yord's microbots to escape. The seabed subsidence and the ooze produced by these invisible mouths were in evidence only at Well One. Yord had applied his microbots only to Wells One and Three. Fortunately, he had developed an artificial bacterium, a "countermeasure" called TOTO-12X3, to destroy TOTO-12.

On the internet, Kyle read about METAL EATING BUGS and experiments in creating "synthetic microbes"—one with the droll name of Synthia.

⊰⊱ ⊰⊱

On the evening of the day the Navy took Joseph Yord away, Dawton stood on the catwalk of the 02 deck.

Kyle stared at the sea as if expecting anything at all to rise from it. Their tumultuous caldron of good and bad luck. Black clouds off to the west had seemingly formed out of nowhere. Serpentine streaks of lightning cut brilliantly through the dark cumulous: electromagnetic energy little understood, though scientists cited windcurrents and the crash of particles that stripped electrons from atoms and produced voltage on an awesome scale. Those ragged flares made him think of Joe Yord's microbots. It took almost a minute for the rolling thunder to reach *Morgainne*.

Why did the Navy want Yord? What went on at that place Yord mentioned: *Dubna?*

What did the Office of Naval Research have to do with him?

Nothing came "out of the blue," or the dark, as it were.

He watched those clouds, that lightning. Few people in the world would be happy with the prospect of environmental meddling of the kind that had been considered for years by various warfare agencies, least of all those who lived or made their living on the sea.

Something quivered in Kyle's memory, blinking like a distant diver's light moving in and out of a wreck. Here in this region known for vanished ships and planes, lost gold and forgotten ghosts, the flickering faraway lightning became the promise of other realms, other realities moving around the edges of awareness; portals to places unknown.

Beckoning.

Feeling his mood, his consciousness change, the sea he was looking at became one that rose countless feet skyward. Within this waterwall's turbid depths flashed hieroglyphic images that morphed into bands. The bands twisted into varicolored streams, veins in a living tapestry, that undulated and folded in on itself finally to part and reveal a quickening torrent of chaos: a great city sinking beneath the sea, upheaving earth and crumbling mountains, a sky blood red and convulsing . . .

He veered away—from the sea and from the vision. His imagination, yes, yes —

Victoria stood on the catwalk watching him. Her presence was enough to jolt him back to lucidity. "I thought you were in the decom chamber," he said. "Are you okay?"

"I am. I heard you were banged up pretty bad. You're white as a sheet."

"Umm."

"You want to lie down?"

He grinned. "Only with you." But he sagged into one of the bench seats against the bulkhead. "You're the best thing I've seen since last I saw you."

She leaned in close and whispered, "How would you like to see a lot more of me?"

"I've been longing for that since the night we met."

"The same for me for you."

The junior archeologist with whom Vic shared a room here on the 02 deck was coming up the ladderway. "Hi," she said lightly. "Sorry if I interrupted something nice."

⊶⊷⊷ ⊷⊷⊶

The next day a new salvage ship named *The Argonauta* arrived from Miami. She was another gift from J. J. Harwood; and it included two ROVs and a new deep-submergence submersible more sleek and powerful than *Wallbanger* or *WBS-3*. On board were Wayne Chizzick and Ed Sanchez. Wayne was still using crutches and the prognosis for his leg and foot indicated that he would not dive for a long time, if ever again. This, of course, did nothing to improve his troubled temperament but with him came his physical therapist, an attractive and amiable young woman who exerted an upbeat and calming influence over volatile Chiz, and curried good relationships with everyone she met. In addition to keeping Wayne's moods on an even keel, Carla Johansson kept his spirits and determination up. Though she officially bunked in the lower staff quarters, she spent a lot of time in Wayne's cabin that was adjacent to Kyle's where, afraid of sleep and nightmare, he heard the sounds of therapy glorifying the wee hours.

Tossed against indurate instrumentation in *Wallbanger's* cockpit, Dawton himself had been banged up worse than he knew. In addition to a mild concussion, numerous cuts and bruises, a sprained left hand and a stressed right forearm required rest that put him out of commission for days. Inactive, he fell prey to visits by Tony Corro who wanted to talk about coverups and conspiracies and undersea sinkholes being used by aliens as portals to subterranean bases.

Alone, he fell prey to moments in which the visions came.

From where? he wondered. Did the past—and for that matter, the future—exist in some "eternal present" posited by visionaries, philosophers, mystics, even quantum physicists? What kind of antenna or radar was in Kyle Dawton's head, or mind, that enabled him to go tripping off willy-nilly into events in a time long gone or a time yet to come? That part of his thinking that was grounded in materialism and logic wanted to find some explicable correlation, connection, between the two. But all he could come up with in such pondering was the region itself, as if *that* held some trove of past and future events to which he somehow had experienced sporadic access.

That laughing phantasm would appear, his own version of Father Time, holding not a scythe but the keys to past and future. The keys would begin to whirl and then vanish, to be replaced by that round stone he'd seen at times— with a fierce face in the center.

He had tried repeatedly to tell himself such was his imagination at work, drawing on copious sources he'd read. But recalling what he'd seen of the Haitian woman, the trawler, the minisub, all that—before any of it materialized in ordinary reality—he could not dismiss such things as fanciful. And even when he'd tried to do so before the recent calamities occurred, a part of him was aware that the visions came as if of their own will and not his.

He would arise from his bed in a sweat and, in order to escape the spell, go to the dive room or one of the labs or out on one of the decks and engage someone, anyone, in conversation about what was going on with the salvage op. But avoiding Victoria. Because he had fallen harder for her than he wanted to admit. He wanted her deeply and was as wary of that as he was of becoming lost to the Unaccountable.

Trying to escape himself, he learned the dive teams were working around the clock while the JJO spraying operation continued. He learned the localized quaking in the seabed along the canyon mouth had ceased but what remained of the galleon still sat at a perilous slant on the canyon's slope and was now near the edge of a monstrous sinkhole that had opened to the east of it. Under sonar probe, the hole varied between 600 and 700 feet in depth.

Thus, with *Ogler* and *Wallbanger* in serious need of repair and *The Morgainne* laden with salvage, the three partners decided that while Wayne would stay with *The Argonauta* at the worksite, Kyle and Victoria would take *Morgainne* to Nassau.

CHAPTER 33

Gold Box

WITH BAHAMIAN COOPERATION, the hoard of artifacts brought up and taken to Nassau began to be offloaded as soon as *The Morgainne* was securely moored and its cargo booms and cranes warmed up at a section of wharf cordoned off and guarded by Bahamian dock police.

It was only a question of time before word reached the consulate offices that would try to lay claim to what their countries had risked nothing and done nothing to discover and resurrect from the deep. The morgainners had found and restored, or were in the process of restoring, gold and silver originating in Mexico and Peru, emeralds from Columbia, pearls and other precious or historical artifacts from Cuba, Mexico, Spain, Portugal, England, France, The Netherlands, and the United States. The governments of any or all of these countries might file claims and petition an international maritime court for seizure. Under the revised wreck permit with the Bahamian government, the latter was entitled to 20% of the first $50 million and 50% of the rest of the proceeds of sale. The collection by all estimates was nearing the half-billion mark. If all went well, much of the treasure would be sold to dealers and collectors and much of it would be on contextual display in some of the world's most famous museums.

From the wharf, bars and ingots of gold and silver; jewels, coins, candleware; cutlery, crystal and plateware made of precious metals, weaponry and other items of high value were transferred by forklift in stainless steel or plastic containers and wooden crates to trucks that conveyed them to a chartered jet waiting at the airport for flight to the Argos warehouse in Miami. At every step, security guards provided around-the-clock protection, turning away the media, the curious, and more-than-curious as the tedious work progressed. The Bahamians had a vested interest in cooperating with the salvors and arrangements had been strengthened with the Bahamian authorities to keep confidential any find made by Argos in Bahamian waters. Until Admiral Chizzick and the three Argos partners had all their legal ducks in a row, they wanted to keep the staggering prize under wraps.

The word nonetheless was soon out. Officials from the Spanish, French, Cuban and Peruvian consulates showed up wanting to see what was already gone—excepting what still lay in the archeological lab yet to be readied for transport. With representatives from the Bahamian Maritime and Tourism Ministry, the Nassau port authority, and Her Majesty's Bahamian Defence Force to back him up, Kyle forbade the consular bunch from boarding *Morgainne*. They left in a huff to acquire court orders for access and inspection.

⋯⟫⟨⋯

Late that evening, he was in the ship's library, once again poring over books and internet sites related to court cases involving disputes over ownership of salvaged goods from the sea when he heard her voice behind him.

"Kyle?"

The clasp of her hands on his shoulders was magnetic and he felt like he might levitate. With elation and dismay, he turned and looked up. The dismay evaporated the second his eyes met hers. Her subtle fragrance made him think of wildflowers in the spring. Her smile was radiant enough to melt his last shred of restraint. She wore shorts, a tanktop with a tropical-print shirt over it that was unbuttoned and slightly parted. Around her neck was a leather lanyard at the end of which dangled several keys. "I have something to show you," she said.

She led him down to the archeological lab. It was almost 22:00 and the lab was empty for the night. She closed the door and locked it.

"No escape?" he joked.

"No escape," she answered with a grin as she took his hand.

Kyle hadn't been down here for several days. On the lab walls were pictures of sixteenth and seventeenth century sailing ships: galleons, brigantines, caravels and carracks. The worktables, cabinet tops and benches were almost cleared of relics he'd seen earlier in various stages of cleaning and restoration, tagged with description and date.

But on one table lay a piece of planking Kyle had seen brought up but had not seen cleansed until now. Etched into its aged wood was the flamboyant lettering, faint but unmistakable, that said *Trouv.*

She was watching him and said, "What?"

He shook his head. "Just . . . where was this found?"

"In the debris field."

"Oh, yeah. I remember now—when it was brought up."

She watched him a moment more, then said, "Come on."

She opened the door to her office. It was small and windowless, its walls covered with photos and drawings of the debris field and the canyon wreck and artifacts found in them.

She went behind her desk and lifted the lanyard from her neck. She inserted a key in a drawer and lifted from it first a bottle of brandy and two snifters, and then something wrapped in waterproof plastic. She stood erect and broke open the plastic and pulled out a gold box. "The contents of this were sealed with candle wax and well preserved . . ."

As she poured the brandy, he recognized the box as the one she'd fought so desperately to retrieve from the canyon wreck before *Wallbanger* smashed half the galleon to pieces. Gold did not corrode or encrust unless it was near iron and iron had to have lain near this one. Expert hands had cleaned it. About a foot long and a little less than a foot wide, its top was decorated with a simple image that looked like an amateurish carving of a rifle telescope's crosshairs. Both circle and lines were roughly wrought and not deep. He stared at it, knowing that like the truncated word *Trouv,* he'd seen it before.

Vic said, "A rather crude representation of what's been known as the Pagan Cross, the Sun or Solar Cross, the Wheel Cross. Probably carved by the box's owner using a knife. Something someone with a lot of time to kill might do . . . while on a long sea voyage. But curiously pre-Christian for a Catholic priest."

Catholic priest?

She handed him one of the snifters across the desk, raised her own, clinked it against his and drank the amber liquor in one swallow.

Kyle did the same.

She moved around the desk to stand beside him, put on a pair of tight cotton gloves, opened the box's lid and pulled out its contents. Her hands were trembling slightly with excitement, with veneration perhaps, for what she was about to show him. He took that trembling hand in his own and closed his fingers over it. She turned to face him, eyes locked on his, her voice now tremulous as the hand that placed the items on the desk: "A rosary, a small dark-brown book with a cross on the front, and a larger book, leather bound, with nothing on its front cover. Look." She opened the book to the first inside page. On it was written in an ornate script:

El Diario del Padre Mateo Olivas de Pedraza
de la Compañía de Jesús
en la Nueva España
1687 Anno Domini a

"This diary is now completely translated. In it, the questions that have nagged us—did we have one ship or two and, if so, why either ship was off the Joulters when the galleon routes didn't go near this area; or how a storm could have blown a treasure ship so far off its normal route, and so on—are answered."

Her closeness and the desire it stirred clashed with what she'd just said; threatened to rip him from his precarious moorings.

"Mateo Pedraza was a Spanish Jesuit, though at the time, 'Jesuit' was not yet a title used by his order. He was with conquistadors in Guatemala, an army of adventurers and plunderers who put down the last Maya rebellion. Pedraza was an amateur archaeologist; a collector of artifacts, anyway, despite papal policy demanding the destruction of 'heathen idols,' books and artifacts. At the Mayan ceremonial center of Tayasal, they found a circular stone that, based on the description in Pedraza's diary, was much like the famous Aztec Calendar Stone, or Time Wheel, uncovered in Mexico City in 1790. He argued with another priest who wanted to destroy the 'devil stone.' Pedraza wanted to take it back to Spain and, with the help of the conquistador captain, prevailed."

Kyle's spine crawled as he recalled the vision he'd had of two priests on the hill above the burning village. Arguing over a "devil stone."

Vic must have sensed his alteration of mood. "What?" she said.

Feeling all at once weak in the knees, he moved away and sat down in the chair in front of the desk. "Go on," he answered. "Tell me about the stone."

She watched him silently for a few seconds, then continued uncertainly, with wariness cutting through her earlier excitement. "It . . . the Aztec stone in Mexico City is three feet thick and about twelve feet in diameter and weighs over twenty-four tons. The Tayasal stone was a much smaller version. About a meter in diameter. Still, it required four slaves to lift it into a wagon that was pulled by a team of mules through the jungle from Tayasal to the coast; and six slaves working ropes and hoists to get it aboard the ship and down to Pedraza's cabin. The Indian slaves regarded it as sacred and were beaten and flogged and threatened with torture before they would touch or move it."

Huehuetque! Huehuetque! De Los Viejos!

"Kyle?"

"Go on. Please."

Vic sat down on the edge of the desk, watching him keenly. "The pack train made it to the coast where ships were waiting. Three of them. They sailed to Havana to join four others and from there headed north for the Gulf Stream in the Florida Straits, bound for Seville. Pedraza was on one of the heavily laden galleons called *La Estrella del Caribe*. On the fifth day out of Havana they were struck by a storm north of the Biminis and became separated."

Storm . . . a horrendous gale . . . tossing decks . . . sails ripping apart . . . men flailing the sea wash, falling overboard . . .

"The *Estrella* became stuck on a shoal. Alone. As her crew worked to repair sails and free her from the shoal, 'like a black mirage, like a smoking pillar,' wrote Pedraza, came a two-masted brigantine armed with cannon. It flew a Spanish flag and was approaching the galleon at full sail with the wind at its back. Seeing the flag it flew, everyone on *La Estrella* began to cheer. But when it came within good cannon range, the brigantine was soon changing flags. The

Corona de Castilla came down and the Skull-and-Crossbones went up. *La Estrella* had been deceived with a trick the Spanish themselves often used: flying a false flag to 'bamboozle' an enemy."

Kyle was no longer in Victoria's office. He was on the *Estrella*, or maybe hovering somewhere above it.

"Pedraza says the slaves aboard *Estrella* were often mistreated. Signs of an impending revolt were recorded by him days before the storm and the brig's appearance. His last diary entry was only four words: 'Pirates attacking. Slaves revolting.' Pedraza and others may have been killed by slaves before the brigantine's pirates ever got aboard. The slaves could well have joined the pirates in subduing *Estrella's* crew."

He saw the crippled galleon with her starboard gun decks facing north, her port decks south, and her two smaller cannon on the third deck in the stern to the west, her only defense in the way of cannon the lighter swivel guns on the main deck . . . with the square-rigged brigantine—a favorite of pirates—hoisting the *Jolie Rouge*, swinging its bow northward and turning its port guns to face the galleon's forecastle as the slaves began taking over—the priest at his desk and the axe coming down.

"Kyle? Are you with me?"

"Ah . . . yeah. I am. Go ahead. What happened then?"

"It's our guess that after the pirates attacked the galleon, they were able to get it off the shoal, man her and, with the brigantine, make for the Tongue to hide the *Estrella* in one of the many pirate hideaways in the Bahamas, probably on Andros where they could offload its treasure, hide it, and sink the ship. But another powerful storm, likely a hurricane, could have driven them back west or southwest toward the reefs and shoals northeast of Andros before they could reach their hideout."

He had a flash of that partial name again: *Trouv.* But this time he saw the full name emblazoned on the brigantine's tossing stern, turning sideways: *Trouvaille.*

"The brig could have been carrying a hoard of pirated goods even before it attacked the galleon. Judging from where we've brought up the smaller cannon and other artifacts from the debris field and the larger guns and so forth salvaged from the canyon wreck, I think we can be reasonably certain that the former was the brigantine and the latter *Estrella.*"

"Have you come across the name of a brigantine called the *Trouvaille?*" He spelled it for her.

"No. Why?"

He didn't answer.

Giving him a curious look, she removed the gloves, went around to the back of the desk, sat down and raised the lid of her laptop. Typed the name in her browser's search field.

Kyle was tempted to try peering again through that flitting crack in reality yet at the same time not wanting to. Instead, he peered over the desk and noticed the huge plastic-covered calendar on the wall behind her. It was big enough to accommodate large handwritten notes made with a felt-tipped marker over the date slots. He saw that the dates with the most notes were:

January 1—*Kyle said he sensed a wreck off the Joulters*

January 12—*Anniversary of the earthquake in Haiti. We found a debris field!*

January 17—*Kyle and I found a pyramid-shaped wellhead shelter 400 mtrs from the debris field, saw dim shape of intact wreck abt 100 mtrs NE of wellhead; the yacht Melanie Rose hijacked, the C Team overcame the hijackers; fought off Russian commandos who wanted Joseph Yord of JJ Oil.*

Jan 27—*Russians captured, removed by Navy; in 1699, Wreck of Estrella*

With a start, he realized that the dates having the most notes were the very numbers he'd seen flash the brightest when diving off the Joulters on New Year's Day. Numbers he'd forgotten till now. Only one was missing: A second *one.* Today was February the first.

"*Trouvaille* means," Vic said, reading the information on her laptop, "a valuable discovery or lucky find. From Old French."

She turned around and looked at what had him fixated. "Kyle?" she said.

"Ummm. Sounds a lot like 'travail,' doesn't it. Which means something quite different from . . . but maybe 'trove' derived . . ." His voice faded as he started to fall again into that swirl of long ago.

"Kyle? What is it?" she said. "You keep zoning out. Are you tired? That concussion—maybe we should go to the infirmary."

"No. No, I'm all right."

"What is it then? You've got to tell me."

Instead of mentioning the numbers, the dates on her calendar, he said, "That stone, Vic, that 'devil disc.' Rich in symbols?"

"Yes."

"With a face in its center, its tongue sticking out?"

"Yes. The Tongue of Tonatuih or Tlaltecuhtli. Tlaltecuhtli was a sea crea-ture that appeared after the Fourth Great Flood, symbolizing the chaos preced-ing creation and the demand for human blood. Tonatuih is generally believed to have been the God of the Sun. So the tongue represents the obsidian blade the priests used to cut out the hearts of those sacrificed to the god. The stone Pedraza found may be a precursor of the one in Mexico City. If so, and if we can find it down there in the *Estrella*, it would set Mesoamerican archaeology on its head because nothing of the sort has ever been found in Mayaland. But—you've seen the Aztec stone in Mexico City?"

"I don't think so." He hesitated, as he'd done before. Only this time, he finally said, "But I've seen it." He hedged again. "I mean, maybe I saw a picture of it in a book or on the internet or somewhere else."

"Kyle, love, there's something you're holding back, something you're not telling me. It will stay just between us if that's the way you want it."

He thought about that, still hesitant, but finally said, "Okay. Take the name *Trouvaille*. I saw part of that name at times, in my mind—or somewhere. Just the first five letters of it on a piece of planking. Like the piece we've found, that you have here in your lab. I've seen a lot of what you've been telling me that's in the Pedraza diary. Some things more clearly than others. I've seen people hanging in a burning village in the jungle. A storm at sea. A ship or ships blown . . . but I've seen things not just in the past—I saw that Haitian trawler sinking. I saw *The Melanie Rose*. I mean, before we saw it in—in reality. I saw that Russian mini-sub, its mother sub lying on the sea floor. Bits and pieces, sometimes murky, sometimes . . ."

"I've been waiting a long time for you to talk to me about this." Perhaps to encourage him to go on, she said, "I think we all have paranormal experiences from time to time, in various ways."

He nodded. "I know. And we forget we had the experience or we suppress it because skepticism's ingrained in us or we don't know what to make of it or we dismiss it as coincidence or a weird twist of the mind or an accident of circumstances. And it's hit and miss. That leaves the door open for all sorts of quackery and phony claims."

"But," said Vic, "some have such experiences more often and more acutely than others. You're obviously a case in point. The wreck you felt that was off the Joulters was there. Not just one but two. And the other visions you've had . . . the ones that proved out, proved to be genuine clairvoyance. But go on. Talk to me."

He sighed. "I'll admit I'm both fascinated, amazed, by it and afraid of it. But I've started to fear I'm a safety risk; to worry about my rep as a professional diver, that I'm losing my grip—salvage diving's a damned risky business for anybody but, like when I've scared you when we've been down—like I'm a risk both to myself and to anyone with me.

Dangerous for the dive op. Dangerous for the company, for the work that's to be done."

"I understand."

"I know you guys can manage without me but . . . in any case, this stuff has me spooked. I'm not sure what to do. I want to be rid of it and I want to learn more, get to the bottom of it, and that scares me too and, bottom line, I don't know how to wrestle it into any kind of . . . how to analyze it, make sense of it." He sat forward in the chair with his eyes on the floor.

"Go on," she said.

"When I try to pursue something that's coming up, try to get hold of it and chase it down, I lose it. It falls away, back to wherever it came from." He looked up at her. "Like I can't get hold of it with that part of my mind that's rational, that wants to make sense of it. Though I saw some things coming, I didn't really know what to make of them and foreseeing them in such fragmentary, incomprehensible ways didn't help us deal with them. And there have been times when I felt like I was going off somewhere else and wouldn't be able to come back. Sort of like narcosis. I keep getting this sensation that I'm on an edge where I could go over—like our poor smashed-up galleon sitting on the edge of that canyon—over into somewhere that's not here. Part of me wants to take the plunge and part of me's afraid to do it, like maybe I won't come back. But I keep thinking that if I do drop, maybe I'll be able to get this stuff out of my head, or maybe grasp it better, control it . . . I don't know."

"How long has this been going on?"

"I can't remember exactly when I first—I had these episodes at times when I was a kid, I think—on into adulthood. But I never had them quiet as . . . seen them so confirmed as I have here. Maybe there's something to this Devil's Triangle lore after all."

"Whatever the case as to that—Kyle, your ability is exceptional. With training, it could be strengthened, honed, better directed and more controlled. Made more understandable, reliable. It could significantly contribute to what little we know of a very elusive . . . wonder. You know there have been studies of extrasensory perception going on for a long time, precognition, retrocognition, remote viewing. Archeology has used psychics and though successes with that have been spotty, there have been some."

"Yeah. I've read about that." He suddenly saw himself entering a room where *several people sit at a long table in a brightly sunlit room. They smile and rise to greet him and introduce themselves. They wear variously styled clothing, some in business attire, some not. They are of mixed ethnicity and farflung in origin.*

We are here to share, to learn, and to serve.

To serve who?

He shook himself, sat erect and put a hand to the back of his neck to ease the tension there. "I don't have any desire to be a subject of study for anything."

"Okay." Vic was about to close the lid of the laptop when she saw something on its screen that stopped her. She let go a low gasp."

"What did you find?"

"The *Trouvaille.* I just saw at the bottom of this document that it was, yes, a French brigantine taken by pirates in 1693. And according to accounts pieced together by the few survivors, it went down in a storm on February the first,

1699." She turned around and looked at the wall calendar. "Today." She faced him again and they stared at each other, for a moment, mirror images of wonder and puzzlement. Then she did close the laptop lid, returned the contents to the gold box and the box to its drawer, stood and came around the desk to stand behind him. She put both hands on his neck to do what he'd been doing.

"Um, that feels good." But he soon rose from the chair and turned to face her.

They slammed together. He put his mouth to hers, wanting to breathe in her breath, her being; and wanting her to take his, wherever the joining, the mergence might lead. She too met the kiss hungrily, ready to take and give all.

They helped each other peel. His one good hand roaming over her skin felt as if it were exploring the sensual equivalent of gold. Hers over him kindled blazes of passion wherever they touched. And on that desk, with things shoved away or falling to the deck around it, their bodies moved like waves in the sea, licking at shoal and shoreline, lapping at crevice and headland, in a desire to reach through the physical to something beyond.

THE END